THE COLDEST BLOOD

Praise for Jim Kelly

'Kelly is fast gaining a reputation for his literate,
atmospheric novels' *Daily Mail*

'A significant new talent' *Sunday Times*

'A rare combination of poetic writing and a gripping plot'
Sunday Telegraph

'The sense of place is terrific: the fens really brood.
Dryden, the central character, is satisfyingly complicated . . .
a good, atmospheric read' *Observer*

'A masterful stylist, Kelly crafts sharp, crisp sentences so
pure, so true, they qualify as modern poetry' *Publishing News*

'A sparkling star newly risen in the crime fiction
firmament' Colin Dexter

'Superb . . . Kelly has produced another story rich in plot
and character, with a bit of history as well' *Publishers Weekly*

'Kelly is clearly a name to watch . . . a compelling read'
Crime Time

'Beautifully written . . . The climax is chilling. Sometimes a
book takes up residence inside my head and just won't
leave. *The Water Clock* did just that' Val McDermid

'An atmospheric, intriguing mystery with a tense
denouement' Susanna Yager, *Sunday Telegraph*

'Excellent no-frills thriller with a real bite. 4 stars' *FHM*

'A story that continuously quickens the pulse . . . makes every nerve tingle. The suspense here is tight and controlled and each character is made to count in a story that engulfs you while it unravels' *Punch*

'Kelly's evocation of the bleak and watery landscapes, provide a powerful backdrop to a wonderful cast of characters' *The Good Book Guide*

'A thriller debut of genuine distinction. Kelly is a name to watch and this is a compelling read' *Crime Time*

'*The Water Clock*'s praise is well deserved . . . highly recommended' *Washington Post*

ABOUT THE AUTHOR

Jim Kelly is a journalist. He lives in Ely with the biographer Midge Gillies and their young daughter. *The Coldest Blood* is his fourth novel, following *The Water Clock*, *The Fire Baby* and *The Moon Tunnel*. His new novel, *The Skeleton Man*, is now available in hardback from Michael Joseph.

He has been shortlisted for a number of awards, including the CWA John Creasey Dagger for *The Water Clock*, and Theakston's Old Peculier Crime Novel of the Year Award for *The Fire Baby*. In 2006 Jim Kelly was awarded the Dagger in the Library by the Crime Writers' Association for a body of work 'giving greatest enjoyment to crime fiction readers'.

To find out more about Jim Kelly and other Penguin crime writers, go to www.penguinmostwanted.co.uk

The Coldest Blood

JIM KELLY

PENGUIN BOOKS

PENGUIN BOOKS

Published by the Penguin Group
Penguin Books Ltd, 80 Strand, London WC2R ORL, England
Penguin Group (USA) Inc., 375 Hudson Street, New York, New York 10014, USA
Penguin Group (Canada), 90 Eglinton Avenue East, Suite 700, Toronto, Ontario,
Canada M4P 2Y3 (a division of Pearson Penguin Canada Inc.)
Penguin Ireland, 25 St Stephen's Green, Dublin 2, Ireland (a division of Penguin Books Ltd)
Penguin Group (Australia), 250 Camberwell Road, Camberwell, Victoria 3124, Australia
(a division of Pearson Australia Group Pty Ltd)
Penguin Books India Pvt Ltd, 11 Community Centre, Panchsheel Park,
New Delhi – 110 017, India
Penguin Group (NZ), 67 Apollo Drive, Rosedale, North Shore 0632, New Zealand
(a division of Pearson New Zealand Ltd)
Penguin Books (South Africa) (Pty) Ltd, 24 Sturdee Avenue, Rosebank,
Johannesburg 2196, South Africa

Penguin Books Ltd, Registered Offices: 80 Strand, London WC2R ORL, England

www.penguin.com

First published by Michael Joseph 2006
Published in Penguin Books 2007
1

Set in Monotype Garamond
by Palimpsest Book Production Limited, Grangemouth, Stirlingshire
Printed in England by Clays Ltd, St Ives plc

ISBN: 978-0-141-01864-5

For Peggy and Brian, who are together

Acknowledgements

This is a work of fiction but several experts have been generous with their time to ensure that technical details are as accurate as possible. I am particularly indebted to Dr Alan Whitmore, of the Institute of Ophthalmology at University College London and Moorfields Eye Hospital; Neil O'May, head of the criminal law department of Bindman & Partners; and the Forensic Science Service, for guidance on issues pertaining to blood. Thanks also to members of the Fen Skating Committee, who were welcoming and gave freely of their memories. Let's hope that, despite climate change, their sport thrives for at least one more generation. All information on the national electricity grid and the network of pylons which are its backbone came from the internet – beginning with the indispensable Pylon of the Month website. Would-be pyloneers should start here. The National Farmers Union in East Anglia was helpful in explaining the use of commercial kites to replace more traditional bird-scaring devices.

So much for specific areas of expertise. Others have given constant help and encouragement. My wife, Midge Gillies, has provided a wide-ranging consultancy throughout the writing of *The Coldest Blood*; from plot, through character, to setting she has made an indispensable contribution. Beverley Cousins, my editor, has continued to keep me on course with her combination of experience and skill. Faith Evans, my agent, is an ever-present guide to good writing.

Trevor Horwood, my copy-editor again, combined meticulous attention to detail with a watchful eye on continuity. Other friends have provided help selflessly: Jenny Burgoyne read the manuscript with forensic intensity and Bridie Pritchard brought an overview to the final draft; Martin Peters set me on the right road from the start with some commonsense advice about the properties of blood. My brother Bob Kelly provided a vivid insight into the realities of an ice storm.

And finally, the landscape – the English Fens and the cathedral city of Ely. As in Philip Dryden's earlier adventures, *The Coldest Blood* combines entirely fictitious characters and plot with locations blending real and imagined geography. This has allowed me once again to be creative with place names, institutions and traditions in order to enrich the story and facilitate the plot, a liberty I hope will not infuriate my loyal, local readers too greatly.

The Dolphin Holiday Camp, Sea's End
Thursday, 29 August 1974

The dagger lay on his naked thigh, its blade as cold as a rock-pool pebble. Lying back in his bunk, he raised the weapon with one hand and splayed the fingers of the other across the muscle of his upper arm, stretching the suntanned skin taut as a drum. Outside, the water of the saltmarsh slapped against the Curlew's *hull, rocking him on the incoming tide.*

He tasted salt on his lips as he bit down on the leather belt in his mouth and pressed the dagger's V-shaped point into the biceps, wincing at the gritty sound of the metal penetrating the flesh. He knew he mustn't scream, but his stomach rolled at the thought of what must come next.

The holiday camp was a mile away but he'd seen kids wandering at dusk in the marsh, four of them, torches dancing amongst the reeds. No one must hear. No one must know.

He held his breath and bit down again on the strap, drawing the blade through the skin, revealing a hint of the meat of the inner arm, a single artery exposed, then severed. Blood flowed like poster paint, dripping from his elbow, as the pain – sudden and electric now – jolted his nervous system and made him drop the dagger and cry out, despite himself.

He gagged on the strap, wanting to weep, and spat it out. 'Two more,' he said. A jagged S, like a lightning bolt. Three cuts. But he knew he couldn't see it through, not then, so he lay flat, matching his breathing to the slow cadence of the sea beyond the dunes, and for comfort placed a hand on the cold metal of the box at his side, a finger outlining the double locks.

If he could just do this, he told himself, it would be perfect. Not for the first time in the twenty-three years of his life he felt God-like, weak with control. Nothing could stop him if he had the courage to finish it; so he felt for the blade again.

But the touch of the metal brought him to the edge of uncon- sciousness. He reached out for the warm wooden ribs of the old boat: it had been his home for thirteen days now: but he would be rid of it soon enough.

The sounds of the coming night began. The distant jukebox at the camp drifting on the wind, and the tinny loop of metallic tunes from the funfair.

In his mind he danced with her then, beneath the dubious glamour of the glitterball, his thigh gently kissing her crotch with the beat, her lips braiding his hair.

He smiled, for he'd be dead soon, and they'd be together.

Letter M Farm, near Ely
Tuesday, 27 December, Thirty-one years later

The hoar frost hung in the curved canopy of the magnolia tree, a construction of ice as perfect as coral. The weight of it made the trunk creak in the still, Arctic air. Below it the dewpond was frozen, steaming slightly in the winter sun, a single carp below the powdered surface dying for air.

Joe stood, admiring its gasping beauty, each of his own breaths a plume which drifted briefly, catching the rays of the sunset. Lighting the cigarette he had made indoors, he drew the marijuana deep into his shattered throat. He sat on his bench with a rowan at his back, heavy with blood-red berries.

'Christmas,' he said to no one, surveying the circular horizon of the Fen.

He expelled the smoke, and replaced it with a surge of supercooled air, willing it to purge him of the cancer that was destroying him.

The house was fifty yards to the north and the only visible building: Letter M Farm was – he had long admitted – as good a place to die as any.

Inside the foursquare Georgian building the lights he'd left on shone into the winter afternoon, and through its double-glazed windows he could see the twin reflections of the open fire within.

He stood, turning to go back, swinging his sticks round

to keep him steady. A wave of nausea made him stop, closing his eyes and wishing again he wasn't alone. With eyes closed he drew deeply on the dope, letting the sweet relief flow like a current through his veins.

When he opened his eyes his wish had come true.

A man was at the house, coming out of the front door, putting something in his pocket. In his free hand he held a black bag, like a doctor's, and Joe wondered if he'd come from the unit. He tried to shout but his throat failed him. Then he saw that the man's head was obscured by a hood.

The man walked back towards the road where a small white van Joe hadn't noticed before was parked amongst the uncut Leylandii. Joe hadn't heard the vehicle approach and a thought insinuated itself: had it been there all day, waiting?

His eyes swam with the strain of focus. When they'd cleared the man was walking back towards him, a spade in one hand, a bucket in the other, the bag gone. From the way the man swung the pail as he strode over the frozen field Joe knew it was empty.

He shivered, aware that something had been planned, planned without him. He lifted a hand to take the cigarette from his lips knowing that even now, when he knew that death was coming anyway, fear could be a pungent emotion. Feebly he took another step forward, straightening his back and raising his arm in greeting when the man was almost upon him.

But there was no response from the face hidden within the shadowed hood. Joe scanned the fields, but the landscape was empty, a lifeless network of ditches, drains and reeds smoking with the mist of nightfall.

The man's measured stride did not diminish. The pace of advance was relentless and suddenly Joe saw his eyes: a smoky grey-blue, the whites clear despite the shadow of the hood, the line of the mouth uncertain, a tongue-tip showing.

Joe took a step back but the man had timed his attack precisely. The spade swung out in a practised arc and crashed, the face turned flat, against his knee, which buckled and splintered beneath the wasted skin. He fell, the pain in his leg oddly distant. His cheek lay on the frozen peat, tiny perfect orbs of ice rolling away from the impact of his body. A hand gripped him by the collar and jerked his head round so that a small gold crucifix on a chain spilled out from around his neck and lay on the peat.

'Who's this?' said the voice, younger than he'd expected, and perfectly modulated, stress-free. Its casual authority told him what he'd begun to suspect: that he might be granted his greatest wish, to die before his illness killed him.

Into his face was thrust a photograph, in a wooden frame, taken from the drawing-room mantelpiece. Four children pictured in the sun, a rolling beach, reeds, and a distant floating buoy in the middle of a channel cut through the sands.

'This one,' said the voice again, a gloved finger stabbing the figure of the child on the left. The boy with black hair and the immobile face.

'We never knew,' said Joe, desperate to understand. 'We called him Philip – just Philip.'

Savagely the man let his victim's head drop to the frozen earth and placed two fingers on his jugular, feeling the strength of his pulse. His assailant stood, surveying the horizon, silently listening.

'You're dying,' he said finally. 'I can't wait.'

He took the spade and freed the fish from its icy prison in the pond, filled the bucket with glacial water and poured it carefully over Joe's body, starting at the waist and working up to the chest and head.

The shock made Joe's limbs jerk wildly. The second bucket stilled them.

2

Ely
Thursday, 29 December

Dryden had been unable to sleep, his propane gas heater failing to stop the frost penetrating the steel hull of his floating home – *PK 129*. Long before dawn he had turned his head and watched as his breath melted the frost on the porthole. He'd gone up on deck in the moonlight and stood, crushed under the weight of stars, looking along the pale sinuous ribbon of the frozen river towards the distant cathedral two miles to the north.

After making a cup of coffee, he wrapped himself in his winter trench coat and sat in the open wheelhouse. The river was white, the swans dark by comparison, lined up exactly in mid-channel to survive the night-time visit of the fox. Across the silent landscape the only sound was the creak of ice, compressing the hull of the moored boat. In the distant miniature city of Ely nothing stirred except for the trundling amber light of a gritter, glimpsed intermittently on the edge of town. A single house, still decked in Christmas lights, blinked back.

For the thousandth time since he'd bought his floating home he ran a gloved hand over the brass plaque above the wheel.

DUNKIRK 1940

It was a romantic touch which had sealed her purchase. He caressed the cold metal once more, feeling history, seeing again in his imagination the boat weaving in the shallows between the flailing, desperate soldiers.

A seagull, the first of the morning, screeched over the cathedral's Octagon Tower.

Cradling the hot mug Dryden traced with his eyes the outline of the town, west from the cathedral to the Victorian mass of The Tower Hospital. There his wife lay between cool linen sheets, locked still in the coma which had brought both their lives to an abrupt halt: stalling them in this twilight world between the past and the future.

Dryden stood, trying to shake off the depression which always lurked in the hour before dawn, and stepped out over the frozen water to the riverbank. His coarse jet-black hair was already iced white by the frost, a frame around the stone-like geometry of his face. The features were medieval, a Norman brow dominating perfectly symmetrical cool green eyes – a face from one of Chaucer's tales. He could have passed for thirty-five, but by nightfall he'd look a decade older.

The moon cast a long shadow from his 6' 2" frame and he paced the riverbank with it, trying not to think of the past. A sound brought relief, the crunch of tyres as a car left the high road and began to zigzag across the Fen towards Barham's Dock, the long-abandoned inlet where *PK 129* was moored. He checked his watch: 7.25am. His other life had begun.

The light was greyer now, the stars fading, as a lifeless colour crept into the December landscape. The white blanket of frost held more light than the pre-dawn sky.

He began to prepare the ritual round of coffees, looking forward to the egg sandwich which would be his in return. When he got back on deck Humph had parked the cab half a mile from the dock and was outside, circling it, his only daily exercise. The cabbie was not hard to see, even at that distance. He carried his startling weight lightly on ballerina's feet, a skipping gyroscope teetering around his beloved Ford Capri, the only two-door taxi on the road.

The third circuit complete, Humph retrieved the greyhound, Boudicca, from the rear seat, taking from the boot the tennis machine Dryden had bought them both for Christmas. The cabbie set it on its tripod feet, putting a fluorescent green ball in the slot, leant back on the Capri's peeling paintwork and pulled the handle, shooting the ball fifty yards along the riverbank. Boudicca, unleashed, moved like a swallow over the black peat, a graceful thudding icon of speed.

The ball returned, Humph loaded it again, and fired.

Dryden zipped up the green tarpaulin covering the wheelhouse and joined them. They drank coffee wordlessly having extracted their egg sandwiches from the foil provided by Humph's favourite greasy spoon café. Humph encompassed his in two bites, the oozing yellow yolk the only colour in the dawn light.

'How cold is it?' said Dryden.

'Search me,' said Humph, enjoying the dog's careering run along the floodbank.

Dryden considered his friend's planetary girth. 'We don't have the manpower,' he said.

Boudicca returned and indecently nuzzled Dryden's testicles.

'Another death,' said the cabbie, nodding towards the Capri. 'On the radio.'

'The cold?'

The cabbie nodded. 'Some poor bastard on the Jubilee. Dead in his flat.'

The Jubilee was Ely's sink estate, a warren of brick terraced streets enlivened by the occasional outbreak of ill-judged stone-cladding. Humph had a house there, his home since an acrimonious divorce, which he contrived hardly ever to visit, sleeping instead in the cab in a series of convenient lay-bys.

'What time?' said Dryden, pulling open the Capri's passenger door and bracing himself for the familiar screech of rust from its hinges.

Humph let Boudicca into the back seat and then lowered himself into the driver's seat by holding on to the door and the roof. The Capri listed alarmingly, the suspension twanging underneath.

'Neighbour found him late last night when he saw the windows open,' said Humph.

Dryden tried to imagine it. The flat, up in the sky, with frozen air blowing through it.

He checked his watch again. *The Crow*'s deadline was still hours away, but it was press day and the journalist in him needed a decent tale.

'Let's take a look,' he said, and their moods lifted, buoyed up by the mutual relief that they had somewhere to go.

3

At the foot of the stairwell of High Park Flats a puddle of urine had frozen solid. There was another puddle in the lift, frozen too, but the colour of no known bodily fluid.

Dryden pressed the button marked 12 but the lift didn't move. The doors did a shimmy, closed once, and then retreated. Out on the tarmac he could see Humph in the Capri, smirking.

Dryden trudged up the first flight of stairs, the walls a maze of graffiti except for a Day-Glo yellow poster offering help for the aged during the cold snap. Twenty-four flights of stairs later Dryden arrived on Frobisher, the level where Declan McIlroy had lived until the early hours of that day. There was a wind up here, and it took another five degrees off the temperature. Dryden's breath billowed, and the air made his throat ache. The cold snap had lasted a week now, a dry blast of Arctic air bringing clear skies and showers of oversized snowflakes.

Dryden wrapped his greatcoat around himself and felt the ice in his hair.

On the drive into town he'd rung the station at Ely for the bare details: a neighbour had come onto the landing to rescue his wailing cat, stranded outside by a frozen flap. He'd noticed that the landing window of McIlroy's flat was open, unusual itself at 2 in the morning, but alarming given the freezer-like conditions. The neighbour found the door unlocked and entered to find McIlroy dead in an armchair in the living room, the TV on, a cup of coffee frozen in the mug beside him. All the room's windows were open. Death by hypothermia had been the doctor's call. There'd be an inquest, but McIlroy had a long history of mental illness, and had attempted suicide twice before: both times using a knife.

Dryden peered over the edge of the lift-shaft wall down at the car park as a seagull flew below him. High Park Flats had been built in the 1960s and was the centrepiece of the Jubilee Estate. Fifteen storeys high it tussled, controversially, with the cathedral's West Tower to dominate the horizon. Each floor had an external walkway linking the front doors of each flat. McIlroy's was No. 126, a corner flat, the last on the gangway.

Dryden walked to the door and tried the handle: locked. He was surprised to find the police and emergency services had already left the scene. There was no sign anyone had died here, let alone lived. He knocked once, twice, and waited, looking south towards the city centre and beyond. The rush hour had begun and headlights in a long necklace stretched out east across the Fen towards Newmarket.

Dryden looked through the window but could see little in the gloom – the dull glint of unpolished taps, orange Formica kitchen units and a rusted gas-fired boiler.

'He's not there,' said a voice.

Dryden turned to find an elderly man, perhaps seventy years of age, wrapped in a tartan dressing gown over a jumper and jogging pants, and clutching a mug of tea.

'I heard – about what happened,' said Dryden, taking a step back. 'My name's Dryden, from *The Crow*.'

'Tell him to fuck off,' said a woman's voice from the half-open doorway behind the neighbour.

Dryden nodded towards the flat. 'Duchess of Kent visiting, is she?'

The neighbour grinned, nodding. 'Don't mind her. Her eyes are bad – shingles,' he said, holding out his hand. 'Buster. Buster Timms. I'm the one what found him.' He nodded at No. 126, and continued to nod. 'Wanna look?' he asked.

'The police?' said Dryden, but Buster was already unlocking the door.

'They ain't bothered. I've been in and out all night with tea. They've gone now – told me to keep an eye on the place . . .' He clicked his dental plate with practised ease.

'What was he like – McIlroy?' asked Dryden, as Buster led the way down a short corridor into the living room. It had two picture windows, one looking out east, the other north. There was a small balcony beyond a french window on which stood a single wooden chair, an ashtray beneath was full of ice. The sun up, the room was flooded with light.

Buster ignored his question. 'I found him there – in the chair. Stiff as a board – honest.' Buster beamed. 'Tragic. He wasn't forty.'

'Right – but what was he like?'

'Declan? Mad, I guess. You know. Mental – problems all along really. We're just neighbours you know, there's no point getting involved.'

Dryden nodded. 'There's no doors,' he said.

Buster looked round, running his finger down a door jamb to where the hinges had been. 'He took 'em off. They're in the spare. Don't ask me – but I can guess.' He winked, clicking the plate of his false teeth up to reveal a sudden glimpse of cherry-red gum. Dryden's stomach flipped the egg sandwich. 'Reckon he'd been inside, you know. But he never said.'

Dryden walked into the kitchen. On a Formica-topped table a bunch of carrots lay, the roots still entangled with clay. On the draining board some newspaper was spread under a cauliflower.

'Liked his veg then,' said Dryden, opening the fridge, which was switched off and empty.

'Eats nothing else. He had an allotment – down there.'

They looked out of the greasy window, away from town towards the distant gash of the railway line. Sheds and huts dotted a landscape of bean poles and serried frostbitten greens, a far-flung shanty town of rotting wood and plastic sheeting.

Dryden opened the cupboard over the sink. This was where he'd kept his tea – Darjeeling, Earl Grey, Peppermint, Camomile.

'Blimey,' said Dryden, examining one of the packets, which was almost empty.

Buster leered, and Dryden felt a rare emotion stirring: acute dislike.

'What's funny?' he said, making Buster take a step back.

'He drank,' said Buster. 'Booze. The tea kept him going when he was outta cash.'

Dryden picked up a single glass tumbler on the draining board and wafted it under his nose: it had been rinsed but the aroma of whisky clung to it like the scent of apples.

Buster's teeth were beginning to rattle.

They went into the hall. There was an electricity meter and Dryden noted that the black enamel dial showed it was nearly full: £22.50.

The first door off the corridor was a single bedroom, a sleeping bag on top of a mattress, no carpet. Next was the spare, or rather it had been used as the spare, but had been intended as the master bedroom. Tea crates held an assortment of wiring and electrical circuitry. By the wall were two old TV sets and a video recorder. There was a sturdy wooden table – the only decent furniture in the flat – set out as a workbench and covered in newspaper. Four of the flat's five internal doors stood against the far wall.

'He could fix anything,' volunteered Buster, crowding in by Dryden's shoulder. 'Mostly for thems that lives in the flats. He was cheap.'

'And this?' Dryden pulled an easel from the wall, below it a sheet spattered with several colours of paint.

Buster shrugged. Back in the hall, Dryden filled his lungs with the damp air. There was a storage cupboard, but when Dryden tried the handle it was locked.

'Key?'

Buster shook his head: 'I only had the front. We swapped the spares. The police didn't seem bothered.'

'Short of money a lot, was he?' Dryden asked, heading back into the living room.

'Yeah. But he got benefit – for the illness.'

'Sick?'

'Coughing. TB, he said. That's when I knew something was wrong last night – I listened, but there was no coughing. He always coughs in his sleep. Drives her mad,' he added, nodding towards the partition wall.

'But you didn't check?'

Buster clutched the dressing-gown cord. 'He liked his privacy.'

Over the tiled fireplace hung a framed picture, two men on a bench by a magnolia tree. The wide Fen stretched behind them, a pond in the foreground. Dryden touched the frame.

'That's his mate – Joe,' said Buster. 'Haven't seen him much. Declan said he had throat cancer, that he couldn't travel no more. He's got a place out there . . .' He nodded to the window that faced north towards the open Fen.

Dryden studied the faces: Joe, white close-cropped hair, expensive, quality shirt and shoes, a cigarette trailing smoke in the summer air. And Declan, slight by comparison, shoulders turned forward, chest sunken, wrists narrow and frail.

Despite the friendship Dryden could sense the loneliness in the flat. 'Any other friends? Christmas, whenever?'

Buster shook his head, but Dryden was pretty sure he'd missed the question, so he asked again.

'A sister. Marcie. She brings him some food, checks on him. She came yesterday.'

There was a cheap pine sideboard in the lounge. On it was a bowl of nuts, the only festive touch in the flat. Inside, Dryden found glasses: odd wine goblets, dimpled pint mugs and a single cracked Champagne flute. Each one sat upside-down, precisely over a dust-free circle. All except one: a whisky tumbler.

4

Dryden sat at his desk, looking down into Market Street through the motif of *The Crow* etched in the frosted glass of the newsroom window. Below the strutting bird ran the paper's motto since its foundation in 1882: *Bene agendo nunquam defessus* (Never weary of doing good).

'That's me,' said Dryden, searching under the desktop clutter for his mug.

He retrieved a 1 euro coin from the plastic tub under the coffee machine and let it drop through the slot. The machine hissed, the steam puffing out into the nipped air. The cathedral's bell tolled 9.00am and the radiators began to reverberate as the near-freezing water ran to the shuddering boiler.

Cradling the cup, Dryden looked out again into the street. Sunshine cut down the pavements from the east, and the rooftops opposite steamed. Icicles hung from *The Crow*'s gutters, but none of them dripped, while a single snowflake, an inch wide, fell like a feather.

He sat and booted up his PC. This is how he liked offices: empty.

But it wouldn't be empty for long. It was press day and, though *The Crow* rarely buzzed, it was nevertheless likely to hum by lunchtime. Each of the three journalists' desks was obscured by creeping glaciers of paper through which punched the occasional metal spike. A subs' bench ran along one wall complete with two cumbersome layout computers which predated the flat-screen era and were three feet thick.

Two ashtrays sat between the PCs and were on the same scale, being slightly too small to double up as hubcaps. The room held little of the romantic appeal of newspapers which had made Dryden choose his trade more than a decade before. That had been on Fleet Street, and the office had shuddered every time the presses ran in the basement. But now the smell of printer's ink was just a memory, like yesterday's headlines.

On Dryden's lap the office cat, Splash, slept on its back, its pink paw pads extended. He stroked her, envying the independence as much as the fur coat.

His phone rang, making them both jump.

'Got five?' He knew the voice, feminine and forceful, and could almost smell the acrid scent of the builder's tea in the big no-nonsense mug.

'Vee?'

'Pop over,' she said. 'I've got something you'd like.'

He slipped out the back of *The Crow*'s offices into the old print yard and around into Market Street, then down a treacherously iced alleyway to High Street. Vee's office was over one of the town centre's myriad charity shops, this one by the Sacrist's Gate, the Norman gateway into the cathedral grounds. A Gothic shadow had left this darkened archway in permafrost since the cold snap had brought even the noontime temperatures below freezing. Beneath the cobbles here Dryden recalled that builders in the sixties had found the skulls of the cathedral's monastic community, stacked in a charnel house. He shivered, wrapping his great black trench coat more closely to his thin frame.

In the charity shop a pensioner was trying on hats. A two-bar electric fire provided the shop assistant, who was asleep, with some warmth. Before her on the counter lay an offertory plate sprinkled with silver and copper coins. Up a spiral stone staircase Dryden found Vee's office. Even here, amongst the damp cardboard boxes and the unstripped floorboards, Vee was patently top-drawer, a real-life living remnant of old money and radical liberal politics. She was a pocket battleship amongst pensioners: compact, with sinewy hands and an outdoor tan. One of her eyes had been blinded in youth, and the pupil was now a single white moon, which watered slightly. She rented the office, headquarters of the Hypothermia Action Trust, which she had founded, and a single bedroom above. That, and a £1m bank balance, was all anyone needed to know about Vee Hilgay.

'Another one this morning,' she said as Dryden came in, folding himself into a wobbly captain's chair.

'I know. I've been out – to High Park.'

She nodded. 'That's the eighth in a week,' she said, setting down a pint mug of tea decorated with a picture of Tony Benn. She poured Dryden a cup from the brown pot on her desk. Then she went to a narrow lancet window set in the stone wall, opened it and retrieved a thermometer.

'Minus 3 degrees centigrade. The average for the month is minus 2 – that's the lowest since '47. Last night it fell to minus 10 out at Mildenhall. This could be a disaster; someone else will die today, and tomorrow . . .'

Dryden made a small indecipherable mark in his notebook to help him remember the quote. 'What do you want me to say?'

'Look at this one,' she said, dropping a file on the table. Dryden opened it, bracing himself for emotional blackmail. There was a picture of an elderly woman, white hair recently set in a geriatric helmet, the skull just showing through.

'Millie Thompson. Eighty-six. Found dead in bed at Manea three days ago,' said Vee. 'On the mat three cheques from the social security and her pension. She was too cold to go out and she had a fault in the gas boiler – she'd rung the board but told them not to bother to rush out. She went to bed instead – that was ten days ago. Ten days without hot food, or heat. The cottage was damp. When they found her she was frozen between the blankets.'

Dryden took the head and shoulders picture. 'I can do something – wrap it up with this morning's.'

Vee smiled, knowing that Dryden's career as a journalist had been severely hampered by a conscience. She checked her notes. 'Declan McIlroy. Psychiatric patient – so, confused, or desperate?'

Dryden slurped his tea. 'I guess . . .' He held Vee's good eye for just a moment too long.

She caressed the Tony Benn mug. 'You don't think the cold did it?'

'Didn't say that, Vee. Just think the police are a bit quick to tie up the paperwork on deaths like this . . . I mean, if I was a murderer I'd grab my chance. You'd never get spotted. It's like the Blitz. You can't tell me a few scores didn't get settled on the bomb sites . . .'

'And Millie too?' she said, tapping the file.

'I didn't say that. It's McIlroy I'm talking about – just McIlroy.'

Vee let the silence stretch. Dryden looked out the window, the West Tower of the cathedral dominated the view, frozen water glistening like slug trails down the Norman stonework. Another giant snowflake fell.

'Neighbour says he's broke most of the time. He does part-time electrical work – but it's smalltime stuff. He's on sickness benefit. But the meter's jammed with coins – more than twenty quid's worth. Most people wait till the coin drops and the lights go out . . .'

'But he's confused . . .'

'I guess. And he drinks. So perhaps he stuffed his benefit in the meter to make sure it didn't get spent at the offy. And . . .'

'Would you like it to be murder?' asked Vee astutely.

Dryden bridled. 'No. Not really.' He stood. 'I'll run something – with the usual advice and emergency numbers. It's all I can do . . .' Dryden was less than enthused by the cold-snap story, partly because the whole of eastern England was hit so there was little unusual in the situation in the Fens, and partly because *The Crow*'s readership shared a deep-rooted, immoral disregard for anyone who wasn't a star in *Neighbours*.

Back at *The Crow* the A team had arrived. The editor, Septimus Henry Kew, was installed behind his glass partition checking the proofs. The news editor, Charlie Bracken, was at his desk, sweating into a blue shirt he'd had on all week. There was an aroma of stale alcohol in the air, which emanated from Charlie's skin and the half-open deep drawer in his desk where he kept an emergency bottle of Bell's.

Dryden brought his screen to life with a single touch of the keyboard and began, instantly, to type:

An Ely man was today found frozen to death in his armchair – the latest victim of the cold snap which has claimed the lives of eight vulnerable, frail or elderly victims in a single week.

Dryden tapped on as Garry Pymoor, *The Crow*'s junior reporter, arrived enveloped in his habitual full-length black leather coat. Garry's balance was poor, having suffered from meningitis as a child, so as he threw himself into his chair he nearly missed.

'Got a goody,' he said to Dryden, trying to knock a

cigarette out of a packet with one hand while clipping his phone headset over his head with the other.

Dryden braced himself. Garry's news judgement was as sound as his semicircular canals.

'They've issued a warning to parents that there's a dope supplier targeting kids. The schoolgate market. Cheap cannabis for young teenagers – twelve- to fifteen-year-olds mainly. They reckon someone is growing locally and flogging it cut-price. Probably a farmer. What d' ya reckon?'

Dryden nodded. 'OK. Get a quote from the NFU. Tell Charlie – it's got to be worth the front.'

Dryden put his story on hold and hit calls: the last round of checks with the emergency services before the final deadline of *The Crow*. There was an RTA on the bypass and a small house fire at a village near the edge of town. And one item worth a par at least – a warning from the police for householders to watch out for bogus plumbers touting for work on burst pipes. A pair of conmen had already made off with one customer's life savings.

'What's the splash?' Dryden asked the room.

Charlie jerked in his seat, realizing it was supposed to be his job to have an answer to this question.

'I guess it's this bloke in the flats – and the rest of the cold stuff. Wrap it all up in five hundred words. And you'd better read this insider on St Vincent's . . . Henry's had the lawyer make some changes.'

Dryden tapped a key on his PC which brought up Charlie's news list. The news editor's judgement was often suspect, especially this close to opening time. Dryden scrolled down the list, checking that he'd called the right story as the splash – otherwise he'd be overruled by the editor at the last minute and Dryden would have to slash his copy and bump up a rival candidate.

* News Schedule: The Crow – Thursday December 29 2005

Front.

Mayor's charity raises £2,000 for Christmas Appeal – PIX. Pymoor

Three injured as car ditches in Thirty Foot Drain – PIX. Dryden

Row over late licence for town club on New Year's Eve. Pymoor

Cold snap claims fresh victim: wrap up on the big freeze. X-ref pix inside. Staff and PA wire copy.

Page 2.

LEAD: New victims come forward in child abuse probe at St Vincent's. Dryden

Village school hit by Christmas arson. £12,000 worth of damage. PIX. Pymoor

Dog which bit baby put down. Dryden

Eight drunk and disorderly cases dealt with by magistrates. 'Binge culture' attacked. Pymoor

Page 3.

LEAD: TV star to open bingo hall revamp – PIX. Pymoor

Littleport man 'made life misery' for whole street. PA court copy

Fen Skating Committee meets on go-ahead for race . . . file PIC.

My View: bishop writes blah blah . . .

Class Snap: Little Downham Church School 1923.

Page 5.

LEAD: Chittering man convicted of bigamy – again. File pix of all three weddings. Pymoor

Ice buckles sluice gates at Denver – PIX. Dryden

Lantern School tops county league tables – PIX. Dryden

News In Brief

Insurers reclassify Fenland properties after survey shows flooding would inundate 100,000 homes. (lift from nationals)

Christmas burglaries round-up. Pymoor

Courts may reopen 30-year-old murder case – PA

Bolting horse destroys greenhouse at Manea. Dryden

OAP heated tea mornings – listing for the week: includes cathedral Lady Chapel.

Dryden filed the list away. 'Bloody hell. It's a bit thin.' He noted in particular that any story tagged 'TV star' clearly involved a nonentity as they hadn't used the real name. Ely typically attracted those who had never made the A-list, but would one day see the Z-list. What was worse, the news editor had missed a good story. The magistrates warning over binge drinking could have been run up into a bigger story ahead of New Year and spliced in with the row over late opening. He sent Charlie an internal e-mail suggesting the change.

Then he called up the story he'd written on St Vincent's, the latest wriggle in a long-running saga surrounding a local orphanage. The intro had been significantly altered from the original by the lawyers – toning down the drama. Dryden cut out his own byline and put in a generic replacement. If they wanted to butcher his copy he'd rather it didn't carry his name.

By Our Own Staff

Lawyers probing abuse of children at a Catholic orphanage in Ely have uncovered evidence from two further potential victims who were at the home in the 1970s.

A spokesman said yesterday that they were now dealing with five separate cases of mistreatment of children aged 9–15 involving beatings, solitary confinement, and withholding food and bedding.

'We feel the weight of evidence is now such that these complaints must be addressed in court,' said Hugh Appleyard, of Appleyard & Co., solicitors for the alleged victims.

A civil action is planned which would seek substantial damages against the Catholic Diocese of East Cambridgeshire, which ran the Orphanage of St Vincent de Barfleur.

The orphanage, at Lane End, Ely, closed in 1989, although the nearby church is still open.

Fr Ignatius O'Halloran, a spokesman for the diocese, said: 'We are co-operating with the authorities and will do everything we can to ascertain the facts of each of these cases.'

Ely police said they were in touch with the diocese and the county council's social services department over the cases, and that a file may be submitted to the Crown Prosecution Service. Criminal charges may follow.

The priest in charge of St Vincent's during the time when it is alleged most of the abuse took place has not been officially named, and has declined to make any comment.

'The lawyer's chucked a lot of the good stuff,' said Dryden, rolling his cursor down through the 600-word story. Garry booed ritualistically. 'And ditched the priest's name.'

Charlie tugged at the collar of his blue shirt and Dryden guessed he'd cut it – rather than the lawyers – just to make sure the story was doubly safe.

Dryden filed the story back into the production basket, failing to suppress a surge of indignation on behalf of the victims of St Vincent's. His own Catholic education had been largely benign, but there had been enough random violence and institutionalized cruelty to allow him some level of empathy with the abused.

He refilled his coffee, recycling the 1 euro coin which could be extracted from the rear of the vending machine, and then bashed out the rest of the splash, taking in 200 words from the Press Association on the weather, including reports of freak snowflakes due to the exceptional cold but dry conditions. A meteorologist was quoted as predicting that the world record – a flake fifteen inches by eight inches which fell in Montana in 1887 – was unlikely to be beaten.

Then Dryden rewrote Garry's story on the cannabis supplier so that it made sense. Garry, pathetically grateful, offered to buy him a drink at The Fenman bar opposite now that the press-day lunchtime had officially arrived: it was 11.30am.

But Dryden was still haunted by the claustrophobic Declan McIlroy. He shared with him that oppressive fear of the locked door, and was still intrigued by the scent of freshly imbibed whisky. What kind of man has a final drink and then washes up? And whose was the other glass, stashed carefully back in the sideboard?

'A walk first,' said Dryden, standing. 'Come on,' he added to Garry. They headed for the door, both of them showing their mobile phones to Charlie. 'Any questions, we're news gathering.' The news editor smiled, dreaming of his first pint.

5

The long shadow of High Park Flats fell just short of the allotments Dryden had seen from Declan McIlroy's front room: the vast penumbra lay instead across wasteland, the centrepiece of which was the rusted chassis of an abandoned car – the make unrecognizable now – blotched with fire marks around the wheel arches and empty windows. Two boys in peaked US-style caps threw stones at the metalwork from a pitcher's mound made of a pile of discarded wooden pallets. Schoolchildren, bored by the holiday and ejected from the warmth of the flats, had lit a fire in an oil drum and were poking it with sticks. A smaller child, just toddling, its skin chilled red under skimpy clothing, played with a plastic playroom oven.

Dryden and Garry crossed quickly into the weak sunlight beyond. Here a picket fence had once marked the boundary of the allotments and remnants of the whitewashed wood remained, interspersed with planks and flotsam, and a vicious spiral of razor wire.

'What we looking for?' said Garry, fingering his spots.

'Let's see if we can find someone. Anyone,' said Dryden, ignoring the question and looking for signs of life. A scarecrow decorated with a child's beach windmills caught his eye – a few sails turning in a sudden breeze – but otherwise the landscape was still.

Dryden crashed a foot down on the earth, managing only to dislodge a few crumbs of the hard-frozen soil.

'Jeez,' said Garry, looking out over the broken-down bean

poles, the clumps of iced pampas grass and the dotted huts and sheds.

They walked down a central path. Most plots were empty now, the heavy clay of the Isle of Ely dusted white while a few carrot tops and gone-to-seed vegetables stood out – burnt black by days of sub-zero temperatures. The only colour came from the random plastic water butts.

In the far corner of the allotments there was a narrow gap in a hedge, beyond which a lazy line of smoke rose into the sky like a twisted gut. They stood at the opening, looking in, but hesitating to break a spell which seemed to hang over the spot. The plots beyond were better kept, with neat, rubbish-free drills, the wide enclave surrounded by a high hedge. Two poles had been erected at either side of the entrance and from a rope hung between them a row of dead crows dangled, together with a fox and a desiccated cat.

'Guess they couldn't afford a welcome mat,' said Dryden.

A shed at the centre of the field was larger than the rest and boasted a stove pipe, from which the smoke was churning, occasional black mixed with orange-tinged white. The windows of the hut were misted, but inside Dryden could see figures moving.

'Carrot City,' said Dryden, as Garry fumbled for a cigarette in the pockets of his oversized leather coat.

Then Dryden saw the dog. It was chained to a ring slipped through a spike in the ground. It was a regulation Dobermann, with regulation retractable lips. Dryden, a physical coward of considerable range, took a step backwards. Dogs – other than Boudicca – were just one of the things he was afraid of. But they were one of the things he was afraid of most.

The guard dog hadn't barked, always – in Dryden's experience – a very bad sign. It stood, waiting to see if the intruders would persevere. Dryden tried to gauge the length of the chain, drawing a virtual circle across the allotment's shanty-town geography.

He edged forward, aware that his most terrifying nightmare was to be seen as a coward, and that dogs can smell fear. The Dobermann was up and running in a terrifyingly short second. Dryden, rooted, felt his guts heave and his pulse rate hit 120 before the hound was six feet away, where the chain snapped rigid and wrenched at the dog's throat, tumbling it back in a heap. It rose, dazed, and exposed rosy pink gums and a set of textbook canines.

'Back and sit.' It was a woman's voice, resonant but not masculine. The dog folded itself down, sphinx-like, and rested its chin on its giant paws.

She was standing outside the hut with what looked to Dryden's tutored eye like a pint of beer – even from fifty yards. Garry pushed him in the back and they edged past the dog, Dryden's eyes fixed firmly on the stove-pipe smoke in the sky.

They passed two 'PRIVATE – MEMBERS ONLY' signs en route to the shed and an auxiliary notice which read: 'BEWARE – POISONS USED'.

'Can I help?' said the woman when they were up close, in the tone of voice which means the opposite.

Her face was extraordinary – or rather her skin was. Dryden guessed she was in her late thirties or early forties, but in many ways her calendar age was irrelevant: she just looked weatherbeaten. Her tan was that specific shade of ochre which is the result of exposure to wind and rain as well as sun, the face patterned by systems of small lines – especially around the eyes, which were wet and a vivid green. In many ways she was beautiful: the thick black hair sucking in the light, the skin, Dryden imagined, carrying the exhilarating scent of sea salt. It was a face that had spent a lifetime under an open sky.

But the eyes held him. There was something mesmeric about the eyes. Why was she looking over Dryden's shoulder? He looked behind. High Park Flats stood like a gravestone on the near-horizon, a single Christmas tree lit in a dark window.

Suddenly he remembered she'd asked a question. 'Yes. Sorry. My name's Dryden – I work for *The Crow* – it's about Declan McIlroy.'

A man appeared at her shoulder, wrapped in a donkey jacket. He had a narrow jutting head like a vulture, held forward and low between his shoulders, and his hair was shorn to a grey stubble. He put his arm around the woman's waist and rocked her so that she leant against him.

'It's OK,' she said, touching his free hand, and turning back to Dryden. 'You can come in. We know about Declan.'

She went first, reaching out with both hands to touch the sides of the door frame, the fingertips fumbling slightly to find the wooden edges. Which is when Dryden realized she was blind, that the green eyes which reflected everything saw nothing.

Inside it was hot. The stove pipe didn't rise directly through the ceiling but crossed the shed in a diagonal to reach the external chimney. It radiated the heat, and around it on various chairs and wooden crates sat half a dozen men. In the corner stood a large plastic barrel and the heavy air was scented with a perfume Dryden knew well: home brew.

'Welcome to the Gardeners' Arms,' said the woman, with a tired smile. 'I'm Marcie, Marcie Sley.'

Dryden couldn't stop himself glancing at the barrel. 'Who's the brewer?'

'It's a co-op,' said the man in the donkey jacket who'd stood by Marcie. He held out a hand like the bucket on a mechanical digger. 'John Sley.' Dryden noted the grey stubble on his chin and guessed he was a decade older than his wife. Sley took a swig of beer, and Dryden glimpsed wrecked teeth. 'There's an association – of allotment holders. This is the clubhouse, if you like. We do tea as well . . .'

Garry beamed. 'Beer's fine.'

Two more glasses were found and filled. The beer came flat, but tasted malty and Dryden sensed the alcoholic kick. 'Strong?'

'Six point five per cent,' said Sley, and Garry whistled happily.

Dryden nodded. 'I'm sorry – you're Declan's sister?' Marcie sat down suddenly, letting the silence say yes. 'I just wanted to know a bit more about him. I know it's very soon – too soon – but the health people are keen to flag up the dangers of the cold for the elderly . . . the vulnerable. It's a terrible accident. What do you think happened?'

Marcie fingered something at her throat. A crucifix, Dryden noted.

'Declan wasn't well,' she said, sipping the beer. 'He'd been confused and he drank – drank too much. Sometimes he'd open the windows to ease the anxiety of being inside.'

Dryden let the silence lengthen, knowing that the less he pushed the more they'd talk.

'What did the police say?' said Marcie eventually. 'I rang this morning, when we heard . . . I'll have to clear the flat.' Her voice caught, and her husband refilled glasses to give her time to recover. Then he sat next to her, one of his bony hands gently massaging her neck.

'Not much. They think it's an accident too. But Declan had a drink with someone last night,' said Dryden. 'Perhaps

31

yesterday afternoon. Anyone visit?' he asked, letting them think the police might have their suspicions too.

Marcie stood and flipped open the cast-iron door on the stove with a length of kindling. The sudden flare of red flame cast half her face into shadow: 'I popped in with his lunch, but we didn't have a drink. Why did they say that?'

Dryden could sense the atmosphere tipping towards antagonistic, so he ignored the question. 'How was he?' he said, sipping the beer and guessing that John Sley's estimate of the alcoholic content was wrong by a factor of two.

It was Marcie who answered; all the other heads were down, examining the beer. 'Declan's been low, we all knew he had problems. The winters were always worse – nothing to do down here.'

Dryden nodded. 'He liked it then – being outside? I saw the flat – there's no doors . . .'

'Claustrophobia,' said Marcie. 'He wanted to be outside all the time really. But the TB was bad . . . he's had it since childhood. We had to make him stay in over the cold snap. I should have popped back . . .'

John Sley shook his head. 'You couldn't have done anything. If he'd decided –' He stopped the thought there and the silence was profound, marked by the cooing of a wood pigeon.

'He'd tried to kill himself before, hadn't he?' asked Dryden, happier now the subject had been broached. 'The windows of the flat were thrown open when they found him. Did you, any of you, ever think he'd try to take his own life?'

Marcie Sley's hand went to her throat. One man, thin, with a small, silent dog held by a rope lead, lit a roll-up cigarette.

'Like you said, he'd tried before,' said Marcie. 'But when I saw him I thought he was well – almost happy. He hadn't been drinking – I know that.'

Dryden thought about the electricity meter stuffed with cash, and the malt whisky.

'There was a friend in particular, wasn't there – Joe, was it?'

Several heads nodded. 'I'd really like to talk to him – you know, some more background, Perhaps he visited him?'

'Joe likes his privacy,' said John Sley. 'We could pass a message.'

Dryden jotted his mobile number down on his card. 'He can ring any time. What did you say his surname was?'

'We didn't,' said Sley, seeing them to the door, where he called the dog to heel.

'Thanks for the beers,' said Dryden as they edged out. 'Security's good round here. Kids nick the veg, do they?'

'If they do, they don't do it twice,' he said, shutting the door in Dryden's face. Beyond the frosted glass he saw Sley's back retreat towards the convivial glow of the fire; but for them the Gardeners' Arms was closed.

6

Charlie, *The Crow*'s lightly soused news editor, rang Dryden before they'd got off the Jubilee Estate.

'That you?' Dryden noted the edge of panic and the subtle background noise that could only be the bar of the Fenman. He heard glasses kiss in a toast and the sickly notes of the Christmas number one.

It sounded warm and friendly – but he wasn't going there.

'Henry's read the piece on the child-abuse claims – it's all fine,' said Charlie, taking a slurp. 'But the lawyers sent him an e-mail. They wanted to know – you did put this stuff to the priest, yeah? You said no comment in the copy – but was that no comment after he'd heard what we were going to say or no comment because you couldn't get to him?'

'The latter,' said Dryden, as Garry danced on his toes, eager to join the ritual Fenman session.

'Shit,' said Charlie, aware that he should have asked the question sooner.

'But we didn't name him,' said Dryden.

'The lawyers say that might not be good enough. Anyone who knew the set-up at St Vincent's knows who we are talking about. Henry says can you get round there and have another go – if you can't get through, drop in a note with the details on it and tell him to get back asap if he wants to make a comment. That way we're covered. Well, we're better off than if we don't do it, anyway. OK?'

Dryden felt the beginnings of a headache, and the cold

was penetrating between his shoulder blades, inserting a sharp pain like a knife wound.

'It's pointless,' he said, clicking the phone off. 'Arse coverer.'

Dryden rang Humph and set Garry free, the junior reporter heading off towards town. The cabbie picked Dryden up at the bottom of the steps that led to Declan McIlroy's flat. The Capri's interior was now heated to Humph's preferred temperature: 82°F. There was a smell of warm plastic, bacon and dog. Boudicca lay on the back seat, the greyhound's great head the only part of her body on the tartan rug.

'She was sleeping,' said Humph, reproaching Dryden for the call.

'Sorry. It may have escaped your notice, but I have to work for a living. Lane End. Chop-chop.' Dryden ran a hand through his thick black hair, letting the fingers stick like a comb. This was the kind of useless errand he'd become a journalist to avoid. If the priest objected to anything in the story it was entirely academic as the paper had already gone. The presses were turning, there was no going back.

He looked at his face in the rear-view mirror: the green eyes dimmed, the immobile medieval face set on precisely geometric lines beneath the shock of black hair: he ran a hand through it again and tried to relax.

Humph edged the cab through the Jubilee and out down a long drove which turned regularly at right-angles to zigzag out of town into the Fen. They passed a derelict pumping station and a clay pit before reaching a hamlet of discarded council houses, now owned by a local housing association. Entertainment consisted of a telephone box and a bus stop, both of which had been vandalized. Just beyond stood St Vincent's, another stunning example of the modern Catholic

Church's inability to build an inspiring place for worship. It looked like the living quarters from Noah's Ark, a brick shed, the only decoration a life-size copper figure of Christ on the cross over the door which now bled green blood down the façade and over the doors.

Next door was the presbytery: a Victorian house, not unlike a seaside B&B, with bay windows and some stone decoration at the pinnacle where another simple cross was hung. The garden was over-neat and stone flagged and if it had been a B&B it would have had a sign in the window saying 'No Vacancies'. A young priest, a gold and purple football scarf covering his dog collar, was hurrying towards the church. 'Excuse me, Father,' said Dryden, stepping out of the Capri. He felt an overwhelming memory of guilt, the legacy of that Catholic childhood.

'Father,' he said again, catching the young man up. He was in his mid-twenties, his face blank and devoid of charity, but a wave of well-cut blond hair hinted at vanity.

'I'm looking for Father Martin. Is he in?'

'He is here for those that need him,' said the young man, and Dryden imagined a thunderbolt delivering instant retribution for the odious piety.

'At home?' he asked, nodding towards the presbytery.

The young priest's eyes flickered towards the church.

'I'll be brief,' said Dryden, walking on.

The young man dogged his steps: 'He's praying . . . I really think . . .'

But Dryden was through the padded door and into the body of the church. A single candle burnt in the gloom by a side altar and the crucifix which hung over the main altar was brutally bare: an oak cross without decoration. A Christmas tree stood in a side chapel, unlit. A crib of cardboard stood in the nave, but most of the two-dimensional figures had fallen over. Father Martin was sitting alone on one of the plastic chairs close to the confessional boxes. Glancing in the stone dish which held the holy water, Dryden noted that it was frozen.

He let his shoes slap against the polished parquet flooring and Father Martin stiffened as he took the seat behind: the priest's hair was cut cruelly short at the back, the exposed neck red and sore.

'I'm sorry,' said Dryden, trying to take his eyes off the flickering red light beside the altar.

Father Martin didn't acknowledge him.

'I'm from *The Crow*. There have been further allegations about St Vincent's during your time as principal. I did call yesterday – at the house – but there was no answer. I should put these allegations to you in case you wish to make a statement.'

The priest turned. Dryden tried not to react to the birth-mark, a livid red scar which covered one cheek and encircled the left eye. In compensation for this disfigurement the rest of Father Martin's appearance was immaculate: the still-black hair combed flat, any grey obscured by Brylcreem, the dark cassock dust free. He smelt of coal-tar soap, and Dryden saw that his fingernails, where his hand rested on the chair-back, were white and trimmed, the skin underneath a baby-pink.

'I am told by the lawyers employed by my diocese that I should not talk of these things.' Dryden's eye caught a shadow moving by the altar.

The priest stood and left by a side door on the far side of the church from the presbytery. Outside there was a memorial garden, some battered roses frozen against their sticks. Beyond the Black Fen stretched, scorched by the overnight frost. Where the ice was gone the grass on the peat was a deep green, like seaweed.

Father Martin buttoned up a heavy coat and raised a finger to point north. 'The Catholic Orphanage of St Vincent de Barfleur,' he said. A mile distant, on a slight rise, stood the ruins of a house. The building's shadow in the low winter light was as substantial as the house itself.

Dryden nodded. 'But you're not saying anything on the record at this time. That's the case?'

Father Martin nodded. 'I'm sorry. Those are my instructions.'

Dryden flipped open the mobile and rang Charlie. The call was answered, but for a few seconds Dryden could hear only the sound of festivities in the Fenman; Garry's voice, excited by alcohol, shouted for a drink.

'It's me,' said Dryden. 'It's no comment. That's official.' He cut Charlie dead before he repeated an invitation to join them at the bar.

Father Martin extracted a silver cigarette case from his overcoat and offered one. Dryden sensed a moment of communion and took it, and a light from the priest's hand, noting the acrid scent of menthol.

'I walk at this time . . .' said Father Martin, about to excuse himself.

'Why St Vincent de Barfleur?' said Dryden, trying to keep his witness talking.

'He is one of the most admirable of the martyrs.' Father Martin smiled. 'Would you like to know how he died?'

Dryden nodded, avoiding the priest's eyes.

'He was crucified upside-down. A lingering death, but he never cried out to denounce his faith.'

Dryden felt the old antagonisms rise. 'Which is admirable, is it?'

Martin nodded, not hearing. 'Do you want to know why they crucified him?'

'I suspect you are about to tell me, Father.'

'They crucified him because he refused to let them twist his words. They were actually anxious to avoid the spectacle of a crucifixion, so they offered him a way out – a form of words. He wouldn't take it, he said the words of Christ were sacred.'

Dryden swallowed hard. 'I'm doing my job.'

Father Martin shrugged, happy to have hit his mark. Dryden drew heavily on the cigarette and let it drop to the grass, where the sizzle was audible. 'I could walk with you,' he said.

Father Martin smiled. 'As you are so interested, Mr Dryden, perhaps we should visit the ruins of St Vincent's?' Dryden returned the smile but felt manipulated, beaten, and in a curious way, as he followed Father Martin across the Fen, a victim too.

7

Out on the peat the soil was silent, the usual trickling of water petrified by the permafrost. Dryden's battered brown leather shoes were still dry when they got to the ruins, a lonely landmark it took them ten minutes to reach. A single snow flurry came and went, leaving the peat peppered with unmelted flakes of ice.

The orphanage had stood on a low island of clay in the Black Fen reached by a one-track drove which ran beside a deep drain. The building itself had been surrounded by a wall topped by iron spikes, now punctuated by falls of rubble. The entrance gates had long gone but over them a wrought-iron frieze held the name still.

The Catholic Orphanage of St Vincent de Barfleur.

Dryden nodded, unnerved by Father Martin's brief excursion into Catholic history, and wondered out loud why it had been closed down.

'Orphanages were out of fashion, and the Church's reputation was hardly pristine. Numbers fell, too far in the end. The diocese tried to sell the building, it's still trying to sell the building, but it's been closed for a decade, more.'

Dryden looked at the priest's profile, the jutting Gaelic brow in contrast to the weak nose. He'd guessed he was close to retirement age – perhaps sixty or more. The black cassock beneath the heavy overcoat made him look more substantial than he was.

They skirted an outer fence of wooden stakes and barbed wire which had been thrown up to provide some security.

One of the fenceposts had taken root, a tree now the height of two men.

'Good God,' said Dryden, stopping and running a finger along the sapling's bark, regardless of the blasphemy.

'Yes,' said Martin, the face brightening for the first time, the birthmark less visible now the priest's skin had reddened with the cold. 'A poplar. The posts must have been very green; it's taken root. A little miracle . . .'

Dryden returned the gaze and the smile vanished.

They were in the shadow of the building now and, out of the blinding low-slung rays of the sun, Dryden could see it clearly for the first time. The floorplan was a letter H, and only the forward two wings were, in fact, in ruin. The rest of the house had been secured with corrugated iron over the downstairs windows and doors. It looked like a workhouse: functional architecture with the single flourish of the grand doorway over which stood a marble canopy on two pillars, one of which was bending outwards alarmingly. Ivy, now white with ice, had colonized the façade.

'I didn't realize it was so big,' said Dryden. 'How many boys?'

Martin crunched out a cigarette on the flagstoned court-yard. 'Twisted words, Mr Dryden – our lawyers were quite specific. I should say nothing.'

Dryden held up his hands. 'No notebook. I'm just trying to understand.'

Martin nodded. 'I've read your stories, Mr Dryden. I detect a marked sympathy with the alleged victims.'

'A Catholic education, I'm afraid. It leaves scars,' said Dryden, struggling to keep the conversation uncharged.

The priest nodded, classing himself effortlessly as a victim too. He retrieved another cigarette and Dryden recalled the priests of his childhood and the acrid stench of nicotine; the jaundiced fingers.

'Just over two hundred in 1970,' said Martin. 'That was the centenary. It had been there, or thereabouts, for years. There was a great need, you see – especially amongst the urban poor. Our boys came from many places, sent by their churches.'

'And the priests?'

'Numbers? It varied. When I was principal we never managed more than a dozen. Class sizes were on the large side – but then the education was on the poor side.'

They laughed, and the space echoed like an empty room.

'I will deny this conversation, Mr Dryden – if anything ever appears.'

Dryden nodded. 'It won't.'

Martin stiffened, a palm at the base of his spine. 'There was never any sexual abuse – you do know that? The allegations all refer to what – these days – can only be described as inappropriate attempts at imposing discipline.'

'That's a plus point, is it? A badge of honour? It's certainly a novel brand image. St Vincent's – we beat them but we never fuck them.'

Dryden was pleased he'd said it. Martin coloured, the birthmark almost disappearing, the hand holding the cigarette vibrating slightly. Dryden felt he'd reclaimed a little bit of his own childhood, if nobody else's.

The priest produced a set of keys and wrestled briefly with a large padlock on the corrugated-iron sheet covering the front door. He swung it back, almost violently, as if airing the place, and then unlocked the door behind, which was studded with nails in mock medieval grandeur. Then he was gone, swallowed by the shadows, without looking back.

By the time Dryden had edged over the threshold the

42

priest had thrown open a shutter, the light revealing in the gloom of the entrance hall an ugly ironwork candelabra suffocated in cobwebs.

'I was thirty-one when I arrived here as principal in 1970,' said Martin, shivering despite himself. 'I think the diocese knew something was wrong and I was supposed to put things straight. The outsider. And that's how they treated me.'

Dryden climbed halfway up the stairs to look back down on the priest, noticing the neat natural tonsure of scalp surrounded by the short, oiled hair. The floor was cold stone in a chessboard black and white design. Despite the dereliction two smells still tussled for supremacy, both remembered from Dryden's childhood: beeswax polish and rotting carpet. The walls too were horribly reminiscent: split by a dado rail between purple below and lemon yellow above.

'The winter of 1970,' said Martin, lost now in his own memories.

Dryden nodded, climbing further despite the creaking wood. A bird fluttered somewhere in a loft and some leaves around an open fireplace blew themselves into a tiny whirlwind. On the landing a threadbare carpet ran off into the darkness in both directions: ahead a large stained-glass window looked out into the rear courtyard. Martin overtook him, turned left, and opened a door into one of the rear wings. It was a dormitory, and here the windows were without curtains or blinds and largely intact, bathing the long gallery in a flat, institutional light. Bedsteads had stood here in two lines against both walls, the linoleum still bearing faded stripes where the sunlight had fallen between them.

Martin stood, his large frame twisted slightly. 'I didn't know,' he bowed his head. 'Not for many years. The teachers had mostly been here for a lifetime – the youngest for twenty years. Several had been boys here. It had been a brutal place, and I often think the only real mark of their guilt was that they felt they had to hide it from me.'

'You don't mind if I find that hard to believe,' said Dryden, walking the length of the empty room to a shoulder-height wooden partition. Beyond was another bare room, the floor tiled this time, and the walls showing the scars of a row of urinals. 'It's medieval,' he said to no one.

'Yes,' said Martin. 'Yes, it was. There were four dormitories – each a separate school house. Leo, Pius, John, and Paul. A priest ruled each – tiny kingdoms, really. The tradition, I was informed, was that the principal was expected to enter only at the invitation of the priest in charge. I never challenged it. I was expected to live apart, to preserve the authority of the office.'

'Where?' said Dryden, running a hand along the ice-cold tiles.

'In one of the forward wings. There's a flat. The rest of the staff lived in the other – except those with house responsibilities who lived here.' He nodded to a single door in the far wall. Dryden tried the handle but it was locked; he rattled it, listening to the echo.

They retraced their steps to the hallway outside, down the half-lit stairs to the tiled lobby and into what had been an office to the side of the main doors.

'My kingdom,' said Martin, switching on another bare lightbulb. There was a desk in the middle, grotesquely decorated and on a grand scale, while above it a great picture had hung, its shadow still visible on the scarlet and gold wallpaper.

'They can't get the desk out. It was probably made in this very room.'

'When *did* you know?' asked Dryden, tired with the contemplation of furnishings.

Martin shrugged, turning out the light. In the sudden shadow he paused and Dryden could see his eyes, and the water that suddenly filled them. 'It doesn't happen like that. We aren't innocent and then suddenly guilty, not when it really matters. We're corrupted, by degree. It's how evil works, Mr Dryden, through a series of tiny victories over good. I was institutionalized, and the institution allowed those things to happen, and then suddenly it was too late. I do remember when it was too late.'

'What happened?' said Dryden.

'The school was empty, I can't recall why. Perhaps a service at the church, or sports day – yes, sports perhaps. I knew I was alone. I was working in my office when I heard this persistent noise. It is very distinctive, the crying of the defeated. I won't pretend it was the first time I had heard such things. I went upstairs and broke the rule.'

'What did you find?' asked Dryden. They were by the main door again, in front of a large hall mirror built into the wall in which the silver had begun to blacken in ugly blotches.

'Beyond the wash basins were toilet cubicles. In Pius. The boy was in one. He said he'd been there for several days. He'd been given a Bible, I remember, and a cup to drink the water from the cistern. He was naked, crushed in many ways. I tried to get him to leave but he reiterated the punishments which awaited him if he dared. It was hard to believe, but there was no doubting his sincerity.'

'What did you do?'

'Nothing. It was too late. I knew it had been happening, I had been protected from the knowledge by the rules. I said something ineffectual, to salve my conscience, and we carried on.'

He looked at Martin in the mirror, the face more sinister now that left and right had been transposed.

Outside, the sky was cloudless, the visibility icicle-sharp. They walked back towards the church along the old track which had been the drive, Dryden annoyed that the priest had succeeded in saying so much without making anything clearer.

They stopped at a low stone wall which edged a small graveyard.

'As I said, two more victims have been identified,' said Dryden, trying to inveigle the priest into specifics, into confronting the reality of the police investigation.

The priest opened the graveyard gate. 'Yes. They are contacting others, I believe – Hugh Appleyard is a good man. Many more will come forward, I'm sure. Some will embellish the truth, some will invent it – but there is enough shame in a hundredth of what they say to damn the guilty.'

Again, effortlessly, he had distanced himself from the children who were in his care.

'The priests in charge. What of their stories?' said Dryden, encouraging him to implicate others.

Martin laughed then, and Dryden sensed the corrosive cynicism which had been his punishment for those decades of responsibility.

'Ask them,' he said, spreading his arms wide. 'They're all here. Remember, I was thirty-one when I arrived. The youngest priest was twenty years older. The last died two years ago.'

Dryden rubbed the lichen from the nearest grave and saw that each stone bore a simple cross and the diocesan crest.

Father Martin looked at the sky. 'That is my sentence, Mr Dryden. To be left alone amongst the accused.'

Or your salvation, thought Dryden, filling his lungs with the frosted air.

8

Dryden slept happily in Humph's Capri, his dreams refusing to take flight thanks to the ballast provided by six pints of Isle of Ely Ale and a four-star curry which had given him hiccoughs. The session in The Fenman bar had been particularly lively, culminating in Garry's ill-fated attempt to dance a Highland reel in anticipation of New Year.

When Dryden finally awoke the moon was up and ice covered the Capri's bonnet. He stretched, aware that a hangover hovered, and cleared a porthole in the condensation of the window. Outside, against the stars, the black outline of The Tower Hospital loomed like an exam.

Humph was listening to one of his Estonian language tapes, repeating with care a long list of pastry delicacies available only in Tallinn, while flicking through his bilingual dictionary, unnaturally excited by the section devoted to pies. Each year he applied himself to some obscure language, in the almost certain knowledge there was little danger he would ever need to speak it in Ely. Then each Christmas he would flee the unspeakable horrors of the festive season by flying out to some forsaken European capital for a few days to try out his new vocabulary. He had just returned from Zagreb, having spent the previous year mastering Serbo-Croat menus.

He flipped open the glove compartment to extract a miniature bottle of Croatian hooch he'd bought at the airport. It was purple and tasted of lighter fuel.

Dryden peered out again at the lit foyer of The Tower.

A former workhouse, the building had become a lunatic asylum throughout Victoria's reign. It boasted a single turret, complete with an interior-lit clock and fake battlements, the whole encircled by grounds full of institutional trees.

Laura Dryden, thanks to the continued support of the Mid-Anglian Mutual Insurance Company, was one of fifty paying 'guests' in the private hospital. It was a situation Dryden knew could not last for ever. One day the insurers would politely point out that their responsibilities were close to an end, and suggest a less expensive regimen of care involving what they called 'home' – a concept with which Dryden would have struggled if he had allowed himself to think about it at all.

He pushed open the cab door before he had time to reconsider his decision to begin his ritual daily visit. The rust in the hinges screeched, as he knew it would, and he slammed the door closed without saying a word.

Inside, beyond the overheated and over-lit reception, the carpeted corridors muffled his steps. There was an expensive silence, in which high-technology machinery hummed, spoilt by a solitary cry from a patient's dream.

Dryden knocked on Laura's door, a little ceremony which marked out her right to privacy despite the certainty that she would not answer, would almost certainly never answer. He had not heard his wife's voice for six years: since the night their car had been forced off a wintry Fen road by the oncoming headlights of a drunk driver, and down into the black water of Harrimere Drain. Dryden had escaped but Laura, trapped on the back seat, had been left in a diminishing pocket of air for three hours: three hours in which she must have struggled with the fact of her abandonment, three hours in which the horror of reality had forced her to retreat into a protective coma, a retreat from which she was only painfully emerging. For this was no ordinary coma. Fate had reserved another twist of the knife.

Locked In Syndrome (LIS) was still a little-understood condition, but medical experts were at least now agreed that it existed. Victims usually entered the coma under extreme trauma; however, the peculiarities of LIS were connected not to the outward symptoms, but to the inward realities. Sufferers exhibited no signs of mental or physical activity, but those who had emerged from LIS reported varying degrees of consciousness – from fleeting dreamlike visions to a state very close to normality. Those able to move a finger – or more often an eyelid – were able to communicate using the latest technology. After three years of immobility Laura had managed to move the small finger on her right hand and had learnt to communicate using a machine – the COMPASS – which had been installed by her bed. It constantly displayed a grid of letters and by flicking a switch placed in the palm of her hand Laura was able to select them. As her slow recovery continued she had mastered the COMPASS using a suck-and-blow pipe which could be placed between her lips. Her messages were often fluent and rational, but interspersed with prolonged periods of either silence or a dreamlike surrealism.

Dryden entered the room, turning the dial on the dimmer to illuminate the figure on the bed draped in a single white sheet.

The COMPASS jumped instantly into life, a spool of paper trickling out of a printer like ticker-tape.

One of the refinements Laura had learnt was to prepare a sentence on screen and then activate the print key as her husband entered the room.

HI. LOVE YOU.

It was a ritualistic greeting, but welcome none the less.

Dryden's spirits rose, and he edged on to the bed, insinuated an arm under Laura's neck, and raised her head higher on the pillows. Her hair was an exuberant pile of auburn, which he noted had been freshly brushed. The nurses, who maintained an optimism about their patient which Dryden struggled to match, often applied some make-up as well, adding colour to the Latin tan which had paled so visibly over the years.

Laura's eyes, a liquid brown, swam slightly as she fought to focus on his face. He felt a surge of optimism and clutched her tighter. The year had been marked by a steady improvement in her health, and the first spasmodic movements of muscles in her right arm and foot. They'd been enthusiastic about the suggestion from the consultant that she might leave The Tower – a brief excursion into the outside world, a weekend perhaps, or more, but somewhere close to medical care if her condition caused alarm.

Dryden turned her head gently towards the window. 'It's so warm in here,' he said. 'You've no idea. Outside it's minus 10 or something. The river's freezing up by the Maltings, the boat's locked in.'

While he held her there was no way she could operate the COMPASS, an enforced silence he knew Laura enjoyed. He spilled out news of the rest of the day, making sure he included the kind of details she loved: Humph's diet, the minutiae of *The Crow*'s eccentric personalities, and – most difficult of all – how he felt.

But more often he escaped by telling her what he'd done.

'I got the splash again,' he said. It was one of their jokes. On Fleet Street, on the *News*, he'd fought every day to get the lead story. Once, perhaps twice, a month he'd land the honour. On *The Crow* it was his by default.

'Guy, in his late thirties, froze to death in his armchair at home. Twelfth floor of a block of council flats, with all the windows open. I guess he didn't care if he lived or died but I can think of easier ways to end it.'

He stopped, sensing he'd strayed on to forbidden territory, and tried to fill the silence by uncorking the wine bottle he'd opened the night before. This was one of their small ceremonies: the shared glass of wine. As Laura's condition had improved she was able to take liquids through a drinking funnel.

'Anyway. Police have it down to suicide. Bloke had a history: depression, self-harm, the usual gloomy litany. But there's something more there – perhaps he did do it, but I still don't understand. He had plenty of cash, and he'd been drinking – and not alone. He's got this mate called Joe, so perhaps they hit the bottle together.

'I took Garry down to the allotments by the flats where the dead guy used to hang out in the summer. There's this kind of little club there, and they meet in this shed with a stove. There was something really . . . exclusive about it. It wasn't the Garrick or anything, but it was odd, like they were all there for some other reason . . . They wouldn't tell me where Joe was, either, even though it was obvious they all knew him; said they'd pass on a message, but I bet they don't. People never do.'

Dryden laughed at himself and shook his head, holding the funnel so that he could let Laura sip the wine.

'Then I went out to Lane End again – to St Vincent's.' Laura was the daughter of a north London Italian Catholic family who'd run a small café. He'd shared the whole long-running saga of the orphanage with her, knowing she understood his deep-seated reservations about such institutions, and the imposition of fear and guilt which held them together.

'The priest in charge – Father Martin – took me round the place. He's the only one left of all the priests there in the eighties. He actually made me feel sorry for him, which is a bit of a bloody miracle in itself. Anyway, two more kids have been found so the inquiry has enough evidence to move to court. His head will roll – but I doubt he cares now; he may not even live that long. Social services will probably get the real drubbing, and the police.'

He brushed her hair then, having slipped a CD into the player attached to the COMPASS – *Il Trovatore*.

Outside he could see grainy snow falling in the super-cooled air. The drop in temperature with nightfall reduced the flakes to pellets of lightweight hail, blown with the wind.

'It's too cold to snow properly,' he said. 'But the water-meadows have got plenty of ice on them so they may race this weekend – or sooner. Remember when we skated at Burnt Fen?'

He always paused for an answer, keeping alive the hope that one day there would be one.

'I'll dig the skates out just in case. I could run into town on the river – give Humph a day off. God knows what he'd do with it, mind. Probably drive round in circles.'

He switched the brush to his left hand, trying not to think, trying to concentrate on the details of his day that didn't matter, but the central faultline of his life was inescapable. After Laura's accident he had been able to hope that one day they would be as they had been before that winter's night. That he would go back to his job on Fleet Street, that she could return to her career as an actress – at that point a very promising career. Childishly he had held on to this dream longer than his wife. By contrast her hopes were a compromise, a deliberate attempt to lower expecta-tions, to hope only for the next improvement, the tiny, almost unnoticeable triumphs which made her life worth living.

Triumphs he had begun to despise. He suspected now that 'recovery' was a relative term, that he would never have his life back, never have his wife back, that the best they could hope for was an extended convalescence, a lifetime spent waiting beside a wheelchair or a hospital bed. And he despised himself for finding that that was not enough.

She had sensed the change as well, despite being immersed in her battle to make her brain re-establish contact with her body. He could only imagine the hours she spent dwelling on her predicament, and on theirs. One evening earlier that winter he had found a message on the COMPASS screen. He wondered how long it had taken her to compose, for it was free of the literals and errors which marked her usual attempts to operate the machine.

I CAN'T ASK YOU TO STAY FOREVER. THIS IS MY LIFE NOW. GO IF IT'S BEST. I'LL LOVE YOU ALWAYS.

He'd held her that night, crying freely at the thought she had doubted him, promising that he would always be there. And she'd been honest about her life, admitting that the long periods of silence, sometimes stretching out over days, were not always lost in a dreamlike coma. Depression, as debilitating as the coma itself, sometimes made it impossible to think, or write.

She'd asked him, then, about the life she often found unbearable:

IF I WANT YOU TO END IT PROMISE THAT YOU WILL.

He'd promised too quickly, as if to a child.

One day, when the black depression had been with her for a week, she'd told him something else.

I DONT WANT TO DIE HERE.

Which begged the question, where did she want to die?

The Dolphin Holiday Camp
Friday, 30 August 1974

Tonight, the last they would play the game, Philip lay still, willing his pulse to slow. Around him, in the other chalets, he knew the children slept. Soon he'd hear the footsteps on the wooden walkway that ran between the huts. Then the face would appear at the window, the quick professional look sliding over his bed, before the Bluecoat moved on to complete the round.

Then it would be time.

He listened to the sounds of the adult night: a jukebox in the bar played 'When Will I See You Again' for the third time and a wave of laughter rolled out from the camp's club, down the long avenue between the chalets, and broke with a whisper no louder than the swish of the sea beyond the dunes. A klaxon sounded at the funfair and screams marked the descent of the big dipper.

Philip gripped the sheet at his chin and pressed his eyes shut, willing the game to begin.

An amplified voice, distorted beyond coherence, interrupted the music as the floorshow began. He'd seen them often in his head: his uncle and aunt, in the darkened audience now, their heads thrown back with the rest, cigarette smoke trailing like clouds at sea. Through the door to the next room, in the half-light, he saw their beds, waiting, crisply made.

Outside, through the gap he'd had made in the curtains, the stretched-blue sky of a summer's day had already turned to mauve. A seagull called, dashing across his field of vision, and a bell tolled twice from the floating buoy which marked the deep-cut channel through the sands.

And then he did hear the footsteps. The pattern familiar: the crunch of sand and the gritty shuffle of deck shoes on wood, the metallic stutter of the master keys clanking against the brass dolphin. Then the window, left just open, creaked wider, and the curtain rings clicked.

A second passed, lengthened impossibly by the tension of the moment, and then the Bluecoat was gone, whistling tunelessly with the Three Degrees.

Philip swung his legs down onto the bare boards, pulled on shorts and T-shirt, and bundled his pyjamas, a beach bag and ball under the sheet. He walked soundlessly to the door and turned the handle and the Yale key simultaneously. Clicking up the catch, he looked out at the chalet opposite, the one with the metal numerals screwed to its blue painted door: 10.

Dex was there, standing too, scared by the secret they shared, twisting a length of kite string in his hands. Philip felt the now familiar sense of belonging, an only child suddenly enveloped in the wordless rituals of a family. The game was about to begin for the last time. But for a second they paused, holding a look across the twilight of a summer's evening neither would ever forget.

9

Humph pulled the trigger on the tennis machine and sent another ball skittering along the frozen river bank. Dawn was still some way off but a little light was creeping out from the east under a sky the colour of wire-wool. Dryden watched Boudicca's thrilling run, and then fetched coffee from the galley below.

Friday. A tombstone of a day for Dryden; with *The Crow* now behind him he had four days to kill before publication of its sister paper – the *Ely Express*. Time was something Dryden feared, possibly even more than dogs and heights. It offered an opportunity for introspection which was wholly unwelcome.

He set the coffee cups on the Capri's roof and considered the distant skyline, expertly locating the brutal shadow which was High Park Flats. He visualized Declan McIlroy, freezing gently to death in his own armchair. *The Crow* wanted him to write a feature for its sister paper on the cold snap, while Dryden was keen to find out more about Declan's untimely death. He decided to combine both tasks.

As Humph bundled the greyhound back into the rear seat of the Capri, Dryden used his cell phone to ring Vee Hilgay at the Hypothermia Action Trust. It was still just 7.00am but he knew she'd probably be at her desk. She answered on the first ring, a slight sibilance signalling that she was already sipping tea. Did she have a volunteer on the Jubilee

Estate? Not in the flats, she said, but certainly on the estate. Could Dryden meet them, perhaps visit some of those most vulnerable? They fixed a meeting spot for 8.00am. The trust had put posters up at the flats a week ago asking that anyone who needed help combating the cold ring a freephone number. The flats had then been leafleted two days previously and the trust had a list of twenty residents who had agreed to a visit from an expert who could offer professional advice on insulation, diet, and state benefits.

They had an hour to kill. Humph massaged his tummy under the nylon embrace of his Ipswich Town FC replica shirt. 'Brunch?'

'You mean another breakfast,' said Dryden, slipping on the seat-belt by way of affirmation.

The Box Café – known more popularly as Salmonella Sid's – was a greasy spoon hidden behind the riverside's newly renovated façades. Humph stayed in the cab, to which an indulgent staff ferried his mug and plate while Dryden demolished a full English and completed a quick run through the downmarket tabloids.

He was at the bottom of the stairwell leading to Declan McIlroy's flat at precisely 8.00am, his lips still stinging slightly from the heat of microwaved sausages.

Vee trudged towards him across the deserted car park. She wore Doc Martens with red laces and a tattered donkey-jacket with lapels to die for: badges included CND and Troops Out of Iraq Now. She brandished a printed list. 'These are the residents who responded to the flier,' she said.

Dryden read down, trying to remember if he'd seen a leaflet in Declan McIlroy's flat. 'Perfect,' he said, stabbing a finger on the name Buster Timms. 'Great hook: a man who lives next door to the latest victim of the killer winter.'

Vee nodded, her eyes hinting at disappointment. She liked Dryden, loathed his trade. 'I'll come with you; the field worker here doesn't want the publicity. Pictures?'

'Yeah – I'll ring the 'toggy once it's in the bag,' said Dryden, jiggling his mobile by his ear.

The lift had been cleaned and was working, despite a dent in the aluminium back wall the size of a dustbin lid. A wind was blowing on the twelfth floor and the air was so keen that when Dryden put his hand on the safety barrier of the walkway his skin momentarily froze to the metal. He knocked on Buster's door, then stepped back for Vee to make the pitch. Dryden turned his back on the door to look down on to the car park below: it held three vehicles, two cars which were necessarily stationary owing to a 100 per cent deficiency in the wheels department and a small white van which Dryden could not see clearly from above. It trundled to the exit and out of sight around the flats.

The door rattled open on a chain. Buster was still in his tartan dressing gown, with several layers of padding beneath.

'What?' he said, leering at Dryden.

Vee held up the Day-Glo yellow flier: 'Hypothermia Trust, Mr Timms. You rang our number. We might be able to help warm you up. This is Mr Dryden – from *The Crow* – he's going to put some of the advice in the paper for those we can't visit. Would you mind?'

Dryden admired Vee's doorstep technique, which he couldn't have bettered.

Buster shrugged. 'She's just gone out – clinic for her eyes. Why not? I've met chummy before . . .' he added, nodding at Dryden. Buster walked off towards his front room, the bow of the legs beneath the dressing gown suggesting childhood rickets. There was a hatch between the front room and the kitchenette and Buster was already making tea, a cloud of steam around him like dry ice.

Dryden knelt down before a five-bar fire. 'What's wrong with the central heating?'

Buster appeared with a tray. 'We save that for the evenings. Keeps the bills down – that's why she's out, really; after the clinic she'll go to that drop-in centre off the town square. Then there's a new centre in the cathedral as well. Coffee, biscuits, she'll be hours.' He shrugged with unconcealed happiness.

'The sister called,' said Buster, nodding at the partition wall to Declan's flat. 'She's taken a lot of stuff. Boxed the rest up. Left me his keys – all of them. Even the cupboard.' Buster winked at Dryden. 'It's worth a look.'

Vee sat, taking out a fat Manila file from her satchel.

'This isn't gonna cost, is it?' said Buster, eyeing the file and forgetting Declan's flat.

Vee shook her head, taking the tea and turning aside the sugar bowl. 'No. Not a penny. I need to do a heat audit on the flat. This electric fire, for example – it's really very inefficient. You'd be better running the radiators for an hour in the morning . . . Can I have a look?'

Buster showed her the immersion heater and the gas boiler in a hall cupboard. She checked the windows, letting the cool air which slipped through the ill-fitting metal frames play on her lips.

Dryden wandered round, making an effort to collect the kind of detail that would bring the feature alive. The plastic Christmas tree with fairy lights unlit, the three cards on the mantelpiece, the puckered wallpaper in one corner of the ceiling where the damp had got through. A goldfish bowl stood on the bedside table, complete with underwater castle apparently without a resident. He flicked the bowl with his finger.

'Belly up,' said Buster from the doorway.

Dryden noted the slight sheen of ice on a family snap-shot which stood framed on the window ledge.

Back in the front room Vee ran through the couple's shopping list with Buster, trying to see if she could slip them on to the council's meals-on-wheels service. That could save them enough cash to run the heating for longer, and stock up the cupboard with some soups, fresh vegetables and fruit. She did some sums on a pocket calculator, expertly summarizing their pension position and eligibility for winter fuel payments and the cold-weather bonus.

'We might be able to get you a grant, Mr Timms – on top of the payments. It's worth £2,500 – you could get double-glazing. And you know the hospital does sessions as well?' she asked. 'They do some very light physiotherapy – hot drinks. Just going would be good for you.'

Buster looked stoically unimpressed. 'Your man did that already,' he said.

Vee paused, sipping tea, thinking she'd misheard.

'The doc. Called the other day with your flier. Did miracles with her shoulders, checked her temperature, pulse, the lot.'

'And you?' asked Dryden, catching Vee's good eye.

Buster tucked the tartan dressing gown more securely around his waist: 'He scarpered when I got home, I'd been down the bowls club. He was off then. Didn't believe she was seventy-one, she said. Said she could run a marathon.' Buster nodded, looking at them both. 'Bit of a tosser, really.'

'Did he visit Declan too? Next door?'

Buster's eyes were wary now, sensing that something was wrong but unable to guess what to hide. 'After us. I heard him knock anyway and he didn't walk back past the door for an hour – maybe more.'

'This was the night he died, wasn't it?' said Dryden.

'I didn't tell the police,' said Buster, one step ahead now. He raised a hand to his forehead. 'I just didn't think.'

'Don't worry. I can pass it on if you like . . .' offered Dryden. Buster pushed his teeth forward in a smile. 'What was he like – the doctor? Not your own GP then?'

'I only saw him for a minute, like – he'd done with her, and he said he had to finish his appointments. Bit odd, really. No tie or anything. But smart. About fifty, perhaps not. My age, everyone looks young. She said he had very strong 'ands, when he massaged her neck and that. Medium height – pretty solid. Don't expect that, do you? Our one's a streak of piss.'

'How about his face?' asked Dryden, knowing the police would press for more, even if they had already filed Declan McIlroy's death firmly under suicide.

Buster pursed his lips. 'Sorry, she had the TV on by then – *Countdown*, we never miss. Mousy hair? Dunno. Short, I think; shortish, anyway.' He clicked his fingers. 'She said he had lovely blue eyes, silly cow. He had a black bag too, and a clipboard.'

'And he just knocked, Mr Timms?' asked Vee, aware that the purpose of their visit had shifted. 'No preparatory call? We insist on that,' she added, looking to Dryden.

'Nah. She heard this noise from the landing, someone going past . . . Bastard was halfway to Declan's flat so she got him back, said we were needy. He said he'd planned to do us next but she told him we didn't answer the door after dark.'

'So this was what? Five, six?'

'Yeah. We watch the repeat of *Countdown* – so that's got to be after 5.15 yup?' Suddenly Buster looked less sure. 'Or did we give it a miss that day?'

Dryden struggled to contain his frustration. Why was it

that in the real world witnesses could hardly confirm their own names, let alone recall telling details about someone else?

'Perhaps your wife would remember more about this doctor?'

Buster laughed. 'Doubt it, mate. Eyes,' he said, tapping his temples with both index fingers. 'Can't see a thing up close – she saw *his* when he had a look in *hers* with one of those light things.'

He slurped the rest of his tea. 'There was one thing,' he added, pushing his hands out to catch the feeble warmth from the fire. 'He went to the loo just before he left so I peeked in the bag. Guess what?'

Vee and Dryden shook their heads, shocked by Buster's casual dishonesty.

'I only had a sec. There was pills and stuff, and the kit – like for blood pressure. But there was a bottle too. Whisky. Unopened.'

10

Buster made a second pot of tea when Vee left, and they refilled their mugs before going out on to the balcony. The cat made figures-of-eight around Buster's ankles as he fished the keys out of his dressing-gown pocket and let himself into Declan's flat. There were several tea-crates in the front room, one of them full of crockery and glasses shrouded in old newspapers, and the taint of rancid grease had been scoured from the kitchen.

'The sister did all this?' asked Dryden.

'I helped. Missus made her a hot drink. You got to help, but it's amazin' how she gets about.'

'You mean even though she's blind?'

'Right. Makes you realize how lucky we are,' said Buster, and Dryden could see that it hadn't, not until now. The old man looked around the flat. 'We should have helped more. But like I said, he wanted his privacy.'

Dryden put his head in the bedroom. The mattress and sleeping bag were gone, the single bed up on one edge. 'Did she find anything, anything she didn't expect?'

Buster shook his head. He was standing by the locked cupboard in the hall with the keys. He turned the Yale silently and stood back: 'She said I could have one of these, but I'm not bothered.'

The lower half of the cupboard contained canvases, tacked on stretchers and stacked on edge. The smell of turpentine was pungent. Dryden flipped them forward, craning his neck to see each composition – some vivid landscapes, a field of Fen rape, a view from the lounge down onto the allotments, a still life of a table top with a single apple. And there were nudes, female, the skin colour dominated by angry reds, the faces indistinct.

But the top half of the cupboard held a canvas on a stretcher which had been pegged to a cross-wire to dry.

'Jesus,' said Dryden, taking one edge of it in his hand.

It was of two men, naked, standing waist deep in a pool. The colours were dark, soiled and crude, but the brush work adept. One of them had white hair and Dryden recognized the same box-like features as in the painting that hung above McIlroy's fireplace: the elusive Joe. Was the other man Declan? Dryden found it difficult to tell, the features here were smudged and chaotic. But the picture's real impact was not in the composition but the colour of the pool. It wasn't blue, grey or white but a startling arterial red, and from each man a trickle of blood ran down from wounds on the arms to replenish the pool beneath.

'That's Joe, I guess?' said Dryden, pointing. Buster nodded. 'Don't know where he lives, do you – or his surname?'

'Just Joe. Lives on the Fen, that's all I know. He didn't come much; they met down at the allotments. He just called when Declan was sick, 'cept this time of course.'

'Did you know Declan painted?'

'No idea. I asked Marcie – that's the sister – and she said it was therapy. No – therapeutic, that's what she said. But she didn't want the pictures, coz he'd given her one with loads of paint on she could feel – a landscape, she said; reeds and stuff. And he'd always said to burn 'em anyway. Said I could have one of 'em for being neighbourly, to remember him by.' Buster laughed: 'Must be fuckin' jokin'.'

'It's blood,' said Dryden, leaning forward to look more closely. 'Can I take this one?'

Buster was shivering. 'Be my guest. She's gonna pick up the others tomorrow for the tip.' He watched as Dryden took down the canvas and rolled it.

'What do you think it means, then?' asked Buster, backing off.

'Looks like a nightmare to me,' said Dryden.

They went back into the lounge. 'Bloke from the council said they'd have someone new in by the end of the month,' said Buster, picking up his tea mug from the table. 'Missus says it'll be a bunch of darkies with loud music. I hope it is, give her something to fuckin' moan about 'cept me.'

Dryden felt the cool wind from the north blowing through the gaps around Declan McIlroy's picture windows. 'I don't think Declan did kill himself, Buster. What do you think?'

Buster held his dressing gown to his throat. 'If the police are happy, I'm happy. Why make trouble, eh?'

He was watching Buster's face when it froze, the eyes looking over Dryden's right shoulder. He wheeled and saw what he'd seen: through the frosted glass of the hatch to the kitchen, a face, the parallel opaque lines distorting the features.

The intruder sensed that the sudden silence signalled discovery and bolted for the door, heavy boots thudding on the cheap lino.

Dryden was ten feet behind him as he made it to the balcony in time to see him take the steps down by the landing. As Dryden followed he heard the lift wheezing, the doors clattering on the floor below, then the lift again.

Heart creaking, Dryden vaulted the concrete stairs two, three and four at a time until he reached the ground floor where, doubled up, he waited for the lift to arrive. It thudded finally to rest, and the doors clattered open to reveal Buster's cat.

Looking up, Dryden saw a head jerk back from a balcony a few floors above, then running footsteps receded, muffled as they turned a corner and were gone, heading for another exit.

From the top balcony Buster waved lamely: 'Tea?' he shouted.

I I

Dryden threw himself into the Capri's passenger seat and slammed the door, tossing Declan McIlroy's canvas on to the back seat beside the dog. The cab swayed, crying out on its geriatric springs. Humph, oblivious, had his earphones on and was repeating with painstaking care the directions to the railway station in Kohtla-Jarve. Dryden wiped the sweat from his forehead and, trying his pockets, uncovered a comforting cocktail sausage and munched it, regardless of the fluff. His diet, outside the egg sandwich for breakfast and the occasional full English, was satisfied by a kind of trouser-pocket smorgasbord, featuring pork pies, raw mushrooms and anything else acquired on his travels. In the other pocket he found a packet of wine gums and took two for pudding.

He considered the brutal façade of High Park Flats. He'd rung Vee Hilgay on his mobile from Buster's flat and she was still adamant that the unannounced doctor's visit had nothing to do with the Hypothermia Action Trust. She'd checked with the local NHS Trust to be sure and there was no record whatsoever of such an initiative in the Ely area. Dryden asked her to contact local GPs as well.

Were they dealing with a conman? Dryden recalled the news item in *The Crow* warning of bogus plumbers fleecing the elderly. Or had this conman been heading for Declan McIlroy's flat all along? And had he just made a return visit? If it had been his intention to visit Declan, had he oiled the wheels of depression with the whisky, and then left him to

68

commit suicide – or had he enticed him into unconsciousness and then thrown open the windows himself?

Or was Dryden indulging in newspaper fantasy? Perhaps it had been a low-life conman all along and the return visit was just a bit of unrelated daylight looting by one of High Park's gifted thieves.

Dryden placed a palm on his forehead and felt a fresh layer of icy sweat. Either way he needed to tell the police what he'd learned, while at the same time delaying, if possible, any public statements on the news for the *Express*'s deadline on Tuesday. If he could raise enough questions over McIlroy's sudden suicide he could at least run a story saying the police were – finally – investigating. He was inclined to sit on the information for twenty-four hours – but knew the possibility the bogus doctor would call again raised the stakes too high for journalistic games. He needed to get the information on the record fast.

He hit the dashboard with the flat of his hand. 'Ely cop shop,' he said. 'Pronto!'

Humph finished his reiteration of directions to the railway station in what sounded like a suspiciously Fen dialect of Estonian and then fired up the Capri. A cloud of fumes belched from the exhaust pipe with a bang as the cab swept out of the car park, charging a series of sleeping policemen which lay in its path.

Ely police station was a local monument, a humourless glass and concrete block with a radio mast on top slightly too short to afford regular communication with the outer planets. It was a common prejudice in the town that this impressive outpost of the constabulary was almost constantly empty, local emergency calls being routed automatically to a helpful officer seventeen miles away in Cambridge. The skyscraper aerial was not, however, a complete waste of space as its impressive array of steel hawsers provided a roosting spot for several thousand starlings.

Today the mast was decked in ice, which hung like decorations on a giant Christmas tree.

The automatic doors opened as Dryden approached, revealing an empty counter, glassed in and meshed to meet terrorist attack. There were three seats for the public, across which lay *The Crow*'s ever-vigilant junior reporter Garry Pymoor.

Dryden woke him up.

'Right,' said Garry, brushing aside the embarrassment which would have overtaken lesser men. He sat up, unfolding himself from the ubiquitous black leather coat and releasing a faint odour of Indian Pale Ale and bubblegum.

'They phoned. Said they'd got some stuff for us on the cannabis peddling. I was gonna ring . . .' he said, yawning so wide that his jaw cracked.

Dryden pressed a button by a grille and waited for a disembodied voice to crackle into life, but there was silence.

'Garry Pymoor and Philip Dryden from *The Crow*,' he said. The reinforced door clicked open and Dryden pushed through into a long corridor which was slightly sticky underfoot and smelt of disinfectant.

A man stood at the far end in the customary uniform of the plainclothed detective: grey suit, light blue shirt and dark tie, with polished black slip-on shoes. His hair was white and cropped and his shoulders were set at an angle that exactly matched his career prospects. He welcomed them, offering his hand to Dryden. 'Thanks for coming. Jock Reade, DI Reade. I'm the drugs liaison officer for the force – along with a few other jobs. We've got some film for you . . .' Dryden noticed the acrid hint of nicotine mixed with aftershave and the complete absence of a Scottish accent.

'Great,' said Dryden. 'I'm actually here on another case – the man found dead in High Park Flats yesterday. I need to talk to someone; I've got some information I think you should have.'

DI Reade buckled visibly at the prospect of extra work. 'Er. OK. No one else here at present. But I can take a note – though I've got the CCTV set up for Mr Pymoor.'

'Right. But who's the investigating officer in the High Park Flats case?'

DI Reade rubbed a finger at his temple: 'Pretty sure there isn't one. I mean, bloke had tried to top himself a coupla times – right? We're stretched, you know, on manpower. But I can pass anything up the line.'

Dryden held up his hands: 'OK, OK. Let's see the film.'

Reade led the way through the deserted police station. Stairs led down to the cell block, where they were led into a room with two rows of seats before a console of twelve TV screens. Above them was one larger screen showing a magnified image of one of the dozen pictures below. At the moment a lorry was seen backing into the car park by the Market Square, as a single pedestrian, swaddled in a thermal jacket, crossed towards the town's shopping precinct. Reade hit a switch changing the images. 'This is High Street just opposite the Lamb Hotel. Trouble spot on a Saturday night, of course. Not much happening now.'

Dryden nodded. 'How long do you keep the film?' He'd always suspected that the cameras were empty.

'Usually 48 hours – then we reuse it. Otherwise we'd disappear under the video cartridges.'

Reade sat on the console desktop, playing with a packet of Silk Cut. 'As you know, we've been concerned about cannabis being sold to teenagers in Ely. It happened quite suddenly, about a month ago, and continued for nearly three weeks. There's no fresh reports – but we'd like to nail this in case it's just a brief pause in the supply.

'We picked up a couple of kids out of their heads down by the bypass last Thursday. They'd done some glue, which is nothing new, but they reeked of dope. Let's say we were sympathetic about their cases – and in return we got some information about the supplier. They said he sells out of a car after dark just here . . .'

Reade got up and stabbed a finger into a large map of the town centre. 'Just here. Very clever – it's one of several blind spots not covered by the CCTV cameras. But he wasn't as clever as he thought. Just overlooking this bit of car parking is the rear of Boots – they got broken into a couple of times in the summer so they'd put up a camera of their own. And they keep the film.'

Reade played importantly with some buttons.

The big screen showed a deserted car park at night, a halogen security light reflecting on frosty tarmac. A car was already parked in the shadows, side on, the number plates not visible.

Dryden squinted, leaning forward. 'Did we not see the car pull in?'

Reade shook his head. 'The camera is timed. It comes on at 6.30 and the car was already parked up.'

A single figure in a knee-length hoodie moved in jerky spasms across the car park and miraculously appeared inside the car without having opened a door. A clock on the screen showed the time ticking by. A minute and thirty-two seconds later the figure was out, walking towards the camera, the coat's hood pulled down low.

'Customer number one,' said Reade, freezing the frame.

'Note the wedge-shaped badge on the jacket – it's a designer label. Pretty rare, pretty expensive.'

Garry fingered his spots. 'Did you get the kid?'

Reade nodded. 'Well, we got a kid in an identical top. A week later in Market Square. He'd just had a hit and was trying to take his trousers off over his head.'

They laughed without mirth.

'His dad didn't find it funny when we took him home,' said Reade. 'Nice middle-class semi on the Lynn Road.'

Another figure appeared, moving across the tarmac like an animated clay character from children's TV. Two others joined the first at the car window. This time the deal was over in twenty-five seconds.

'It gets boring after that. Until 7.38pm precisely.'

Reade accelerated the picture forward, a dozen or more customers coming and going in a few seconds. Then the driver's door swung open, a man got out, locked the car, and slipped behind a ventilating unit. A dark liquid stain spread out from the shadows, trickling towards a gutter.

'Charming,' said Dryden, as the man reappeared and Reade froze the frame. He was medium height, thin shoulders under a dark overcoat, one hand in a pocket, the other, massive, hung low like a weapon. The face was split between light and dark, the contrast too great to allow any ID.

'It's not much,' said Reade. 'I've got a statement you can use,' he added, handing Garry a Xeroxed sheet. 'It's got the car make and model etc. When he drove off, the plate stayed in shadow.'

'And the CCTV stuff had been destroyed? No way of following him out of the town centre?'

'Right,' said Reade unhappily. Garry nodded, having lost the plot.

'What's that?' said Dryden, standing and pointing at the rear of the car. It was a four-wheel drive. The rear windows, all the windows in fact, had become clouded with condensation. But in one side pane there was a small black irregular patch of clear glass. 'Can you run the tape back?'

Reade pressed the rewind. The drug seller retreated into the shadows, reappeared, and got into the car backwards. Suddenly the small black window in the misty pane was gone.

'Someone else?' asked Garry.

Dryden shook his head: 'I think it's why a lot of the kids didn't get in the car. When the first punter got in you could just see a dividing mesh – between the back and the passenger seats. It's a dog. Bit of security?'

Reade let the film run forward again.

'Could we have a still?'

The detective rummaged in a file and produced a black and white 'video-grab' image. It was grainy and indistinct, but it caught some of the menace of the original footage.

'Great,' said Dryden, handing it to Garry. 'We'll give it a good run.'

Back upstairs Dryden waited until Reade had given Garry more data on local drug-related crime to boost the story before bringing up Declan McIlroy's case. 'There was nothing on calls, but have there been any reports of a bogus caller in High Park Flats – or on the Jubilee? Someone posing as a health visitor perhaps, or doctor. There was something on a bogus plumber – but that was out of town.'

Reade took them back to the deserted office. He rifled through some files on one of the desktops, then booted up a PC.

'Nope,' he said. 'As you said, we've got a joker pretending to be a plumber, but that's just the older semis on the edge

74

of town. He's never touched a flat. That's pretty rare, of course; there's less to filch and it's much more difficult to get away quickly in one of those blocks if the con fails and they get sussed. High Park is not a good place to upset the natives.'

Dryden nodded. 'Declan McIlroy had a visitor the night he died. I'm pretty sure it was a bogus doctor – he took in the old folks next door as well.'

'Get away with anything?' asked Reade, making a note.

Dryden shook his head: 'Perhaps the motive wasn't theft.'

Reade sat at the PC and keyed in some instructions. He read quickly, then gave Dryden a sympathetic look: 'Not much suspicious about McIlroy's death,' he said. 'Lonely guy, history of mental illness, neighbours heard nothing. Inquest was this morning.'

Dryden felt a hot spate of anger. 'Shit – that was quick. What's the hurry?'

Reade straightened. 'It was today or wait a week – nobody objected. We like to expedite such matters.' He blushed, knowing he'd tried to fob them off with a long word.

'Verdict?'

'Misadventure. Death by hypothermia, but he had enough booze in him to knock out a rugby team plus a dangerous level of painkillers.'

'Any witnesses called?'

Reade was shaking his head. 'Oh. Yeah – there was. Social worker. Ed Bardolph, and a relation – sister.'

Dryden's spirits rose. He knew Bardolph, and he knew where he'd be.

'Thanks. I'll have a chat, I know Ed. Look, I know you're stretched but I really think this case is worth a second look. There's been an intruder at the flat as well – the dead man's flat, today. The neighbour, Mr Timms, can fill you in. A visit would pay dividends.'

Reade nodded vigorously. 'That's one of the problems with the Jubilee. Anything left empty gets stripped pretty quick. I'll get the community man to pop in, no problem. I'd better take some details as well . . .'

Dryden nodded, knowing he'd been brushed off. But for once it suited him. He'd done his duty and reported both incidents; if DI Reade didn't want to take it seriously, that was fine by him. He'd ring on Monday to check any progress but as it stood he could legitimately write a story saying that police were investigating the bogus caller and any possible links with Declan McIlroy's death.

Reade made a note of the facts on the bogus caller and the intruder and got Dryden's signature on both. They left the detective shuffling paper, searching for his coffee mug. The automatic doors at the front counter swished open, expelling them into the cold air, and above them the starlings rose as on a single wing.

Dryden walked down towards the river from Market Square. He wrapped his oversized black coat around him, the buttons and buttonholes overlapping across his narrow chest. Across the Fen a snow squall smudged the black horizon like an artist's finger, while in the foreground skaters criss-crossed the frozen watermeadows watched by a scattered crowd lifted wholesale from a Brueghel landscape.

At the foot of the hill lay the district of Waterside, a collection of warehouses and cottages which had grown up alongside the river's wharves. Beyond that lay the frozen river. Dryden noted that the ice here was patchy and floated in rafts, unlike the solid white crust that had encircled *PK 129* upriver. But even here, despite the tidal ebb and flow provided by the sluice gates downstream, thicker pack ice was creeping out from the banks. By dusk the ice would be solid from shore to shore.

Dryden crossed the river by a steel footbridge as a single rower passed beneath, swaddled in jumpers, heading quickly for the sanctuary of a boathouse, the skiff's hull nudging aside miniature icebergs. On the far bank lay Quanea Fen, a skaters' paradise, lit by a low sun just now breaking through a bank of clouds. The temperature had fallen below minus 6 degrees centigrade for three consecutive nights – the official stipulation before a championship skating event could be held in safety. Sympathetic farmers had opened the field sluices to flood the Fen, preparing the vast arena for the event. Ice already covered the two-inch-deep man-made mere, creating the perfect venue for the championship – a solid steel-grey surface several times bigger than any Olympic rink.

Wooden blocks with flags were being set out along the oval of a 400-metre speed-skating course. On the track itself volunteers worked with wide brushes to clear away the tiny stipples on the ice left by the flurries of hail and snow. Around the arena an ice fair clustered; a couple of burger bars and a tea and coffee stall were already doing brisk business. A small travelling fair, usually mothballed for the winter, had been hustled out of hibernation to make the most of the expected crowds. A coconut shy and a child's roundabout were already up and running. Duckboards had been laid down for those not on skates and a troop of council workmen in fluorescent yellow jackets were stringing lights from posts sunk in the ground.

It was a scene in silver, grey and black, except for a single blazing brazier set on wooden blocks, a glimmer of cold orange like a blackbird's beak in a winter landscape. Then, suddenly, a half mile of multi-coloured lights flickered on between their posts, then flickered out after the test was judged a success.

Ed Bardolph, the social worker who had been a witness at Declan McIlroy's inquest, was chairman of the Fen Skating Committee, the official body which alone had the power to convene the championships and regulate the races. Dryden knew the FSC was due to meet here, on the ice, to make its final decision. In the distance he could see a knot of men clustered around the brazier beside a brace of Land Rovers and a skidoo. As Dryden approached, moving gingerly over the ice and wishing he'd brought his skates, the group formed a circle around a hole in the ice beside the fire, like Eskimo fishers.

Dryden spotted Bardolph crouching, examining a plate of ice they'd levered up from the grass. Bardolph was also the local spokesman for the public-sector workers' union Unison, as well as a self-confessed skating fanatic – two pastimes which had brought him into regular contact with the local press. He was heavily built, with navvy's arms and a lumpy, bucolic face, and easy to underestimate.

'Hi,' he said as Dryden approached, standing and holding out an ungloved hand. He transmitted a smile which was not entirely cynical, for he enjoyed Dryden's company and whenever they'd crossed paths in the courts he'd been impressed by the reporter's work, which combined accuracy with an understated sensitivity.

'Sorry,' said Dryden, turning to walk away from the group and secure some privacy. Bardolph left his companions cutting a second circular plate of ice from the ground fifty yards nearer the river.

Dryden blew a theatrical plume of breath. 'It's about Declan McIlroy – I missed the inquest. It must have been slipped onto the list. We're doing a feature on the dangers of the cold snap, I wanted some background . . .'

Bardolph nodded, clearly struggling to concentrate on anything but ice and the exhilarating probability of a race. They heard a mechanical screech of chains over gears and looked to the river where a crane down by the marina was lifting one of the white boats – a floating tourists' gin palace – from the black water up onto a safe mooring.

'So, misadventure?' asked Dryden, turning back.

Bardolph shrugged. 'What else? There was no note and you know what they're like these days – suicide's a rare verdict; there's too many legal pitfalls.'

Dryden tried to imagine the scene in the small crowded coroner's court. 'The sister came, yeah?' Bardolph nodded, clearly wary of Dryden's questions. Irrationally wary, Dryden thought, but said instead, 'Why were you a witness?'

Bardolph examined his boots. 'I can't say, you know. He was a client, a client for many years, and our relationship is still confidental – even if he is dead.'

'Sure. I just thought you might have said something in court. I'm just trying to catch up . . .' Dryden was playing a practised game, inviting his source to merely confirm what was already in the public domain, while leading him towards its boundaries.

'Declan had some severe social problems which stemmed from a very unhappy childhood. He was in care, an orphanage. He was actually very bright, which didn't help, of course. I put him in touch with a therapist, and he had some treatment. There was a friend, Joe, who had a house out on the Fen, and he spent some time there – but it was a temporary respite. Declan painted too, and I think he was gifted in some ways, even if the work was self-indulgent. He took courses – correspondence courses – hundreds of them, in fact: electrical engineering, IT, computer maintenance, stuff like that, as well as history of art.

'But as I say the problems were chronic. There were always unresolved frustrations which resulted in periodic outbursts of anger. Violence – sometimes against the nearest person to hand, often against himself.'

There was a cheer and everyone on the Fen turned to watch two skaters leaving the starting line to test the course, each with an arm held at the back, the other swinging like a pendulum.

'Do you think he committed suicide, then?'

'I guess. But it wasn't characteristic.'

Dryden was confused. 'You said the violence was often directed against himself?'

'Yes. But that was violence. The manifestation was always immediate and pretty brutal. A slash with a broken bottle, a head-butt into concrete, that kind of thing. This was very . . . passive, I guess. Very controlled. It wasn't what I would have expected. But then the pressures were new . . .'

They walked on, Dryden allowing the silence to acknowledge the fact that Bardolph had led him on.

'The court heard this?' he asked gently.

'No. It was in reports; the coroner will have read them.' Bardolph sighed. 'But they'd have to confirm if you asked – just leave me out of it, OK?'

Dryden nodded. 'Of course.'

'The case against St Vincent's – the Catholic orphanage. Declan was a victim. You know the background, I've read your stories in *The Crow*. That was a pressure in itself. But we'd had to . . . unearth is the right word, unearth the past. It brought out the issues, you know, the causes of his lack of self-respect. It was a painful time.'

Dryden saw the mottled face of Father John Martin, the birthmark livid against the cool blue eye.

'He was one of the victims who had just been identified?'

Bardolph nodded. 'That's right, which means the pressures were new.'

'It might *not* have been suicide,' said Dryden, turning away, looking back at the cathedral, the West Tower now lost in its own private snowstorm. 'Declan had a visitor the day he died. A man claiming to be a doctor giving advice on the cold. I don't think he was there to keep Declan warm.'

Bardolph shook his head in disbelief, but Dryden left the thought hanging, unresolved. 'Was anything else on Declan's mind? Any other worries?'

Bardolph shook his head again, putting a glove back over

his hand, and Dryden knew he'd lied by the flicker of his eyelids and the pinching of his nose.

Dryden nodded as if he understood. 'At the very least it deserves investigation.'

Bardolph nodded, stamping his foot on the ice, impatient to get back to the Eskimo hole.

'Funeral?' asked Dryden.

Bardolph pulled his attention back to his former client. 'Cremation – it's private. Then they'll scatter the ashes. He would have liked that. Claustrophobia – worst case I've ever come across, actually. He had to be sedated in prison. That all goes back to childhood too . . .' Bardolph let his gaze slip away over the ice. 'Spent most of his time out on that balcony, twelve storeys up.'

Dryden nodded, as if sharing an old truth. So Buster Timms was right about his next door neighbour's criminal past. Dryden thought of the doorless flat and the windows thrown open to the night. 'It's getting colder,' he said, his jaw suddenly juddering with a shiver.

Bardolph grinned, watching the circling pair of speed skaters. 'I know. Isn't it wonderful?'

Dryden walked to the riverbank and found a bench free of snow. The more light he let fall on Declan McIlroy's life the more the shadows seemed to deepen. He felt the first lethal pangs of depression. The cold was getting to his heart, the chill in his back making his shoulder blades ache. Closing his eyes, he tried to conjure up a warmer memory, an antidote to the cold. It was that last summer again, always that last summer. His parents had sent him away with his uncle and aunt to the coast while they took in the harvest at Burnt Fen Farm: 1974. They were worried: worried he'd been lonely too long, an only child whose life had encompassed little more than the hamlet around the farm. So they'd decided on the break, just beyond the horizon, surrounded by children, at a holiday camp.

He could feel the warmth now. The hissing white water around his legs where the waves had broken, the sun beating flat down on the footmarked sand, and the glow of the sunburn on his shoulders. He would remember that summer always because of what came next. The return home, the snows of winter, and the floods which took his father away. So it had been his last summer, the last summer of childhood.

13

Humph was waiting on Waterside, the Capri a bubble of vanity light emitting the bass notes of an Estonian folk song. Dryden didn't realize how cold he'd become until he bent his six-foot two-inch frame and folded it into the passenger seat.

'Jesus,' he said, his knee-joints popping like champagne corks. Reaching for the glove compartment, he cracked the top off a bottle of malt whisky – a Glenfiddich – as Humph studied the thermometer he'd hung out the door on a short piece of string.

'Minus 8,' he said, the little bow of his doll-like mouth drawing together to produce a tuneful whistle.

Dryden checked his watch: 3.15pm. By dusk the temperature would be even lower, with every chance that the skies would stay clear. The Capri's heating rattled, churning out warm air which reeked of barbecued motor oil.

Tipping the miniature bottle back, Dryden finished the malt, feeling the heat burning down into his chest. Humph produced an identical bottle and passed it over, while he turned the ignition and choked the engine into life.

'Where?' he said.

Did Dryden care if Declan McIlroy had been murdered? He could go back to the office, polish off a pile of wedding reports and gut some council minutes before hitting the pub with Garry and the subs for the ritual Friday tea-time piss-up – a celebration only marginally less riotous than the press-day binge. McIlroy's case was going nowhere. He checked his mobile but there was still nothing and he wondered if Marcie Sley had really passed on his number to the elusive Joe. Why had Declan's only close friend suddenly stopped visiting the flat? Did he know Declan was dead?

'Misadventure' was a verdict which covered several sins, but was unlikely to prompt the police to invest any more time in checking out the bogus doctor. But then he thought again about McIlroy's final hours, sitting alone as the killing Arctic wind tore through the flat. He thought of the cold enamel washbasins in the dormitory at St Vincent's, and a life disfigured by casual abuse.

Had he committed suicide after all? It was possible, Dryden admitted to himself, familiar with the subtle horrors of an aimless life.

He jerked the seatbelt across his chest. 'High Park Flats. The allotments.'

As they drove north the snow began to fall again, a shower of half-hearted confetti, blurring the windscreen and adding an element of outright chance to Humph's normally erratic driving style.

The allotments looked deserted, although a clutch of vehicles stood frosted by the entrance, like sugar-dusted chocolates. Through the picket fence Dryden discovered that the Dobermann was off duty – which lifted his mood dangerously higher – as he wandered between the stiff winter vegetable tops. Then, from out of the silence, he heard voices. The Gardeners' Arms was clearly open for business. Instinctively Dryden kept himself out of view behind a large water butt. The door of the shed with the stove pipe opened, the sound of voices swelled, and a figure was admitted to what sounded like a party. A wake perhaps, for Declan McIlroy?

Dryden had not, as far as he could tell, been seen. He slipped away towards the perimeter Leylandii hedge, moving in a series of zigzags, using the dotted sheds and makeshift cabins as cover. At the back of the allotments was a dumping area for garden refuse fed by a narrow track which ran behind the hedge. Despite the icy air the aroma of rotting vegetables and manure was astringent.

The sound of voices swelled and, looking towards the stove-pipe shed, Dryden saw John Sley slipping out. Dryden slid sideways and found a new viewpoint, between two tree trunks. He watched Sley, vulture's head forward, shoulders hunched under his donkey jacket. Marcie's husband was bareheaded, the cruelly shorn grey hair barely covering the bones of his skull, cigarette smoke trailing from a butt held between his lips.

Sley approached a large hut at the back of the allotments, checked the lock and turned to retrace his steps to the Gardeners' Arms. Thinking twice, he stopped himself, slipped a key in the lock and moved inside the hut, leaving the door open. A light came on, and in the dim twilight an amber wedge illuminated the frosted ground outside the door.

But no light showed at what Dryden had taken to be a line of PVC sheets set in the roof. Why build a shed with no windows or skylights? Dryden took a further step back into the shadows.

Then the orange light on the grass turned red. The shift in colour was striking, the red tinged with yellow like a burning ball of sodium. Then the light turned blue, not the pale dying blue of the sky but a cold neon blue, this time tinged with the blacker shades of iodine. There was a brief return to red, and then the orange light returned. Sley reappeared, closing the door behind him and double checking the lock.

He stood for a second, patting something in his overcoat chest pocket, and then returned towards the Gardeners' Arms.

Dryden made his way to the hut Sley had visited, and circled it. Up close he realized he had underestimated its size. It had to be a good twenty-five feet long and ten wide. Not a single pinpoint view was open to the inside. The lock was a Yale, new and shiny. At the far end was a water butt, with a pipe cut out to enter the wooden panelling through a sealed port. Dryden swung himself up onto the top of the butt and tried to peer in through the roof. Nothing. Plywood boards were secured under each pane of the transparent ribbed PVC.

The sound of laughter drifted across the allotments, the light of the stove flared within the Gardeners' Arms, and Dryden thought now that he knew, at least in part, the secret they shared within.

14

It was 4.00pm and the day had died. Dryden, within the warm, darkened sanctuary of Humph's cab, struggled to see through the frosted windscreen. A security lamp on one of the allotment sheds caught the glitter of frost forming on the Leylandii hedges. A car backfired on the Jubilee Estate and a car alarm pulsed. Humph moodily considered the distant convivial glow from the Gardeners' Arms. Dryden had made him move the Capri back into the shadows near High Park Flats. Here the air was colder still, the ice forming Spirograph patterns on the inside of the windscreen which the cabbie periodically attacked with a chamois leather.

'You could fetch me back a pint,' said Humph, shifting in his seat and emitting a thin odour of chicken tikka massala.

Dryden, equally tempted to gatecrash, wound down the window to refresh the air. 'I'd love to, but – and I'm only guessing here – they don't do carry-outs. Besides – I'm watching that,' he said, nodding towards a 4x4 parked up with the rest by the white picket fence near the entrance to the allotments. In the grey world of the dusk they could just see enough of the interior to make out the dog-mesh behind the rear passenger seats. Within, a grey shape flexed and stretched before sinking from view.

The first to leave the wake was a thin man with a whippet, staggering slightly over the uneven ground. He found his car, at the third attempt, and drove off without his lights on, local radio blaring suddenly from the onboard stereo.

John Sley was next out, expertly juggling car keys from left hand to right, and enjoying a sinuous swagger. The donkey jacket lapels were turned up against the night as he unlocked the 4x4. He flicked a switch on the dashboard which lit the ground below the car in fluorescent blue.

'Now there's clever,' said Dryden, his heartbeat rising.

Sley went to the back and flipped up the tailgate. He shouted something, and the uncurling form of the dog subsided. Then he heaved out a mechanic's trolley which he dropped by the driver's door, before swinging himself, with surprising agility, down and under the 4x4. Thirty seconds later he was out, the trolley stashed, and pulling away, taking the Jubilee's sleeping policemen at 50 mph before turning down a drove road into the Great West Fen.

Dryden nudged the cabbie. 'Go on then. Follow that car.'

Humph licked his lips, fired up the engine and left half an inch of rubber on the tarmac before attempting to vault the very same sleeping policemen: a stunt which dislodged a complete set of nuts and bolts from the Capri's suspension as the cab briefly took to the air.

As they left the city lights behind darkness swept over the flatlands as if a switch had been thrown. Lights dotted the distant Fen roads, some in ribbons marking the flow of traffic, others cottages and farms. Christmas had brought a now familiar outbreak of the kind of kitsch decoration beloved of smalltown America. As they slipped north they passed a farmhouse topped off with an illuminated Santa and sleigh, complete with two reindeer alternately lit red and green. A mile further on a roadside cottage was beaded with Christmas lights which flashed and appeared to shuffle in an electronic dance. To the east a Christmas tree winked on top of a grain silo half a county away.

After five minutes they spotted Sley's lights ahead,

ploughing on, always in sight along the arrow-straight road.

Dryden rubbed his hand across the windscreen to clear the view and Humph flicked the windscreen wipers. When the glass cleared Sley's car had gone, the road stretching out before them as empty as a runway, the central row of cats' eyes as bright as the stars. Humph trundled the Capri up the roadside bank, Dryden got out, slammed the door to cut out the vanity light, and let his eyes acclimatize. At the foot of the dyke a drain ten feet wide was an ice mirror, reflecting the moon rising behind the distant outline of the sugar-beet factory. Looking back he could see Ely, and as he watched the cathedral floodlights came on, picking out the silver leaded lantern tower. On the opposite side of the road was uninterrupted darkness: the next light going east probably a distant village outside Moscow.

He walked twenty yards along the bank and surveyed the scene again. The dyke's waters were still an unruffled silver to the west, but the darkness to the east had been dispelled by a farmhouse, now glimpsed between high poplars which must have shielded it from Dryden's original vantage point. It looked welcoming: lights burnt in the four Georgian windows which faced the road, a Christmas tree in one. As he watched a security light came on, followed by another, and he saw Sley's 4x4 sliding between the trees and round to the rear of the house.

He ran back to the cab where Humph had wound down his window. 'Wait here. If I'm not back in an hour get Interpol and a helicopter.'

Humph grunted, wound the window up, and closed his eyes.

Dryden walked down the centre of the road in the Capri's headlights until he was level with the farm track. As he walked away from the main road and the comforting lights of the cab he was aware for the first time that the temperature had dropped further – into unknown territory. Pressing a finger to his cheek he felt the skin, hard and numb, and a dull pain had begun to grip his throat. The farmland around him was open and featureless under the moon, except for a single magnolia, unseen from the road, bent over an oval of starlit pond. Soon he was amongst the poplars skirting the house, and he could see the 4x4 parked amongst farm buildings to the rear. By a security light Dryden could see Sley on his back on the trolley again, retrieving whatever he'd stashed beneath the car.

This was the moment Dryden always dreaded: the tipping point between his life as an objective recorder and the less familiar role of active participant. Life for him often seemed to be something to watch. But now he knew he would learn nothing more unless he took an active role himself. The thought made his guts twist.

He was within six feet of the 4x4 when the sound of his footfalls alerted Sley to his presence.

'Joe?' said the voice under the car, untroubled.

'Don't think so,' said Dryden, dropping down on his haunches.

Sley slid out without a smile, turning an oily rag in his hands like a garrotte.

Dryden, aware he might have made an error of heroic proportions, glanced back at the main road where he feared Humph would now be sleeping soundly. He regretted the Interpol joke, like almost all his jokes.

'Sorry. It's me again. We were passing and I saw your 4x4. I've seen it before.'

He'd said it quickly, crossing the line before he had a chance to retreat. Sley stood, one huge hand holding a metal box retrieved from under the chassis, which he folded into a green baize cloth he held in the other. Dryden was struck by the odd contrast, between the bony mass of the man's hands and the deft, almost delicate, precision of the fingers. Silence was clearly a medium he was happy with so Dryden carried on. 'On police CCTV. Someone's been peddling cannabis to the kids. How's the dog?' he asked, nodding at the meshed interior of the rear of the vehicle.

'Hungry,' said Sley, glancing at the house still lit up in the darkness. The lights on the Christmas tree in the window seemed to tremble. 'Look . . .' he said, shaking his head. 'I've got no idea what this is about . . .'

But Dryden knew he was lying. He'd have thrown him out if this didn't make sense.

'You grow it in the long shed at the allotments. Force it, I guess – then plant it out in the summer? That'd be it. I saw the red light – that's sodium. And the blue? Mercury-iodide. There was case up in crown court last year. Very sophisticated. I'm just kinda interested in why, that's all. To kids. How much you make?'

Sley twisted the cloth again. 'Look, I've got to get on . . .'

Dryden turned again and with relief saw that Humph was out of the cab, standing in the headlights firing the tennis machine ball down the deserted lane for Boudicca to fetch.

'That's my oppo. He knows why I'm here. The police have the film, and we know where the stuff was grown. If you're planning on bluffing I think that's a big mistake.'

Sley opened one of his huge hands and revealed the metal box. 'I need to get this to Joe.'

'Joe,' said Dryden. 'Declan's mate, right? Another customer? A bit mature for your market, surely, he must be fifty if he's a day.'

Sley stepped a foot closer. 'He's forty-one. But he won't make forty-two. Cancer – larynx. You should hear him talk.'

Dryden shrugged. 'I was looking forward to it. Marcie said she'd pass on my number. But no go, eh?'

'We left messages,' said Sley. 'But the illness is bad right now.'

'What's that to me?' asked Dryden, sensing that he'd been expertly hooked into the trap of empathy.

'That's why we grew the cannabis,' he said, getting out a packet of Marlboro and lighting one up. The ash at the end, after the first deep draw, was the same colour as his hair.

'Joe started it on the allotment, when he knew the pain was coming. But the supply never stretched through that first winter. That really scared him, and he was too ill to plant again in spring, and he'd bought this place. So I took over the shed: it's not difficult stuff to grow if you get the gear, and there's guides on the net. He needs the supply, he needs to know it's there. This year was good – you know, the wet spring, the clear summer. There's a surplus so . . . it got sold.'

He slammed the door of the 4x4 and the echo ran round the Fen, bouncing back off a brick-built pumping station half a mile to the east. A dog barked four times, rhythmically, and was quiet.

'Why don't you come with me?' said Sley, walking off towards the house. 'Meet the customer.'

Dryden had sat through too many gloomy inquests on the bleak deaths of lonely drug addicts to see anything in Sley's crime but callous greed. But he hesitated now, knowing that to meet the dying Joe would complicate the simple balance of good against evil. Could he leave the cancer victim out of the equation? And other questions remained: had reliving his time at St Vincent's orphanage really driven Declan McIlroy to self-destruction? Was he part of the criminal circle which had grown and peddled the dope? Had he, perhaps, encroached on a market where someone else had enjoyed a monopoly? And why hadn't Declan eased his own pain, and his final hours, with a home-grown joint? Dryden had wanted to talk to Joe all along, and now he had the chance. He, better than anyone, would know if his friend had any enemies who might have shortened his brutal life.

The farmhouse was foursquare, a late-Georgian landmark with elaborate lead guttering and sash windows. A crack ran through the brickwork indicating that the house stood on the unstable drying peat.

Sley was peering into a half-lit hallway at the side of the house.

'It's odd,' he said, when Dryden caught him up. 'He normally comes out when he hears the car.' He tapped a gold ring on the window and a cat – jet black – leapt to the sill.

'Let's try the back.' There was a kitchen door, almost all glass, but all frosted. Inside they could see a light over a work surface and the glow of an oven. Sley flipped up the letterbox and shouted for Joe. Dryden was six feet away but caught the warm smell of roasted meat from within.

Sley stood, rattling the knob. He looked out across the Fen. 'He can't be far.'

'Is there another door?' asked Dryden, the cold beginning to slink between his shoulders.

He followed Sley round to what had been the main door-way of the old house. It had a series of three semicircular steps leading up to the door itself, which had a fanlight above.

Sley stiffened, and Dryden caught him up, walking past and looking around in the splash of electric orange which illuminated the porch. He saw the corpse almost immediately, knowing he was looking at death in the same instant that he recognized the curled form as human. The sleet and snow had accumulated, creating a shroud which covered most of the exposed flesh of the face and one hand, which had tried to cover the eyes but had slipped to reveal one socket, now itself full of marbled ice. Rigor mortis and the cold had drawn up the lips, revealing teeth disfigured by nicotine.

But it was the colour Dryden would remember, or the lack of it. The skin was white, as was the hair, but so were the lips, all coated in frost. The hand that had fallen from covering the eyes was scratched and caked with earth, but where the nails showed they too were white, without a blush of pink to signal life.

They hadn't said a word. Sley tried the door and found that it too was locked. Dryden peered into the front room. A fire had burned in the grate but was ashes now.

Sley produced a mobile. 'I'll get the police. Ambulance.'

'It's an odd way to die,' said Dryden, his eye for the first time picking out across the frosted gravel the scuffed furrow which led to the body from the direction of the distant magnolia tree. He recalled a picture on Declan McIlroy's wall, the two friends on a bench, the distant horizon of the Fen a shimmering line of summer heat.

He saw an image then, the dying man pulling himself along the frozen ground towards the warmth and light of his home. How could the door be locked? An accident? But that was the problem with tragic deaths, thought Dryden; they were inherently unbelievable. There was something about the curled, catlike form on the step which spoke of resignation, rather than desperation.

Dryden pressed his nose against the window again. There was a flat-screen TV in front of which a single armchair had been pulled up. In front of that was a small table from a nest, upon which was a knife, fork, and heatproof mat.

'Dinner alone,' said Dryden to himself.

He made a mental inventory of the room's personal effects. The walls were bare but for a framed map of Ireland, a mirror – the only object of any age – and one richly framed canvas. He recognized one of Declan's landscapes, the black peat tinged with an angry purple.

On a sideboard a wooden gypsy caravan stood, and before the fire a cat's basket with a wool fleece inside. On the mantle there was a gold-framed picture of a woman: fifty perhaps, the smile as smart and sharp as the executive hair, a dark business jacket boasting a cameo brooch. The smile had lost any warmth it might have once had, like the ashes in the grate below.

Something about the picture, its precise alignment, its central position, signalled remembrance. Joe had lived alone. But did he die alone?

15

An eggshell-blue squad car swung in off the drove road, its headlamps sweeping the landscape like a lighthouse beam. Dryden, having fetched Humph from the road, watched from the fusty interior of the Capri, now parked beside the 4x4. He'd been shivering, not because of the ice which had begun to encroach on all the cab's windows, but because death left him cold, disheartened and afraid of the future. He'd applied an antidote to depression: three miniature malts, but the inner glow only flickered, then died. Sley had rung for the police but it seemed they were in little hurry. Dryden dozed fitfully in the Capri while Humph grumbled intermittently about lost suppers.

Sley had sat more comfortably in the heated four-wheel drive: punching numbers into a mobile and, presumably, breaking bad news. Dryden expected others would arrive the next morning, a caravan of condolence.

The police car parked beside the 4x4. The uniformed PC was young, perhaps twenty-five, enveloped in an overcoat which touched the ground. They met him on the gravel. 'John,' he said to Sley, shaking hands. They'd met before and Dryden felt suddenly excluded.

He slipped off a glove and shook Dryden's hand, replacing it immediately. 'Richard Ware. I'm the community officer for the Fen out to Shippea Hill. The station rang. They'd have sent from Ely but they've closed the drove at the city end 'cos of black ice. So I'd better secure the scene – can you show me, John?' He buttoned up the overcoat to his throat, shuddering with the cold. 'It's a record – the temperature. Minus 18 – and that's without a wind. We should be inside . . .'

'He's round at the front of the house, on the step, the door's locked,' said Sley.

Ware nodded. 'OK.' His eyes slipped over the house, checking windows. 'You've both been round the front?'

They nodded.

'Right. Enough footprints then already. Let's try to get to him through the house from the back. Chances are he's locked himself out by accident, but I need to check from the inside, secure the scene. Let's play it by the book.'

They went to the kitchen door and the policeman expertly forced the Yale, sliding a plastic card down the door jamb. Dryden felt the heat hit his skin. Inside the smell of meat was overpowering. Ware flipped down the oven door and retrieved a chicken, the breastbone protruding through the overcooked flesh, while the vegetables stood peeled and immersed in water, but unheated.

'Last supper,' said Ware, moving through to the living room, his eyes dancing over what seemed familiar territory. In the hall, on the high wall which skirted the stairwell, hung a kite in the shape of a kestrel, its tail feathers tacked up in swirls. Dryden lingered in the kitchen, where a cork noticeboard was dotted with memoranda, secured with drawing pins: a hospital appointment card, bus timetables, a few postcards and several newspaper cuttings – he noted one from *The Crow* by the paper's gardening correspondent about the cold snap, and something from the *Lynn News* on Fen house prices. In the middle of the board was an open patch, oddly at variance with the rest of the crowded surface. Two drawing pins, with red heads, had been pressed neatly together in the middle.

Ware came back down the hall. 'There was this,' said Dryden, giving him a copy of *The Crow* and three editions of the *Lynn News* – the local evening paper. 'I took a walk. These were in the post box down by the road.' Dryden had noted the name stencilled on the US-style mail box: Joe Petulengo.

Ware nodded. 'That means he hadn't been down to the road since, what – Tuesday afternoon – late afternoon.' He looked around again, staring briefly into the dead ashes of the fire and along the mantelpiece.

'Something wrong?' asked Dryden.

Ware shrugged. 'Nope. Something missing . . . perhaps.' He knocked his knuckles together: 'So – where is he?'

Sley went out into the hall and pointed to the door. Ware examined the locks – a Yale, and a Chubb below it. The Chubb was open, but the Yale firmly engaged. He turned the locking handle and swung the door in.

The victim lay still, rimed with frost.

'God,' said Ware, kneeling and inching an ungloved finger towards the marble-white jugular. Dryden saw that at the neck was a gold chain, a hanging crucifix. Ware slipped a hand under the outer waterproof coat and within, to a jumper below. The sound of ice breaking made Dryden wince.

The constable stood, regloved his hand and looked out across the moonlit field towards the distant magnolia.

'All his clothes are frozen, they're heavy with ice. He's been drenched.'

Ware stepped out but stopped them following.

'Go back through and come round.'

By the time they'd circled the house Ware had taped off the scene. 'That was his place – down by the water,' he said. 'Every time I went by on the road he seemed to be out there. I tried to tell him it was too cold . . . you too, John,' he said, catching Sley's eye.

Ware produced a heavy-duty police-issue torch and lit a circle around his boots. Across the gravel was the clear trail of the victim's body, the central furrow of the torso, the intermittent scuffs where the elbows had levered his weight forward.

They left the path and walked on the grass towards the mirrored surface of the pond, shattered now by the hole at its edge. Sharp shards were thrust up from the impact, refracting the moonlight into a jagged spectrum of cold rainbows.

The hole had frozen over but the star was clear to see.

Ware stood, his arms crossed over his chest, his hands in his armpits. 'Looks like he fell in. He used to sit here.' He touched the iron seat. 'You can see the slip marks along the edge.'

It was true, Dryden acknowledged it with a nod. 'Suicide?'

'He'd talked about it,' said Sley. 'I asked Richard to keep an eye on the place – but you know, if he'd decided, what could we do? He might have tried, changed his mind, crawled back to the house.'

A single flashing blue light caught everyone's attention at the same moment. It was a mile distant, slipping easily across the night like a ship's light at sea.

'I'll meet them,' said Ware, setting off quickly back towards the house. 'Keep off the gravel and don't touch anything.'

Sley didn't move and Dryden knew why. They watched in silence as a satellite crossed the sky, horizon to horizon in an elegant curve.

'How much of the dope have you got left?' asked Dryden.

'Not much. Joe's supply until the first harvest of spring, I guess.'

'Why did you need the money?'

Sley didn't answer.

'Destroy it. Strikes me you've got a bumper surplus now your friend's dead. Just burn it. The police are giving us updates. Any stuff appears on the street I'll go straight to the station – OK?'

Sley turned to the house where the ambulance had parked by the front porch.

'And I want a lift back into town – we need to talk some more,' said Dryden, troubled now by a double coincidence he didn't trust: two deaths by ice, two regulars from the Gardeners' Arms.

He told Humph to go home and went round to the kitchen door. Ware was in the living room, overcoat off, perched on a double radiator. A phone stood on the window ledge and the PC pressed PLAY for messages.

'Message timed 11.15am Thursday, 29th of December.'

'Joe? It's Marcie. We hope you're feeling better. They said at work you'd taken a few days. Look, it's really important you ring me, Joe; there's some news. Some bad news. I can't just leave a message. Ring please.'

There were two messages and he hit PLAY again.

'Message timed 6.45pm, Friday, 30th of December.'

'Joe. Marcie. John's coming out tonight to see you, OK? But if you get this and are feeling well enough, ring me – the mobile's on.'

'Did he ring?'

Sley shook his head.

'So. That fits. There's every chance he was dead by the time the messages were left,' said Ware.

Dryden went back to the kitchen and began picking his way through the paper in the recycling bin: bills, junk mail, some typed business letters from the bank.

The kitchen units were modern, the oven hi-tech. But like the rest of the house the room felt unused, a showcase. A single plate and mug stood on the draining board, a black recycling bin full of paper by the back door.

Ware came through. 'I should lock up.'

Dryden stood, kicking the bin with his shoe. 'Odd. When does the council pick up recycled paper round here?'

Ware joined him by the bin. 'Today.'

'A week's worth of rubbish but no newspapers,' said Dryden.

Ware nodded: 'And there *is* something missing,' he said, turning back to the living room. 'I'm sure there was another picture on the mantle. He'd picked himself out once when I asked – a faded snapshot from the seaside. This bunch of kids, smiling . . .'

16

A sky like an army blanket hid the stars. In High Park Flats a single bathroom light shone coldly out, joined only by a solitary string of Christmas lights trailing from a window ledge. Sley parked the 4x4 by the entrance to the allotments and killed the engine, checking his watch.

'Two minutes past closing time precisely,' he said. 'I need a drink.'

Beyond the fluorescent lights of the car park the darkness lingered amongst the bean posts and frost-bitten furrows and Dryden stumbled several times as they picked their way towards the dull gleam of the stove pipe. Once, looking back, he saw a pair of car headlights swing into the shadow of the flats, then die.

Sley, playing a torch at his feet, found a log pile and collected an armful of kindling and wood, balancing it expertly with a splayed hand while inserting a key in the door of the Gardeners' Arms.

Inside, the smell of drying fruit was intoxicating, the sweetness of apples mingling with the fusty aroma of yeast from the home brew. Sley stooped by the stove and quickly lit a fire, leaving the glazed door open to light the room. Something rustled in the corner, like an autumn leaf.

Dryden sat on some sacking piled on an old garden stool, aware that the hessian was crisp with frost. He imagined the ghosts of Joe Petulengo and Declan McIlroy just beyond the light, cradling mugs of the tangy double-strength alcohol. The Gardeners' Arms was a refuge, Dryden could see that now, a hidden corner of the world reserved for outcasts, and those who had chosen to join them.

The fire began to draw and Sley added the logs. He lit a cigarette and rubbed at his scalp with the heel of his hand.

'How well did they know each other – Joe and Declan?' asked Dryden, taking an earthenware cup from Sley. The beer was icy, the thud of the alcohol palpable.

Sley held his own full glass but didn't drink. 'It's history. I don't understand what you're trying to prove . . .'

It was an odd word to choose. Dryden set the mug down and retrieved a Greek cigarette from a packet in his overcoat and lit it with a piece of kindling from the fire. He watched Sley's hatchet face, half lit in the firelight, and wondered if he'd regret not going straight to the police with what he knew.

'I'm not trying to prove anything,' he said. 'I've got to write a feature about those in danger from the cold – if they were friends, that helps. This is information I need. But just a reminder – if I don't get it, I'll get something else off the police in return for tipping them off as to the identity of the elusive drugs peddler. How does that sound?'

Dryden realized he didn't fear Sley any more. It was an eloquent admission that he sensed a common decency beneath the brutal exterior.

Sley drew in two lungfuls of nicotine. 'So. How well did they know each other?' repeated Dryden.

'The allotments were a meeting place. For all of us.'

'But before. How long had they been friends?' Dryden could sense the boundary he was pushing at, sure now that just beyond it lay the link he sought. He watched Sley through the drifting smoke from the cigarette, and sensed he was calculating a reply.

Sley stood, drinking savagely, the liquid slopping in the

glass. 'They grew up together, in care. Brothers really, but for the accident of blood.'

Dryden nodded. 'So what's the big secret?' But his thoughts raced: if Joe had been at St Vincent's was he too embroiled in the action against the orphanage?

'There's no secret. It's just private, isn't it? They were orphans. Joe's parents were travellers, Romany. Gyppos – take your choice. Petulengo – a name he was proud of, eventually. But that was the nightmare for him – being in care, being inside, being locked up.'

'And you?'

Sley ignored the question, refilling his glass. 'Joe lived in a caravan, a mobile home really – plush. You'd be surprised. Snug as a peg.' He laughed again, and Dryden sensed a long-held prejudice, finally liberated by death.

'Until . . . ?'

'Last year. He was diagnosed with the cancer, throat. He said he'd always promised himself he'd die in a house. Die in his own home. Crazy. So he bought the Letter M and then spent most of his time on that seat by the water, just looking at it.'

'He had the money then?'

'Oh yeah. He was never short, Joe.' He laughed without a sound. 'And when Mary died he'd nothing left to spend the money on.'

'A wife – I saw the picture,' said Dryden.

'Yeah. She was older, MS. Pretty nasty really. He never really got over it, although most of us thought she was pretty aloof, focused on the money. She'd married it, after all.'

Dryden let the slight pass. 'And the allotment?'

'Outside again. He spent hours here. It was Declan who'd started first. The council gave him that flat but he couldn't stand it. Claustrophobia – much worse than Joe – even when he was out on the balcony. He'd slept rough for years – that's where he really wanted to be. He just used to shrivel up indoors.'

Dryden nodded as if he understood. 'Is that why he drank?'

Sley shrugged. 'Life he'd had, you don't need an excuse.'

'And the cannabis. Anyone else smoke the stuff? Declan?'

Sley shook his head.

Dryden stood. 'You said orphanage. He was a Catholic, Joe – yes? I noticed a cross, a crucifix on a chain at his neck.'

'Sure. St Vincent's, with Declan. It's closed now.'

Dryden smiled, enjoying the inevitability of fate.

'Declan was a victim of abuse in the case against St Vincent's. Was Joe another?'

Sley shrugged. 'Sure. I doubt any kid who went through that place escaped, do you?'

Dryden accepted a second mug of beer. The glow from the stove was more substantial, and he stretched out his legs in the heat. He saw them differently now, these two men whose damaged lives had ended so savagely; saw them at a dormitory window, two pale faces, held close, dreaming of an end to childhood.

17

Dryden set out across town, the stunning canopy of the night sky an antidote to sleep. Wisps of mist trailed from the cathedral's great West Tower like medieval pennants in the moonlight. On Palace Green a single muntjac stood chewing at what looked like a refuse bag. As Dryden crossed the grass the deer looked up and then sprang into flight, its white underside flashing as it headed for the cathedral park. The cold of the night was at its deepest and each shop window glittered with rocket bursts of crystal ice.

As he trudged towards the distant landmark of The Tower Hospital Dryden considered the extent to which he had succumbed to a dubious conspiracy theory. If Declan's death was suspicious, what about Joe's? Had someone really murdered them both? They were both witnesses in the case against St Vincent's — but was that really a motive for murder? A more mundane explanation looked plausible: that a lonely, damaged alcoholic had taken his own life when the bitter winter had offered him the opportunity; and that a benign accident had sped Joe Petulengo to a quick death, where a lingering one had seemed a certain fate.

But what of John Sley? Could the sale of drugs be linked to either death? Was the production of marijuana, so efficiently organized, really just to ease the passing of a friend?

The gravel on The Tower's drive was frozen solid, each stone to its neighbour. The great clock was still lit in its mock-Florentine tower, but had frozen at 11.45, a disc of ice smudging the normally crisp outlines of the Roman numerals of the face. The automatic doors of the foyer swished open and he lingered in the caress of the hot air within, letting his shoulders slump, easing the exquisite pain in his joints. The nurse behind the desk was a regular and looked up only to check the electric clock: 1.02am.

'For Laura Dryden,' he said. The nurse nodded. Dryden's late-night visits were not uncommon. Laura's sleep pattern was erratic enough for it to make little difference to her when he called, as long as he did.

Her room was tropical. As he closed the door the COMPASS clattered into life and he analysed his reaction: was he pleased that his wife was conscious? He walked to the bed and felt the familiar thrill of seeing her face, her brown eyes wide and, briefly, locked on his. He leant in low, and lifted her in an embrace.

He took the tickertape from the COMPASS.

A LETTER.

He searched the screen of the PC and found a new file marked HOLIDAY.

He opened the document, and lay beside her on the pillows to read. Laura's consultant had suggested that she could leave the hospital for a brief break. They'd had to put the request in writing, and this was his formal reply. For more than six months now she had been free of the complications which had once confined her to her room: bouts of pneumonia and a series of blood infections had demanded constant observation. But now her health was stable, the lingering physical symptoms of her illness the only bar to a wider freedom – and even here there had been improvements.

But for Dryden the progress she had made merely doubled her schizophrenia: her world had always been divided between conscious and unconscious – but now the conscious world was divided between those hours when her recovery provided hope of a return to the life they had once had, and those in which it mocked their dreams, promising only the prospect of a slow and imperfect rehabilitation, a struggle back to the rudimentary movements of early childhood.

Tonight her hopes were alive and Dryden shared them, genuinely thrilled that there might be a life for both of them outside this hospital room.

The memo listed the conditions for her release from The Tower for a period of seventy-two hours.

- You will need to either transport a hoist or take the break at a destination which has one on site. We recommend a bridge hoist with a lifting weight of no less than 100lb.

- You will need a supply of waste bags and PEG-feed apparatus. We can provide these.

- We recommend that your destination should be no more than 45 minutes drive from a general hospital. Ideally it should not be more than 90 minutes from The Tower.

- You will need to either transport a wheelchair or have immediate access to one at your destination. We recommend you take one of those used at The Tower which can be adjusted to relieve pain and increase seating tolerance.

- Clearly it is possible to transport the COMPASS, although cumbersome. A small handheld version is now on the market and costs around £2,000. Unfortunately, we do not have this item, but we can order it for you.

- We need both a landline telephone number and a mobile number deposited with us at reception. We will give you the emergency lines for the hospital. We can guarantee an immediate response and retrieval of the patient to The Tower within four hours as long as all other stipulations have been followed.

- You need to contact the Mid-Anglian Mutual to amend insurance cover while not on the premises. We understand that their response is likely to make cover contingent on following these stipulations.

- For the time our patient is outside the hospital our fees will remain unaltered.

'Unbelievable,' said Dryden, tapping a finger on the last prescription. 'Don't forget the fees, eh? We wouldn't want to get away with two days at a cut price.'

He lifted his wife up against the pillows and began the tiny rituals which had made his nightly visit to The Tower an almost religious ceremony. Uncorking a bottle of Italian red wine from the side cupboard, he poured two glasses, setting one down on Laura's tray. If she asked, he would pour a little of the liquid into the drinking tube she was beginning to master. Then he sat, tapping a single white Greek cigarette from the packet out into his hand. He no longer smoked as a habit but Laura enjoyed the acrid smell of the harsh tobacco, and the memories it brought her of a honeymoon spent in the Cyclades.

Taking the perspex tube attached to the COMPASS, Dryden looped it tenderly over his wife's lips. He watched as her cheeks moved with the effort of sucking and blowing the commands which would move the on-screen cursor.

LATE?

They had developed a shorthand language to restrict the agonizing stutter of the computer printout.

'Yeah. Sorry. I should have texted. Sorry.'

He drank a glass of the wine and took a refill.

'Odd. Another death from the cold. Out on the Fen. This guy was just frozen on his doorstep. Under ice. It was like something from a wildlife film, some animal rigid in the Arctic snow. Disturbing, really; much worse than a bloody corpse.'

SUICIDE?

Dryden shook his head: 'I guess – or an accident. But there's a few things wrong. It's like this other one in the flats, the guy who just threw the windows open and died in his armchair. It turns out he'd had a visitor just before he died – a doctor, but there's no record of an official visit from any of the emergency services, Age Concern, nothing. Then, when I go back to the flat there's someone there. Someone who shouldn't be there. I tried to catch him but he did a runner. So what's that about?

'And the one out on the Fen . . . he was locked out of his own house. I know that can happen – I did it once at the flat, remember? But this guy gets an evening paper every day, right? Plus weeklies. And yet there are no newspapers in his recycling bin, even though the bin's full.'

There was a silence and Dryden dribbled some of the wine into the drinking funnel and replaced the COMPASS tube with a feed. He watched as the surface of the wine vibrated, draining slowly away.

'OK. He keeps the newspapers somewhere else. That could be true. And the bogus doctor could have just been a con artist – although nothing's missing from either the victim's flat or the next door neighbour's, not that either was stuffed with treasures. And the bloke in the flat when I went back could have just been looting the place now the owner's dead.'

He unhooked the feeding tube.

'But the thing that I can't let go is the coincidence. They knew each other, these two – the victims. Lifelong friends. Two accidents, two sudden deaths, a shared childhood. That's fiction – and fiction doesn't happen.'

Dryden shook his head again, and walked to the window to raise the blinds.

The COMPASS jumped: CAN WE GO?

He sat, taking her hand, massaging the finger joints where the nurses had shown him.

'Sure. If you want to.' He'd hesitated and he knew why. What if depression came with the journey and the realization that this would be a brief interlude in the rest of her life? What if temptation came with the freedom?

'Where?' he asked, trying to push back the thought, the idea that there might be an end to it.

ANYWHERE THATS NT HERE.

He thought of that childhood summer, the white surf fizzing around his tanned legs, the sea stretching as far as a Fen horizon.

'Give it a month, three. Let the spring begin. Then we can go – to the coast. Let's go to the coast.'

The Dolphin Holiday Camp
Friday, 30 August 1974

They called him Dex but it didn't suit him. He was shy, frail, with a lopsided poor-boy's haircut. Timid too, frightened even, but he punctuated his fear with eruptions of random violence. Philip pitied him, but never turned his back on him. He ran to him now across the grass that separated the rows of chalets and they stood for a second, listening to the sounds of the distant jukebox, the metallic jangle of the camp's fairground, their eyes piecing together the night in shades of black and white. A seagull, almost luminously pale, balanced on one of the lampposts which lit the path to the sea, its body turned into the breeze like the prow of a ship.

Smith appeared in the still-open doorway. Smith was bigger, a full year older, long limbs disjointed by a child's rush to grow. He held the torch lightly, juggling it, smiling at the prospect of the game and scratching at his white, crewcut hair.

They stood together, saying nothing, and Philip was thrilled again by the intimacy this implied. Were they brothers? Philip could think of no way to ask. Why did they share the chalet – while Dex's sister slept alone in a chalet by the pool? It worried him, this inconsistency in a world he thought he understood.

They ran down towards the saltmarsh. The tides had been high all week, the second of the game. Seawater, flowing up the river estuary, backed up through the network of channels to create a liquid maze. Here they had mapped out the rules – between the pumping station and the sluice, the old boathouse and the bird hide. Ahead they saw

the iron sluice gate where they always met, and Dex's sister there, wait-
ing to begin, standing in a pool of light from her downturned torch.

Philip got there first and jumped up to sit beside her on the cool
iron safety rail. He brushed her thigh with his leg, the guilt at this
sudden intimacy almost buried beneath another emotion: a confused
but intense attraction to the cool skin and the stretched mahogany tan.

The sister. Dex called her 'Sis' when he spoke, which was rare, but
he stuck with her; a satellite, always connected by invisible bonds of
gravity. Philip envied him that, and the soft brush of the skin.

So jealousy too: which only made him want to touch her again.

Smith, suddenly unsure, turned his square head towards the marsh.
He took the torch from his pocket and shone it briefly into his own
face.

'Philip. It's Philip's turn.'

Sis looked at him then and he tried to smile. But he felt the fear
return and his mind raced on: mapping out the game. Where? Where
would he hide? He felt for the torch in his pocket, the relief at the
cold touch of metal profound, then he jumped down and ran, know-
ing the minute hand on Dex's watch would be racing on. Sixty seconds,
never more.

The old boathouse was lost in darkness and reeds, behind it a
wooden rowing boat rotted, covered by a tarpaulin. Smith, he knew,
had hidden in the boathouse more than once, and Dex had used the
boat itself. Philip lifted the worn green material and slipped in, turned
the torch on, and imagined what the others would be doing, crowding
his imagination so that the fear wouldn't have the space to get in. He
saw them, by moonlight, spreading out now, each one alone, each one
searching.

He killed the light and the darkness pushed up against his eyes.
Desperate to see out, to see anything, he worked his fingers along the
wood where the moss was dry until he'd got a hand under the tarpaulin,
and raised it an inch.

The moonlight, shredded by a passing cloud, lit up the reed tops.

Beyond the dyke, along the river where they never played, there was a circular light like a bird's eye. It was perfectly round and pale and seemed to hang in the dusk, the eye of a predator watching its prey.

18

Saturday, 31 December

Humph had dropped him by the boat in the early hours and he'd climbed aboard, made coffee, and brought it up on deck to try to fend off sleep. That's when he saw them, the measured footprints which had come out of town during the night, and then appeared to return. Footprints: heel and toe, paced out along the riverbank in the peppered snow. He checked the boat, the painter, the tarpaulin. Nothing. In winter few walked the footpath, and his post was left up at the farm. He'd gulped the coffee, trying not to think, telling himself that paranoia was an illness.

Then he'd gone below, making another pot of coffee, and seen what wasn't there. Against the forward bulwark he'd tacked up Declan McIlroy's canvas. The two men waist deep in blood. It was gone. Until then the cold of the night had not made him shiver. He checked the boat out, the deck and forward through the cabins. Nothing else was gone. So he poured himself a malt and returned to the deck.

He could see only one image: the intruder's face glimpsed through the frosted striped window of the serving hatch in Declan McIlroy's flat. The fear returned and he switched on *PK 129*'s floodlight, illuminating the river and the banks. A pair of black swans, startled, took to the air.

He went below but hadn't slept, the silent landscape beyond the porthole peopled by shadows which seemed to hover on the edge of vision. By dawn the lack of sleep buzzed in his blood like adrenaline and when, a few hours later, he heard Humph hoot the Capri's horn he felt a flood of relief not to be alone.

Over the weekend the cabbie transferred his services to better-paying customers, mostly bar and club workers who needed ferrying at ungodly hours. Dryden didn't resent the desertion but it didn't make Saturdays any easier to live through. But Humph always made it for breakfast, complete with fried egg sandwiches. Dryden ferried out the coffees, trying hard to let the comfort of routine obscure the rawness and fear of the sleepless night.

'Someone's been on the boat,' he said, unable to remove the edge of anxiety from his voice. 'Last night, before you dropped me off. Look.' They walked along the riverbank, the footsteps still clear despite a smattering of newly fallen snow. 'They took the canvas, the one from Declan McIlroy's flat.'

'I told you,' said the cabbie, pausing briefly before attacking his sandwich. Humph had a low view of life on water and had advised Dryden to get a flat in town. 'Water gypsies,' he said. 'Change the locks.' Humph believed that the river's small population of New Age narrow-boat dwellers was responsible for almost all recorded crime.

Dryden shook his head. 'Nah. Why take the painting and nothing else?'

Humph thought about it. 'Stay at mine – there's room.' This was an understatement. Since divorce had separated Humph from a wife and two daughters his semi echoed like a giant oil drum.

'I'm fine,' said Dryden, collecting up the mugs and plates. 'They won't come back.' He looked to the horizon and found the box-like outline of High Park Flats, hoping he was right.

But twenty minutes later, as he watched the cab disappear, a final backfire marking its arrival on the main road, the sense of insecurity made him sick. He liked his own company, and loneliness was not an emotion he normally recognized, but suddenly he needed the distractions of work.

He used his mobile to make a round of calls – fire, ambulance, police, coastguard and the press office number for the county council's social services department which was co-ordinating help for the old and infirm during the cold snap. The police had nothing fresh on the death of Joe Petulengo. His age was given as forty-one, a widower, with no children. Cause of death was confirmed as hypothermia, and an initial examination of the clothes in which he was found confirmed they had been soaked in water. There were also traces of pond weed and clay on his clothes, and several fibres of cannabis. Police were treating the incident as a tragic accident. An inquest would be held that Tuesday.

The news from the cold-weather helpline had been equally bleak. Today's top temperature at sea level was likely to be minus 8 degrees centigrade, falling to minus 14 at dusk. The night would break records, with ground temperatures touching minus 20 in some exposed areas. The short-term forecast was still dry, almost parched, with little threat of any significant snowfall. But the medium-range forecast was ominous. A layer of warm air from the south was insinuating itself northwards. It would lie between the snowclouds above and the supercooled earth below. Storms were gathering and if snow did fall it would melt as it fell, passing through the warm layer, and then reach the ground as iced water, freezing on impact with buildings, cars, roads – almost anything that got in its way. Freezing showers were forecast, with the prospect of a full-blown ice storm at any time in the following ten days. He took a note, but knew it wasn't enough. So he drank more coffee, put on another layer of clothing and rummaged in the forward store for his ice skates, then he hung his shoes by their laces around his neck and skated into town, the exhilaration of the open sky and luminous river lifting his spirits.

The Crow's offices were deserted, like the rest of town. He began to put together a package of information on the weather – a painstaking process of ringing charities, utilities and the emergency services which would save him time come Monday morning when the pressure would be on to find some decent news stories for the *Express*. He found one good line almost immediately: the water board predicted that freezing ground temperatures could threaten the mains supply. Plans were being made for a fleet of water tankers to provide outlying districts, and a list of locations had already been posted online.

The risk of an ice storm, rare in the UK, was worth a standalone story. He needed some background material to paint the picture for *The Crow*'s readers, so he went online and Googled up some facts and figures from a lethal storm which had hit Ottawa and Quebec in 1998. The headline numbers were suitably alarming – 100,000 people had fled to special shelters, nearly 2 million had lost all power at home, hundreds had either died in accidents or been poisoned by fumes at home using faulty heaters after electricity supplies had failed. Transport had been almost entirely halted, the freezing rain making car door locks almost impossible to open. Millions of trees had died, cracked open by the freezing rain which had seeped into the wood only to expand into wedges of ice. The sea had frozen in several spots on the eastern seaboard, and pack-ice had crowded the Great Lakes.

'It's a disaster movie,' said Dryden to himself, his mood lightening further.

He walked to the office bay window and looked out onto

Market Street, past the etched motif of *The Crow*, where snow still fell for now in picturebook flakes. He abandoned work and walked out into town, buying tea from the mobile canteen in Market Square. Then he went to the police station and dutifully reported the theft of the canvas from his floating home, the uniformed PC on duty not bothering to reassure him that the culprits would be swiftly and professionally tracked down. He left with a reference number in case he had to make an insurance claim, although a second search by daylight had revealed that nothing else was missing from *PK 129*.

Back in town a few shoppers moved briskly between the Saturday market stalls, but already some traders were packing away, and a lorry had backed in to load up unsold vegetables. A wind was rising and the awnings and plastic sheeting strung up to protect the stalls snapped like whips. The town Christmas tree, surrounded by security fencing in the middle of the market, swayed. Dryden sought cover in the lee of a mobile fishmonger's counter, and stood sipping the tea. He considered the lives of Joe Petulengo and Declan McIlroy, and he considered their deaths, weighing again the balance between conspiracy, suicide and accident. A large conger eel lay on one of the fishmonger's white plastic trays, its eye flat and sightless. And he thought of the footsteps again, crisp on the towpath. He made a decision then, finished the tea, and headed back to the office.

Using *The Crow*'s online archive he'd checked for references to Petulengo. In May 1994 an article had been published to mark the tenth anniversary of the foundation of a company – JSK – a one-man business dedicated to designing and manufacturing high-performance kites for use on farms. Most models mimicked the shape, colour and flight patterns of birds of prey, the kestrel being the most popular. The flying scarecrows were endorsed, in the article, by a farmer who had used a prototype on his land for more than five seasons. A grainy picture showed Petulengo flying one from what looked like a rooftop, the spiky miniature pinnacles of the cathedral's Lady Chapel just visible in the distant background. A spokesman from the National Farmers' Union lauded the idea, and praised its environmental credentials. The paper described Petulengo as a 'young entrepreneur', and in a less-PC age as coming from a 'well-known gypsy family'. Dryden recalled the lovingly arranged tails of the kite hung in the hallway of the farmhouse at Letter M Farm. He bent an Anglepoise lamp down over the cutting. The picture was good enough to see the face clearly – the statuesque head, the short white hair, the powerful, squat frame. He found JSK in the telephone book and noted down the address.

Twenty minutes later Dryden stood, dizzy now from lack of sleep, outside the factory wire, the view fractured into neat diamonds, gripping the metallic grid with bare fingers. He rested his forehead on the wire, wishing he'd tried to sleep.

The old jam factory had been the site of one of the town's few large-scale industries, founded in the mid-nineteenth century. Fruit had been delivered via a spur of the railway, grubbed up in the 1960s. It was three storeys high, with large lattice windows for light and a set of iron folding doors across the ground-floor loading bays: a windswept spot, a solitary industrial landmark. From the flat roof a single thread of string rose into the air, a long low-slung loop like a washing line, disappearing into the slate grey sky. It swung precariously, as if the wind were fighting to keep it aloft.

Dryden lifted his hands free from the freezing wire, wincing at the slight tearing sensation which came from the skin at his fingertips. He breathed out, the cloud of steam almost fog-like. It was colder, much colder. He looked up at the pendant string. 'Kites,' he said, calling up the memory of one dipping over the sea.

Cars crammed a small car park, none of them aspiring to the adjective executive. To the east was a plot reclaimed from the peat on which stood a large mobile home, immaculately painted in white with green trimmings, with a brace of carriage lamps and a double garage; a tiny bit of kitsch suburbia, set adrift.

Up a set of stone steps and through a reinforced glass door a watchman slept in an overheated cubicle reeking of tea bags. A board on the wall indicated that the building was let to a range of small businesses, had been opened by the local MEP and sponsored by the regional development agency. Dryden slipped past the sleeping sentry, found JSK on the board and climbed to the top floor.

As he trod the cold concrete steps he listened to an echo climbing with him, and something made him stop, one foot raised. For a step the echo was ahead of him, then silence. Climbing on he tried again, but this time the echo, perfectly matched, had no life of its own. In the cold of the stair-well he stood, considering the dangers of paranoia. Around him he could hear the sounds of small-scale engineering: a saw screamed, a mechanical punch produced a rhythmic bass note, Radio 1 crackled.

Dryden shivered and pressed on. The stairs ended at a set of double see-through plastic doors stencilled with the letters JSK. The shop floor within was open-plan, cluttered with work benches over which were draped swathes of the materials used to make kites: wooden canes, aluminium rods, sheets of PVC and lightweight plastics. What looked like an impromptu staff meeting was taking place at one end, with a dozen overalled men clutching mugs, drawn up in a semi-circle. They were being addressed by John Sley, small-time drug peddler and allotment brewer. Beside him was Marcie Sley, who turned her head towards Dryden, the only one to hear his entrance.

Dryden waited, considering the cat's-cradle of ties which seemed to bind together the lives of the two dead men.

A notice board was sprinkled with pictures: a works outing at what looked like Hunstanton, some colour advertising shots of kites being flown, and a PR shot of Joe Petulengo, up close, with a CBI award for exports. And another cutting, from what looked like the *Cambridge Evening News*, of him holding the same award but with an arm thrown around a woman in a smart dark suit. Dryden recognized the face as that in the portrait over the mantelpiece at the Letter M farm.

Suddenly a snaking, crackling sound, like fire running across petrol came from the roof above Dryden's head. Then something heavy and brittle struck directly, the vibration of the impact briefly releasing a shower of dust from the beams. John Sley was first to a metal staircase which ran up from the shop floor. Quickly, everyone followed, Dryden being the last to climb out under the grey sky, almost close enough – it seemed – to touch. Around them lay the open Fen, the city to the north, dominated by the cathedral. There was a low parapet but Dryden, restricted by his fear of heights, moved cautiously to a point equidistant from all the edges. A tangle of splintered wood, mangled metal and plastic lay in a contorted heap on one edge of the creosoted flat surface: whilst across most of it a nylon cord zigzagged and lay in spools. Sprinkled over everything were icicles, a drift of miniature stalactites, although some were more than a foot long – daggers of frozen water.

Dryden was next to Marcie Sley, her eyes tracking the movement around her. Again he was struck by the luxurious black hair and the weathered skin, which he felt the urge to touch but, confused by the emotion, blurted out a question instead.

'What is it?'

She turned towards him, and he could tell she'd recognized the voice. 'One of Joe's kites,' she said, smiling. 'He flew them off the roof – they're super-lightweight. They have to be – farmers need to be able to put them up once, then forget them. He used to sit up here for hours watching, designing. If you can get them high enough they stay up for days in the right conditions. It isn't the right conditions.'

They laughed.

Dryden could see the problem. The superstructure of the box kite was coated in a thick layer of black ice.

'I went back to Declan's flat,' he said. 'The neighbour let me in. He said you'd been working hard, clearing his stuff out. I'm sorry – I took one of your brother's paintings.'

She nodded, sightless eyes searching the pale light in the sky. 'I'm going to bin the rest,' she said. 'It was the act of painting which was important. Over the years he'd thrown hundreds away – or just painted over them. He'd have been flattered . . .'

Dryden cut in. 'Only the canvas has been stolen. I live out on the river, a boat. They got on board and took it, just that.'

She nodded. 'Which one? He used to describe them to me, the colours and the texture of the oil.'

Dryden laughed. 'Two men, their arms mutilated by wounds, standing in blood. Not uplifting, I'm afraid.'

She looked away so that Dryden couldn't see her eyes.

He looked around at the men trying to clear the debris of the fallen kite and bundle it down the staircase onto the shop floor.

'Do they know the boss is dead?' he asked.

'They do now – John's just told them, he's the foreman, has been since the start almost. We don't know what's going to happen. It's a private company so it keeps trading until the estate is sorted out. Who knows then?'

'Foreman?' said Dryden licking ice from his upper lip. 'Must be nice – secure job, decent pay . . .'

Marcie turned her head towards him and Dryden felt something stir in his memory, but saw only a kite flying over a distant beach. 'Look. We both thank you for what you've done. He won't do it again. Money is a problem. It was a temptation, and he's sorry, believe me.'

Sley joined them. 'Dryden. News?' He seemed less menacing in a pair of blue overalls, the powerful hands winding in the kite cord like wool.

Dryden wondered what he was expecting. 'I wanted to know more about Joe. You didn't mention the factory . . .'

Sley held up a hand by way of truce. 'I'll get coffee.'

They sat in the main stairwell, away from prying ears, perched on the ice-cold concrete steps. Marcie Sley reached out her hand and her husband took it, holding it in his on his lap, where a wedding ring with a Celtic pattern caught the light. It was an intimate gesture and Dryden looked away.

Marcie's green eyes were on him when he finally looked back. 'John didn't mention JSK because he's still ashamed of the past. A distant past, Dryden. He got the job here because Declan vouched for him – and he knew him because they'd shared a prison cell.'

'And . . .' said Dryden.

'It's past,' said Marcie quickly, holding her husband's hand tightly. 'He's not proud of it, but it was nearly twenty years ago. OK? Joe gave him a chance – a big chance. Getting a decent job straight out of prison is almost impossible.'

Dryden shrugged. 'Fine. Why didn't he give Declan a job?'

'He'd never have stood it – inside, with all these people. My brother was the loner's loner. It was all we could do to get him to come down to the allotments. Or to stay in the flat. We've had to trawl the streets to find him before now.'

From the factory unit they heard a mechanical saw and the swish of an industrial cutter across a metal tube.

'Why was Declan in jail?' asked Dryden.

Marcie's eyes swung round. 'He attacked a man who stole a bottle from him – while he slept. He caught him doing it – so he smashed the bottle and put it into his face.' She left the statement hanging there, while they imagined the trickling blood, and the serrated slice of the glass through skin.

'I'm interested in them,' said Dryden, deciding for now not to ask how John Sley had ended up in a prison cell. 'They were both at St Vincent's. Victims together. They'd agreed to give evidence in the action against the diocese, right?'

Marcie Sley nodded and her husband leant forward. 'You think someone killed them to stop them getting to court?'

That was exactly what Dryden had thought. 'No. Just interested. Could it have driven both of them to suicide?'

John Sley looked to his wife, then took up the lead. 'Declan was under a lot of pressure. The case brought back memories, things he'd never really dealt with. Issues.' It was what Ed Bardolph, Declan's social worker, had said too. 'Issues' was one of those words Dryden disliked: a euphemism, an Americanism, a screen.

Marcie shifted on the step and Dryden caught a glance from her husband. 'Isn't it all a bit, I don't know, archaic –

orphanages? It sounds Dickensian, what about foster homes, adoption?' asked Dryden.

He noticed their hands tightening. 'It was difficult,' said Marcie. 'Mum was still alive. A psychiatric hospital in London, Claybury. Even back then Declan could be violent. But they tried, I was fostered for a while. But we all ended up back where we started . . . always.'

There was a note of anger in the voice, the first he'd heard from this strangely serence woman. Anger and something else. They talked more about Declan, with John Sley taking the lead, but Dryden watched his wife's face and saw playing across it another story, as yet untold.

They left him eventually and he stood for a second looking at the stencilled letters on the door to the workshop as it flapped closed: JSK. He knew now he'd forgotten to ask the obvious question: surely it should be JPK. What did the S stand for?

19

In the cathedral the Victorian cast-iron heaters hummed in counterpoint to the practising choir. Dryden paused inside the west doors, letting his ears search for the perfectly struck higher notes, while ahead of him a thin layer of mist crossed the nave like the signature of a ghost. He cut into the north transept, beneath the angel roof, and through a side door into the pale stone chamber of the Lady Chapel. A zealous bishop of the Reformation had smashed out the stained glass so here the light was cold, falling without judgement on the mutilated heads of the carvings which crowded the room.

The hum of electric fan heaters set up a whirring chorus. About 150 people were crowded in, swaddled in blankets and seated either in wheelchairs or on pews brought in from the side-chapels of the main cathedral. A wooden trestle table held thermos flasks, and a bank of microwave ovens pinged, the scent of shepherd's pie tussling with the subtle stench of disinfectant. Volunteers ricocheted between the needy, ferrying food, drink and fussy attention.

Vee Hilgay appeared from a side room carrying a thermos of coffee.

'I take it this is professional,' she said, leading Dryden towards one of the stone seats which bordered the room.

Dryden accepted a styrofoam cup. 'Vee. I'm trying to find someone. A Catholic priest – John Martin – I rang the church at Lane End and they thought he might be here.'

Vee nodded, filled the cup with coffee and disappeared into the throng.

Martin appeared suddenly, his dog collar discarded for a comfy sweater. But the punctilious neatness was still apparent, the hair Brylcreemed in lines as straight as the pews in the nave.

He sat in the niche next to Dryden, cradling his own coffee.

'Ecumenical, then?' said Dryden, already spoiling for a fight.

Martin nodded. 'It's a generous offer. Most of these are off the Fen; we provide the transport, the cathedral provides the heat.'

'I've got some good news,' said Dryden, smiling. 'Declan McIlroy and Joe Petulengo . . .'

Martin stiffened, looking uncomfortable.

'. . . they're dead.'

Dryden looked into the priest's eyes and realized he'd miscalculated.

Martin stood. 'I'll pray for them.'

'I'm sorry,' said Dryden, standing too. 'Please . . .' He put a hand on Martin's sleeve, letting his weight draw the priest down again.

Martin looked at his coffee. 'I need a fresh cup,' he said, disappearing into the crowd, and Dryden was surprised to see him return. 'How did they die?' he asked, sitting.

'The cold. That's what the police believe. Declan had a stiff drink and sat in his armchair while he froze to death with the windows open. Joe had an accident – they think he stumbled into water near his home, fell through the ice; he was found on his own doorstep. I found him, actually . . .'

Martin crossed himself and Dryden watched the priest's lips moving, a devotion Dryden had faked so many times.

Dryden leant closer. 'Who exactly would have benefited from the case against St Vincent's not coming to court?'

130

'You mean anyone other than myself?'

Dryden crushed the styrofoam cup. 'Father. I need your help. I don't think these men died by accident. They were key to the case against the diocese – both for the civil action, and any subsequent criminal charges. Now they're dead those actions will – at the very least – be stalled for some time. The whole thing may collapse. So. Who else?'

Father Martin shrugged, outlining with a finger the blood-red birthmark on his face.

'The diocese, clearly – but that was purely monetary. The action would have entailed substantial damages – but hardly a motive for murder. The police were enjoined to the action as well – for failing to respond adequately to complaints – as were the county council's social services department. I suppose there may be individuals whose careers were at stake. But . . .' He laughed. 'It seems far-fetched?'

Dryden considered the divided loyalties of Ed Bardolph – Declan McIlroy's social worker. But Father Martin was right: finding a suitable motive for murder if the case against St Vincent's went ahead was a challenge he was failing to meet.

He tried another tack. 'Do you remember them? Joe and Declan?'

'Yes. Yes, I remember them. They were close – both in John's I think. They left in the early eighties. At sixteen.'

Something Marcie Sley had said echoed in Dryden's mind. 'Was that unusual – to spend their whole childhoods at St Vincent's? Declan's sister said she'd been fostered for a while but then returned to care. So she never got away either . . . none of them did.'

Martin reached for his dog-collar to ease the pressure at his throat, forgetting it wasn't there. 'Look. I really think this *is* private . . .'

'But it was unusual, wasn't it? There was a reason, wasn't there? A reason why they stayed in care. What was it, Father?'

'I can't,' said Martin, standing. 'I really can't. It's down to her, really. Did you ask her?'

Dryden couldn't stop his eyes sliding away from the priest's. 'No. But you're right, it is private. I'm only trying to find the truth, to find out who they were before they died.'

Martin scanned the room. 'Ask her. Ask her about the Connor case. But please – we didn't talk.'

'Connor?' asked Dryden, but Martin spotted an elderly woman stranded in a plastic seat stretching for a coffee cup on a table just beyond her reach.

'Mrs Edwards . . . please, let me . . .'

He touched Dryden on the shoulder before he went. It was a blessing, and for once Dryden didn't recoil.

20

The day had died and redundant Christmas lights winked in shop windows. High over the cathedral a flock of rooks were a thumbprint on the sky. It was a lost weekend, between Christmas and New Year, and the town centre was empty, a scarab street-cleaner criss-crossing the now deserted Market Square, which echoed to a pre-recorded rendition of 'Hark the Herald Angels Sing'. In the butcher's window a toy dog in tartan did somersaults.

Dryden stood in the lee of the giant Christmas tree. 'The Connor case,' he said out loud, his breath a cloud as tangible as candyfloss. He'd read something about it in the last week – perhaps two. But where? It had to be either one of the quality broadsheets, one of the tabloids, the two local evening newspapers – or *The Crow*. Unless he'd heard it on the radio. He made his way to the office and let himself in through the print yard door. The building was silent, Jean – the paper's half-deaf receptionist – having closed the front counter at noon. Dryden put the 1 euro coin in the coffee machine and made his way to the large cupboard that the editor grandly referred to as the paper's 'library'. Here Jean pasted up cuttings in thematic folders – crime, weather, churches etc. She also bound copies of the nationals and tabloids for reference.

Where should he start?

Quite early in his journalistic career Dryden had developed a useful skill. On his first local newspaper in a small Midland town it had been his job to read the nationals to spot any story which might be followed up locally. After a while he found he could pick the town's name out of a page of print without having to read it. The word just jumped out, a semantic Belisha beacon flashing 'story'. For several years after moving to Fleet Street he was still haunted by the word, but he'd adapted the skill to pinpoint other key words, and always let his eye roll over a page before starting to read.

The nationals. He'd start with them. The story was unlikely to be local – they were rare enough and he'd written half the paper himself anyway. He ran through the broadsheets and the tabloids for the last two weeks. It took him twenty minutes and he found nothing. He felt tired and in need of a more convivial environment than a draughty newspaper office. Jean had not yet found time to bind copies of the local evening papers and *The Crow* for the last week so he took copies himself, stuffed them in a spare paperboy's bag and set out for the riverside.

Out on the water meadows a few skaters circled the course marked out by the wooden posts Ed Bardolph and his fellow volunteers had set out on the two-inch-thick ice the previous day. Reaching the riverbank, Dryden turned north along the town-side towpath. After half a mile he came to a deserted Victorian dock called The Hythe, built to take the imported bricks which had fuelled the expansion of the city's suburbs in the 1890s. By this miniature docklands the developers had built a pub – the Frog Hall – a riot of ill-judged Victorian taste dominated by ceramic exterior tiles which made it look like a giant public lavatory.

Dryden nudged open the door, smelt the aroma of stale beer and last night's cigarette smoke and immediately felt better. The only customer, he took his beer into the tiny snug where a coal fire pulsed with warmth. He thought about his floating home out at Barham's Dock, beached on ice, and he edged closer to the coals, producing a copy of *The Crow* from his trench coat pocket.

He read newspapers backwards. Starting with the small ads and personal column and ending with the front-page splash. The best advice he'd ever been given as a reporter was to read your own newspaper: very few did, missing plenty of stories in the small ads and failing to keep up with those written by the rest of the staff. *The Crow* posed less of a challenge, but the principle held.

He found a story he wasn't looking for almost instantly and put a red ring round the tiny item . . .

LOST: Buffy, much-loved nervous Labrador, missing since December 24th. Must be found before New Year fireworks. Tel 66689.

'Nice little tale,' said Dryden, ringing the item with a pen. The barman, a morose Ulsterman, moved further down the bar.

Half an hour later he'd reached page 5. He picked out 'Connor' and reread the item at normal speed. It was a single paragraph in the flight of 'News in Briefs' laid out down the side of the page. He could see why he'd missed it: it had been taken off the Press Association wire service and was technically from outside *The Crow*'s circulation area anyway.

NEW WITNESSES IN MURDER CASE

The wife of holiday-camp killer Chips Connor, who has launched a campaign to win a re-trial 30 years after her husband was jailed for a brutal seaside murder, said today two witnesses had answered her appeal for new information on the case. Connor, born in the Fenland town of Whittlesea, was jailed at Cambridge Crown Court in 1975. Campaigners now plan to petition the High Court to hear an appeal against the life sentence in what has become a celebrated case.

Dryden checked the *Cambridge Evening News* and found that it had taken the item earlier that week on the Monday – at the same length – adding a thumbnail description of the victim – Paul Gedney. He folded the paper and looked in the fire. What had the case got to do with Declan McIlroy and Joe Petulengo and their childhoods spent in care?

Were Declan and Joe, the victims of St Vincent's, the newly discovered witnesses in the Connor case? Thirty years ago they would have been children, thought Dryden, each with another decade before them at the orphanage. What might they have known that would have set Chips Connor free?

21

In the West Tower's shadow a line of cabs sat, most with
their engines dead. The cabbies had congregated in a licensed
people-carrier halfway down the queue to save on fuel and
conserve heat. A lone shopper, emerging from Argos,
struggled across the High Street with a package slightly
smaller than a postbox towards the black cab at the head of
the rank. Dryden was surprised to see Humph's Capri at the
rear, with the cabbie firmly wedged into the driver's seat,
unsociable to the last. Humph was listening to the football:
Ipswich Town versus Luton at Portman Road. He had his
club strip on and in his lap a notepad on which he'd set out
the team names in their proper formations. As Dryden
pulled open the passenger-side door Humph fidgeted with
the club scarf which he'd wrapped round one wrist.

'Score?' asked Dryden, flipping open the glove compartment. His mood lifted as he spotted a catering-sized packet
of prawn-flavoured crisps in the footwell.

Humph flexed his miniature fists. 'One all. Ten minutes
to half time. Good job they invested in that undersoil heating. We could win this.' The tones were clipped, warning
against further conversation.

They sat in silence until half time, then they said nothing.

Dryden sipped a malt whisky, wondering where Chips
Connor was now. He abandoned the memory. Until he could
talk to Marcie Sley – or possibly Ed Bardolph – he could
make little progress in trying to understand how the case
was linked to Joe Petulengo and Declan McIlroy. He checked

his watch: it was still too early to catch Bardolph before the skating began down by the river. And he'd have to leave Declan McIlroy's sister another day at least before trying a fresh pitch for information.

'The Tower?' he asked Humph, pulling the seatbelt across his chest.

Humph pointed forward along the parked-up rank. 'You'll have to wait.'

There was nothing quite as rigid as the etiquette of the taxi driver. They sat listening to the second half as the cabs edged forward until Humph was able to pull away from the head of the queue. By the time The Tower came into sight the day was over, unlike the one-all draw which was limping into its final minute.

The foyer's Christmas lights winked expensively in the gloom. The Tower's heating system, always efficient, was as plush as the carpets. Laura's room was a few degrees cooler, and Dryden went to the window to watch the last of the light draining from the sky. The sight lifted his spirits and he raised his wife from the bed, hugging her close until he could hear her heartbeat. He felt an echo of what home had been like, finally banishing the anxiety which had been with him since he'd found the footsteps in the snow alongside *PK 129*.

He poured wine and lit a cigarette, going back to the window to drop the blinds.

'It's night now,' he said, the need for sleep almost overwhelming. 'You've no idea how cold it is out there. The monkey puzzle tree – the big one on the lawn – that's just crystal, like one of those cheap trinkets we used to buy on the coast. And I can see Humph in the Capri – he's asleep. He's been listening to the football – I think the excitement wears him out. He's got the dog on his lap – or it could be the other way round . . .'

He drew deeply on the cigarette, the nicotine bringing tears to his eyes.

Laura's auburn hair lay in a fan on the pillowcase. He lay down beside her and ran his fingers through it, smelling the rich natural scent of the oil, as pungent as a child's.

'Why do you think some kids never get adopted? They spend their whole lives in foster homes, or care. I guess it's like animals – people always want the perfect one, the youngest one, the one they can mould themselves. They don't want a history, they don't want issues.' That word again.

The COMPASS jumped into life, the roll of paper clattering as it fed out of the computer printer.

HOLIDAY PLEASE.

She never said please. Dryden sensed that she felt the word was too much; a symbol of dependency and need.

'Of course. I'm sorry. It's just so cold, and we can't go far. A cottage, perhaps – the coast, like we said? How about one with an Aga?'

There was silence then, and he knew this was a reproach, for making her plead, and for failing to disguise his reluctance – a reluctance which sprang not from any rational fear, but from anxiety about what might happen if he took his wife away from The Tower. The leaving in itself would be good for them both, even if it suggested the possibility of not returning.

22

Humph dropped him on the riverbank, where the ice was now thick and pitted with the tracks of pebbles and stones pitched across its surface. A pair of ungainly swans strolled in midstream like cowboys. Dryden walked south past the Maltings and the Cutter Inn to a terrace of Victorian houses which looked out over the watermeadows. At the end of the row was a boathouse, the temporary HQ of the Fen Skating Association. The ground floor had originally housed the boats, while upstairs there was a balcony outside a function room behind a single picture window. Here Dryden had watched the Cambridge crew in training the previous year during a press event before the annual Varsity boat race, a memory clouded by six large glasses of Pimm's No. 1 sucked through a straw.

The wooden doors which ran the entire length of the boathouse frontage were shut, leaving a small wicket gate as the only entry point. Inside, trestle tables had been set up between the low-hanging boats, piled high with skater registration forms. The space was crowded with men in Christmas sweaters and other assorted festive knitwear. Fluorescent yellow stewards' jackets hung in lines, above a rank of metal lanterns. There was a small kitchen at the rear and soup was being decanted into thermos flasks. Dryden found Ed Bardolph unwrapping loudhailers from a packing case.

Dryden shook his hand. 'Ed.'

Bardolph's face was flushed with the cold and adrenaline, and the room buzzed with childlike excitement.

'The river's nearly solid,' said Dryden.

Bardolph nodded, checking a small oven crammed with heating pies. 'Should be safe by 8.00pm we reckon. We might try and rerun the long-distance race to Cambridge. They did it in '63.'

'Time?'

'Late. Maybe midnight. We could wait a day but the forecast is not 100 per cent – there's warm air up there, if it touches ground level we could lose the lot and freezing rain would ruin the ice.'

'I'm sorry . . .' said Dryden, stepping closer. 'I've got some bad news that you may not have heard yet. Can we talk . . . in private?'

They climbed the stairs. Bardolph had clearly been dividing his time between his real job and his passion, and had set up an impromptu office on the bar in the function room complete with fax, laptop, mobile charger, and file case.

'I can work pretty much anywhere,' he said, as if trying to convince himself. 'And we only get the weather once in a blue moon.'

They went out on to the balcony. The view across the frozen Fen was breathtaking, a living Dutch masterpiece of gliding figures.

'It's Joe Petulengo, Declan's friend. He's dead.'

'What?' Bardolph leaned back against the low balcony rail.

'An accident, probably. Out at his farm. He fell, into water, and froze to death.'

'Jesus,' said Bardolph. 'That's dreadful. You know the link . . .'

Dryden nodded. 'Petulengo was one of the victims of abuse at St Vincent's – like Declan. They grew up together, in care. Did you meet him?'

'No – never. I didn't talk to Declan about the case either

141

– except right at the start. It's difficult. I work for the social services department and they were likely to end up in the dock too over St Vincent's . . . but Declan was my client. I advised him to see a third party before agreeing to give evidence against the diocese – a colleague from outside the county. We played it by the book.'

'I didn't say you didn't,' said Dryden. 'So what's Chips Connor got to do with it?'

'Connor! How . . . ?' Bardolph looked out over the frozen Fen, knocking his gloved fists together in frustration. 'Look. Wait there.'

He went inside and Dryden could see him rifling through the box folders, before returning with a single Manila file. 'You need to understand,' he said, 'the two cases are linked.' He retrieved some reading glasses and scanned the first page of the file.

'The friendship between Joe and Declan was very important, but they were vastly different characters. Declan had been inside, he'd become very timid, a kind of recluse in many ways. Joe was a very confident man – at least that's what Declan always said. He'd made a success of his business, he had power – something Declan never had. Anyway, several months ago one of the evening newspapers ran an appeal for new witnesses in the Connor case – Connor's wife had decided to mark the thirtieth anniversary of his sentence with another attempt to get him freed. She'd always said he was innocent, and she wasn't the only one. So Joe saw the story and got in contact. The Connor family solicitors . . .' here Bardolph flicked through the pages. 'Holme & Sons – of Lynn. They interviewed Joe and asked him to try and get Declan to come forward as well. If it had been the other way round, if Declan had seen the appeal, he would have kept quiet – I'm sure of that.'

'But he was a witness too, and he agreed to step up?'

'Joe was very important to Declan – a mentor, I guess. If Joe was happy to do it – so was Declan. George Holme interviewed them both, separately, and took statements. They were in care at the time they were staying at the holiday camp. It became clear during Holme's questioning about what happened at the camp that they had been badly treated at St Vincent's – I can't tell you exactly why because it involves the sister – but it all came out.'

'There was abuse in the holiday camp?'

'I didn't say that. Anyway, the important thing is that Holme knew about the action being co-ordinated by Hugh Appleyard against St Vincent's – solicitors are a pretty close bunch. So Joe and Declan found themselves under pressure to come forward. I don't think Joe thought twice about it. After a lot of soul searching, Declan also agreed to give evidence against the diocese, to tell a court what he'd suffered at St Vincent's.'

'So it's not a coincidence that they are involved in both cases?'

'No. Not at all. It's all down to Joe coming forward. Then one thing led to another.'

'So what happens now?'

Bardolph looked out over the ice. 'St Vincent's? They would have been compelling in court, I think – especially together. I never actually met Joe, but it was clear they were close. Brothers, almost. They'd shared that childhood, that sense of being victims, a very intense emotion. I don't think any court could have ignored their evidence, or put it aside as hysterical, or contrived. But they were not the only victims. There'll be delays, but it'll come out in the end. The abuse – you know – was pretty widespread, institutionalized, really. That was the problem.'

Dryden nodded. 'And the Connor case . . . how exactly were they involved in that?'

'The basic facts aren't disputed: Joe saw the appeal in the newspaper for evidence in the Connor case, as I said. The article included the last known picture of Paul Gedney – that's Connor's alleged victim. In essence their statements would have been simple, as I understood it: that they had seen Gedney.'

'So?'

Bardolph laughed, buttoning the jacket at his throat. 'They saw him a month after the prosecution said Chips had beaten him to death at the holiday camp at Sea's End. He was holed up in some old boat in the marsh along the coast. The police never found the body, you see. If they'd been able to make that ID in court – between the face on the poster and the face they'd seen, well then Chips would have been freed immediately. There would have been a review at the very least.'

'Sea's End,' said Dryden. 'The Dolphin?'

'Yes. It's still in business, actually – gone upmarket.'

Dryden saw the camp gates, that first sight of the crowded beach of 1974, and a single lit porthole shining in the marsh. 'But this was in '75?' he asked.

Bardolph went on nodding, flipping the page and finding a colour photograph. He looked at it briefly, seemed to make a decision, and then held it out: 'No. No – it was 1974. The summer. The trial was the following year. That's them at the time . . . August.'

Dryden took the snapshot and felt the world around him recede, as if seen through the wrong end of a telescope, as he brought the snapshot close to his face. Three boys and a girl, a sandy path between dunes and a distant view of the sea. The familiarity of his own childhood face staring out of the past was surreal, and the jolt of recognition made his heart contract. He walked to the balcony rail and looked out across the white Fen, hiding his eyes.

'Declan is the one on the far left,' said Bardolph.

Dryden nodded. Dex, the frightened loner armed only with the unpredictability of violence.

'The others?' asked Dryden, trying to keep the emotion from serrating his voice.

'The other boy, the one with his arm round Declan's shoulder, is Joe Petulengo. The girl on the end is Declan's sister.'

Dryden nodded, confused. He flipped the picture over and read the pencilled caption on the back.

McIlroy – Smith – Unknown – McIlroy.

'But it says Smith,' said Dryden. 'Not Petulengo.'

Bardolph was still rummaging through the paperwork. 'Sure. Joe was from a traveller family; Smith was their adopted name. It's common amongst the Romany: helps in business and avoids some nasty racism. He was plain Joe Smith until his marriage, I think. Times change, and by then he was on his feet, JSK was up and running. I guess he decided he was proud of his past, even if it was too late to change the company brand.' Dryden saw it now, the stencilled logo on the factory unit door: JSK. Joe Smith Kites.

'And the girl is Marcie Sley?'

Bardolph grunted. 'Yup.'

The skin, Dryden thought, dusted with sand. 'And the third boy – the one with the black hair?' he asked.

Bardolph shrugged. 'No idea. All we know is that his first name was Philip – which, as you will appreciate, is not an uncommon first name. He played with the others, but they never got his full name. The camp's records haven't survived – at least not the bookings. They had to leave early . . . they didn't swap addresses or names.'

No, thought Dryden. There'd been no time for that. The picture had been taken on the second day by the woman Marcie had called 'Grace', when it seemed as if they had a lifetime in which to play together.

'And Marcie's not involved because . . .'

'Because she's blind. Identification is the key. She could have provided some corroboration of timing and so on. She was sighted at the time. But that's not much good now, is it? What she can't do is stand up in a court of law and identify the picture of Paul Gedney as that of the man she did see. She's never seen that picture – she's no use at all as a witness.' Bardolph shivered. 'Look. We need coffee – hang on a minute.' He disappeared inside to fuss over one of the thermos flasks.

Dryden knew then: knew when they'd seen what they'd seen. That last night of the game.

Bardolph reappeared with coffees and another file, which he held awkwardly, leafing through the typed pages. 'Once Declan decided to go up with Joe to see George Holme I talked through his evidence with him to see if it stacked up. Back in '75, during the trial, the prosecution alleged that the victim died on the night of 5 August 1974 – at the Dolphin. But Declan and Joe's evidence would make it clear that Gedney was alive a month later – on the 30th. Friday, August 30th.'

Dryden rested a fingertip on the image of his own young face. 'Did he see what they saw? Could this . . . Philip . . . be a witness?'

'Possibly. Joe and Declan seemed unsure. I guess they might run the picture again – see if they can find him. Holme could even take the statements they've got to appeal – but I doubt that would get very far.'

Pellets of hail began to fall and Dryden wrapped the

trench coat more closely to his bones. Had someone killed Declan McIlroy and Joe Petulengo to keep Chips Connor in jail? Did anyone know that he, Philip Dryden, was the missing child from the snapshot? And if they did, did they fear that he too had seen what they had seen the last night they'd played the game?

The Dolphin Holiday Camp
Friday, 30 August 1974

In the saltmarsh, under a covered boat, Philip lay still.

The dilemma was always the same one — an excruciating tension between the fear that he would never be found, and the fear that he would. Switching on his torch, he played the beam on his wristwatch: a Timex Christmas present with half-hearted luminosity. 8.42pm.

Twenty-five minutes had passed since he'd left the others by the sluice gate. He'd heard some footsteps almost immediately, timidly padding round the old boathouse. Dex. Almost certainly Dex. Then nothing, except the distant barrel-organ leitmotif of the fairground.

He lay, curled in a ball now, hoping above all that it wouldn't be Smith. Then he'd have to lie still with Smith, waiting for the others. That was the game: each one had to squeeze in until the last one was left alone, searching.

Let it not be Smith, who smelt of the cloying tang of the chemicals they made him rub in his hair. Let it not be Smith, who would clamp a hand over Philip's mouth if the others got near.

Or the sister? Philip's heart leapt. The last time, she'd held his hand to stop him crying out. She smelt of the sand, and of the natural oil in her coal-black hair.

The tide, resting at the full, began to ebb. He could hear the black water slap the rotting planks of the old boathouse, and somewhere the sea began to trickle back through an open sluice. He thought again of the single lit porthole in the marsh, and wondered what lay within.

And then, as sharp as a seagull's violent screech, a single cry of *pain. Philip's hair bristled and his heart creaked in his chest. Then a sob, but not the one he would have expected after the pain – there was relief, satisfaction, even joy. What pain gave joy?*

Had something happened in the game? Dex, almost certainly Dex, falling and snapping one of his narrow bony ankles. Or Smith, vaulting a channel, breaking an arm. Would they leave him now, forgetting him, running home?

He lay, praying for it to end, praying for it not to end, and a second before it did he knew it would. A rattle, loose change in a pocket, gave him away. The tarpaulin, ripped back, showed Smith against a sky of stars.

'Come on,' he said, shining his torch in Philip's face. 'We've found something. Something by the river.'

They ran along a bank head high with the bristling moon-splashed reeds. Then the pale eye of the porthole was ahead of them; closer now, and impossibly bright. Against the yellow circle of light he could see Dex and his sister at the glass, peering in. Smith roughly put an elbow round his neck and a hand over his mouth, dragging him down to his knees: 'Quiet. Did you hear it? He's in the boat, we've seen him.'

He was afraid then, realizing again how lonely he was with these children, how much he didn't know about what they shared.

They started to crawl forward to join the other children and Philip was close enough to smell Dex's fear when they heard the second cry of pain, like the first, laced with that after-shock of satisfaction.

There was a single beat of silence before Dex screamed, his small head jerking wildly, while the sister pulled him down, away from the light.

Philip knew then that he wouldn't get to see, that like so much else of his childhood, and his life, the night would be defined by what others had experienced, and by what he had missed.

But they'd been seen, and they were running now, all of them, back along the dyke. He found Dex's hand in his and they ran together, back to the sluice, the jagged gasping of their collective breath louder than the waves beyond the dunes. But here Philip, haunted by what he'd missed, turned and saw the distant silhouette of a man on the boat against the sky, one arm cradled by the other.

The sister pulled him back, down the path to the leap, then over and on between the chalets. When they reached the lamp by Philip's they stood for a second, listening, and he saw that the sister had gone.

From the fairground came the ritual screams from the falling big dipper.

Philip waited to catch Dex's eyes. 'What?' he said, knowing he would answer. But Smith dragged the younger boy away. 'Tomorrow,' he said. 'Tomorrow.'

23

Flares had been lit on the floodbank, throwing a guttering light across the crowd that had gathered for the races. Dryden, still struggling with the innocent collision of the past and present, left Ed Bardolph with the rest of the volunteers at the boathouse making final preparations for the long-distance skate to Cambridge. He'd found Humph still parked up on the riverbank, the cab resounding to the ritual intonation of the football results being repeated on the local news. He'd rifled half a dozen miniatures from Humph's glove compartment, grabbed Boudicca's lead, his skates, and set out for the ice fair.

Railway sleepers had been piled into a makeshift grandstand for the traditional start of the championships: the Flying Mile, four circuits of the oval course Bardolph's men had earlier marked out. Other spectators were already crowding along the high floodbank, between the flares. Sparklers, sold at the gate, cascaded silver where children stood. Skaters zigzagged between the fairground stalls and the tea bars, one with a hand-held flaming torch which left a wake across Dryden's eye.

The night sky, clear and crowded, was crushing. Dryden drank one of the bottles from his overcoat pocket, the aroma of the malt sharpened by the frost. Ice was forming in his hair and he took a black woollen hat from his pocket and drew it down over his brow. After buying a ticket, he took a seat on the sleepers at the top. There was a breeze here and he could feel the moisture turning to ice in his eyelashes. The malt made his blood rush, so he had another.

Looking out over the winter scene he tried, once again, to conjure up the heat of that lost summer. He'd met the others on the first day, let loose by his uncle and aunt to wander the camp and find new friends. Taking a book, he'd gone down to the beach and watched the three strange children, the siblings – Dex and the sister – and the brooding presence of the older Smith, with his bleached white hair. And he envied them the familiarity of the triangular world they shared. They'd dammed a stream which crossed the sands, creating a wide deep pool on which Dex sailed a paper boat. Smith had dragged logs from the dunes to reinforce the sand, while Marcie had stood, almost motionless, in the centre of the pool, waiting for the water to rise, as insubstantial as her rippling reflection.

He'd been sitting on a log that Smith wanted. So he'd stuffed the paperback he'd been reading inside the belt of his shorts and helped him haul it down to the sand. Wordlessly he'd followed him up to the dunes to find more. When they'd finished Dex had sailed the boat to him across the newly formed lake, a thrilling act of friendship. After tea in the clattering canteen, in the hour of dusk before bedtime, they'd toured the camp. The boys' chalet was opposite Philip's while the sister had one to herself down by the pool, next to the one where the woman she called Grace slept beside a double cot for the baby boys. There was a man, too, Grace's husband, but he seemed disengaged and never spoke to any of the children, immersed – whenever Philip saw him – in a newspaper, putting red circles round names in the close, dense print of the sports pages. And they'd seen him once, glimpsed through the club door, under the strip-light of a snooker table. Grace was always outside, her florid, intelligent face blighted by anxiety. Philip had never understood, never understood how this disparate family fitted together.

At breakfast on the second day Philip had watched them all, eating at one of the Formica-topped tables in the canteen. He'd told Uncle Roger that he had found some friends to play with, pointed them out, and could still recall the way the man's cheerful smile had faded. 'OK, Philip,' he'd said. 'That's fine.' Fine, nothing more.

They met again in the dunes above the beach, and the intoxicating excitement of belonging had overwhelmed him. Once, he'd seen his uncle by the coastguard's hut, watching them play. He'd waved, then stepped back beyond the horizon.

Dryden closed his eyes and tried to squeeze meaning out of the idyllic memories he had: the Gothic sandcastles, the tide sweeping in the paper boats, Smith and his kite. And the game after dark – Smith's brilliant idea. Of course it had been easy for them, the boys in their chalet, and the sister too. But for Philip the game held an edge, for he alone was taking a real risk of discovery and punishment.

A bell rang, breaking the trance. A man skated across the ice below, ringing a bell and clearing the ice for the race. Four men slowly traversed the course pushing a home-made wooden snow plough which brushed clear the loose snow and ice, flattening out the stipples left by the frozen rain. At the start a dozen skaters straddled the line, then a klaxon set them free, the crowd cheering as they wheeled past, completing a circuit before they were able to break from their prescribed lanes. Boudicca stood, barking at the un-natural sight of men sweeping past, arms like metronomes. The biting cold had reduced the crowd, but perhaps 400 had come, the steam of their collective breath drifting across the track. The floodlights were harsh, the scene entirely coloured in white, silver and the chilliest of blues.

He watched three races, then, tiring of the people around him, he climbed down and through the tunnel under the railway line back to the riverside. A makeshift set of halogen floodlights lit the frozen surface where a line had been scoured across from bank to bank. Clearly the 17-mile dash to Cambridge was on – for the first time in more than forty years. A blackboard by the footbridge announced the start would be at 10.30pm – and that all competitors had to register at the boathouse. Dryden found Humph parked on the far side of the river, his lower body obscured by a giant bag of chips. Dryden decanted the dog into the rear seat and took a handful of chips, using the mobile to ring Mitch Mackintosh, *The Crow*'s staff photographer. The paper could use some pictures of the start – and Mitch could alert the *Cambridge Evening News* to get some snaps of the skaters finishing along The Backs by King's College.

'I'm gonna skate home,' said Dryden. 'I want to think.'

Humph took the slight with good grace, embracing the chip bag for warmth as Dryden laced up his skates.

Dinner finished, Humph produced the *Cambridge Evening News* late football edition and, using a delicate pair of nail scissors extracted from the Tardis-like glove compartment, he snipped out the report on Town's match against Luton, and the new league table, carefully adding it to a scrapbook he kept in the driver's side door pocket.

Dryden watched the cabbie reading the now eviscerated newspaper, recalling the cuttings on Joe Petulengo's kitchen noticeboard. Had the killer snipped a version of the Connor case story out of the *Lynn News*? With the holiday camp bang in the middle of its circulation area there was every chance it would have been a substantial one, not like the paragraph *The Crow* had run. Had Joe's killer decided to remove it from the scene, only to realize that it could have come from one of the old copies of the paper in the recycling bin, leaving a tell-tale hole for a diligent detective to spot? Was that why all the newspapers had gone?

By now the starting line was obscured by a crowd of skaters a hundred strong. They steamed like cattle, jostling for position. Behind them half a dozen of the organizers were out on skates too, each holding a burning red flare. Mitch arrived and fussed, setting up two cameras on tripods which he could activate automatically to catch the off. He was decked out with the latest gear, including four further cameras strung round his neck, and Dryden advised him not to go on the ice or he might go through it. A klaxon brought the skaters to toe the line, a second marked the off, accompanied by a cheer. Mitch's cameras all flashed at the same moment, a blinding intervention which reduced the first fifty yards of the race to a chaotic muddle of stumbling half-blind competitors.

Dryden lost himself briefly in the crowd of spectators watching the skaters make their way down the long straight cut, dug out of the peat by the Normans nearly a thousand years before. Then the field swung east past the Cutter Inn and was gone.

A three-quarters moon had just risen as Dryden followed, skating south. Away from the harsh yellow lights of the riverside his eyes switched to night vision and he saw before him the sinuous track of the white river, and nothing beyond the black shadows of the floodbanks until, a mile downstream, he was able to turn and see the cathedral's Octagon Tower, a construction of ice itself in white sodium light. Ahead, on another long man-made straight of the river, he glimpsed a flare-holder marking the tail-end of the race. Then it flickered out, and he was alone.

155

Overhead the constellations wheeled. He thought about Dex and Smith and for the first time felt a personal sense of loss, a realization that they had been his friends, and that he'd lost part of his childhood when they'd died.

He skated for twenty minutes until he knew he was close to home, then he stopped again and looked back at the city. The Octagon Tower disappeared as the time switch cut the power to the floodlights, and across the silent landscape Dryden heard a bell toll eleven times.

And something else, the scrape of a skate on ice, the echo bouncing along the frozen river's surface. He looked along the glimmering ice but it was clear, criss-crossed only by the marks of the skaters who had gone before. He stood, wondering if he was alone, at the centre of a vast landscape which seemed empty of life. Overhead a goose flew, creaking, heading east towards the reserve at Wicken.

He skated on, waiting for Barham's Dock to open up to his right. As he came level he saw *PK 129*, its bilge pump spluttering and keeping the ice from locking round the hull. He skated into the dock to a wooden staithe – all that remained of the dockside where vegetables from the fields had once been loaded directly into barges. The moon was up now, the landscape lit, and he regretted not asking Humph back for a drink. The boat, his home, looked cold and anti-septic: icicles like bunting on the hawsers to the short mast.

Dryden peeled back the tarpaulin over the wheelhouse, cracking the stiff frost from the green material. Dropping into the cabin, he fired the electric generator into life and felt the vibration through the steel hull. The propane heater he'd lit before going out that morning had kept the frost out of the cabin, but only just. Now he switched it on to high and held his fingers to the orange flames while the kettle boiled.

He thought of Laura and wished he could slip into bed beside her now, feeling the warmth of her skin and the welcome of her breath. Looking up from the flames he caught the reflection of his face: the short black hair white with frost, the skin immobile, the eyes as cool as glacier ice.

He made coffee and added the last of Humph's miniatures. Above the small writing table against the bulkhead hung the picture taken by his uncle on the last day of the holiday in 1974. It hung, Dryden failed to notice, precisely at the horizontal, unlike all the other pictures, maps, and framed cuttings on the wall which had – over time – come to list with the boat. In the picture he clutched his aunt's hand, which lay too lightly on his shoulder.

Something caught in his throat making him retch, so he finished the coffee and flipped open the drinks cupboard, lifting a bottle of Talisker clear of the wire rail which held it securely in place. His glass was in the galley and he spilt in two inches of the peaty liquid, drained half, killed the lights and slumped on the bunk, resting the glass on his chest so that the moonlight caught the liquid like an amber stone.

He slept, perhaps for a minute. When he woke he knew, almost instantly, that it might be too late. Smoke filled both his lungs and as he tried to draw in air he knew he wouldn't find it. His body hinged at the waist in a convulsion and as his head came up he gripped the edge of the porthole and looked out: on the ice, a figure stood, checking a wristwatch.

Then he fell to the deck. Here the air was worse, thin wisps of smoke rose up through the boards, and he felt a dull pain behind his eyes which had begun to blur his sight. He crawled towards the stepladder to the wheelhouse, found the step by touch, and dragged himself up.

Below, somewhere, he heard the unmistakable crackle of

fire, and briefly, through a crack, saw the tell-tale yellow-blue hint of a flame.

He sat for a second, knowing that to lift the double covers to the wheelhouse took two precise manoeuvres: the sharp drawing back of the heavy brass bolt and a well-judged upward blow with the shoulder. He'd done both a thousand times, and if he could do it again he knew he'd live through the night. So he waited a precious extra second, focusing on the bolt, drew it back, then rose from the knees, putting his full weight behind his shoulder. The doors didn't move.

He fell backwards into the cabin and lay looking at the polished wooden decking above. Smoke filled the air and he felt warmth at his back. His mistake was obvious now: he should have smashed through the heavy porthole glass while he had the strength.

Focused on his consciousness, he lay still. Outside, unseen, he heard the professional sharp hiss of an ice-skate turning on its heel, and he imagined the figure gliding away, a single arm swinging like a metronome.

A minute passed, then three. The lights of a car swung through the darkness, the beams sweeping over the interior of the boat. The pain had stopped now but the moving lights reminded Dryden that he wanted to live. Inside his pocket he could feel his keys, so he made a fist with them, rolled over, pulled himself up by one of the brass guide rails on the bunk and drove his hand through the glass port-hole. For some reason there was silence still, and he watched as a wound on his hand opened to reveal the white knuckle of the bone.

He heard a dog bark once, and remembered nothing more.

Interlude

From the *Lynn News*, 10 March 1975

By Angus Murden, courts reporter

Holiday camp killer Chips Connor left his victim to bleed to death, Cambridge Crown Court heard today.

The prosecution allege that Connor killed 22-year-old student nurse Paul Gedney in a rage after surprising him trying to rob the camp safe.

Charles Frederick Connor – known as 'Chips' – a 23-year-old Blue Coat at The Dolphin Holiday Camp, Sea's End, denies the charge of murder.

Today prosecution counsel Mr Robert Asquith, QC, outlined the chain of events which he said led to Gedney's death on the night of 5 August last year.

He told the jury that Gedney, a nurse at Whittlesea District Hospital, Fenland District, had left his home in the town earlier that day by motorbike, taking with him only cash and a holdall of personal items.

Whittlesea police would confirm, said Mr Asquith, that Gedney was a suspect in an ongoing inquiry into the theft of drugs from the hospital. He had been interviewed three times over allegations he was involved.

Witnesses said Mr Gedney appeared at the camp, 30 miles north of the town, that evening and asked a member of staff where he could find Mrs Ruth Connor, the defendant's wife, who was the manager of the Dolphin.

The court would hear, said Mr Asquith, that Chips Connor, Ruth Connor and Paul Gedney were well known to each other, all having attended Whittlesea Catholic High School.

Mr Asquith said that Mrs Connor would testify that Gedney pleaded for help, admitting he was on the run. She and her husband reluctantly agreed to let him stay at the camp for one night – evidence the defence accepts.

At 1.25 the next morning police were called to the camp and told by 'Chips' Connor that he had discovered Paul Gedney attempting to rob the safe which, ahead of the weekly payday, held in excess of £1,400.

Connor told police he had struck Gedney with a heavy office stapler as he was making off with the money, drawing blood. The stapler would be produced in evidence, said Mr Asquith.

Chips Connor told police he chased Gedney, lost him amongst the chalets, but saw him leaving by motorbike, eastwards on the coast road. Gedney's description was circulated to police forces in the east of England.

Evidence from police officers who visited the Dolphin that night and the following morning indicated that Connor was suffering from severe symptoms of stress.

They were informed by his wife that he had learning difficulties and was prone to anxiety attacks. A police doctor attended the scene and administered tranquillizers.

The prosecution now alleges that Connor had in fact lied to police; that he had pursued Gedney through the camp to the nearby beach where he had violently assaulted him, dragged his body into one of the camp's beach huts and left him to die.

Later, said Mr Asquith, Connor disposed of the body and the money – almost certainly at sea. The court would hear that Connor was a keen fisherman and owned a small open boat moored at the camp's river wharf. Forensic evidence would show that traces of Gedney's blood, skin and hair were found on the boat.

Six weeks later, on the evening of 15 September, vandals lit a fire beneath one of the beach huts. All the huts were affected by smoke damage and on the morning of 16 September Mrs Connor ordered winter staff to repaint and clean the worst affected.

Mr Jack Cley, a painter, of Sea's End Lane, unlocked the shutters of Sun Up House – Hut 16 – and saw that the interior was blood-spattered, an empty holdall lay on the mattress, and several items of discarded clothing were scattered on the floor.

Blood had dried on the mattress, and soaked through to the wooden slats beneath. There were also deposits of blood in the sand under the hut.

Forensic evidence would be presented to the court showing beyond doubt that Connor had been present at the scene, said Mr Asquith. His fingerprints were found on a metal bed-frame in the room, while fibres from his clothing were embedded in the dried blood.

The prosecution would suggest that Connor, who held keys to the huts so that he could open them for guests prepared to pay a weekly fee, had planned to make sure the hut in question remained empty for the season.

However, Mr Connor's plans had been interrupted by illness. On 31 August he was admitted to a private clinic in King's Lynn suffering from stress. On 16 September he was arrested and charged with the murder of Paul Gedney.

Mr Asquith told the jury that the forensic evidence collected at the scene of the crime was the key to the prosecution case. Experts would testify that the blood on the stapler used as a weapon by Connor – which was the same group as Gedney's – was identical to that found in the beach hut.

Mr Asquith conceded that the prosecution had not only a duty to prove beyond reasonable doubt that Connor was the killer, but that Paul Gedney was dead, as his body had never been recovered.

He told the jury that medical opinion would be brought before the court to the effect that the blood loss sustained at the scene – in excess of five pints – was undoubtedly fatal.

North Norfolk coastguard had searched for Mr Gedney's remains, he said, but currents may have taken his body out into the North Sea. There was, further, overriding circumstantial evidence Mr Gedney was dead, he told the jury.

This included a substantial, untouched bank account, and the absence of any known sighting of the victim since the night of the robbery. Evidence from Mr Gedney's doctor and close friends would be put to the court showing that the victim had no known history of depression, and had never exhibited suicidal tendencies.

The case continues.

24

The Dolphin Holiday Spa
Sunday, 8 January

'That's nasty . . .' said Ruth Connor, sliding a microchipped keycard across the counter.

Dryden turned his wrist where the jagged scar of the wound was still red, the criss-cross stitches picked out in white across the skin.

'Accident: DIY. I'm useless.' They laughed, but Dryden noticed she didn't let the warmth reach her eyes.

The woman stepped back to punch some details into the PC. 'Everything seems to be fine, Mr Dryden.' The pale blue tracksuit she wore was expertly tailored to show off a narrow waist, a model's tapered legs, and a cantilevered bust. To one side of the panelled reception area a full-length black and white picture, framed in steel, showed a blonde in a bikini with a sash: Miss Holbeach 1970.

As she turned back, Dryden nodded to the poster. 'That you?'

She laughed again, and Dryden realized for the first time what was so odd about her. Everything was colourless: the bone-blonde hair, the pale skin, the perfectly modulated ice-cube coloured teeth. Even the lipstick, a bubblegum pink, hinted at ice. Dryden calculated her age quickly. She might be eighteen in the picture – so early fifties now, even if she looked ten years younger. He doubted that Chips Connor looked as good after thirty years in prison for the murder of Paul Gedney, and he doubted even more that Ruth Connor's long campaign to free her husband had been marked by celibacy.

'Hard to believe,' she said, inviting the compliment.

Dryden had done his homework on Ruth Connor. He'd found a feature piece online from the *Lynn News* a year after her husband's conviction for the murder of Paul Gedney. She was the daughter of the camp's founder, John Henry, a local celebrity who'd once earned a living as a stand-up comic. He'd ploughed his life savings into founding the Dolphin in 1952. By the early 1970s he'd been fighting a losing battle against diabetes and his daughter had left school at eighteen to learn the ropes running the office. By the time Dryden had come to stay in 1974 she was the manager, while John Henry limped on to an obscure death in 1980.

'I stayed here once,' said Dryden, dropping down on to his haunches so that he could check the neck brace under Laura's chin. His wife's brown eyes swam slightly, and he noted again that they were unusually bright, each reflecting the harsh cold sunlight that flooded in through the foyer's plate-glass windows.

Out at sea waves broke on a distant sandbank the colour of ash, and in mid-channel a red buoy heaved on the swell. On the beach a line of snow marked the extent of high tide.

'I'm sorry – I don't recognize . . .'

Dryden laughed. 'You're forgiven. It was in 1974. I was still in short trousers. I'm surprised the old place is still here . . .'

The eyebrows, thinly pencilled, arched. 'It isn't the old place. We've invested a lot over the years. New markets now – although it's still very popular in the summer months –

especially in the school holidays. But the rest of the year we don't take children.'

She seemed excessively pleased with this arrangement and her eyes wandered to the plaque on the wall which indicated that the Dolphin Spa – as it was now called – had been awarded four stars by the English Tourist Board. They watched as an elderly man swaddled in a fluffy bathrobe shuffled across the foyer towards the plate-glass doors to the indoor swimming pool. As they closed behind him a waft of damp, scented air billowed out. One part of the foyer had been converted into an internet café, and three of the latest Apple Macs sat on crisp white desktops. A middle-aged woman in walking gear tapped at one while sipping a small espresso.

'In winter it's mainly the health spa market now. And nature lovers, of course . . .'

Dryden's eyes widened.

'Oh no,' the hand wandering to the throat. 'Not those kind of nature lovers. Birds, the marsh flowers, the seals out on the point.' She let a hand touch her breast, briefly outlining the upward curve. 'There's a conference hall as well – seats three hundred. So there's trade all year now.'

As if on cue they heard the distant patter of polite applause.

'Estate agents,' she said with a smile straight out of the brochure. Dryden wondered how often she visited her husband in jail. If she dressed like that she'd cause a riot.

He'd found the details for the Dolphin Spa online. The camp had six purpose-built chalets designed with wheelchair access and a bathroom modified for those with mobility problems. They could all double up as ordinary chalets in the height of the season but this was one new 'market' Ruth Connor had tactfully avoided mentioning. Extras included a physiotherapist who visited daily, and a hoist at the pool for those unable to descend the steps. That, and a 24-hour chalet-monitoring service had helped bump up the cost, which more than handsomely reflected the facilities and had made Dryden choke. He disengaged the brake on Laura's wheelchair and turned towards the doors. Ruth Connor grabbed a padded fleece and led the way.

Outside, despite the sunshine, the wind was bitter. Dryden re-zipped Laura into a thermal one-piece suit. Her face was slightly blushed with the cold, and one eye was watering as the wind blew in from the north, but she looked more alive than Dryden could remember since the crash six years earlier.

'That's the buoy we used to swim out to,' he said, pointing.

Ruth Connor nodded, before realizing that Dryden had been talking to his wife. 'The huts were over there . . .' He pointed west, beyond the new indoor swimming pool and the leisure complex which had supplanted the old prefab offices. A white van, emblazoned with a blue dolphin, pulled up and a posse of chambermaids alighted, giggling.

A mobile trilled and Ruth Connor located it efficiently in her tracksuit pocket. She registered the number. 'Oh. Will you excuse me? One minute.' She took a few steps away, colour flooding back into her face as she listened to a crackling voice.

'Good. Good. That's wonderful, love. It's what I want and it's best . . .' She stepped away a few more feet and Dryden lost the thread of the conversation. It sounded like she was talking to a child, the tone vaguely patronizing, the concern intense.

He cupped a hand under Laura's chin. 'I loved this place, right from the start,' he said, kneeling down so he could speak into her ear. 'When we drove into the car park that first morning I could see the sea. It was high tide, and all the children were crammed into the last few yards of dry sand, and they'd run – you know – back and forth with the waves as they swept in, and we had the windows open in the car so I could hear the sound. There's nothing like it, the sound of a beach in summer.'

Ruth Connor walked back into earshot as she finished the call. 'Now, will you do that for me?' she said, then smiled at the reply and cut the mobile off, the face instantly realigning itself for business.

They set out again as she produced a stylish woollen ski hat which she pulled down low over her hair. 'The sea keeps the temperature up, actually,' she said, answering a question that hadn't been asked. 'Although the wind doesn't help. The chalet's got storage heaters – and some hot air blowers if it needs a boost. They're double-glazed, very snug,' she said, wriggling her neck down into the thermal collar.

Dryden held his overcoat lapels to his chin. The north wind was still freezing, and the danger of an ice storm still hung over the Fens and its coast. Emergency services and the power companies were on constant alert, and councils had stockpiled grit and salt to keep the roads open. Looking along the coast westwards Dryden could see the diminishing line of massive electricity pylons linking the national grid to the outlying communities of The Wash. Each one glinted silver-white in the sunshine, the connecting cables hung with decorative ice.

An elderly woman in running shorts jogged past, her legs a livid red, the flesh juddering with each blow of foot against gravel.

They walked down towards the beach between lines of chalets, brick now rather than clapboard, with modern plastic windows and doors, and set within neatly trimmed lawns

167

scorched by frost. White picket fences separated each plot from its neighbour, potted fir trees and brass carriage lamps adding a further suburban touch. Each had a tarmac parking space and several cars were on the site – mostly expensive 4x4s or people carriers. Through one window Dryden could see a couple on a wicker sofa, both fast asleep, a flat-screen TV showing indoor bowls.

Down by the beach there was evidence that the Dolphin's traditional attractions had not been entirely abandoned. The summer fairground was mothballed: a helter-skelter swaddled in stiff tarpaulins. A blackthorn hedge still enclosed the outdoor swimming pool, an Olympian stretch of 1930s art-deco concrete, now empty except for a kidney-shaped slick of ice on the base and a beached pedalo full of accumulated hailstones.

The eastern perimeter of the camp was marked by Morton's Leam, a tidal channel which ran inland through high sandbanks, a single fishing boat keeled over in the sluggish water of low tide. A footbridge crossed the water where the coastal path met the creek: a graceful curve of timber with double handrails, which took the path east. But Ruth Connor led them west to a line of chalets built on wooden stilts in the sand dunes. Dryden pushed Laura up a ramp and over the specially widened threshold. Connor gave him a brief professional tour of the facilities, then left. He positioned Laura's chair by the window, carefully wiring up the portable COMPASS they had purchased for the trip so that Laura could speak. Then he used the hoist to transfer his wife to a lounger, put a talking book on the tape deck provided, and went out to the verandah with his binoculars. He swept the glasses east and found Humph's Capri easily, parked up beyond the footbridge beside a clump of wind-torn pine trees, with a clear view of the chalet.

A glint of cold reflected light came from the driver's side of the cab. He guessed that they were swapping telescopic images and he raised his hand in greeting. Two miniature fountains of water leapt out like whiskers from either side of the Capri's bonnet and the windscreen wipers swished once in reply.

25

Fear: it was still the emotion which haunted him despite the seven days which had passed since the fire on board *PK 129*. If Humph hadn't tried a social call at midnight with a bottle of malt whisky he'd be a charred corpse on a mortuary slab; dead along with Joe Petulengo and Declan McIlroy. Dryden, recalling the 'accident' which had killed Petulengo, and the 'suicide' which had ended Declan's life, didn't believe in co-incidences – and certainly not when they came in threes.

The police had no time for Dryden's conspiracy theory. The inquest into Petulengo's death had recorded a verdict of accidental death, dismissing any concern that he might have taken his own life. The victim had died of hypothermia, although his fall into the ice had resulted in particularly severe injuries to his left leg. The detective who had taken a statement after the fire on board *PK 129* was dutiful but unconvinced, clearly sensing paranoia and professional opportunism in the reporter's lurid version of events. The fire brigade examined the scene and a full report would be made: but it looked like an accident due to a poorly maintained generator, with the occupant drunk in his bunk.

So Dryden was on his own. He'd spent a night in hospital while a surgeon expertly stitched his butchered hand. Then, for a week he'd slept at Humph's council house on the Jubilee Estate, keeping clear of the boat where shipwrights were repairing the fire damage; and clear of *The Crow*. The editor had agreed a hasty plan: Dryden would take his annual holiday entitlement in one go – giving him time to recuperate, and time to think – a mixed blessing.

One question dominated his thoughts, and was the root of his fear. Had the killer struck because he thought Dryden was a potential witness along with Petulengo and McIlroy in the Connor case, or because the reporter's inquiries into their abrupt deaths was getting him close to the truth?

To Dryden the first possibility seemed outlandish: he had told no one he was the child in Ed Bardolph's picture. It was a secret he held in his head. Had someone guessed? If so, Dryden had moved swiftly to try and reassure his assailant. He'd prepared a story making it clear the campaign to free Chips Connor had been derailed by the deaths of the two key witnesses: all hopes of an appeal were lost, unless the elusive witness, the boy known only as 'Philip' – could be found. But there was no sign – he had written – of that happening.

The second possibility – that he had stumbled close to the truth – was more likely, and more dangerous. Recuperating at Humph's house he had kept a low profile, and nothing had appeared in *The Crow* or the *Express* to suggest he was still on the case. But he *was* still on the case. Now that he knew the victims were his childhood friends, and that he too could have joined them, he could hardly walk away from the case now.

There was one other explanation for the arson attack. Declan and Joe had been victims of abuse at St Vincent's. Could their deaths really be linked to the planned civil action for damages, and the criminal action which might follow? It was true others had come forward with testimony, and more would follow, and Father Martin had admitted as much. Could Dryden's inquiries have prompted the attempt on his life? Ed Bardolph had said the investigation into abuse was *directly* linked to what had happened at the Dolphin in 1974. Why were the boys at the camp in 1974, and who had been looking after them?

The only way forward was to go back to the past. His one living link was Marcie Sley, but she and her husband were – according to an unhelpful secretary at JSK – on compassionate leave following her brother's death. They'd appointed a new foreman to run the kite works in their absence. The office wouldn't give Dryden a number or an address but he'd found their house anyway – a lonely Fen-edge bungalow which echoed to his knock. They'd be back, but in the meantime he needed answers.

Alone in Humph's overheated front room he had worked quickly. The cabbie had supplemented his onboard language tapes with an online course in Estonian. Dryden used the broadband link to research the death of Paul Gedney. One thing was clear: if Petulengo and McIlroy had lived to give their evidence in court, Chips Connor would have been a free man. They had seen the victim alive on the night of 30 August – and the next day Chips had left the Dolphin for psychiatric treatment at the clinic near Lynn, where he had stayed until the police had charged him with the murder on 16 September. That left Chips less than twelve hours in which he could have killed Paul Gedney – and completely undermined the prosecution case that he had done it on the night of the robbery. There was no way the original conviction could stand.

So if Chips Connor was innocent, who was guilty? Although his body had never been found, there was little doubt Paul Gedney had died in the beach hut, beaten to death. The problem for the prosecution was that it had happened after 30 August, not on the night of the robbery. So who framed Chips Connor? Clothing, hair, and other exhibits presented at the trial linked him to the murder scene – and linked the victim to Connor's fishing boat.

And so, inevitably, all roads had led Dryden back to the summer of 1974 and the Dolphin holiday camp. And to leave Ely was no more dangerous than staying behind. He'd already booked their chalet and cleared the details with The Tower when, just 24 hours before their departure, he'd been called into Ely police station by DI Jock Reade.

A polite request, some news, not good, he was told.

Reade had seen him in his office, silent except for the scratching of the detective's pen in his notebook, the starlings outside circling the giant mast above. A square of green tartan framed on the wall hinted at Jock's distant origins.

'Is this official?' Dryden had asked, accepting a coffee.

Reade had put his mobile on the desktop, killing the signal. 'Not at all. Just a chat.'

So Dryden had waited, slurping the coffee. 'Someone has a grudge, Mr Dryden,' Reade had admitted, trying a smile. 'The final report from the brigade,' he said, tapping a small pile of files on the otherwise empty desktop. 'They found traces of a rag, soaked in lighter fuel. Its chemical composition is quite different from that of the marine engine fuel, or the oil for the generator. Arson, I'm afraid.

'And there was this, of course,' he added. From a briefcase on the floor he retrieved a piece of paper. Dryden recognized the statement he'd made after the theft of the painting from *PK 129*. 'You reported an intruder on the boat, on the morning before the fire. A stolen painting.'

'And the man in Declan McIlroy's flat,' said Dryden. 'Did you check that with the neighbour?' Reade's fingers moved towards his computer keyboard, but he managed to stop himself activating the screen.

He pursed his lips. 'Any enemies, Mr Dryden? Anyone

who might have a grudge? I don't expect being a reporter makes you popular with everyone. There's this case against St Vincent's, for example. You've been tenacious, I believe. I understand the DPP is looking at the files. Threats, perhaps – anything we should know?'

Dryden pushed his legs out under the interview table. 'I think they're all linked,' he said. 'The two deaths, the theft, the arson, the intruder. It's about Chips Connor. I told you that a week ago. A PC came out to the boat.'

The detective slipped out a fresh file and flipped it open. Dryden noted a letter headed with the insignia of the Chief Constable's Office. He recalled that Chips' solicitor, George Holme, had been pressing for the case to be reopened, despite the death of the key witnesses and the withdrawal of the appeal.

'A decision's been made,' said DI Reade. Clearly not by him, Dryden noted. 'The Connor case *is* to be reviewed. All the original witnesses will be re-interviewed where possible. The victim's family, colleagues, friends . . . the lot. Everything double-checked. The CC has asked us here at Ely to take the case; the original investigation was based in Lynn, of course. We'll be going through the notes with the officers from the 1974 inquiry. The two deaths here – Petulengo and McIlroy – will be reviewed as well. Although frankly . . .'

He gulped some coffee. 'Anyway,' he shrugged, 'we can provide an independent view. We need to wrap it up.'

He bit his lip then. He'd said too much. The implication was clear: the chief constable wanted the case closed. A perfunctory review, followed by a brief statement, would bury Chips Connor's case for ever. Dryden doubted Reade had much of a reputation within the force for producing unexpected results. But in the course of the review he'd stamp all over the Dolphin, a show of thorough policing with zero chances of uncovering a long-concealed truth.

Dryden sank his head in his hands. 'I want to know who tried to kill me,' he said. 'I'm going to the Dolphin. A short holiday, with my wife. We leave tomorrow. It's all booked.'

Reade bristled, dismissing the idea with a laugh. 'It's a free country, Mr Dryden, but we couldn't let you prejudice our inquiries.'

Reade's eyes darted to the wall rota. Dryden guessed he wasn't a sucker for overtime. 'But you're not starting on Monday morning, right? It's a thirty-year-old case. Resources must be stretched.'

'What the CC wants, the CC gets,' said Reade, not answering the question.

'Give me a week,' said Dryden. 'If I find anything, you'll know.' He held up his mobile. 'It's what you need. An inside track. You're not gonna find out anything turning up for an appointment, are you?'

DI Reade shook his head, but licked his lips.

'And I know something already,' said Dryden. 'Something important. You'll get everything, and you can leave me out.' He'd push him one more time, then he'd reveal that he was the mystery kid in the photo, the one who'd played with Joe, Declan and Marcie. 'Just give me some time. Then, when you do go in, you'll be ahead of the game.'

Reade's otherwise anodyne features reassembled themselves around an ugly mouth. 'I don't like being fucked about, Dryden. I take early retirement in five years and nobody, least of all you, is going to make a mess of my record.'

'This is just a chat, right?' said Dryden, putting his elbows on the desk and smiling.

Reade calculated quickly. 'I will be arriving at the Dolphin with three officers on Tuesday morning. My other team will be calling at precisely the same time at the station at Lynn to take possession of the CID files, original statements and recordings. I will oversee interviews at the camp. That means you've got three days. Which means this conversation never took place. You'll be the first person we interview, at which point I will require you to tell us everything you think pertinent. Is that clear?'

'No appointment?' said Dryden, pushing his luck.

'We don't need one. I'll have a warrant. Good enough?'

Dryden stood. 'Deal,' he said, but they didn't shake hands.

A seagull screeched over Dryden's head, snapping him back to the present. The sea was calm and still, creased only by the tide slipping in towards the creek. He looked at his watch now as he stood on the chalet's verandah. He didn't have forty-eight hours any more.

Looking towards the horizon he suppressed an image: the drifting body of Paul Gedney nudging the sandbanks. Who had killed him, and why? If he could overcome his fears, he told himself, he could think more clearly. He swept the glasses east, panning round the camp's layout: past the fairground, the outdoor pool, the leisure complex and the line of pylons running west. And there they were, the original wooden huts, or at least a dozen rows of them. Ruth Connor's plans for modernization had yet to sweep them away. Green with moss they stood, rimed with frost, black holes gaping in the bitumen-soaked roofs, and from a verandah post a child's swimsuit hung in shreds, bleached by a decade of lost summers.

26

Dryden ran his finger round the curved plastic number: grimy now and chipped at the end: 9. The window had long gone and the sill was green and slippery with lichen. Inside the bedframes were rusted, the lino curled at the edges. A dead seagull lay in one corner beside a rusted bucket full of ice placed under a jagged shard of sky in the roof. He felt nothing, but turned to look across at 10. The stoop was still there, sagging under the weight of sand which had drifted in with the winter storms. He could imagine Dex waiting, waiting for the game to begin, the pent-up violence vibrating in his thin, awkward arms. Edging inside, he put a hand on the bedstead and rattled the metal, lifting the detachable headboard away from the main frame and the wire base. A cloud of rust was released, a blood-red shower of oxidized iron.

Outside again he checked his mobile: no messages. He'd left Laura resting with the monitor switched on. Reception had his numbers and the nursing assistant would look in on her every two hours, until he notified them he was back at their chalet. He'd go back soon, take her out on the sands, under the liberating sky.

But for now he walked on between the dilapidated huts, many of them partly submerged by the creeping dunes. A pile of ashes and blackened wood lay by one, evidence of a surreptitious barbecue, but otherwise there was little sign that the huts were ever visited. Snow began to fall, miniature flakes as dry as sand which blew into his eyes.

He ran for shelter through the lines of chalets towards a large building, a box-like two-storey block with tall metal-framed windows which were still intact. From inside he could hear the agonized sound of something metal being wrenched from a wall, followed by the crackle of splintering wood. There were a pair of swing doors unbolted which he pushed open with his back, wheeling round to find himself in the old camp's dining hall. One wall was still obscured by a giant mural of a desert island, palm trees stretching over white sands, parrots in the tree, and a family playing with Day-Glo red buckets and spades.

The thrill of eating here was with him again. The sheer cacophony of three hundred people at each sitting, the sun glinting off knives and forks, the breakfast plates piled with full English, the pea-green teapots ferried out by the waitresses, reeking of tannin.

A man stood at the far end of the room, trying to prise a radiator from the wall.

'Hi. Sorry,' said Dryden, and an echo returned. The hall was empty, a void as cold as the hard rolled ice cream which had been his favourite pudding.

The man stooped and retrieved a set of plans from the floor. He was stocky and powerful, the musculature accentuated by a close-fitting black leather jacket, his shoulder-length brown hair well-cut, streaked with bleached blond and held at the back in a small pigtail. A beard and moustache crept over the heavily tanned skin of his face. As he walked closer Dryden noticed a necklace of thin black leather.

'Sorry,' repeated Dryden. 'My name's Philip Dryden – I'm staying at the camp.'

The man nodded, producing a packet of Gauloises and knocking out one white-tipped cigarette.

Dryden produced his own Greek equivalent and they lit up together. 'It's a holiday village now,' said the man, the voice older than the bleached hair. 'This was the camp dining hall.'

'I know. I came here – as a kid. So what's happening?'

He shrugged, looking up at the roof. 'Just trying to work out what it would cost to rip it down – this is part of the problem,' he said, thudding a boot down on the parquet flooring. 'This stuff is worth a fortune but it would cost one to rip it up. Built to last, unfortunately. Last time we had people in the old huts was '98 . . . When did you visit?'

'Seventies,' said Dryden.

'Seventies eh? Before my time.'

Not much before your fucking time, thought Dryden, smiling. He'd have guessed the man was forty, but the voice could have been a decade older.

'But this place hasn't been shut down for just seven years, surely?' asked Dryden.

'No, no. The new chalets are largely self-catering. We do meals but on a much smaller scale. This place served its last Sunday roast in the late eighties.'

Dryden sniffed the air but the only aroma was rotting wood. 'I'm a newspaper reporter,' he said, trying to provoke a mutual introduction, aware there was little time for subtler inquiries. '*The Crow*, Ely. I've been following Chips Connor's appeal. But I guess that's all before your time too, then . . .'

The man held out a hand. 'William Nabbs. Estate manager. So this is a business visit?'

Dryden shrugged. 'How long have you worked here?'

Nabbs kept smiling but Dryden could see he was angry not to get an answer. 'Mid-eighties,' he said eventually. 'Summer job in the university vac. Came for the surf.'

Dryden nodded, noting now that he was standing closer the regulation blue eyes to go with the bleached hair. 'North Sea have any surf?'

'Sure. Plenty,' said Nabbs, trying a Beach Boy smile.

'I covered the championships once – at Newquay,' said Dryden. 'Nice little summer job for a mate on the sports desk. I tried it, but I was crap. Couldn't stand up to save my life.'

Nabbs' shoulders relaxed visibly. 'It is tricky. I went down a few years in the nineties. Never really got anywhere. But I could stand up.' He laughed, clearly amused by Dryden's lack of basic skills on a surfboard.

'So you stayed here. Must like the place.'

'Yeah. I did business studies – so I stuck around when they started to expand, modernize. It's quite a going concern now – and they've got bigger plans, a marina is the next phase, then an environmental centre – you know, something like the Eden Project in Cornwall.'

Dryden shivered as they watched a trickle of snowflakes dropping slowly from a hole in the roof.

'I've got to write a feature for the paper on the case, now the appeal has collapsed. I'm just looking for some basic info.'

'You should talk to Mrs Connor,' said Nabbs, collecting a toolbox from a trestle table under the dining hall clock, which had long stopped, its hands frozen over the image of a blue dolphin.

'I will. She seemed busy right now, I'll catch her later. So she's the boss, right? But who owns the place?'

Nabbs slipped an elastic band around the plans and squared his shoulders defensively. 'Technically speaking, the majority stakeholder is Chips Connor. But you know, it's a private company.'

'Technically?' said Dryden, picking out the word and ignoring the warning.

Nabbs laughed as if it was all too obvious for words. 'It's pretty difficult running a business from inside a prison, even a low-security one. Calls are monitored, no access to a bank account, correspondence is restricted to prison notepaper – not a particularly encouraging addition to the brand image.'

'Sorry, I'm lost. I thought Ruth Connor inherited the business from her father – how does Chips end up as the owner?'

'When they married Ruth split her holdings fifty-fifty with her husband. But she's got power of attorney so it's all pretty academic . . .' He ditched the stub of the Gauloise.

'So they both hold a half share?'

Nabbs sighed: 'No – there's another partner: Russell Fleet, the assistant manager – he bought out half of Ruth's holding back in the early eighties. But as I say, Ruth's the boss, talk to her. OK? All clear?'

Dryden laughed. 'Sorry. Inquisitive mind.'

Nabbs stooped, expertly working a chisel between two bits of the parquet flooring and lifting out a single block. 'Look at that. Oak. Breaks your heart.'

'What's she like – Ruth? Efficient, I guess. She must have been young when she took over here – what, mid-twenties?'

Nabbs laughed at a private joke, then slipped on some thermal gloves and made for the door.

'From what she's said it wasn't her choice, Mr Dryden. The old man was ill, couldn't do the day-to-day stuff, so there was no alternative. And she's got a gift for it. Think this place would still be running on the kiss-me-quick brand on the windswept north coast of the Fens when you can fly to Spain for twenty quid? I don't think so.'

'So when did you say you'd arrived exactly?' asked Dryden.

Nabbs led the way out, pushing open the double doors with his back. 'I didn't.'

Dryden nodded, as if he'd got an answer. 'So,' he smiled, 'did he do it? Chips. Did he kill Paul Gedney down in the beach hut? What do the locals say?'

'Chips? Ruth's always said he was innocent, Mr Dryden, and that is more than good enough for me. But you can always judge for yourself.'

Dryden looked around. 'Don't tell me – he's in hut 19?'

'Not quite. Her Majesty's Prison Wash Camp, it's only twenty-five miles. Go if you like. He enjoys visitors apparently, although I've never been.'

Outside the giant snowflakes had begun to fall again now the wind had dropped. They walked between the huts towards the beach, the sky above suddenly clearing to reveal a winter blue. 'Does she visit?'

Nabbs nodded. 'Most weeks. She's stood by him for thirty years, which says something, I guess.'

They'd reached the crest of the dunes and looked out over the mirror-flat sea. 'Still surf?' asked Dryden, trying for flattery.

'Sure, sure. Most days in the summer when there's a swell. I take a class on the beach as well – I enjoy it.'

Dryden could just imagine it: the bleached hair tied back, the high-maintenance tan.

'So if Chips is innocent, who do they reckon killed Paul Gedney? There must be gossip.'

Nabbs took out a mobile and began to enter a text message. 'Gedney was involved in some kind of petty theft – drugs, I think. I guess someone from his past caught up with him. It's not a pretty business, is it?'

'I guess not. I was here that summer – '74. Should I remember Chips?'

Nabbs looked off into the middle distance. 'One Blue Coat's much the same as the next. He was a good swimmer, Chips, a lifeguard and everything. Good looking lad too, like I said. There's some pictures in the bar – Ruth's never taken them down. Bit of a heartthrob. But if you were here you'd have seen him for sure – he did a lot of the entertainment apparently – the poolside stuff, you know . . . games, competitions.'

'Spent a lot of time with the kids then?'

'Part of the job.'

'All very straightforward in those days, I guess. No Criminal Records Bureau vetting, no vetting full stop.'

They'd reached the beach and Nabbs turned west. 'Sorry, Mr Dryden, is that meant to mean something?' His mobile trilled and he stopped to read a text. 'I better go,' he said. 'The Grid are here to look at the pylons. The ice is building up – and this storm's still forecast. Could be a problem for us. I better get back to the office. Good to meet you.'

They shook hands and Nabbs set off, not back to the central complex, but along the beach, over the single graceful arch of the footbridge across Morton's Leam and out towards the cottage by the blackened stump of a distant disused lighthouse.

Dryden looked inland towards the village of Sea's End. A single wooden spire rose from the Norman church, a dogtooth pattern of lead tiles catching the light.

He flicked out his mobile and searched the address book for Father Martin's number.

Just one ring: 'Father Martin. St Vincent's Presbytery.'

'Father. It's Philip Dryden. I'm sorry to crash in on your time. I'm at the Dolphin.'

Silence.

'That's –'

'I know, Mr Dryden. How can I help?'

'Just a couple of details. I just wondered. It's Joe and Declan's holiday here in 1974, I just want to be clear about a few things. Did other children come to the camp from St Vincent's in those years, and if they did, who looked after them and footed the bills?'

'Well, we paid the bills, Dryden, but the costs were minimal thanks to a charitable donation from the management at the camp. Yes, other children had been. Several, in fact, most years from the late sixties onwards.'

Dryden sensed he was still dealing with a hostile witness. 'And who looked after them here, Father? Who was responsible, in loco parentis?'

'Well, most years I sent one of the priests, who gave up their annual leave, by the way, to attend. It worked well, actually; it was used within St Vincent's as a kind of reward, for the children at least. We sent between two and six each year depending on availability at the camp.'

'And there were never any problems with these trips?'

'None. They were entirely beneficial for everyone involved, I think.'

'But in 1974 it was different, wasn't it – there was no priest?'

'No. It was a slightly unusual arrangement, but for the best motives. We sent Declan and Joe in the care of Marcie's foster mother – a woman called Grace Elliot. Things had been going very well with Marcie, and there was even hope that they would take Declan, perhaps even Joe. She was looking after baby boys, I recall, as well – but that was short term. Joe and Declan were inseparable. Grace Elliot wanted to see all the children together. There might have been a happy ending for them all.'

'Father, are any of the allegations of abuse against St Vincent's related to these trips?'

Dryden could hear the hall clock ticking in the presbytery. 'I recall my lawyer's advice again, Mr Dryden. I suspect this conversation is not entirely off the record, unlike our earlier one. You'll forgive me if I get back to work.'

But he didn't put the phone down. Dryden could hear him breathing at the other end of the line, waiting to be released.

Dryden almost whispered it. 'Goodbye, Father.'

27

AIR

The single word was on the printout of Laura's portable COMPASS machine. The nurse had checked on her and moved her to a lounger by the window, adjusting the head supports so that she could see out across the sands. The tide was rising quickly, leaving a thin-stretched world of sand and grass beneath a stormy sky, black clouds torn apart by a high-altitude jetstream. A container ship lay ten miles off shore, white water breaking at the bow. Visibility in the icy air was astonishing and Dryden half expected to see a distant iceberg to the north, drifting in the cold light.

He used the hoist to get Laura out of the lounger and back into the wheelchair, doing it twice before he'd worked out how to position the thermal suit so that he could zip her in once she was seated.

Finished, he touched the sweat under his hairline, realizing once again the physical effort needed to take care of Laura's basic everyday needs. He made some tea in the kitchenette and filled a flask, sending Humph a text message at the same time. Then he rang the Home Office press desk in Whitehall to get the numbers for HMP Wash Camp – a category-D open male prison. Visiting time was daily between 5pm and 8pm, and he called in an old Whitehall favour to bypass the written application normally required to see a prisoner. With less than two days before DI Reade and his team arrived at the Dolphin, Dryden couldn't afford to wait.

Outside the wind had picked up at sea, whipping the spray off the crests of white horses as they ran into shore. 'Where shall we go?' he asked Laura, but the COMPASS was disconnected.

A gust made the picture window flex, turning a whirlwind of dry snow in the lee of the chalet.

'OK. Brace yourself.' He pushed her out onto the ramp and down to the hard sand of the beach below the high-water mark. The sand was slightly crisp underfoot where the seawater was freezing. He left a footprint and watched a thin film of ice form across the flooded mark.

They went east towards the mouth of the river and then over the bridge in the tracks of William Nabbs. Dryden paused at the top to get his breath and looked out to sea: the container ship had slipped across the horizon and was now nosing in towards an invisible coastline to the far west, but another had taken its place.

On the far side of the river the coast swung north-east in a long, shallow arc towards the lighthouse a mile away. In the mid-distance Dryden could see the Capri, parked up in the marram grass, with Humph leaning on the bonnet in his giant insulated Ipswich Town tracksuit. Boudicca skittered around him in wide, ecstatic circles.

Humph tiptoed over the sand, leaving footprints a foot deep. 'Hi,' he said to Laura, in a voice Dryden hadn't heard before.

'Shit,' said Dryden. 'I'm sorry – you've not met.' He'd known Humph five years but he'd never taken the cabbie inside The Tower. 'Laura – this is Humph.'

The cabbie tried a wave, then plunged the hand deep inside a pocket.

'Humph, this is Laura,' he said, completing the introductions. 'And she's as bloody cold as I am.'

Humph trained a pair of military binoculars on the chalets by the beachfront.

'Clear?' asked Dryden.

The cabbie nodded, his tiny mouth forming a perfect bow. 'No problem.'

'Thanks again,' he said.

''S OK,' said Humph, turning abruptly to scan the horizon. 'It's a holiday, really.'

'You OK to sleep in the cab? It must be bloody freezing.'

Humph nodded: 'I keep the heater going – long as I don't run out of petrol I'm fine. Dog's hot.'

Dryden suppressed an image of them cuddled up together under the tartan rug.

'There's this,' said Humph, producing a rolled-up newspaper from his pocket. It was Saturday's *Lynn News*. The page-three lead ran under the headline:

TRAGIC DEATHS END APPEAL HOPES
FOR JAILED HOLIDAY CAMP KILLER
By Alf Walker for the Press Association

The family of convicted murderer 'Chips' Connor has abandoned a campaign to have his case heard by the Court of Appeal following the sudden deaths of two vital new witnesses in the 30-year-old case.

Connor, a seaside children's entertainer and lifeguard at the Dolphin holiday camp at Sea's End, was jailed in 1975 for the brutal murder of Paul Gedney.

Ruth Connor, manager of the Dolphin Holiday Spa, said recently that she was certain her husband would be freed once the new evidence had been heard.

Today she was too upset to talk about the case but a statement issued by George Holme, the family solicitor, confirmed that the file had been withdrawn and no leave to appeal would now be sought.

'It is a tragedy that Chips Connor is now likely to see out the rest of his life in custody because of the unrelated deaths of these two witnesses.'

He said that the police had been notified in both cases, but that there were not thought to be suspicious circumstances in either of them.

The names of the two men are not being released to the press.

Mr Holme said that while both men had made statements outlining their evidence the advice of legal experts was that this would not prove sufficient for the Court of Appeal.

'All evidence in such cases must be open to cross-examination,' said Mr Holme. 'Clearly in this case that will now not be possible. We have reluctantly withdrawn our action.

'Strenuous efforts have been made to contact another potential witness without success,' he added. 'We will always be ready to take up Chips Connor's case, but for now the family would ask to be left in peace.'

The two witnesses, believed to be from the Ely area, came forward after the *Lynn News* ran the original story launching the appeal for fresh information to mark the 30th anniversary of the court case.

Mr Holme said that the contents of the statements made by the two witnesses had been passed to the police and he was hopeful that detectives would at least review the files.

'I have written to the Chief Constable urging him to take a fresh look at this case in the interests of justice,' said Mr Holme. 'But for now we have to accept that we no longer have the evidence to force an appeal.'

'Excellent,' said Dryden. The story made it plain that the elusive third witness had not been found. He watched Boudicca pounding along the waterline, white water trailing her through the shallows.

'Any progress?' asked Humph, producing a paper bag crammed with sticky buns. The cabbie looked at his watch.

'A bit. I've found two people who could have a good reason for keeping Chips inside – his wife and a junior partner. If Chips got out he could call the shots – if he really wanted to. He holds a 50 per cent share, which makes him the senior partner in my book. I wonder what he thinks of all this . . .'

Dryden nodded towards the distant dome of the leisure complex.

'His wife?' asked Humph. 'His wife's got a good reason for keeping him inside? That would be the woman who's been running a campaign to get him out, yup?'

Dryden intercepted the tennis ball and threw it again for the dog, the ball bouncing once before dropping into the oncoming surf. 'I said I'd made a bit of progress, not a lot.'

28

The Eel's Foot lay embedded in the bank of Blue Gowt Drain, a mile south of the marshland village of Sea's End. The long silver line of the frozen dyke cut the landscape in half, running impossibly straight, its ends unseen. The pub, built to feed and water the Dutch prisoners of war who had dug the ditch more than 300 years before, was low-beamed and dark, the windows looking away from the water and across the black expanse of peat which ran south to Ely.

Alf Walker sat in a window seat nursing a half pint of fresh orange juice and a copy of *The Complete Birdwatcher*.

'I hate pubs,' he said, as Dryden sat, having already drained three inches of his pint of Osier's Ale.

Outside, the Capri stood alone in the car park, the cabbie inside asleep with his language tape headphones firmly clamped over his ears.

'Sorry,' said Dryden. 'It's a bit tricky meeting at the camp.'

Alf took a file from a rucksack on the seat beside him. Inside was the cutting Humph had ripped out of the *Lynn News*. 'Thanks for this,' said Alf. 'Most of the local evenings took it – and *The Crow*, of course. I presume that's why you stipulated a Friday embargo?'

Dryden nodded. He might be on leave but he wasn't in the business of scooping his own paper. He'd spent many a dreary afternoon in Alf's company on the press bench at the magistrates' court in Ely. Alf was the wireman for the Press Association in eastern England and had a daunting patch: from Lincoln Cathedral to the Thames Barrier, from

Luton Airport to Southwold Pier. Alf had held on to his job for twenty-five years, despite stiff competition, by carefully avoiding vices such as alcohol. His passion was birds, and if the court case was dull he'd fill his neat shorthand notebook with immaculate sketches of wrens and sparrowhawks, swallows and marsh waders.

Dryden drained his glass. ''Scuse me.' He ferried out a double all-day breakfast to Humph and returned with a fresh pint for himself.

Alf's pre-ordered salad sandwich arrived with an offending handful of crisps, which he cordoned off with a delicate shuffle of his napkin.

'So,' said Dryden, spilling nuts across the table. 'I need help, Alf, and I haven't got much time. I need to know about the first story – the one that started all this off, about the appeal being launched for fresh information. When was that – last summer? Did the PA run it – or did it start with the *Lynn News*?'

'Started local,' said Alf, folding a leaf of lettuce neatly into his mouth.

'And Ruth Connor just rang 'em – or was it Holme, the solicitor?'

'Neither. Far as I know, the first story had very little to do with the family. It was silly season – you know how it is – there was nothing much happening anywhere. So they did what you and I have done a thousand times, they went through the files looking for an anniversary. Anything: triplets born ten years ago, a child missing a year, a National Lottery winner five years ago. Then you just go back and do an update. So they latched on to the thirtieth anniversary of the Connor case – the sentencing, anyway; the murder was actually the year before, of course. Connor had always said he was innocent so they rang the family and said they were going to run an appeal for people to come forward with any information which might help spark an appeal – there'd been none at the time so legally they still have the option. Then they got a quote off the wife backing the campaign, and that was that.'

'Until . . .'

'Right. Until someone came forward with fresh evidence. Frankly, they were amazed. They thought they'd get a coupla stories out if it, tops. Then the lawyer rings and says two reliable witnesses had come forward and there were high hopes the original verdict would be called into question.'

'And Holme was clear – I take it. That the witnesses had seen the newspaper story and then come forward?'

'Right. Either that or they'd seen one of the posters.'

'Posters? Why'd they print posters if the story was just a run-up to fill space?'

'They have a monthly campaign – a poster each time. It's just for advertising, really; there's a different sponsor for every one. Missing people, mainly, appeals for witnesses at crash sites, that kinda thing. So that month it was the Chips Connor case.'

Alf rummaged in the rucksack. 'Here,' he said, unfolding the poster, which they spread out on the table.

The picture Dryden had seen in the *Lynn News* had been a thumbnail, and he'd wondered at the time how anyone could have come forward on the strength of such an indistinct image. But the poster was quite different: pin-sharp and in colour. Paul Gedney had thick brown hair cut stylishly for the seventies, a powerful muscular neck and clear taut skin. But it was the eyes that were extraordinary, and dominated the face completely.

'Bloody hell . . .' said Dryden. 'You'd think he was the killer, not the victim. Talk about mad staring eyes.'

Alf nodded. 'It's called exophthalmia. If you'd ever kept tropical fish you'd know all about it. "Pop eye" is the common term; you have to put stuff in their feed to stop it.'

'Well they didn't put it in his,' said Dryden, holding the picture up to the light. The whites of the eyes clearly encircled each of the blue pupils, the centre of the eye protruding, the sockets round and full. The flashbulb of the photographer had caught the fluid in both.

'He wouldn't have made much as a door-to-door salesman, would he?' said Dryden. 'He'd frighten the kids.'

'Yeah. Perhaps. My daughter reckons he's a dish.'

'What?'

'Well, she's a teenager. The haircut's back in style. The eyes a bit mad but some women like that, you know, a sense of danger. And his face is distinctive: there's a strong jawline, lean features. Anyway, that's what she said when I showed her. The benefits of a daughter's-eye view, Dryden.'

Dryden nodded. 'Maybe you're right.' He noted that Alf's plate was clean and the juice drunk, so he stood. Neither of them had time to waste. 'I might have something else soon – on the case. I'll ring you first – OK?'

Alf smiled. 'Sure. How's Laura?'

Dryden lied, swiftly and proficiently. 'Good. It's her first trip out, so yeah, good.'

The truth was different. When he'd got her back to the chalet after the walk on the beach he'd fixed up the portable COMPASS and tried to get her to talk. But there'd been nothing: a well of silence, several feet of blank ticker tape. Which meant one of three things: she was in what her doctors liked to call a 'blank state' – a temporary return to complete coma; she didn't want to talk; or she was too depressed to try.

Dryden checked his watch. 'I'd better get going. Appointment. Can I take this with me?' He held the poster at arm's length.

'It's not a face you'd forget,' said Alf, nodding. 'However hard you tried.'

29

The Capri sped south across the Fens to the tune of an Estonian folk song while Humph's fingers, as nimble and slim as his feet, danced on the fluffy steering-wheel cover. Dryden rummaged in the glove compartment and complemented his two pints of Osier's with a malt whisky. The combination of the alcohol and the stinging cold made his skin hum. The sun, struggling on the western horizon, was a crisp purple disc, the frosted landscape lost in the glare.

'Tropical fish,' said Dryden, wiping his mouth with the sleeve of his coat. He glanced at himself in the rear-view mirror, noting that the sub-zero temperatures had only whitened his natural pallor. But his green eyes shone, radiating satisfaction at being in motion again.

'What about 'em?' asked Humph, annoyed Dryden had interrupted his language tape.

'Their eyes bulge if you don't look after them.'

Humph turned up the volume on the tape deck by way of comment and wriggled down into his seat. 'You don't need more pets,' said the cabbie, and Boudicca yawned, the sudden clamp of her gums closing oddly hollow.

'She's yours,' said Dryden. They sped on, happy to be at cross-purposes.

HMP Wash Camp was not signposted and lay hidden behind a new gas-fired power station on the outskirts of the Fen market town of March. Four plumes of water vapour rose from the power complex's quartet of squat aluminium chimneys, obscuring the sun and throwing elongated shadows across the Fen. The prison itself was modern, single storey and enclosed by a suspiciously well-kept garden. As Humph trundled the cab forward a single floodlight popped on and an entry barrier, unguarded, rose automatically.

'Welcome to Devil's Island,' said Dryden, as they slid beneath and into a car park.

Dryden got out and followed the signs to reception. His Whitehall telephone call had paid dividends and he had only to sign a request form for a visit. In the box marked 'purpose of visit', to be read by the prisoner, he wrote 'friend of appeal witnesses Joe Petulengo and Declan McIlroy'. Presumably Connor knew his hopes of freedom were over, that the two men were dead, but Dryden was counting on hooking Connor's curiosity, if not his sympathy. As the form was processed Dryden watched a bus pull in to offload a shambling line of visiting families, clutching bags. Dryden got ahead of them to be decanted through the usual system: a cursory electronic scan and search before admission to the inevitable spartan waiting area. For an hour he sat in the ill-lit room with the others, one toddler riding a tricycle around the chairs, while a no-smoking sign became the object of concerted abuse. As darkness fell the view outside of a featureless brick wall was replaced by the reflections of the waiting families, eyeing themselves belligerently.

Dryden had not seen a uniform since his arrival and the male warder who eventually appeared to shepherd them into the visiting room was, likewise, unaccompanied by the jingle of keys. This room was large and well lit, comfy seats were arranged in little clusters, and the children could play in a brightly painted Wendy house at one end. A trestle table had been set out with winter vegetables, clearly grown by the prisoners, and cleaned and polished to perfection. The inmates sat, some smoking, most leaning back in their chairs, thighs spread, their eyes searching the faces of the visitors who poured into the room.

Dryden let them find each other until only one was left; he stood, one hand on the back of his chair, waiting too. Dryden was surprised by Connor's height, perhaps an inch below his own six foot two, and the athlete's build: a white spotless T-shirt drawn across the chest, the leg muscles stretching the cloth on the jeans. The biceps were exposed on the arms and overdeveloped, the occasional vein knotted near the surface.

'Hi. Chips Connor? My name's Philip Dryden. Thanks for seeing me. I wanted to talk about Declan and Joe. I'm sorry; you must know they're dead.'

They shook hands, and Dryden noticed the dampness of sweat, the heat of stress. They sat and Dryden saw that Chips had something in his hand, held lightly.

'I never knew their names,' he said, then looked about, distracted. 'Most times I only see Ruth.' The voice was unexpectedly light, even gentle, and clashed with the overtly masculine build. He shook his head just once too often, suggesting a conversation with someone within. 'I don't like visitors,' he added, and Dryden was sure he was unaware of the insult. 'And I never go out, not to see people. I could – but no.' He shook his head again.

'Why?'

Connor shrugged. 'Breaks the routine.'

'And you like the routine.'

'I can't swim, that's the only problem.'

Dryden nodded. 'You used to swim a lot, didn't you? At the Dolphin. You were a lifeguard by the big pool under the clock.' Dryden remembered the poolside organized games, the Blue Coats extracting limp cheers from crowds of shivering, goose-bumped children.

Chips nodded happily. 'There's only the gym here – so I do weights. Sometimes we run, they let us out for that, but only on the Fen. But I'd prefer to swim.' He rubbed the T-shirt sleeve up to reveal his biceps. 'Could you ask them if I could swim? Ruth asks every time but we don't get anywhere.'

'Sure,' said Dryden, eager to push on. 'But everyone's more interested in getting you out. You know, for good.'

'But that's not gonna happen now, is it?' There was an edge to the voice, overriding the childlike cadence of the sentence.

Dryden nodded. 'There's still a hope, I guess. Perhaps they'll find the other boy – the one they called Philip.'

Chips let the paper ball in his hand unfurl. It was the application form Dryden had completed at the barrier gate.

A door clattered open and a woman entered with a trolley, metallic and gleaming, hissing with steam. Connor crunched the paper ball again, placed his hand on the coffee table between them and withdrew it quickly, like a card player laying a bet. The ball of paper was left behind, unfurling gently.

'Do you want a drink, Chips? A biscuit?'

He nodded rapidly. 'Yes please. Orange juice, no added sugar. They sell wine gums too.'

Dryden fetched a tea for himself and spilt the sweets on the table by the paper ball.

Connor began to eat them, methodically, like a bird pecking at grain.

Dryden studied his face, which was oddly featureless, like Action Man's. While his body had successfully fought the onset of age his face had taken the burden of the years. He'd been handsome once but the blandness had deepened to the point of being threatening: like a photofit. Over one eye, curving out of the hairline, was an old scar.

'Do you remember them, Chips – Declan and Joe?'

An almost imperceptible nod.

'They were in care – I guess you know that. St Vincent's; it's a Catholic orphanage.'

'I don't wanna leave, anyway,' said Connor, ignoring him, stretching back in the chair, a yawn cracking his jaw. Dryden was struck again by the odd mix of the juvenile and the adult, an almost adolescent confusion.

'Why don't you want to leave?' said Dryden, caressing the mug of tea.

Connor looked round, trying to find a rational answer. 'I have a room here,' he said eventually. 'TV. No one can get in.'

It was an odd compliment to pay a prison, that its principal attraction was that no one could get in. He could understand now why Ruth Connor had not led or initiated the campaign to free her husband: it was, possibly, the last thing he seemed to want.

'I used to go to the Dolphin,' said Dryden, deciding to try and push the boundary back, back thirty years to the summer of 1974. 'In the seventies. You probably gave me a swimming lesson in that very pool.'

Connor nodded, but didn't smile, and finishing the sweets he began to sip the orange juice. Around them now some groups were breaking up, moving off through double doors and further into the prison. The woman at reception had told Dryden that if the prisoner wanted he might take him to his room, or to see an exhibition of art in the gym.

Dryden looked at Connor's hands and noted they were powerful and still, a single wedding band the only jewellery.

'I'm sorry. I know you answered all these questions before but Declan and Joe were my friends – I want to know who killed them.'

Chips stiffened in his seat, unable to stop the bland features of his face jerking suddenly into something like shock. 'George, my solicitor, he said there'd been an accident, and a suicide.'

Dryden shook his head. 'I don't believe that. So I need to know more, Chips, more about that night of the robbery. You've probably told the story a thousand times, but can you tell me what happened? Can you tell it again?'

'You're a newspaper reporter, yup?'

'So?' Dryden considered how efficiently the Connors kept in touch.

'So I shouldn't talk. Ruth called. We speak every day, like I said. There's no one else to speak to on the phone and I get a card. I have to use it up – I think it's a rule.' Again the casual, unconscious slight.

Connor laughed at something private and then leant forward. 'I swim sometimes, in my head. I can show you.'

He stood and Dryden followed, despite the tea left steaming on the table. As Dryden rose he swept the rubbish and uneaten sweets into a bin but pocketed the ball of paper Connor had left to unfurl.

Beyond the doors a corridor ran round a courtyard, benches arranged in a square with a single dry fountain as a focus. A covered walkway led across lawns, the hallway antiseptic, the lighting brutal. When they got to what appeared to be a residential block they climbed the stairs to a corridor. They could smell ground coffee, and somewhere the trickling notes of Schubert. Connor led the way into his room but left the door open, kicking a wedge into place. In one corner a towel lay over an exercise bike, and several pairs of trainers were lined neatly along the skirting board. The walls were bare except for one which held a large poster of a swimming pool seen from above, the figure of a lone female swimmer in a white swimsuit gliding vertically between the lane markers.

Dryden took the only chair, Connor the bed, then he looked at the poster. 'It was night time. I was passing the long pool – the one by the clock like you said. I was on the way back to our chalet, Ruth had gone to bed . . .'

He stopped suddenly, sipping the orange juice carton that he'd brought with him, remembering something.

'And I was just doing the last round, checking the kids. Some of the parents were still in the bar so I had one or two left in the huts by the dunes. Two: Taylor and Atkinson. Girls – June and Rosie.'

Dryden nodded, remembering the ritual of the twitching curtain. 'That's a good memory.'

Chips looked at him again. 'I remember everything. When I got to the office the light was on and the door was open when I tried it – which was wrong. I always locked it – even when someone was inside who should have been inside. He'd got the safe open when I came to the door, they said at the station he'd lifted the office keys out of Ruth's bag in the bar, but they couldn't explain how he'd opened the safe. He had the notes in little piles – ones, fives, tens, twenties. I thought he'd run, but he didn't. He put the money in one of those boxes you clip on to the back of a motorbike – like panniers. Then he just kind of walked past me . . . like I wasn't there, like I didn't count. He didn't think I'd do it, you see. Didn't think I was capable of it.'

Dryden nodded. 'Capable of what?'

Connor cracked his knuckles. 'In the office we had a desk stapler – big thing, with a solid wooden base. So I picked it up and I hit him, from behind. Hard.'

The prisoner was breathing faster now. 'That's why there was blood there when the police arrived – and the splashes on the path outside, and the skin and hair on the stapler . . .'

'Did you like Paul, Chips? You were at school together, yeah?'

'I liked Paul. He could talk to the girls, but I couldn't. They said he looked like a pop star.' Chips was silent, a smile surfacing slowly.

Dryden tried to imagine the scene at the holiday camp on the night of the robbery, playing back in Connor's memory. The warm night, the distant laughter from the bar and the casual cruelty of being ignored.

Connor ran a tongue along dry lips. 'He ran after I hit him. I followed for a bit but he cut between the huts, towards the car park. He had a motorbike. I heard the engine and saw the tail-lights on the coast road . . . So I ran to our chalet and told Ruth and we called the police. That's what I told them happened, because that's what happened.'

The last sentence lacked emotion, a pro forma recital.

'Why do you think he came back, Chips? Why did he end up on the boat in the marsh?'

'The *Curlew*,' he said.

'The *Curlew*? Was that what it was called?'

He nodded. 'Ruth's dad owned it, John Henry. We were gonna rent it out but it needed a lot of work. She shipped water, and she was well stuck in the mud. Big job, that, so we left it a season. She's still down there, Ruth says – but she's gone to rot now.'

'But why did he come back, Chips?'

A gentle buzz came from a device on the ceiling by the grille for the hot-air system. Connor looked up. 'That's the timer. You've got ten minutes. Never more, they trust us.'

Dryden leant forward. 'The newspaper story said you talked to Paul Gedney earlier that night, didn't you – with

Ruth. That he needed somewhere to stay. Did you think he was afraid of anyone? Because if you didn't kill him, Chips – someone else did.'

Connor was agitated now and Dryden could see a disturbingly ordered line of sweat drops along his brow, just below the hairline.

He fingered the arc-like scar which crossed his forehead. 'He said he thought someone would get him, someone who'd helped him steal the drugs. He said he'd got involved with people, that he'd got in too far and that was why he needed to get away, make a fresh start. So we let him stay that night.'

'Did he name names?'

'He said they'd find him. So he couldn't stay longer.'

Dryden nodded, even though he hadn't got an answer, while outside in the corridor a family went by, several conversations networked into one.

'Can you think of anyone who would want to keep you in here, someone who would want to stop you coming home?'

He grinned then, an adult's cynical smile. 'What about me?'

'Don't you want to be free? See your wife?'

'I see her every week. I saw her yesterday. I'm looking forward to seeing her soon.' His eyes widened. 'Really soon.'

Dryden found it hard to believe the simplicity of Connor's emotional life. He sensed a keener intelligence hidden inside the child. 'What about the life you've missed, Chips? Children – don't you regret that? You were good with children, weren't you, Chips?'

'Ruth couldn't. We tried those first years,' he said, suddenly standing and looking at a heavy-duty diver's wristwatch. 'They said we should adopt and we talked about it, but then . . .' He looked out of his window at the night, studded with institutional lights, touching the scar again.

They didn't shake hands but Chips did look him in the eyes for the only time. 'Thanks for coming. I'm sorry about your friends.'

Later, outside, in the cold but reviving air, Dryden leant on the cab's frosted roof and retrieved the ball of paper from his pocket. Connor hadn't touched the application form, but he'd written on the blank side, in capitals, each stroke of the pen incised into the paper, overrunning its prescribed length.

I DIDN'T KNOW.

30

Dryden sat in the dark with Laura, the view beyond the picture window lit by a moon which had just risen from the sea. Ghostly white lines of surf ran into the beach below them, while further out a green light momentarily obscured a red one: ships eclipsing each other in the night. Despite the chalet's double glazing Dryden could sense the coolness of the glass, a hint of the Arctic temperatures beyond.

Laura looked out, the hand-operated extension to the portable COMPASS machine lying unused in her hand. Dryden had hung a PEG-feed bag above the chair for her evening meal and he'd talked as the nutrient levels fell: a rambling dissertation on the mystery of Chips Connor which had elicited no response. He'd tried to hold the swimming brown eyes for a second: 'If you're unhappy here – tell me. We don't have to do this.' Nothing. They'd been at the Dolphin for twelve hours and she'd said nothing except the single word AIR.

Finally, he stood. 'I'll leave the lights off so you can see the view. There's some videos up at reception. Art-club stuff as well as the usual – I'll get something you'll like. We can watch it later before bed. I'll be ten . . .' He flipped on the monitor by the bed, checked the PEG-feed, and double-locked the door on the way out.

On the step he looked east towards the dunes where he knew Humph was watching. He took a torch and flashed it three times, the immediate response a precise triple reflection. On the ghostly white beach he saw Boudicca, a sudden flash of jet-black shadow.

He looked up at the moon. A day had gone, but he felt further from the truth, unsure even if there was a truth. DI Reade's arrival would destroy any chance he had of finding out what lay beneath the placid surface of the little community which was the Dolphin. It was up to him, but he felt he was failing, floundering amongst half-truths and lies.

A gravel path led inland, each pebble welded to its neighbour with a tiny coating of ice. Dryden picked his way past the camp's new chalets, the deep sense of silence eerily complete. At reception the lights were on but the desk deserted, airport Muzak polluting the silence. He took a seat in the internet café and logged on, calling up from memory the website for Companies House. He was enough of a journalist to know that there were certain facts worth checking with official sources. He paid a £3 fee online by credit card and called up the last annual return for the Dolphin Holiday Spa.

'Now that I didn't expect,' he said.

Two owners listed: Charles Frederick Connor – 50 per cent, Ruth Josephine Mary Connor – 50 per cent.

So much for Surfer Joe's degree in business studies, thought Dryden. Three quid and he could have checked for himself. Either that or he had a decent reason to lie.

Dryden walked out through a carpeted lounge which smelt of synthetic lavender and followed the sign to the bar.

It was a shock, seeing it again, after thirty years: the polished dark wood panels, the art deco lights and wall fittings, the deep semicircular sofas, the polished parquet ballroom floor. He could still see his uncle and aunt sat on the high stools, as clear now in his memory as a family snapshot. It was an adult world, shadowy and darkened by the polished wood, infused with the aroma of beer, perfume and cigarettes, and splashed with evening sunlight. He'd never been inside, seeing it all from the garden beyond the French windows, with a glass of squash and a packet of crisps; a pre-dinner ritual which had briefly separated him from his newfound friends on the beach – a separation he had endured with grace, coveting the secret of the game to come.

In his memory something timeless played, but tonight the bar was silent. On one stool sat the only customer: Ruth Connor. Behind the bar was a man in a crisp white shirt, open at the neck, who had been leaning in close to share a private conversation and straightened as Dryden approached, rubbing his hands with a bar towel.

But Dryden had heard the last words he'd said, and they weren't a whisper: 'There's no way he will – relax. OK – just relax.' The tone had been angry, the emotion largely suppressed, the words spat out.

'Mr Dryden,' said Ruth Connor, recovering quickly. 'Our very own roving reporter . . .' She was still in the tracksuit, but the perfectly brushed blonde hair was unruffled by exercise, although Dryden noticed two blotches of red skin at her neck.

'I've missed the rush then,' said Dryden, looking round, wondering if Nabbs had told her he was from *The Crow*, or if she'd known all along.

'Our estate agents are out for the night. Coach, into Lynn,' she said.

'Lets hope *they* get charged 5 per cent commission upfront,' said Dryden. 'And then find out they've been gazumped for a table.'

She smiled, the teeth revealed catching the light.

'This is the old bar, isn't it – from the camp? It's nice – opulent. It's got character.'

Ruth Connor laughed. 'Yes. In other words the rest of the camp hasn't. It's the Floral Bar. It's the only bit of the 1930s original buildings, along with the offices above. The rest is gone, history now.'

There was an awkward silence. 'I'm sorry,' she said. 'This is Russell. Russell Fleet. He runs all this with me. We're just catching up – Russ has been on holiday. Now I can relax a bit. He makes great cocktails,' she said, jiggling the glass. 'If you're nice to him he might even make one for you.'

They shook hands, the assistant manager's flesh flabby and moist. Russell was a stone overweight but still powerful: middle aged, medium height, with the kind of limpid blue eyes usually reserved for people in recent receipt of a telegram from the queen. His skin was blotchy and overheated, discoloured by liver spots. His head was shaven in the modern style: a mistake as the stubble was prematurely grey and the cranium revealed was shallow, lacking the high dome which can make the skull noble. One eye was inflamed, an infection edging the eyelids in red.

Dryden knew a picture of health when he saw one.

'How about a White Lady?' asked Fleet.

Dryden nodded, wondering if he was missing a private joke. 'Sure.' He turned back to Ruth Connor as Fleet fussed with the cocktail shaker, brushing aside an offer of help from a young barman who had appeared from a back office.

'You've been talking to William Nabbs,' said Dryden.

'Yes. He mentioned your – interests. Can I take it your visit is partly professional? . . . I'm sorry – perhaps I should have recognized the name. George Holme, Chips' solicitor, sends us the cuttings. It's been a great help, the support of the press. Thank you – I don't get the chance to say that very often to a reporter in person. There was a story today, I think – in the *Lynn News*, but that wasn't you?'

Dryden shook his head, impervious to the flattery. He'd written one story about Chips Connor and he doubted she'd even noticed his name. 'No,' he said. 'I saw it too. So the appeal is off? The lawyers seem to think there's no hope now.'

'What do you think, Mr Dryden?' said Fleet, setting the drinks on the bar. 'Ruth's lost hope too – it's been cruel these last few weeks. She thought Chips was coming home.'

Dryden could sense the electricity in the air, a conversation hidden within another. He picked up the cocktail. 'To estate agents – the only profession the British public distrusts more than journalism.'

Ruth Connor coloured slightly and took a gulp, glancing at a framed picture on the polished wooden panel beside the bar. Dryden stood, taking a closer look, letting the alcoholic thud of the cocktail take effect. It was Chips, a teenager, posing on the edge of the pool in trunks, the sunshine catching his natural summer tan.

Dryden turned. 'Could have been a film star, eh?'

She nodded, turning her chin to catch the light on what Dryden imagined was her best side.

Dryden threw some money on the bar and bought a round, excluding Fleet, who had been cradling an orange juice anyway. Ruth Connor's assistant manager moved off down the bar with a sheaf of paperwork once he'd conjured up two more of the lethal concoctions.

'I visited him today,' said Dryden, still watching for a reaction.

She didn't miss a beat. 'I know. We talk most evenings when I can't get over. If this is a working holiday, Mr Dryden, there seems to be very little holiday involved.'

Dryden shrugged as if it were a decision made by others. 'It's handy – having the prison up the road,' he said. 'So –

do you think he's resigned to seeing out the sentence? What's that – another five years? He seems like a model prisoner, but no remission?'

She siphoned up some more cocktail and Dryden thought there was suddenly something desperate about her, a tension which made her hand vibrate as she shuffled an errant hair from her cheek: 'It's been obvious to anyone who's talked to Chips for the last thirty years that he's an innocent man. But the judge stipulated that he should serve the sentence. And, frankly, he is not interested in going in front of a parole board. All we want is for the verdict to be quashed – which would be as much justice as he could hope for. After that, who knows what will happen? There's money, he can choose.'

Dryden sipped his White Lady. 'I'm sorry – can I ask a personal question?'

'You can try.' The tone was as hard as the old ballroom floor.

'The newspaper reports that I've read said Chips had learning difficulties. Today – well, it's clear that he has some problems. Were those problems as marked when you were married?'

She smiled the clinical smile again and retrieved a hand-bag from the bar. A Filofax, businesslike, held a snapshot wallet. Out of it she took a colour picture, a couple dancing, both faces together for the camera.

'Our wedding day,' she said. 'August 31st, 1971. We were eighteen.'

Dryden recognized the face but everything else was different. She danced with arms thrown free at her side, her hair turning and rising, both feet just clear of the ballroom floor.

'It's here,' he said, tapping his shoe on the wooden polished boards.

She nodded, reaching out to reclaim the image.

Fleet appeared with the third round of cocktails and she took an inch off the top. 'I don't think anyone approved – but Chips was good looking, great fun. He loved the camp, wanted to make a go of it too. We'd been at school together, so there was nothing of the whirlwind about it, quite the opposite. I was very lucky, actually, and very happy.

'But there was an accident.' She touched her forehead at the precise spot Dryden had noted the scar on her husband's forehead. 'He was diving – in the main pool. We had a high board then . . .'

Dryden nodded, remembering the falling bodies, the thrill of danger.

'A child, just toddling, pushed one of the pedalos on the poolside into the water. It drifted under the board – Chips didn't see it until he was falling. There was a lot of blood . . .' Dryden thought how pale she always was. 'The skull was split, there was some damage to the brain where it had been crushed up against the serrated bones behind the forehead – it's a common feature of car-crash injuries. He came back quickly enough, that was Christmas '73, and in many ways he seemed unhurt. The good humour was there, but there was something childlike after that . . . and there were childlike fears. He seemed to find people very frightening, especially close up, and he was genuinely terrified by emotions. There was a loss of something. He'd always been so good with people . . . but now, he was very cold. It was like he couldn't imagine how anyone else felt.'

She lifted the crease of the perfectly laundered tracksuit bottoms.

'There were panic attacks, crises of anxiety which just swept over him for no apparent reason. We'd find he was gone, and we'd search the camp – which was embarrassing

212

in season – and then they'd find him, usually in the dunes, as far away from the crowds as he could get. It wasn't just the people – it was the unpredictability, the not knowing if he'd have to meet someone new.

'Anyway. We carried on, hoping it would get better. He still enjoyed the pool work – I think that was because he was in control, and he was with the children. And he was very good at some things – in fact he'd got better at some things. He had an amazing recall for names, which is a real plus in this work. And we put him in charge of the beach huts because it was mainly paperwork, and he was meticulous, really. But I didn't know what to do . . . he was still very afraid of the world.'

'He doesn't want to leave prison,' said Dryden, sensing at last some real emotion. 'Why try to get him out?'

'I've said. There's a difference between innocence and freedom. I'd like to see the record straight – and so would he.'

'Mrs Connor, if your husband didn't kill Paul Gedney, who did? You must have thought about that.'

Outside they heard a coach returning, the babble of corporate voices heading towards them. She shuffled the glasses and collected the mats. Then she stopped and looked Dryden in the eyes. 'If you'd met Paul, I don't think you would have asked that question, Mr Dryden.' She'd raised her voice, and Dryden detected the edge of suppressed anger beneath. 'He collected enemies for a hobby, he had a level of natural arrogance which most people found repellent, and he'd do anything to get what he wanted. It's a volatile cocktail,' she said, draining her glass.

'He'd fallen in with some dangerous people. It's obvious that he ended up hiding in the marshes, in the *Curlew*. Clearly, someone found him.' She stood. 'I'm sorry. Russell will need a hand. This time of night we're short of staff – and there's some illness about, flu and suchlike. We're a bit stretched.'

Dryden stood too. One more question. 'I understand the Dolphin paid most of the cost of having the children from St Vincent's for the holiday. Kids like Joe Petulengo and Declan McIlroy. That was very generous.'

'Yes. It was. Anything else?'

'Chips wrote this . . .' said Dryden.

He put the piece of paper on the table, spreading it out. I DIDN'T KNOW.

'Didn't know what, do you think?'

She shook her head, but she didn't move. Dryden watched the estate agents heading in for nightcaps. 'What do you think Chips would think if he walked through that door right now?' asked Dryden.

It was a random question, but Dryden could see it had hit home. She couldn't stop herself looking across the dance floor. 'I think he'd be angry, angry that he'd lost thirty years of his life, and I think this room would remind him of that. Angry, Mr Dryden, very, very angry.'

31

He held Laura's head to his chest and, propped up on the pillows in bed beside her, looked out to sea. The moon was high now and the sea an unruffled field of silver. On the beach towards Lighthouse Cottage a figure Dryden couldn't recognize stood, pitching stones. The dune grass where Humph's cab was parked up was dark except for a hint of the Capri's vanity light amongst the reeds. Dryden felt his wife's breath on his neck, and, leaning back, allowed her head to drop to his shoulder, her lips to edge closer to his skin.

'What do I know?' he asked.

The ritual pause.

'I know that Ruth Connor is one tough customer. But then it's been a tough life. She marries golden boy Chips Connor, the rippling lifeguard, and within two years he's suffered an accident which has left him with brain damage – not enough damage, to be cynical, to consign him to a hospital or a home, but enough to turn him into an emotional iceberg. There she is, the blushing bride, with a life ahead spent with a selfish child.'

Dryden looked at Laura, her head turned from his, the COMPASS switch held lightly, and realized it was too late to change the subject.

'But murder? It's bizarre – to pick off Paul Gedney as a victim just to get Chips out of her life. There were so many better ways. Divorce, desertion, subterfuge. She'd given him half the business by then, but even in the best of health

Chips wasn't a mover and shaker. She was still in control, she didn't have to do anything stupid.'

Dryden shook his head. 'It's much more likely Paul Gedney was killed by someone from his past, someone involved in his sordid little racket, stealing drugs from the hospital dispensary. I need to know more about Gedney if I'm going to find out who killed him. The hospital's at Whittlesea – it's a run – but I've got Humph. I'd be away a few hours, no more.'

A seagull, ghostly white, fluttered against the window, confused by the reflection.

'All that presumes Gedney is dead, of course, but the forensic evidence was, is, overwhelming – he'd lost enough blood to satisfy a Halal butcher and even Chips Connor's defence lawyers in the trial didn't try to argue that no murder had been committed.

'And the night he fled to the Dolphin he told both Chips and Ruth Connor someone was after him – and the some-one he had in mind didn't wear a blue uniform. I think whoever it was caught up with him – tracked him down to that boat in the marshes and beat him to death. Perhaps he ran, and they caught him on the beach. Who knows?'

Dryden threw his head back in frustration. 'More to the point, how the hell do I find out? I'm thirty years too late and I'm running out of time.'

He knelt beside Laura's chair and rested his head on her knee. 'Perhaps I'm worried about the wrong crime. Smith and Dex didn't die thirty years ago – ten days ago they were both alive. Did Paul Gedney's murderer kill them? Or is someone else desperate to keep Chips Connor in jail?'

Dryden watched the sea crease as a wave came in from the north, and he stretched out, sensing Laura had slipped into sleep.

The day had multiplied the questions, but provided few answers. He knew more, but understood less. So there was only one thing left to do. Slipping from under the duvet he dressed quickly and grabbed his overcoat and mobile, edging out the door to the verandah. The air was totally still, but cold enough to instantly freeze the hair on his hands as he fumbled with the phone. Looking down he could see that the receding tide was freezing on the sands, ridges of ice forming in waves.

He rang directory inquiries and got George Holme's office number. He waited a full minute when he got through until the answer phone clicked in: 'This is the office of G. W. Holme & Sons, solicitors. Our office hours are 9.00am to 5.15pm Monday to Friday. If your call is urgent, please leave a message.'

'Hi. This is a message for George Holme. My name's Dryden, from *The Crow*. It's the Chips Connor case. I wanted to let you know that I can help. There were four witnesses that night the children found Paul Gedney in the *Curlew*. Joe Petulengo, Declan McIlroy, Marcie Sley, and a boy called Philip. They never saw Philip again, and there were no records left to trace him when the appeal got under way. Joe and Declan are dead, Marcie can never be a credible witness. But I know where you can find Philip. I'm at the Dolphin now – but you can ring me on this mobile: 07965 4545445. Goodbye.' He checked in his notebook and found the office number for JSK, the company founded by Joe Petulengo. He left a similar message for John and Marcie Sley. 'If you're back, and feeling up to it, I'd really like to talk again.'

Then he buttoned the trench coat up to his neck and looked eastwards to the lighthouse. The single figure on the beach was no longer alone. A couple stood, their arms locked, watching the falling tide.

The Dolphin Holiday Camp
Saturday, 31 August 1974

With the light of dawn Philip slept, to be woken by a voice opposite. 'Just get dressed quickly, boys.' Philip looked at his Timex: 7.35am. He crept to the window. On the stoop stood Grace Elliot's husband, his back to the open door, with one of the Blue Coats and a security guard. They said nothing, avoiding each other's eyes.

The Blue Coat stayed behind. He had one of the poolside swimming poles and he sank to his knees and worked it under the wooden chalet, in the sandy shadows, pulling something out of the cool dark space: a canvas bag, knotted with the blue rope the fishermen used. He should have taken it away then, Philip had sensed that, but instead he'd tugged the neck loose and pulled out a box. He could see it was of dark wood, polished, with a brass plate where a key had once gone. The Blue Coat had opened it and Philip could still hear the tiny, metallic tune: 'Greensleeves'.

They were missing at breakfast. An empty table by the window where the family had always sat. He ate quickly with his uncle and aunt and returned to the chalet. His aunt said she'd pack and he could have half an hour: a last half hour, but that he couldn't go on the beach because of his shoes, his jelly-moulds already swapped for school brogues.

He'd run then, down towards the sluice, hoping they'd be there. He wanted to know what the man had found, and why he'd found it, and what they'd seen the night before and if they'd been seen, but most of all he wanted to say goodbye. He'd rehearsed this last morning many times: an only child struggling with the manners of friendship. Would they come again next year? Would it be the same two weeks? In a schizophrenic, oddly adult way he knew that it would probably never happen, that hoped-for repeat of the summer, but he was young enough to crave, desperately, the possibility that it might. Fuel enough for a year of dreams.

But the marshes were empty. He ran to the poolside, deserted on changeover day despite the sunshine. In the distant car park families were loading up, cases being strapped to roof racks. By reception the first newcomer had arrived, a small child in shorts running ahead of a man with two suitcases. Just inside the doors there was an amusement arcade, they'd come here once with Smith, bringing coins they'd found on the beach. Philip slipped in and stood alone on the plush blue carpet, the machines winking silently, unplayed.

He heard Smith's voice first, oddly muted. 'Don't push.'

Philip stepped between the machines and stood behind a cabinet where a mechanical crane fished for prizes. Through the glass he saw the children outside in a single line led by Grace Elliot: Sis, Dex and Smith, with one of the camp's security guards, a different one this time, at the back. Philip padded behind, aware that the rigid formation was part of some wider punishment. They'd been seen the night before, recognized. But had the man who'd seen them seen him? There'd been no early knock at his chalet. But what had the children said? Had they betrayed him now?

Philip inched out into the sunshine of the car park, skirting a line of cars, mostly black and already humming with heat. The three children stood by a Morris Minor Traveller. Grace Elliot talked with the security guard, shaking his hand, crying, her face red and wet. Inside the car her husband sat at the wheel, a map spread out concertina-style.

Philip edged closer, seeing them through the windows of a VW camper. He caught Sis's eye, but she shook her head: just once, but he could see the plea, the urgency of the signal to keep away. Dex clung to her, Smith stood apart, his shoulders rigid with the fear he was hiding.

Then, released by a command he did not hear, the children bundled into the back seat of the car. Windows down, they joined a queue at the gates. Dryden watched them go, willing them to acknowledge he was there, afraid they would. But their heads never turned, not once, to look back at the sea, or to look back at him.

32

Monday, 9 January

The façade of Whittlesea District Hospital boasted a brace of Palladian pillars and a portico complete with a carved heraldic shield. But if the front hinted at grand ambitions the rear shouted poverty. Steam gushed from a vent, rising up the blackened brickwork and melting the snow in the guttering above. A skip marked 'clinical waste' tumbled soiled paper onto the tarmac and a gang of seagulls launched sporadic raids on a tumbled rubbish bin. By a pair of plastic swing doors a male medical orderly sat swaddled in a shell suit smoking a cigarette like an addict. The insistent hum of extractor fans provided a constant soundtrack to complement the crackle of the radio from beyond the steamed windows of a laundry.

A pair of female nurses stood arm-in-arm on the doorstep engaged on separate mobile phone calls. Dryden, extracting one of his Greek cigarettes, stood close to the orderly and lit up.

It took five seconds for the orderly to speak. 'Visiting?' He was in his twenties, unshaven, his eyes haunted by lack of sleep and overindulgence in something liquid.

Dryden shook his head. 'Looking for the union rep – Unison. Any idea?'

'Not on site. This place is closing – not enough patients to justify the staff, not enough staff to justify the funding. Lynn's got the nearest full-time rep.'

'I was after a bit of history, actually – someone who used to work here as a nurse. Anyone still around?'

'Yeah. Loads – that's the problem. Nurse, you said?'

'Yeah – male, a trainee. With access to the dispensary. This would be '74, perhaps a bit earlier.'

He whistled, as if Dryden had asked to speak to Queen Victoria. 'That's going back a bit.' He ground the stub of the cigarette out on the tarmac. 'Come on.'

The change in temperature was astonishing: the heated fug of the hospital interior settling instantly on Dryden's frosted skin. The smell turned his stomach, the memory of custard weaving round that of urine and floor scourer. They picked their way through a hallway strewn with dirty linen and out into one of the hospital's main corridors. Sixty yards ahead of them an overweight nurse pushed a patient into the distance on a trolley: otherwise the long vista was empty, the dully polished floor reflecting noise from the wards at each side. A TV buzzed a sports commentary, while somewhere a tap gushed into a bath, the plumbing banging as it dealt with the rush of hot water.

At the far end they descended damp brick steps under a sign marked DISPENSARY. At the bottom was a windowless room with some plastic seats and a matching pot plant. A counter behind meshed glass took up one side of the room, the service hatch was open and deserted except for a single tea cup and saucer. It was even hotter here and Dryden could feel through the soles of his feet the hum of a boiler somewhere in the basement.

Dryden's guide smacked the counter with the palm of his hand: 'Shop! Marina, shop!'

His guide retreated, leaving Dryden to wait alone. He paced the room, reading posters on the walls, many of which looked like they'd been printed up for the launch of the NHS in the forties – a diagram of a dissected eye, a list of do's and don'ts for diabetics and a gruesome set of pictures showing the progress of malignant melanomas. He checked his watch: Laura was in the pool at the camp doing hydrotherapy, but he felt the gentle tug of guilt.

'Yes?' The woman was black, a kind of red-mahogany colour, and Dryden guessed the genes were Cameroonian. There was something imperious about the long, graceful neck and the precise angle at which she held her elegant head, the hair cut short and grey. Dryden estimated she was sixty.

'I'm sorry to bother you – you must be busy. I was look-ing for someone who might remember a nurse who worked here in the seventies. My name's Dryden – Philip Dryden. I am a journalist, with a local paper in Ely.' He let that sink in and, when she didn't throw him out, carried on. 'It's about a nurse called Paul Gedney. The police were after him – something to do with stealing drugs? He was here then – in the summer of '74.'

She picked up the tea and came round the counter, sitting elegantly on one of the plastic chairs, expertly balancing the cup in its saucer. 'It's a long time ago.'

'But you remember him?'

She shook her head as if trying to dislodge a persistent image. 'What's this about?' she asked, fiddling with a long amber earring.

Dryden told her about Chips Connor's case, and the hunt for witnesses to free the convicted man. He said he didn't have much time, and he checked his watch to prove it. But it seemed she'd decided to talk anyway, because she cut in before Dryden had finished his pitch.

'Paul – I remember Paul, yes. I'd just qualified, so I was a few years older, but we got on well. There was something very odd about him, you see.'

She paused, waiting for Dryden to invite the disclosure. 'Which was?'

'Unlike the rest of the population, he was not a racist.'

Dryden didn't need this, and he suppressed an urge to pick up the point. He wondered if she'd mixed up racial discrimination with the innate Fen antipathy to newcomers of all colours. In the mid-1970s they probably hanged people with ginger hair in Whittlesea.

'Right. But what was he like?'

'An outsider, like me. He would have been eighteen or nineteen years old, I think, when he first came here. Very self-contained, you know, almost arrogant really. He always made it plain that he'd chosen to be a nurse, that it wasn't second best to being a doctor, which was a bit disingenuous because while he was certainly smart he'd missed out on a formal education. He was that type: a kind of undisciplined intelligence. I think he resented that lost opportunity.'

'Did he resent anything else?'

She sipped the tea. 'People who got in his way. There was something slightly malevolent about him, you see. I got the feeling he'd do anything, you know, if he'd judged the outcome as correct. He was one of those people with their own moral compass – he decided what was right and wrong.'

'And he stole drugs? He'd decided that was right, had he?'

'Yes,' she said, tilting her chin. 'Yes he had. He was very close to his family – his mother, actually. She was ill, and had been for many years – diabetes, I think, but I could be wrong. Anyway, she needed support and help at home. He tried to manipulate the bureaucracy, the red tape, to get her extra cash and visits. But it didn't work. I think he stole to finance a carer, the medical treatment. She had private care at a clinic, I think, which didn't come cheap.'

'Regular Robin Hood, then. What kind of drugs?'

'Anything he could sell. Tranquillizers. Painkillers. It was very cleverly done – just small amounts, but regular as clockwork so that the system could factor in the losses.'

'Is that possible? Surely everything is balanced up – drugs in, drugs out?'

Her hand went to her graceful throat.

'Yes. Good point.' She tried a smile but gave up. 'The books showed no discrepancy.'

Dryden nodded to fill the silence. 'Who kept the books?'

'My predecessor – the senior pharmacist.'

'And what happened to him?'

'*She* took early retirement – medical grounds. Parkinson's.'

'Right. So Paul Gedney gets to face the full weight of the law and does a runner while the chemist gets to flick through the time-share brochures?'

She held out her hands, palms up, and Dryden noticed how pale the skin there was. 'I don't think anything could be proved in that respect, at least not beyond doubt. And the pharmacist was ill, although the disease was at a very early stage. Bringing a criminal action against a clinician or a professional within the service is very difficult. But Paul had been seen selling the drugs – on several occasions. There was a dossier on him, pictures, statements.'

'Is the pharmacist still alive?'

'She died. Her husband was a doctor – an eye specialist – and we see him sometimes. But they separated soon after she left the NHS. He's based at the Royal in Lynn, but there's a visiting clinic here.'

Dryden stood. 'What was her name – your predecessor?'

She stood too, again the tea cup and saucer beautifully

poised. 'Lutton. Elizabeth Lutton. Actually, I can show you . . .'

Leading the way, she quickly climbed the stairs to the main corridor above. She took him to an echoing Victorian entrance hall dominated by a Grecian bust, which was dusty and unnamed. On the wall there was a framed colour photograph of a man in a suit cutting a ribbon.

'The day they opened the day clinic, it's out the back across the car park. A Portakabin. That's her.'

She pointed at a woman amongst the dignitaries gathered in the background. She was younger than Dryden expected, perhaps thirty-five, an unsatisfied smile lighting up a broad face, framed in buttery-yellow blonde hair. Something about the hair conjured up a memory for Dryden: two pale bodies moving together in the dappled sunshine of the dunes.

'And the husband?' he asked.

'Dr George Lutton. Not pictured. I doubt if he'll talk, Mr Dryden.'

'Any of the family left – Gedney's mother?'

She shook her head. 'She died. Very soon after Paul's disappearance. There was a funeral, I remember that, at the Catholic church. The family was a sprawling one – there was another brother, and two or three sisters, I think. All of them – except the other brother – were younger than Paul and the father couldn't hack it so they all went back into care. It was dreadful to see.'

The hair on Dryden's neck prickled. 'Back into care? These children were fostered by the Gedneys?'

A minibus arrived outside the main doors and a group of elderly patients began to bustle through, filling the marble hall with voices.

'Yes. She was a foster mother, although I think the illness

228

made it difficult in the last few years. That was why Paul was so determined to try and support her. There was a lot at stake. He'd come to her when he was pretty young, I think. Before that he'd been in care – not locally – more your part of the Fens, I think – Ely.'

33

Humph pulled the Capri over into a lay-by on the edge of town. Beside the road a dyke lay frozen, smoking in the midday sun, a starburst of cracks where someone had lobbed a lump of concrete onto the surface. To the south-east the Fen stretched, iced furrows and the occasional wind-cowed hawthorn the only features on a landscape rolled flat by a heavy sky. Dryden's trained eye skipped along the spirit-level of the horizon until he found the distinctive double bump of Ely Cathedral – the Octagon and West Towers visible from twenty-five miles, and as familiar as Humph's lugubrious profile.

Dryden nibbled the pastry edge of a pork pie while Humph rummaged in chip paper. He rang the number for the Dolphin and got the daytime receptionist: Laura was still in the pool and would then be taken back to the chalet for a rest and sleep. Then he retrieved a text message from the mobile.

DRYDEN. WE'LL BE THERE 9.00AM TOMORROW. BE AVAILABLE. READE

'Shit,' said Dryden.

He turned to Humph. 'You said you'd seen someone on the beach last night?'

'Yup. The woman who runs the place, with the blonde hair. She walked along the beach about 11.30 after the lights went out at reception. Met a bloke on the sands – compact, black leather jacket, pony tail. They went back to the cottage by the lighthouse. Lights on downstairs, then upstairs, then just upstairs. She reappeared this morning – sevenish. Different jacket, different jogging pants.'

'Bravo,' said Dryden. 'You could do divorces – pays well.'

Humph licked the chip paper as Dryden considered the implications of Ruth Connor's nocturnal stroll along the beach. He was hardly surprised she'd found solace somewhere, perhaps anywhere, after thirty years of virtual widowhood, but he wondered how much Chips Connor had been told.

But first he had some more questions for Father John Martin. Urgent questions: and this time he wasn't going to let him dodge those questions down a telephone line. 'Let's go home for a bit,' said Dryden. 'St Vincent's – Lane End.'

Paul Gedney's foster mother had been buried a Catholic and her fostered son had been in care in Ely sometime in the sixties. It seemed that St Vincent's might be more central to the story of Chips Connor than Dryden could ever have guessed. He wondered what else Father Martin had seen fit to keep from the reporter, on the convenient pretext of protecting other people's interests.

They sped south, a miniature motorcar on a giant Monopoly board, untroubled by any variation in height or direction, across the reclaimed miles of the Great Soak, a journey calibrated by the passing shells of forgotten windmills. At one point they passed a sign on the roadside: 'Cabbage 20 miles' – the kind of detail that made Dryden revel in the landscape. Ten miles from the edge of the city Humph swung the cab out to overtake a tractor and, untroubled, stayed in the middle of the road for a mile, whistling tunelessly.

Dryden's mobile rang, and noting that the number was unknown he flipped it open.

'Mr Dryden? This is Mr Holme's secretary – I'll put you through.'

Dryden heard an old-fashioned purp-purp of a desk phone ringing. 'Mr Dryden? I'm glad I've caught you. Thank you for your message. Can you talk?'

Dryden looked out on the limitless expanse of black peat, calculating swiftly what he should say. 'Sure.'

'You have our witness, I understand. Clearly I need to interview him, perhaps informally at the first meeting. Can we do that?'

'I think so, yes. I need to talk to him, of course – but I can't see a problem. Can I ask if you've told anyone else about my call?'

'Er. Well, my client, of course, is Chips Connor, but I don't feel it would be appropriate just now – the fact that we were forced to drop the petition to appeal was a great disappointment. He's a fragile character – as I understand you may appreciate. A visit, I'm told.'

'Yes. I see. Not Chips. But his wife, then. You've told her?'

'Indeed. I think that's best for now.' Dryden had banked on the news filtering out; if the killer was close he needed to flush him – or her – into open country.

He looked out of the cab's passenger window at the limitless horizon. 'I'll get back to you,' he said. 'You'll want him to come to the office, I take it?'

'Ideally. But we could come to him, if that's an issue.'

Dryden said he'd ring and killed the signal, shivering. They'd arrived: Lane End was deserted, the only movement a sluggish line of black smoke trickling out of a chimney pot in the single crescent of council semis. Three children, hands linked, skated on shoes down the drain which ran beside the road.

The presbytery door was opened by the novice with the purple and gold football scarf. 'He's not in,' he said, before Dryden had spoken.

'Tell him I've come about Paul Gedney. He'd be really pissed off to miss me.' Dryden noted that the profanity brought some colour to the young priest's face, and an unattractive hardening to his eyes. Dryden hoped his first parish would be poor and violent, somewhere so bad nobody could believe the statistics.

Dryden stood on the step, daring the novice to shut the door in his face. They heard a light footfall in the hall beyond and Father Martin appeared, dabbing his mouth with a linen serviette by way of apology. 'Daniel didn't know I was in my room. Come in, come in . . .'

The hallway was familiar to Dryden: identikit Catholic interior decor from the seventies. A cold tiled floor was scrubbed clean, an ugly telephone sat on an MFI table, a hatstand hung heavy with overcoats. On the wall Christ exposed his Sacred Heart, and a landscape shot of the Connemara Mountains hung in a heavy dark wood frame, the colour leached out by light. The house reeked of Pledge edged with incense. There was also a strong aroma of stewed tea, the tannin obscuring something less wholesome, something a lifetime past its sell-by date.

'Please . . .' They climbed the stairs and crossed a landing creaking with lino, to a study bedroom. The bed was a single, neat as a prayer, and made up by someone who did it for a living. The desk faced the window looking towards the ruin of St Vincent's. On the leather blotter stood a glass of milk and what looked like a cheese sandwich made, Dryden guessed, by the same professional hands which had produced the bed's crisp hospital corners.

Father Martin turned the captain's chair around, resting the milk and sandwich plate on his knee, the heavy grey sky behind him. Dryden took the one other seat, a straight-backed dining chair as uncomfortable as any pew. There were books, but not too many, a single Gaelic football banner over a black and white picture of some boys in shorts.

'Daniel's only trying to protect my privacy,' said the priest.

Dryden nodded, thinking how thin it sounded, how self-pitying.

'Paul Gedney. Why didn't you tell me he was an orphan at St Vincent's?'

Martin turned slightly to rest the plate on the desk. 'The smart answer you know . . .'

'Because I didn't ask,' said Dryden.

'Quite. Paul Gedney came in 1957, I think. He'd be five or thereabouts. His mother had died, an only parent. There was a place at St Vincent's, and the doctor was a member of the congregation here at Lane End. In those days such human details counted for much. He was with us for more than a decade.'

He took a single small bite of the sandwich and tucked a crumb back between thin lips.

'You weren't troubled by this double coincidence. That two of your boys should be the witnesses in the case of the murder of another?'

'Well – it isn't as much of a coincidence as you might think. Perhaps I can explain?'

Dryden nodded. 'You didn't seem keen to explain on the phone, Father.'

'Ah, well. A different question. There are some things I must not discuss. But history is history.'

He put his fingertips together and closed his eyes, shutting Dryden out. 'So. Paul found a foster home in 1967 at Whittlesea. A woman known to the diocese – Gedney was the family name – she'd taken several children and in fact took Paul's older half-brother a few years before she took

234

Paul, which is something St Vincent's always encouraged, of course.'

Dryden nodded, wishing he'd taken a notebook.

'Anyway, he did very well with the family – at school and so on, given his background and the inevitable emotional problems. In fact he did much better than the older brother. That didn't last – he came back to us before moving on, although the brothers were in touch. But Paul was adopted, finally. He was an intelligent child, highly intelligent in many ways.'

'I'm sorry – how do you know . . . this is all before your time here, isn't it?'

'Files. We have files. I had anticipated some interest. And I got to know him much later – after he'd begun his train-ing, actually, to become a nurse.' He stopped eating, and Dryden sensed he was enjoying the exposition.

'And very laudable that was. I should have said that it was a peculiarity of his character that this coldness was allied to a sincere – I believe – a sincere wish to protect his adopted family, and indeed to help others generally. He was intensely close to his adopted mother, and the other children. One of his mother's great interests was in help-ing make life easier for those pupils here not lucky enough to find a home. She was in constant touch with St Vincent's – indeed, she was a governor for a short period – and she ran outings and suchlike – trips to the seaside, the zoo, the pantomime at Christmas, that kind of thing. Remarkable, really, considering their straitened circumstances and her worsening health.'

Father Martin sipped the milk, which left a white slick across the glass like medicine.

'At school – in Whittlesea – Paul met Ruth Henry, as she was then. They were all friends, Chips too. Paul's foster mother asked Ruth if it was possible her father would set aside a few chalets in the summer for children from St Vincent's at the Dolphin. She agreed to ask – her father was by then a very sick man I have to say. Anyway, he had taken great solace from the Church and was happy to agree, and so for a few years at least we were able to send children on a holiday, a rare opportunity for them in those days, believe me. We paid a vastly reduced rate – as I think I mentioned to you on the phone only yesterday – a few pounds to cover costs. The year Declan and Joe went was the sixth year – unhappily the last, as I also mentioned.

'Usually I sent one of the priests too – but that year Declan's sister, Marcie, was included with her foster parents as I've explained. Not the kind of arrangement we could get away with today, of course, but I think everyone's motives were for the best.'

Father Martin, stopped, peeling back the sliced bread to examine the cheese within. They both watched as snow fell against the window.

'I tried to revive the holidays a few years ago but Mrs Connor declined – insurance, apparently – and they did other good works which suited them best. A young-offenders scheme, I believe; such is progress.'

Dryden stood, the noise of the chair scraping on the lino echoing in the empty house. 'You said Paul Gedney had a half-brother, Father. What was his name?'

Father Martin ran a fingertip along an eyebrow: 'Paul's family name was . . .' he flicked through the file. 'Ah, here, yes: Earnshaw. But he and his half-brother shared a mother, and as I say he was ultimately adopted by another family. I can dig it up if it's helpful. Can I ring? I've got your number.' He glanced at the desk and at a notebook with an alphabetical staircase opposite the spine. Beside it lay a green file, with the diocesan crest in gold on the front, tied with a red lawyer's ribbon.

'I don't suppose I can see Paul's file?'

Father Martin shook his head. 'I don't think that would be appropriate. There's a picture, though.' He pulled the bow free and slid out a passport-sized snap; Paul Gedney aged ten.

'Those eyes,' said Dryden.

'Yes. A thyroid complaint, I'm afraid, which may well explain some of the behavioural problems. He was seen by doctors here, but there was little they could do. Painful, I think. A tortured life, Dryden, but there were many. I will pray for his soul.'

Dryden nodded. 'You do that, Father. I've got twenty-four hours to find out who beat him to death.'

34

Back at the Dolphin Dryden craved sea air to clear his head. Lighthouse Cottage clung to the horizon on a narrow spit of wind-tossed dune grass. Dryden picked his way along the beach between the clumps of marram, retracing Ruth Connor's brief journey of the night before. It was time, he'd decided, to find out more about the private life of William Nabbs. The path was well-worn, a sandy twisting alley between the overarching sea-thorn. On the beach the tide was piling shards of ice towards the high-water mark, a jumble of miniature icebergs stained with yellow seafoam.

The cottage itself had been partly buried over the decades by the creeping dunes which protected it from the sea, the garden encircled by a dry-stone wall, a barrier which had kept alive a solitary sheltered palm. Dryden clattered the gate and rapped the door. Satisfied Nabbs was out, he peered in through the double-glazed windows. The kitchen was high-tech and stylish, the appliances black, sleek and edged with chrome. To the seaward side there was a sitting room with a large window looking out over the sand and the surf. Before it was a Mastermind-style black leather chair with kick-out foot support. On one wall an eight-foot-square canvas of a wave breaking mirrored the reality beyond the glass. There was a flat-screen TV, a CD and DVD deck. Fitted bookshelves covered the walls, the volumes neat and precise. Dryden couldn't be sure, but he'd guess they'd be in alphabetical order.

It looked like a bachelor pad, but there was something

distinctly feminine about the sofa, covered with a silk throw, and on the coffee table two mugs sat, a copy of a celebrity magazine on the glass top.

On the seaward side a wooden garage stood low in the sand, the roof weighted down with rocks and pebbles from the beach. Through a small glass pane in the door Dryden glimpsed the dull white gleam of a surfboard, its skeg like a shark's tooth. Further back a machine, covered with a tarpaulin. Black, with dull rust-dotted chrome, and the glazed emblem of a starburst on the petrol tank: a British motorbike, without number plates. He didn't bother to try the door, which boasted two padlocks and a triple bolt.

'Did he come back here?' Dryden asked himself. He imagined the wounded Paul Gedney taking refuge on the night of the robbery, watching the distant blue light of the police patrol car on the coast road to the south, answering Ruth Connor's call. Had the motorbike lain for three decades untouched? Surely not. Unless someone had wanted to keep it hidden in those first few weeks when the police had been trying to track Gedney down. After that it was perhaps too dangerous to sell, or even risk dumping without the plates.

From the top of the wide garden wall Dryden looked inland across a landscape of brittle frosted seagrass. Half a mile to the south stood one of the huge electricity pylons. High security fencing ran round its four splayed girder feet, while by a gate a blue electricity company van was parked, an amber light pulsing silently on the roof.

By the time Dryden got to the wire the engineer was climbing the encased ladder within to the pylon's lower gallery. William Nabbs was outside the wire looking up, swaddled in a heavy-duty yellow thermal jacket, charting the climb through binoculars.

'Hi,' said Dryden, exhilarated by a sudden squall of hail-stones. 'What's up?'

'Snow and ice,' said Nabbs, not lowering the glasses.

'I was always terrified of these,' said Dryden, looking up through the concentric squares of the superstructure to the high ceramic insulators which held the wires nearly 150 feet above. 'We'd fly kites – down on the beach. They always looked closer to the wires than you'd think. I guess that's what the fencing's for, eh?'

'Four hundred kilovolts,' said Nabbs. 'One touch and you'd fry.' He let the binoculars fall on a chain round his neck, but continued to look up, knocking his gloved fists together for warmth. The engineer was on the first tier of the structure, about 120 feet above them, his harness clipped to a metal rail. He'd a set of tools held on a belt and with a hammer he was dislodging compacted ice which had congealed on some of the transmission gear. The splinters fell, glittering in the air, and smashed into the rock-hard grass below.

'So. What's up?' said Dryden, emphasizing the repetition.

Nabbs straightened. 'They're worried. It's so cold the snow gets compressed and forms ice. There's enough up there to put a real strain on the girder structure. If we get freezing rain as forecast, that can coat the gear, moisture can seep into the electrics and . . . bang!'

Dryden jumped. 'What about the wires?'

They both looked south towards the next pylon half a mile away. The cables looped towards it, each one decorated with occasional icicles. The pylons marched to the horizon, daring the eye to see for ever.

Nabbs shrugged. 'The wires are high tension – in fact they help hold the pylons up. One of those wires snaps, I'd duck first, then I'd run. One pylon goes, they start crumpling down the line. Especially one like this – its a deviation tower, it's

240

where the pylon lines change direction. It's bigger than the others – it has to take the tension in the wires from both directions.'

Dryden tried to imagine it, the wires snaking in the air.

'Hear that?' said Nabbs.

Dryden listened and picked out a high electrical buzzing.

'As the weight of ice builds up the hum changes – the note rises.'

The vibration had an edge, like a wire shorting inside a plug. Dryden thrust his hands deeper into his overcoat pocket. Across the dune grass by the camp's reception building he could see the staff minibus disgorging the next shift of cleaners, the blue dolphin etched on its side.

Nabbs looked out to sea where the surf was beginning to rise. The grey water buckled, built a black shadow where the wave was rising, and then fell with a blow on the sand.

'Bit cold for catching a wave,' said Dryden, reeling him in, trying to get beneath the well-tanned surface.

'Yeah. Even I'd have second thoughts . . . I normally go in Christmas Day though – local tradition.'

They turned back towards the camp reception. 'I thought you'd be off when winter came, chasing the sun, chasing the swell.'

Nabbs ran a hand through the dyed blond streak in his hair. 'Once, perhaps. And there's nothing wrong with British winter surf that a decent wetsuit can't normally cure.'

Dryden smiled, thinking about the young William Nabbs, arriving in the eighties, becoming part of the world Chips Connor had left behind. He nodded towards Lighthouse Cottage. 'How long you lived there? It's quite a spot. The cottage yours?'

Nabbs nodded. 'I've been here fifteen years – the house is a perk.'

'And Ruth Connor – she lives on the site still? I seem to remember an old house, is that right?'

Nabbs nodded, running the field glasses along the line of pylons to the west. 'That was Dolphin House, her dad built it in the fififties. There's a picture in the bar. It went in the redevelopment – there's a flat now, above reception. Very swish.'

Dryden nodded, waiting to see if his witness would incriminate himself. 'What about the other partner – Russell?'

'A semi on the edge of Sea's End. He's got kids, they go to the school at Holbeach. Wife works down in Whittlesea; he's always lived off the camp.'

'So in winter it's just you and Ruth Connor on the site.' Dryden knew he'd hit the wrong note, so he pressed on quickly, making it worse. 'Ruth Connor. She's a good looking woman, I wondered . . . it seems odd . . . Her husband's been locked up for three decades, I guess no one would blame her if she'd found someone else.'

Well, you cocked that up, thought Dryden, as Nabbs' face hardened.

'That is something you could ask her,' said Nabbs. 'If you had the decency and the guts. I'd like to see you try. If they sold tickets I'd buy one. As a point of information, several people live on the site – including a security guard and a caretaker. OK? Otherwise I guess Ruth deserves the same level of privacy the rest of us enjoy. Don't you?'

There was nothing quite like pompous self-righteousness to get Dryden fired up. 'Fancy her, then, do you?'

Nabbs turned to go, then wheeled back. 'Anything you'd like to tell me about your life, Mr Dryden? Married? Wife love you? Kids?'

Dryden shrugged. 'Difficult to tell. She was in a coma

for five years after a car accident. You could ask her – although I can't get any answers at present. I think she's becoming suicidal. She's over there – in the last chalet.' Dryden pointed, both his voice and his finger trembling slightly.

Nabbs held up a hand by way of truce, then took a deep breath of the freezing sea air. 'Look. My private life is discreet, OK, but it's not a secret. No doubt you've been talking to the kind of people who like living other people's lives for them. It's a small place, and a lot of people have got small minds. I didn't have you down as one of them, that's all.'

Dryden turned. 'The two witnesses, the kids who saw Paul Gedney that night in 1974, before someone spilt five pints of his blood in the sand. You know what I'm talking about, yeah?'

Nabbs was suddenly wary. 'Sure.' The hum of the transmission lines above shifted up a note.

'They're dead, like it said in the paper. They were friends of mine, in a roundabout sort of way. I think someone killed them. Someone who didn't want Chips Connor to come home.'

Nabbs coloured visibly, despite the cold. 'Jesus. You're mad. It's 2005, not 1805. Do you think anyone – least of all Chips – thinks he's coming home to the loving wife he left thirty years ago? Look, that marriage was over long before they took Chips away, OK? Christ – she's visited him every week for three decades. He's pretty happy in a room six by eight. I don't think dealing with the wide open world is really on any more, do you? It's not about whether he can get out of an institution – it's about which institution he's going to spend the rest of his life in.'

'So he knows, does he?'

They heard the tap-tap of the engineer's hammer on the metal superstructure of the iced pylon.

'It's not part of his life any more, Dryden, OK?'

'But if he came home – what about the business?'

Nabbs shook his head, laughing, exasperated. 'You don't give up, do you? Ruth and Russell run the business. If Chips ever gets out he'll be rich thanks to the work they've done. What would he have done differently if he'd been here? Plenty. But I doubt he's bothered, do you?' But he looked away then, hoping perhaps that Dryden didn't have an answer.

Dryden squinted, watching a small fishing boat crossing the sea in the mid-distance. 'Just to give you the picture: Declan McIlroy, one of the witnesses who was going to get Chips free, the killer got him drunk, then they left him to die of the cold. Hypothermia. The police found him frozen to death in an armchair. The guy had no life to speak of – alcoholic, depressive, a childhood in care. But they took it away anyway.'

'I'm sorry about your friends.'

'Thanks,' said Dryden. 'But I'm more interested in Paul Gedney's friends. What does Ruth Connor think happened? She must have discussed it. Pillow talk,' he added, trying to make him angry again.

But the interview was nearly over. 'Gedney was low-life, all right? They'd been friends at school, the three of them. Chips was popular, a gateway to other friends. Ruth was going to be rich one day – at least by standards around here. He used them: he used everyone. Then he did a runner, but Ruth always thought there were others involved. She said it wasn't his thing – crime – that he was subtler than that. But he needed the money, perhaps he helped himself to more than his share, so some other specimen tracked him down and beat him to death. It's what low-life is all about.'

They'd reached reception and Nabbs turned to look back at the pylon. 'I think about him sometimes – Gedney – when I'm out on the surfboard. I think about his bones – what's left, you know – rolling over each other on the sea bed. Cheers me up.'

He smiled at last, while above them a wire hummed, as taut as a drawn bow.

35

Marcie Sley looked out to sea, her green eyes reflecting the surface of the water. Her husband stood six feet behind her on the beach, a precisely calibrated distance which seemed designed to let her remember alone, but to offer the consolation of company. Dryden watched them from the verandah of the chalet for several minutes as the physiotherapist worked inside, massaging Laura's back, oiling the skin and filling the small room with the sleepy aroma of almonds. The handheld COMPASS lay on the bed, the tickertape still blank.

It was a break, he knew that. And just in time. DI Reade would be there in the morning, but first he had a chance to talk to the one witness he was certain could tell him so much that he didn't know. What exactly had the children seen that night through the single porthole? And why had they been sent home in disgrace, while he had been spared?

Out on the sand the wind was rising and John Sley wrapped himself tighter in his black donkey jacket. Dryden briefly spoke to the physio, organizing another trip to the pool, then slipped out on to the verandah, jumped down on to the sand below and walked towards the distant couple, trying to imagine what Marcie was seeing through unseeing eyes: her brother Dex perhaps, unpicking the string on one of Smith's homemade kites, or the young Philip, staggering down the sides of the sun-splashed dunes with logs for the dam the children had built.

John Sley saw him first, and a word passed between the couple, the cigarette smoke dripping out of his mouth. In his other hand he held a key with a solid brass dolphin attached.

By the time Dryden was beside Marcie she was smiling. He felt again the urge to touch the skin, to be closer to the dense black hair.

Instead he stood, looking out to sea as well. 'So you're staying? First time back?'

Her hand rose, seeking her husband's. 'Yes. The phone call – you've got news?'

Dryden checked his watch, ignoring the question. 'You came quickly. Thank you. We don't have much time.'

'I wanted to come.'

They listened to a gang of seagulls fighting over a fishtail in the shallows. 'There was a boat – in the marshes, that summer. Can we see if it's still there?' she said. He nodded and took her arm, noting the deliberate use of the metaphor of sight.

They walked round the chalets and down towards the old camp. Dryden could almost feel the presence of the ten-year-old girl who'd held his hand within the covered boat, and he wondered if she too felt anything of the past.

John Sley had yet to speak, the cigarette still held in his shattered teeth.

There was a small bridge now over the ten-foot drain they had once jumped. They edged across it until they stood by the old sluice, rusted shut, while an ugly electric pump stood in its place in the dunes, humming.

'We're at a sluice,' said Dryden, his voice in neutral.

'We met here each night – the children,' said Marcie, bringing her shoulders up towards her ears like a child treasuring a memory. 'The boys were always late, and too excited. I could hear them coming through the dunes, it's a very boyish thing – that mixture of fear and bravado.'

Dryden turned south as the north wind brought in a flurry of snowflakes.

'Who was bravest?' he said. 'Smith? He would have been the oldest.'

'Yes, always,' she said, looking at him intensely now, the eyes shining. 'Declan could live with the fear because Smith was there. And Philip was there because he was too scared to say no – he never looked scared but I knew he was. There was a kind of electricity, a shell of anxiety.'

She looked around her, smiling. Dryden felt the pain of recognizing himself, not just then, but now.

'So we played the game,' she said. 'Sardines. Smith adapted it for the saltmarsh. One would hide, the others would spread out to find them. If you found the one who was hiding then you squeezed in and waited for the rest. It was ideal – the maximum injection of fear and excitement. There were only a dozen possible places, really – unless you took your chance in the reeds – so we always had time to finish. That night it was Philip who went first. It should have been Declan but there was a fight, and so we chose Philip instead. We gave him 100, then we killed the torches and spread out . . .' she said, taking a step towards the edge of the drain.

Dryden took her arm before her husband could, and she gripped his hand as if to tell him something. 'Which way?' he forced himself to ask. A seagull screeched overhead.

'The boat was to the south,' she said.

For half a mile they wove between the channels of the liquid maze, where the last high tide had left little crystal palaces of ice, paper-thin canopies hanging in the freezing air, abandoned by the retreating seawater.

At first Dryden thought the old boat was gone. Thirty years of wet rot and the sluicing of the tidal water must have slowly rubbed it out, an artist's mistake gently erased from a watery canvas. But as they stood on the bank he saw in the wet sand revealed by the tide the low-pitched roof of the *Curlew*, the seawater edging down her side to reveal the first graceful curve of the porthole, the glass as murky as a jellyfish.

Marcie's husband had hung back, his great fists loose by his sides, reluctant to share the past.

'There's a boat just here,' said Dryden. 'A porthole's showing.'

She nodded, living the memory within. 'We'd been searching for ten minutes, perhaps a bit more. Then we all heard it, a cry. It seemed very close, and very real. Within a minute we were there – everyone except Philip because he was hiding – and there was a boat moored in the reeds, the porthole lit, so we crept forward to look inside.'

Dryden imagined himself listening too, still hidden beneath the green tarpaulin.

'We didn't normally go that far – down to the river. There were boats passing sometimes, and a path. So Smith had said no, right from the start, that it was out of bounds for the game. But I crept forward anyway, and the others followed. The water was gurgling out with the tide and the fair was on at the camp so there was plenty of noise to cover us.'

Dryden slipped a hand through her arm and she shifted her weight so that they leant together.

'Paul Gedney was inside,' she said. She touched each eyelid with her fingertips. 'Smith and Declan saw him too. He had this mousy hair, cut short, and his shirt was off and he was well built, sort of marbled with muscle, grotesque really.'

'What was he doing?'

She shrugged. 'I think he'd passed out. He was lying in a bunk. There were loads of books, and food – biscuits, crisps, fruit. There was a generator running, and a single light, and clothes scattered about, and one of those plastic drinking barrels with a tap. And this box . . .'

Dryden led her down the bank towards the boat which, inch by inch, was emerging from the black water as the tide ebbed.

'What kind of box?'

'It was metal – aluminium perhaps: that white, blanched colour. It was ribbed and patterned on the outside, and it had a lid with two locks, about the size of one of those coolboxes you take on the beach. Perhaps that was it. His hand lay on it as if it was precious.'

She stood still, rebuilding the memory. 'Where's the boat?' she asked suddenly.

Dryden led her along the sand, crisp underfoot with ice. The *Curlew* had tipped to port over the years, lifting its starboard rail above the riverside bank. Dryden took her hand and put it on the frozen wood, edged with frost. On the stretch of exposed deck black crabs scuttled across the ice.

She gripped the rail. 'He was just lying there, but the sleeve of his shirt was rolled up and the arm was covered in blood, dripping down. There was a clean open wound – two inches, perhaps three.' She licked her lips and looked back, as if sensing her husband's presence against the skyline. 'The boys went back then, to find Philip – there were only a couple of places we hadn't checked. But while they were away it happened again . . .'

She brought her other hand up beside the first. 'He opened his eyes and he took the knife. The porthole was to his side, very close, but he was looking ahead or to the side where he'd strung up the light from the cabin roof. He cleaned his arm with a dressing – a medical dressing – and I could see the fresh wound still oozing the blood, and beside it another wound, still raw but not bleeding. The two wounds made a V-shape pattern on the muscle. Then he took the knife, put the point to the end of the fresh wound and drew it across his arm, again a few inches, opening up a third cut. Here . . .' She touched her upper left arm just below the joint with the shoulder. 'For a second the wound just gapped, and then it filled with blood, and he cried out again, that dreadful cry.'

Dryden heard the scream in his memory, with its hint of triumph. A zigzag wound, thought Dryden, and he saw another memory from that summer, of the subtle urgent rocking of white bodies in the sand.

'I heard the boys coming back then,' said Marcie. 'Behind me, but I just couldn't stop watching. Gedney's eyes were closed, but the pain made him jerk his head to one side, and when he opened them he was looking at us. That's why we remembered the face, and the eyes. It's what Declan said when he saw that poster the newspaper printed: "I'll never forget the eyes."

'We panicked then, and ran back through the marsh to the chalets. I was terrified, I think we all were – even Smith. We heard footsteps behind us, I think Declan always did.'

Dryden nodded and looked seawards, where a bank of black cloud stood on the horizon like a mountain range. 'Do you think he knew who you were – that night, I mean? Do you think Paul Gedney could have known who you were?'

'I know he did,' she said, breathing in the air, heavy now with damp as the ice storm finally edged towards the coast. 'Because of what happened the next day.'

36

Humph swung the cab off the coast road and up on to the sandy verge, the exhaust pipe whacking the grass with a dull thud. A flock of seagulls circled the Capri and Dryden guessed the cabbie had been jettisoning food at regular intervals from the driver's side window.

'I was asleep,' said Humph, brushing crumbs from his Ipswich Town top with a delicate hand.

He'd said nothing more when Dryden had rung twenty minutes earlier to ask for the pickup.

'Back to the Eel's Foot,' said Dryden, checking his watch. Flipping open his mobile he found another text message from DI Reade – another reminder to be available for interview the next morning. What he needed first was to hear the rest of Marcie Sley's story, to take it beyond the point where his childhood self had left the other children that summer's night.

They drove on in silence, the black, peat-black winter fields so featureless there was a powerful illusion they were standing still. The chimneys of the Eel's Foot came into view along the floodbank. He was at the bar when he heard the tyres of John Sley's 4x4 on the car park gravel. Dryden met Marcie at the door and found a table in a corner. Marcie's husband left them, sitting at the bar nursing a pint of beer and a local paper.

'Thanks,' said Marcie. 'I needed to warm up – and John's worried about me. Bronchitis, it comes and goes.' She turned her head towards the fireplace where the logs crackled, the source of the radiating heat.

Dryden lowered his voice. 'You said that you know for sure that Paul Gedney recognized you that night – how?'

Marcie patted the seat beside her, an unconscious effort to find her husband's hand. 'It's best if I just tell you what happened, all of it. In retrospect – now – we can see why it happened. But then, it was just baffling for us – for all of us. We were only children.'

The eyes had filled and Dryden was startled to find the question had brought her to an emotional edge. He wanted to hold her, to tell her quickly who he was, but the promise of the story to come held him back.

She pushed the base of her wineglass a few inches across the table top and Dryden guessed she didn't trust herself to lift it.

'I was woken up by Grace Elliot, my foster mother. It was just before seven on the morning after we'd run away from the boat. I can remember leaning over and reading the alarm clock, and then remembering two things, two really dreadful things: I remembered the night before, and then that it was the day we were going home. And then I was afraid, because she'd never knocked on the door before. Grace had two other kids – boys, toddlers, and they'd slept next door with her and Jack, her husband. Anyway, I got up and there was this man there on the stoop outside, a security guard.'

'What did you think?'

'I thought they knew – you know, that we'd been out at night.' She went for the wineglass and it tipped alarmingly as she took a sip. 'Anyway, he asked Grace if they could look under the chalet.'

'They?'

'There was a Blue Coat there too. He didn't say a word. But the security guard said there'd been a complaint about us – he didn't mean the whole family, he spelt it out – he meant us . . .'

'You, Dex and Smith . . .' said Dryden.

'Yes,' she said, suddenly smiling again, that secret smile. 'He said there'd been a spate of thefts in the camp and that they'd had information – that's exactly what he said: "information" – that it was us. That someone had seen us, after dark, out amongst the huts.'

Dryden leant back and drained his pint.

'He said they didn't want to call the police. I can remember the relief even now – pathetic, really; I should have just gone on saying we were innocent. He said it was probably all a misunderstanding, but they needed to look under the huts. So Grace said they could.'

She laughed. 'It was underneath, of course. We'd got a string bag, for the beach things. It was usually stuffed under the steps. But they found it buried, full: biscuits and sweets, some cash – I remember a five-pound note – a couple of watches, and a single ring – a gold wedding ring. He laid it all out on the bed, on my bed. I just looked at it and Mum looked at me.'

Dryden refilled their glasses at the bar and checked that Humph was still happy, the cab gently vibrating to an Estonian nursery rhyme.

'Grace left the kids with Jack and took me to the office. Smith and Declan were already there and on the table was another bag – Declan's bag from St Vincent's, I remember the purple crest. And there was more stuff: a fountain pen, a hip flask, a musical box with a silver lock, just a magpie's haul really. The kind of stuff kids love.'

'No police?' asked Dryden.

She shook her head. 'No. Not even then. They said they didn't want the publicity. Declan said thank you. He was crying, and Smith held him. The security guard was different this time. I guess he was the one in charge. He said they couldn't just forget it. They had to do something, just to make sure we never came back, in case the police did get involved. So he wrote a letter, setting out what had happened, and he put a statement with it from the Blue Coat as well. Then they copied them on a machine, three copies, and gave Grace two.'

'What did she do?'

'She drove us all home – that morning. We went back to the chalets and packed. Grace had got most of it all sorted anyway the night before. We just got our stuff into the car and piled in. I can't remember much . . .'

She looked towards the wineglass. 'She drove to St Vincent's first and dropped the boys off. We all saw it. She gave the letter to the priest. Declan looked so fragile, Smith was better. He was strong enough for both of them, otherwise I really don't believe my brother would have got through it.

'Then she took us home. Nothing happened for a week. I didn't ask, but I knew. She'd been talking about taking Declan as well, so we could be together. But I knew that wouldn't happen now. And then the next weekend – on the Saturday night – we heard this row downstairs. It was her and Jack shouting, and it was a real shock because they never argued. Then the next day she just told me to pack, that I was going back to the council home. I'd been with her three months, which was the trial period, but they'd decorated my room, and we'd talked about holidays for the next summer. I'd have stayed, I know that. But it changed everything. She said she'd never see me again, and she hasn't. She might be dead now and I wouldn't know, she wasn't that strong.'

She covered her mouth and lifted the wineglass, so Dryden looked away. 'You told them you didn't steal those things?' he asked.

'We did. But only once, that first morning. After that it wasn't the most important thing. The most important thing was avoiding the police, getting away from there. And we didn't want to say where we were – out in the marshes. That would just have been admitting we were not in the chalets, that we could have been out thieving. We couldn't talk together so we didn't know what we'd said. It happened so quickly I don't think any of us had the wit to see the link – between what we'd seen the night before and what had happened the next morning. But it's clear now, isn't it? That they'd done it to get us away, before we could go back to the boat. If we'd told someone, they wouldn't have believed us – and there's no way Gedney would still have been there – not that day, not that morning.

'So we just went along with it, their version of what we'd done. Except for one thing. They asked who the other boy was. But we never told them that.'

Dryden felt that sense of loss again, for the children who had refused to betray him. 'And the Blue Coat?'

'Well – yes. An irony. It was Chips Connor. Mum had paid for swimming lessons, so we knew him. We were terrified, of course, so I can't remember much, but like I said, they gave him a kind of statement to sign – you know, just setting out that he'd gone to look under the huts and that he'd found the bags and what had been inside. And we all watched, and his hand just shook, like a leaf, shook so much he could hardly hold the pen.'

37

Out at sea, the bank of advancing cloud was now an almost tangible barrier. It appeared to drop to the surface of the water itself, and Dryden watched as a falling curtain of snow turned a red container ship grey before obliterating it entirely.

Dryden and Marcie Sley sat in a perspex shelter by the Dolphin's swimming pool, shielded from the wind. The blind woman was still, the wind buffeting the shelter at her back, while Dryden described the scene.

'There are clouds at sea,' he said. 'Creeping in. But it's snow still, no sign yet of the rain.'

Marcie's husband had gone back to their chalet, but Dryden still sensed his antagonism. Humph had retreated to the sand dunes with the Capri, the dog and a bag of chips.

Dryden was acutely aware that Marcie Sley had yet to ask again about the witness he had uncovered, the missing boy. Trying to postpone the moment further, he found his own question.

'Tell me about John,' he said. 'Have you ever seen him?'

She laughed. 'No. No, I haven't. But I could tell his face in a thousand,' she said, stretching out her fingers inside her gloves. 'I trust him with my life, Dryden – quite literally. But he doesn't trust you. Forgive him, he's not a sociable man at all, but he loved the Gardeners' – and he could spend time with Declan and Joe. They were happy there, and so was I.'

She ungloved her right hand and reached out, taking his own. 'And he doesn't trust you because he doesn't know who you are. But I do. *Philip.*'

Dryden laughed, strangely elated by the moment of recognition. She held out both her hands, palm up, and he meshed his fingers with hers. 'I wondered why you hadn't asked. A guess?'

A blast of snow peppered the perspex. Her face, suddenly animated, looked younger, and Dryden saw again the girl who had played in the dunes.

'Perhaps, at first. There was something when we met – at the Gardeners'. I don't know what it was, but first names are odd like that. I always think you can end up liking people you should hate just because their name reminds you of someone you liked. I've always liked the name – perhaps that's down to you.' She smiled. 'When you called it made me think – but it seemed such an extraordinary coincidence, that you should be . . . our Philip. But it isn't, is it? You're a reporter, they died in Ely. Then today, down by the old boat, you called Joe plain Smith – but I thought that might be something you'd found in the files, or a cutting. But Dex – I knew then, I don't think anyone has called him Dex for twenty years.'

In the distance, through the side window of the shelter, Dryden saw John Sley standing under the canopy by the camp's reception, a flare of light briefly illuminating his face as he lit a cigarette.

'I'm sorry. When we were children . . .' He stopped, recognizing what an extraordinary statement that was. 'When we were children – I didn't think there was anything wrong – with your sight, I mean.'

She nodded, and released his hand. 'When I left the home in Peterborough – that was in '82, Christmas – I just walked out, I was old enough, past my eighteenth, anyway. There were schemes, a hostel, all sorts of safety nets I guess. But I knew better. I had a friend who'd gone into a squat in a terraced house down by the river. It was unbelievably exciting, being free from . . . from everything, and it outweighed what I should have seen, that the house was dangerous, that the drink and drugs would crush me like they crush everyone.

'But I let it happen. It is really disorientating, that kind of experience. I can't really remember anything concrete, real, about the next three years at all. I drew benefit and I know that one day someone from the council tracked me down and said that there was still a place in the hostel. I laughed in his face, and then when we'd chucked him out I locked myself in the bathroom and cried. I just didn't have the guts to do the right thing.

'One day in summer we crashed out down in the park, all of us, and when we got back the landlords had moved in and boarded the place up. There was tape over the windows and new locks. I had this box, a writing box, which Grace – my foster mum – had given me before I'd left and it was on the lorry. I lifted it out but this bailiff just pushed me over and took it back. After that I ended up sleeping rough, around the city centre mainly, there's a place under the inner by-pass where they let you sleep in cardboard boxes. I had this dog and we begged on the pedestrian subway.'

Dryden found his hip flask and sipped the malt. 'Were you in touch with Dex?'

She shook her head and dropped her chin. 'I wasn't in touch with anything. The last time I'd seen Declan was in '81. He was still at St Vincent's then – and so was Joe. Declan was fourteen. We had a day together, in Peterborough. They dropped him off by mini-van. He cried most of the time – they'd punished them, you see – for the theft. They'd taken them off the register for adoption and fostering – Declan said they were losing kids and the place was running down and he thought they'd done it just to keep the numbers up. And they abused them. Because they could. They'd locked him in a toilet cubicle; he said they often did it, that he'd be there for days. It's incredible, isn't it? That's where the claustrophobia came from, of course. I could tell how scared he was when they came to pick him up.'

'And that was because of the letter that was sent home with them, from the camp?'

'Yes. As far as I know they did nothing to check it out, they just took it for the truth. That was wrong too, Dryden. Another injustice.'

She accepted the flask. 'I was never an alcoholic. I hated it really – even what it did.' She drank and handed it back. 'Then one day I went down to the exchange to pick up the benefit and they gave me this form to fill in – they did it most times. And I looked at it and I couldn't see bits – they were just like black patches in my vision, moving, slipping. I was frightened then, so when they gave me an appointment at the clinic I went. But it was too late.'

A gust hit the shelter like a blow, whipping over and dashing snow into the empty swimming pool. Through the perspex Dryden could see a jagged white seascape.

'Toxocariasis,' she said. 'You catch it from dog shit. There are worms, and if the eggs get in your eyes you get this disease. I had it in both – and the retinas were damaged. They tried to stop it but by the winter I couldn't see at all.'

Dryden nodded. 'And John?'

'Being blind saved me. I couldn't survive down there any more, not on the street. I got the place in the hostel and a disability allowance with the benefit. They found Declan for me, he was on benefit, and he came to Peterborough. He said he had these friends and that there was somewhere I could stay. I said no to the flat, I needed to be alone, but it was spring then – 1987 – so they put up a bed in the Gardeners' Arms. Joe's business was going well: like I told you, he'd given John a job at the factory. He was part of the crowd. We got married that winter. He saved my life.'

Dryden nodded. 'You didn't say what John had done to get put away.'

'He'd been in and out most of his life, mainly burglary, but he had good hands too . . .' She smiled. 'Safes. It's a dying art. He'd got five years for the last one. And that *was* the last one. But he still has good hands.' She shivered, clasping her coat at her neck.

Dryden's shoulders began to shake in the suddenly damp cold.

They stood. 'I must get back to him,' she said. 'Can I ask you something? The solicitor said you'd found the missing witness. I think you let him presume something, didn't you? That young Philip had seen what we'd seen that night?'

Dryden pressed her hand. 'It's a presumption he made, yes. And it might be true. I can't think of any other way of finding out who killed them.'

She tried to find his eyes with hers. 'I'm sorry, it was unfair of me, it's *brave* of you. They ruined our lives, didn't they, just as they could have ruined yours. Have you asked Ruth yet? Asked her who told Chips Connor to look under the huts?'

Dryden shook his head. 'No. But it's not the only question she has to answer, it's just first in the queue.'

38

The lorry driver was trapped inside the cab of the HGV parked on the tarmac outside the Dolphin's glass-fronted reception block. Steam from the engine rose in clouds which obscured the lorry's windscreen. Russell Fleet, embedded in an oversized fluorescent green windjammer, was working on the passenger side lock with a hair dryer. Through the side window Dryden could see the driver reading the *Sun* spread out on the steering wheel.

'Freezing locks. The windows are jammed too,' said Russell. 'The snow's damp. The forecast says we'll get the ice storm tomorrow.' The flaccid skin of his face was flushed and, despite the cold, a sheen of sweat glinted on his forehead. Dryden was struck again by the almost tangible odour of illness which hung over the Dolphin's assistant manager. It looked like he'd been out in the weather for hours, his hair matted with ice and the outer fabric of his windjammer flecked with water.

The lorry's rear lights glowed in the gloom, the sign on the side of the container read: *Propane Direct – Heat in a Hurry!*

'Hasn't the camp got its own generator?' he shouted to Fleet over the wind.

'Sure. But it's for emergency lighting and the freezers. The Grid's just been on with a warning. They can't guarantee power if they can't get the ice off the pylons. We'd be pushed to run electric storage heaters in the chalets on the generator. These are a back-up.'

Dryden looked up and let his eye trace the looping lines of wire overhead. The electric hum of the power, audible even above the storm, was clearer now, a jagged whine, like fingernails across a blackboard.

Suddenly with a thud the locks on the HGV sprung, liberating the driver. He dropped the tailgate to reveal a stack of gas-fired portable heaters, each one a foot-long cylinder on a stand connected to a high-pressure container. In the sub-zero air Dryden sniffed the intoxicating scent of lighter fuel.

Fleet ran back into the office and reappeared with a gang of daytime staff and they started to offload the heaters onto a trailer slung behind a miniature tractor used in the summer months to run the camp's 'train' between reception and the beach. It was nursery-school yellow with Disney characters on each side and a red bell on the bonnet, but now the paintwork was ribbed with streaks of ice.

Fleet raised his voice against the wind. 'We'll take one to every chalet that's occupied,' he told his reluctant workforce. 'You've got master keys. If there's someone in, explain – I've sent 'em an e-mail on the TV with instructions. Remember – tell 'em not to panic. It's just in case. And tell them to keep an eye on the flame – if it gets blown out they need to relight it, otherwise the gas can build up.'

A battered Citroën estate swung through the camp gates and pulled up alongside the HGV. A woman at the wheel, brushing mousy hair back from her eyes, peered out through the windscreen. In the back two children fought between car seats.

Fleet's shoulders sagged. 'Bloody hell. Now what?'

The woman dropped the passenger-side window. 'Russ.' The voice was tired and edgy. 'School's closed; no prep, either. The heating's failed. Can you?' She looked behind her at the brawling children.

'Jesus,' he said. 'How long? Not tonight, Jean, please.'

'I'll pick them up about eight – OK? There's a crisis at work . . .' She tried a grin but Fleet's eyes hardened. 'If you'd learn to drive it would make life a lot easier,' she said.

Fleet pulled open the rear door. 'What's the point of paying the bloody fees?' The children untangled themselves from seatbelts. 'OK, kids. Come on. You can go on the machines.' A ritual cheer greeted the news and the young teenagers, a boy and girl so close in age and looks they might be twins, ran towards the Dolphin's foyer doors. They didn't say goodbye as the woman swung the Citroën violently in a semicircle and bounced over the speed hump at the security gate. In the falling snow the tail-lights were lost within twenty yards.

'She works then, your wife?' said Dryden, as they both headed for the warmth of reception.

'She's my partner, actually,' said Russell pointedly, then he bit his lip. 'Yup. School fees – they're crippling. They stay late for prep and stuff, otherwise it's not fair on them, you know – latchkey kids and everything. But we didn't want them to board, no family life that way. Jean's got a business too . . . accountants, they work all hours.'

The light in the sky was gone, the chalet lanterns picked out in rows running down towards the sea. Briefly, beyond Lighthouse Cottage, the buoy flashed red twice, and then white. They could hear the sea now, distinct from the wind, a howl of sand and pebbles.

Dryden took one of the heaters off the trailer. 'I'll take one of these now, if it's OK,' he said.

The reception doors whisked open automatically and they met Ruth Connor, clutching her elbows in the sudden wedge of cold air which came in with them. 'Russ, the kids? Is that sensible tonight?'

Fleet unzipped the windjammer and ignored his boss. 'Mr Dryden,' she said, still looking at Fleet. 'George Holme phoned about Chips' appeal – can we talk? Ten minutes in the bar? It looks like I owe you a drink.'

Fleet rubbed his face with both hands and watched her go. 'It's gonna be a long night,' he said. 'I'll join you.'

The Floral Bar was warm and low-lit, a haven from the rawness of the night outside, its dark wood panelling reflecting the art deco lamps. Behind the bar was one of the staff, a teenager in an ill-fitting white shirt and a strangulating black tie. Fleet's children were playing on a bank of machines in an alcove off the old ballroom floor.

Dryden watched as Fleet ordered two bottles of luminescent pop and grabbed a brace of crisp packets. Returning, he went behind the bar and poured Dryden a whisky and a large vodka for himself, which he downed, and then refilled the glass. They listened in silence to the electronic shuffle of the gaming machines and the gentle chug of coins dropping.

Fleet seemed uncomfortable with the absence of conversation. He shrugged, as if he'd made a silent decision. 'So – like Ruth says, the lawyers have rung. Holme. Good news?'

'I think so. I'd better fill her in first, though. Courtesy.'

Fleet licked his lips. 'Sure.'

'How's business?' asked Dryden, playing for time.

'Well – considering it's the worst winter on record – bloody great. We've got fifteen chalets taken. It only needs five to cover our costs. That's the real point, you see – usually this kind of operation you have to lay off all the summer staff, mothball the place. That way you never get any better, you just have to retrain new staff every spring. It's like Groundhog Day. Nightmare. This way we can keep people ticking over – and they can get away, holidays and that, which means you

265

can keep the people who work, the ones that really care. The quality of the service improves, you get better customers, you can charge them higher fees. Off you go.'

Dryden considered Fleet and thought how dreary it was to find someone motivated by making money to the point that they'd live with an accountant.

'Must be worth a few bob, then – the Dolphin.'

'Yeah. Some of the big leisure groups have shown an interest – you know, Center Parcs, Warner's . . . but it's not for sale.'

Ruth Connor came in and joined them, armed with another smile from the brochure. She'd clearly heard the end of the conversation. 'So. Russell's been filling you in on the business. Our business.' She handed Fleet a pile of correspondence. 'Post just in off the van, Russ – could you?

'Let's talk,' she said turning to Dryden, waiting only for the barman to pour her a glass of wine before shepherding him into one of the booths surrounding the ballroom. Fleet took the pile of letters and went to the far end of the bar to sort them, taking with him a large bunch of keys.

A gust of wind made the window beside them flex. 'So, good news,' she said. 'You've found our elusive witness. That's unbelievable. Chips deserves this, you know, after everything that's happened.'

'Yes,' he said, noting how she sipped the wine, sensing a genuine electricity, a spark of excitement, perhaps – or fear.

'Tell me. How did they come forward?'

'I've spent some time on this case, Mrs Connor – there are some surprising twists and turns. Let's just call it fate. I think you can look forward to the possibility – at the very least – that your husband will be coming home soon.'

He smiled, knowing she was smart enough to read between the lines.

She was looking at him when her eyes filled suddenly with tears.

'I know you think I'm a fraud, Mr Dryden.' She held up a hand before Dryden could deny it. 'William tells me you've taken an interest in my private life. It is none of your business, of course, but I think you'll find there are no surprises here for Chips. What happens when he gets out is up to him. The important thing is that he'll be free to do what he wants. You may not believe it, but that is very important to me – and to William, actually.'

Dryden took his telling-off like a man. 'I realize that your main concern is getting Chips out – but I'm quite interested in the question that comes next: if he didn't beat Paul Gedney to death, who did? The morning after the children saw him in the old boat they were sent home – they were accused of a series of petty thefts in the camp. I presume you'd made the connection, that you recall the incident? In the circumstances it was all the more remarkable that they came forward at all. Can you remember anything about that – who accused them, for example?'

She creased her brow as if trying to reconstruct the scene. 'It was quite a minor incident, Mr Dryden. We had to deal with that kind of thing a lot then.'

'It was the morning after they'd seen Gedney – you must remember . . .'

She rose. 'Must I? Must I really?'

Dryden sensed anger again and held up his hands by way of capitulation. 'Sorry. I know it is a long time ago.'

She took her seat again. 'Yes. And don't forget, we didn't know any of that then. It was just another case of petty theft, as I say – and not the first.' She downed the wine and picked up his empty tumbler. 'Can I get you another malt?'

While Fleet poured the drinks they talked in low whispers.

When she ferried them to Dryden's table she'd recovered her composure completely, her chin held elegantly high. 'I do recall it, of course, and I know why. We'd asked the security guards to keep an eye out after dark – there was always some petty theft, as I said, but things had got worse. The problem was keeping the police out – it's not a great advert for a fun-filled holiday. And the staff get jumpy too. That night there'd been a disturbance in one of the chalets and the guard had gone down to check things out. A domestic, of course; people always take the opportunity to throw our ornaments on holiday rather than their own.'

Dryden let the whisky burn his throat.

'Anyway, he was down there and he saw the children running back through the camp – this was late, after 10.30. He didn't see where the boys went but the girl's chalet was by the main pool, and he said he saw her putting something under the hut. Next morning he asked Chips to have a look . . . Once they'd found the stuff, they checked the brother's hut, too.'

'Why Chips?'

'First up. It was one way he avoided people. He'd do the pool, checking the chemicals, netting any leaves or rubbish. I was usually up for seven – but Chips had been up an hour by then, more. He'd just creep out of bed with the dawn.

'Anyway, they found plenty of stuff. Sad, really – we couldn't take kids like them ever again after that – kids from the orphanage. But we take young offenders, outward bound in the autumn – so we do our bit – but they come with their social workers so we don't have to worry.'

Dryden nodded. 'Why was it unfortunate that Chips was involved?'

'We didn't call the police – nothing like that; it's hardly ever worth it, and, as I said, we don't relish the publicity.

But Chips had to face these kids, and he had to make a statement which we sent to the authorities – the council for the girl and a Catholic orphanage for the boys. It was very stressful for him, too much really. We'd been considering getting him away all that summer, but that was the trigger. I guess these days we'd say he had a breakdown. We found him in the dunes later that day. So he went away – a private clinic near Lynn.'

'Which is where he was arrested for the murder of Paul Gedney.'

'Indeed.'

'This guard – the one who spotted the kids – do you have a name?'

'Um . . .' She looked towards the office. 'I'm sure we'll have it on record. Dad was meticulous about the staff. I could check . . . tomorrow perhaps?'

Dryden smiled, leaning forward, thinking that tomorrow DI Reade would be running the investigation. 'No chance tonight? I'd really like to get something wrapped up for my paper. If someone framed Chips then there's a good chance they framed the kids as well. This security guard has never been interviewed, none of this was part of the original inquiry.'

She smiled, not moving. Dryden realized she had the strength and the will to defy him. He listened to the clock over the bar chime the hour.

'There is still a chance, Mrs Connor, that the police will be forced to reopen Chips' file. George Holme is pressing the Chief Constable's Office to at least review the case. If they do they will want to talk to this man. Whoever framed the kids almost certainly killed Paul Gedney. Wouldn't it be a bright idea to try and find him now?'

She couldn't fault the logic. 'Bring your drink,' she said,

standing. They went behind the bar and down a short corridor with panelled walls to the foot of a narrow staircase which led up a single flight to a landing.

Ruth Connor struggled with a double lock to the only door. 'This is daft. I can see that man as clearly as I can see you. It's just his name . . . I think it was Jack – but that's not much good on its own, is it?'

The office was spacious and modern – the 1930s art deco ceiling design obscured by a thick coat of white paint. Two PCs and a laser printer hummed on a desk suite. A TV monitor in the corner showed the bar, and Russell Fleet still bent over the post. One wall was covered with a staff rota; framed sunshine publicity shots covered the rest: minor celebrities pictured hugging total strangers.

'Is this the original office?' asked Dryden.

'Yes. Indeed. But there's not much left from the old days, I'm afraid – it didn't have the *charm* of the bar,' she said, laughing. Dryden, distrusting the sudden upbeat mood, failed to return the smile.

'The safe?' he asked, knowing it was the right question.

She laughed again, but this time Dryden sensed she was playing for time. 'When was the last time you saw someone pay for a holiday with cash?'

Dryden nodded, recognizing that he hadn't got an answer.

'Here. Staff wage records.' She swung a drawer out from a filing cabinet and put a ledger on the table, beginning to flick back through the large pages covered in copperplate. 'I don't think he was ever on the database. I'll know the name when I see it.'

Dryden stood waiting, wondering if it really took this long. He studied the pictures on the wall and his eye was drawn to one: Ruth Connor had mentioned an outward bound course for young offenders and here they were, a group of six, arms thrown around necks, posing on the windswept sands, and in the background one of the course leaders – Ed Bardolph, Declan McIlroy's social worker.

'Here . . .' she said, stabbing a finger on the page. 'Potts. Francis Peter. That was him – Frank Potts. Told you it was Jack! Dad took him on, but he was good, absolutely straight as a die.'

'Remember anything about him?' asked Dryden, wondering about Bardolph, trying to concentrate on Frank Potts, feeling again the unnatural caress of coincidence.

Outside they heard the wind drop, the gritty patter of the falling hail suddenly silent.

She smiled, putting the book back. 'I do, actually. He liked being a security guard so much he decided to make a career out of it. He became a policeman. You might still be able to find him.'

'Any idea where I could start?' asked Dryden.

She let the file drawer close with a crash. 'I think we got a card at Christmas for a few years. New Zealand, Australia? Yes – Melbourne, or Sydney. Somewhere like that.'

The internal telephone bleeped from the desk and Ruth Connor hit a button. A loud static-scarred voice filled the room. 'Mrs Connor? You asked me to let you know. Mr Nabbs phoned in, he'll be with you in ten minutes.'

'Kate, thanks. Can you send him straight up to the office – and we'll have a pot of coffee.'

Ruth Connor didn't bother with a smile this time. 'If you'll excuse us, Mr Dryden. An evening's work, I'm afraid.'

'Right. I'll get on the track of Frank Potts, then. Just about anywhere in the southern hemisphere, right?'

But she wasn't listening any more, or even pretending she was. Dryden saw himself out and went back to the bar, where he sat on a stool for ten minutes, thinking about where you would hide a safe. He saw William Nabbs arrive and head for the office, walking quickly, carrying a single holdall, unmarked, and obviously heavy.

39

From the verandah of the chalet it looked as if the sea had deserted the coast for good. Moonlit sand stretched to the horizon, where a glimmering white chalk line hinted at breaking surf a mile offshore. The air was still, the wind blown out for now. According to teletext on the chalet TV the ice storm was still twelve hours offshore, wheeling in with a deep anticyclone.

He'd sat with Laura for an hour until he knew she was asleep; waited another, sipping malt.

The bedside radio beeped the hours and the incantation of the shipping forecast began. In nine hours DI Reade would be at the camp with his team, and the following morning he would have to take Laura back to The Tower. Dryden would make his statement, then step into the background. The detective would play it by the book, tie up any loose ends left by the original inquiry, test out Declan and Joe's story. But Dryden knew now that the heart of the mystery was still impenetrable, and would certainly defeat the half-hearted inquiry DI Reade was determined to conduct. Dryden had failed, failed the friends who had refused to fail him.

He flicked on the bedside monitor and stepped outside: flashing the torch three times into the darkness. Carefully descending the ice-covered steps he set out along the beach towards the high bank of marram grass where he knew Humph lurked in the Capri. It was time to send the cabbie home.

Dryden stood on the high-water mark amongst fractured

sheets of ice left by the receding sea. The beach was a land-scape revealed, a foreign country normally hidden beneath the North Sea. The power and swiftness of the falling tide had left the wide sands incised deeply with miniature valleys, channels, coves and hills, a country of black shadow and gentle curves as seductive as a desert. The red buoy, which at high water rode out the waves in the middle of the bay, lay on its side in a trickling brook. There was a single island, a sandy outcrop in the shape of a teardrop topped with grass. Here, in the summer, the lifeguards flew their flags. Tonight a red flag lay frozen to the staff.

A dog barked and, turning west, Dryden saw Boudicca, briefly cresting a moonlit sandhill before falling again into a lightless hollow. Humph hove into view, as substantial as the beached buoy in the channel below.

Dryden joined him, his footsteps up the incline marked by deep shadow-filled footprints.

'A ball?' said Humph, when he joined him, pointing inland.

They were above the stream that was all that was left of Morton's Leam at low tide. Trundling down the brook was a round glass fisherman's float – colourless in the moon-light, held within a rope harness. It bobbed as it weaved along the sinuous line of the S-bends, catching occasionally on the sand, before bolting on towards the sea.

'Any progress?' asked Humph, taking the tennis ball from Boudicca's jaws and sending it skittering off downhill again.

'A bit, but not enough. There may be a motive – or two. Scratch a place like this there's all sorts of hidden stories just beneath the surface. I can think of several reasons why someone would want to keep Chips Connor inside, but when it comes to finding who killed Paul Gedney the cupboard is virtually bare. There is only one person in the camp who was here that summer – and that's Ruth Connor. She's lying about something, and her husband was a burden to her, but for the life of me I can't think she had a decent motive for murder.'

'There's you,' said Humph. 'You were here that summer.'

'Right. So I did it? Thanks.' He shivered, sensing the temperature falling beneath a clear sky. Looking inland he saw something else following the float down to the sea. 'That's odd,' he said. It was two things, something round like another float, but behind it something smaller, pointing up out of the water. The two bobbed together, a few feet apart, clearly tied beneath the surface.

'Come on,' said Dryden, dropping quickly down the face of the bank to the stream's edge.

Whatever it was, it was in midstream, moving swiftly with the icy water. Just below the point where the stream cut through the dunes the channel widened into a pool, and here the objects circled, waiting for the stream to nudge them out into the final stretch to the sea.

Dryden edged out in the water, feeling the icy coldness at his toes. It looked like the float was wreathed in weed, but the other smaller object was suddenly clearer and Dryden's heart missed a beat upon recognition: it was a glove, grey-green in the moonlight, the fingers vertical.

'Humph!' he shouted, wading out, the water stingingly cold. He tracked it now as it swung past, and the glove, leading, caught an incline of hidden sand which slowed it, bringing the float towards the bank in a graceful arc.

He was six feet away now and he saw the weed-encrusted fisherman's buoy for what it was: a human head. Between skull and hand an expanse of black material spread, just submerged. The head, the weeds revealed as matted hair, was face down. Humph was at his side, the rasp of breath painful.

'Shit,' said the cabbie. He trudged in, grabbed the arm beneath the glove, and hauled the body round and half out on the sand. The water ran out of the clothes and an eel zigzagged back towards the safety of the black pool. The body was clad in a thermal tracksuit, Dryden saw now, dark blue with fashionable piping.

The corpse was splayed like a starfish: the head wasn't turned down as Dryden had thought but ricked violently to the left, the face obscured by the hair and weeds. The left arm was flung back like the right but at the elbow bent back again, the hand turned up as the rigor contorted the limbs. Between the thermal glove and the tracksuit sleeve a chunky sportsman's wristwatch showed.

Dryden pulled the body up by the shoulder, fully into the moonlight and lifted the hair clear of the face. The pallor was purple-white, like a beached jellyfish. There was some ugly black bruising at the neck, below the ear, and across one cheekbone, but it was clear enough who it was, or who it had been. The last time Dryden had seen that face it had been peering dreamily into a make-believe swimming pool, where a woman in a white swimsuit swam languid lengths. Chips Connor had come home.

The Dolphin Holiday Camp
Saturday, 31 August 1974

Philip ran to the dunes and climbed them to a place he knew where a bowl of sand like a seat looked out over the sea. Here he'd often sat after breakfast waiting for the other children to come, whooping, out from the chalets and down onto the beach. He sat this last time, letting the minutes of summer tick away as the waves swept in across the empty morning beach. Soon he'd be home on the Fen, with a new horizon, home for winter, and this world would not be his again. He knew that now, but dug his hands down into the sand, as if clinging to the surface of the earth, and felt the coolness beneath.

The cry, when it came, reminded him of the night before: the pain, with pleasure in the release. It was close, in the dry grass, and the voices were so low that they seemed to be inside his head. He edged forward, careful not to breast the crest of the dunes where he could be seen against the sky, until he saw below a miniature valley in the sand, blown out by the winds, an amphitheatre unseen from the beach. In the centre were the ashes of a fire. There was a rug of green, a bedspread, and two bodies intertwined as one, seen through the dry grass.

He heard her first, the words in a rhythm as if kneading dough. 'I told you, they're gone. Relax now.'

She sat up on his waist, her hair in a red scarf, wisps of blonde hanging free, her face turned away. Philip didn't understand the way they moved, the man's hand played on the sun-splashed skin. But only one hand. The other lay beside him curled, the fat bicep turned outwards so that Philip could see the jagged angry thunderbolt of the scar.

Then he ran.

40

Tuesday, 10 January

Within the hour the sea had spilled back into the pool, edging up towards the sand dunes. Dryden and Humph dragged Chips Connor's body to the high-water mark, pulling it through the broken ice and flotsam onto the sandy path beyond. A police squad car, answering Dryden's mobile call, edged down through the seagrass, its tyres crunching in the frost. The moonlight shone into Connor's open and unblinking eyes. The black body bag, stiff with ice, cracked as they zipped it up. In his memory Dryden saw another corpse, curled on a doorstep, shrouded in ice.

The wind, blustery now, threw spray over the pathologist, whose examination was cursory. Chips Connor's pale hand, reclaimed from the frozen glove, seemed to call the tide inland. Lighthouse Cottage was requisitioned as a temporary morgue, and Dryden told to wait there for the arrival of the duty inspector from Lynn, while Humph was allowed to retreat with Boudicca to the privacy of the Capri. Dryden left them there, hugging each other.

Lighthouse Cottage bustled with discreet activity and the edgy electronic static of police radios. William Nabbs gave Dryden coffee and threw driftwood on an open fire set quickly beneath a brushed aluminium hood in the kitchen: the clock above read 1.30am. Chips Connor's body had been taken inside first, through to the front room. Outside, a group of uniformed PCs, conducting a fingertip search of the beach, dunes and riverbank in relay teams, made periodic appearances for hot drinks and shelter.

Nabbs drank coffee too. His hair was matted and wet, the blond dyed streaks in stripes through the natural brown. By the door stood a sea rod and tackle, while on the deal table lay a brace of cod glistening in the flickering light, more life in their iridescent scales than in their dead eyes. Dryden, vaguely aware that Nabbs had put something strong in the coffee, watched in fascination as blood dripped from the open mouths to the quarry-tiled floor beneath.

'You OK?' said Nabbs, fussing with the wood.

Dryden nodded. 'Fine. I like midnight walks, I deserve what I get.'

A DI arrived, a raincoat stiff with ice plastered to his legs. He was young – mid-thirties – and would have been keen if he hadn't just worked forty hours straight. He had weak eyes, close together, in a face which looked worried at rest. He introduced himself as Detective Inspector John Parlour of King's Lynn CID, and tried to suck some nicotine from a packet of low-tar menthol cigarettes.

'Where is she?' asked Nabbs, giving the detective coffee too, complete with whisky.

The DI leant his back against the door. 'She's with a WPC now, up in the flat. They won't be long – then they'll bring her here.'

They all glanced at the living-room door.

Nabbs nodded. 'I just don't understand . . . How can it be Chips?'

He looked at Dryden for an answer while the DI consulted a notebook. 'There's some confusion at Wash Camp,' said Parlour. 'The governor is talking to his people now but Connor was counted in at lunch and out again at 1.30pm, went to his room and then to the gym for an hour, that's his daily routine. Then there was a run, outside. Then the weather turned bad, the light went, they brought them in early. The next time there was a count was back in the showers at 3.00pm – he wasn't there. They were running in tracksuits and that's what he's got on now. Plus a wedding ring and the watch.'

'It's twenty-five miles away,' said Nabbs. 'More.'

The DI shrugged. 'He could have hitched – he could have run and walked. He had the time. Map?'

Nabbs spread an Ordnance Survey sheet out on the kitchen table, edging the fish to one end, cleaning the trail of blood away with a piece of kitchen towel. Briefly Dryden imagined he could smell the haemoglobin, a rusty metallic edge which made him wince.

With a finger Nabbs traced the course of the main river back inland. One tributary led towards the prison, stopping short by five miles.

'He could have fallen in there,' said Nabbs. 'Suicide?'

DI Parlour shook his head, the cigarette clamped between his lips. 'I'm afraid not,' he said, launching the stub into the flames of the fire. 'Pathologist says the neck was broken, the head twisted round and back over the left shoulder. He's only making an educated guess but there appears to be little fluid in the lungs – so it's probable he was dead before he hit the water. Hypothesis has to be he was attacked from behind, his chin wrenched round, then dumped.'

Parlour put down the coffee cup and, interlacing his fingers, cracked the bones.

Dryden nodded. 'A few problems with all that. You'll find the channels up inland are frozen – they have been for a week. He's got to have fallen into salt water, below the tidal reach of the main channel – about a mile inland, or in the marshes over here.' He pointed to the intricate tracery of channels to the west of the camp. 'When you get the water off his clothes or out of his lungs I bet you very little of it's fresh. And there were strands of weed on the body – that points to the marshes too.'

'Right,' said Parlour, making a note.

'So he got here sometime this afternoon – probably late,' said Dryden, just – he thought – as Paul Gedney had done more than thirty years before.

The door opened and a WPC brought in Ruth Connor. Naturally pale, she'd blanched further, some hastily applied lipstick a gash across the face. Dryden, who relied almost entirely on first impressions when judging character, thought she looked genuinely shocked, her eyes fighting to keep focused on the real world around her. Dryden felt she made a conscious effort not to look at William Nabbs, but took a chair by the fire and a whisky she hadn't asked for.

'One moment please, Mrs Connor,' said DI Parlour, opening the living-room door just wide enough to slip beyond. The WPC stood guard, a puddle of meltwater forming at her feet.

'It's Chips?' she said, turning to look at Dryden as Nabbs stood behind her, both hands on her neck.

'You'll have to make sure – but yes, I'm sorry, it's Chips.'

She put a hand across her mouth, and when it dropped her lips had left a kiss on the palm. 'Why?' She twisted her head to look at Nabbs.

'We know someone didn't want him to come back,' said Dryden, dropping his voice. 'But he did come back – why do you think he did that?'

She looked into the fire and Dryden could see her fingernails digging into Nabbs' palm.

'You called him in prison, you said. Perhaps . . .'

Nabbs stiffened. 'Is this the time?'

'You tell me,' said Dryden, standing and walking to the window. 'I don't know how much time you've got.' He came closer while the WPC answered a radio call. 'I think it's probably time to stop lying . . .'

The living-room door opened and Ruth Connor jerked visibly in her seat. 'Mrs Connor? Would you . . .' The WPC came over and took her arm, but she held on to Nabbs and allowed him to encircle her waist as they went through the door.

DI Parlour let them go first. 'If you'd wait a little longer, Mr Dryden – we need a statement.'

The door closed and the silence in the cottage was complete. The clock on the kitchen wall ticked on: 2.15am. Dryden closed his eyes and felt a rush of nausea. Why had Chips left the security of his prison cell to come back to the Dolphin? Dryden dwelt again on the message the prisoner had left scrawled on the unfurling paper ball: I DIDN'T KNOW. Chips had helped, perhaps unwittingly, to set the children up for a crime they didn't commit – the punishment for which had haunted them throughout their lives. Dryden remembered then what Chips had said: 'I never knew their names.' But he had known their names, he'd signed the statement at the time confirming he'd found the stolen goods beneath their chalets. What he'd meant, of course, thought Dryden, was that he never knew the names of the witnesses who had come forward thirty years later. Once Dryden had told him, his remarkable memory had pieced the past together: he'd helped to frame them, helped to frame himself.

The outer door opened and a uniformed PC appeared with John Sley.

Dryden helped himself from the malt whisky bottle Nabbs had left on the kitchen table.

'This is ridiculous . . .' said Sley. 'It can't be a crime to walk on a fucking beach.'

'Sir. Please. Just take a seat for a moment. This is a crime scene. A man has been murdered. I'm afraid we just need to ascertain that we don't require a statement from you – OK? Just routine, if you could wait a moment.'

From the living room they heard a sob and a low murmur of sympathy, and the PC slipped back out, leaving them alone.

'Murder?' said Sley, subsiding into a chair by the fire, his donkey jacket flecked with ice. 'Jesus,' he said. 'Who?'

'Chips Connor. Early-morning stroll for you, is it, or late-night?' said Dryden.

Sley looked to the door. 'We'd been talking, but Marcie's asleep now. I couldn't – too much to think about.'

'Now there's a bit more to think about. Tell Marcie – tell her tonight. Chips got out of prison and came home, then someone killed him and chucked him out with the tide.'

They heard movement beyond the door and Dryden decided it was time to see John Sley in action. 'And tell her something else. Tell her the safe's still there, the one Paul Gedney robbed. I'm sure it's still there because Ruth Connor wants me to think it isn't. You could talk about that. About how interesting it might be to know what's in it.'

John Sley held his hands in his lap, the fingers unlaced and still.

The PC returned and began taking down a brief statement from Sley so that he could return to his chalet. Dryden closed his eyes again. Sleep swept over him as if he'd been drugged. When he opened his eyes he was still alone and the clock read 3.15am. Then he remembered DI Reade, who would no doubt arrive unannounced at 9.00am. He fished out his mobile and called the number Reade had given him. Typically, the detective's mobile was off.

'Hi. This is Philip Dryden. There's something you need to know. Your colleagues from Lynn are all over the Dolphin. Chips Connor's body has been found on the beach. Someone broke his neck. This might change your plans. Sorry about that. Ring me when you can.'

Dryden wondered what the murder of Chips Connor would do for Reade's career prospects. The chief constable was unlikely to view the appearance of a fresh corpse as a suitable opportunity to wrap up a troublesome case.

Dryden let his head loll back, his eyelids fighting gravity. Under the deal table the fish had bled again, creating a second pool on the quarry tiles as blood bled on blood. Something malevolent stirred in Dryden's subconscious and he struggled to rationalize his fear. When sleep did come he dreamt of the black blood again, this time dripping from the beaten, jagged lips of Paul Gedney.

41

At dawn the snow was falling again from an inkblot sky. A brisk wind blew and helped offset the effects of a fitful sleep in William Nabbs' kitchen chair – interrupted only by a laborious and studious interview with DI John Parlour. Dryden had kept his statement brief and factual, leaving more tortuous matters for the arrival of DI Reade, who had not returned his call. Finally, released to return to his chalet, he found Laura asleep, the COMPASS blank, the comforting light of the monitor blinking red in the dark.

As he walked between the chalets the air was as cold as a butcher's fridge. A North Norfolk Electricity van was already parked in the staff car park beside two squad cars and a police van. Ruth Connor sat in reception, behind the downlit counter, drinking from an espresso cup. Her pale fingers encircled the thin china, and Dryden expected to see it shatter under the suppressed anxiety which radiated from her like a colour. A WPC sat in one of the foyer's comfy chairs by the internet café, arms folded, with a stare as blank as a bank teller's. Dryden let his shoulders sag in the sudden damp heat which seeped into the room from the misty heated pool.

Ruth Connor looked up, looked through him, and turned to the WPC. 'You don't have to wait, really . . .' She caught Dryden's eye. 'There's work to do here, I'll be fine now.'

As if to prove it they heard a shout from the indoor pool followed by a splash.

The policewoman checked her watch. 'No problem – I'll

stick around till your partner gets here. About seven thirty you said?' Dryden noted that apparently some truths may have been told during the night, if not all.

He pulled a high stool up to the reception counter. 'You all right?' he said, wanting to hear her talk, wanting to see her struggle to maintain that remarkable façade. She looked like she hadn't slept, the hair failing for once to divert attention from the spider's web of wrinkles by her eyes.

She nodded. 'William's out with the engineers, at the pylon. We're going to take a break away; a few days, when the police are done.'

They both tried identical insincere smiles. The phone rang and she grabbed it, her relief palpable as she became immersed in taking down a booking. Dryden was more convinced than ever that she was hiding something, but other than her discreet relationship with William Nabbs he'd got no closer to finding out what it was.

Tyres crunched over snow outside as the Dolphin's staff minibus edged up to the foyer. Russell Fleet dashed over the tarmac and in through the automatic doors. He swapped a glance with his boss, a nod with Dryden, and headed for the bar.

She finished the call and before Dryden could resume the questions she stood. 'Excuse me. Russ phoned earlier – I need to get him up to speed – he'll be running the place for a few days.'

Dryden sat down opposite the WPC, who continued to examine a spot in the mid-distance. Outside, the minibus idled, waiting for its return passengers to Whittlesea and the surrounding villages. Dryden considered his options: for a day at least the Dolphin would be crowded with police, a team working inside the taped-off scene of crime area by the beach, while a separate search was being carried out by frog teams and foot parties across the saltmarsh. DI Parlour, he knew, planned further interviews, and they'd swapped mobile numbers. And then there was DI Reade. But Dryden calculated that a fresh corpse outranked a thirty-year-old miscarriage of justice. The review of Chips Connor's conviction would have to await the completion of the inquiry into his murder. Dryden's role, as witness, victim, amateur detective and, for all he knew, suspect, would be central. He didn't relish being around when DI Parlour discovered just how many details Dryden had left untold, or having to watch the tussle for power in the investigation.

And there was still one place he wanted to go: one central character in the tawdry tale of Paul Gedney who remained a cipher: Elizabeth Lutton, the pharmacist who had made his crime possible and then slipped away from the scandal of Whittlesea Hospital. She was a crucial link to the real story of Chips Connor. Her successor at the hospital had been circumspect. What Dryden desperately needed was a more immediate witness, someone who could tell him how she had felt, who else might have been entangled in their deception, how she'd lived out the rest of her short life. He logged on to one of the screens in the camp's internet café and punched in her husband's name. From the website of his private clinic at Lynn he took up a weblink to Whittlesea District Hospital's outpatients clinic.

'Bingo,' he said, waking up the WPC. George Lutton's NHS clinic ran every Tuesday and Thursday morning.

He took a decision then, and deserted the warm embrace of the Dolphin's foyer. The minibus was fugged up, the onboard heater gently cooking the only occupant – the driver. Dryden tapped on the window. 'Sorry, I know this is a bit cheeky – I need to get into Whittlesea – any chance?'

The driver was a middle-aged woman, big-boned with a

moon face and a nylon uniform bearing the Dolphin's blue motif. 'Sure. At your own risk, mind – we saw three accidents on the way up, and I don't normally drive this old tub. And these don't help . . .' The windscreen wipers had locked, and the glass was a web of cut-glass ice, like a Victorian fruit bowl.

She passed Dryden a can of de-icer and he sprayed the wipers free, before taking the front passenger seat.

'Philip Dryden,' he said, as she pulled out onto the coast road and then almost immediately turned south on the long road to Whittlesea. 'So, if you don't normally drive, what do you do?'

'I'm Muriel,' she said. 'I run the cleaners, chambermaids.' She let a silence lengthen that threatened to last the whole journey. 'Muriel Coverack – it's Cornish.'

On the dashboard was a bunch of keys attached to a key ring in the form of a small plastic photo frame: two children, teenage girls, leered into the camera, clutching each other.

Dryden tapped it. 'Yours?'

'Nope,' she said. 'Sister's. But they come for the hols.'

Dryden nodded, sensing the presence of a lonely life.

She checked the rear-view again. 'You're the one with the wife – in the wheelchair. We don't clean those chalets without a call first – perhaps tomorrow? We'll be really quick.'

'Sure. Thanks.'

Another silence in which Dryden imagined sympathy welling up. 'So, what happened?' she asked, embarrassed too. 'There was something on the local radio – we all heard it on the way. Russ said it was Chips – that he'd been found on the beach. That right?'

'Sure. I found him, actually – someone broke his neck.' He nodded inappropriately, realizing that the image of

Chips' contorted hand, reaching out from the water, had haunted him since he'd woken that morning. He still felt cold from the night, and began to shiver violently.

Muriel turned up the heating. 'There's a rug on the seat behind – use it. You seen a doctor? It might be shock.'

Dryden put the blanket round his shoulders and told her as much as he could, spinning out the story so that he could try and win something back in return. They drove south across the Fens, the thirty miles to Whittlesea like a trek across the Great Plains.

'Odd place, the Dolphin,' he said eventually, as they edged over a crossroads where the traffic lights were out. 'Decent job though?'

She nodded. 'Might all be over soon.'

Dryden turned in his seat. 'Why's that?'

'They're gonna sell it, aren't they? Russ says no when we ask. But last year they had the agents in, and last week they was back. They had guests over Christmas, too – showed them round. They'll do it this time.'

Dryden nodded, remembering something odd. 'Russell always catch the bus in, does he? No car?'

She shrugged. 'Jean drives – I've never seen Russ behind the wheel. We pick him up at Sea's End every morning – six thirty. Hasn't missed a day in twenty years.'

'Settled, then?'

'Yeah – yeah. They've been together nearly as long now. The kids are smart – hardly kids, really. Twins – teenagers. Nice family. Everyone has a row now and then though, don't they?' she added.

Dryden nodded, thinking of Laura again, thinking how wonderful it would be to have a row. When he'd got back to the chalet he'd caught some sleep in a chair and made breakfast as dawn broke. They'd eaten something together:

coffee and a milky cereal. He'd gone to shave and when he got back she'd written something on the COMPASS.

YOU PROMISED. IT'S TIME.

He'd made so many promises, but he knew all too well which one she wanted him to keep. He'd lit the propane heater, set it on low, just in case the heating failed while he was out. He'd smelt it then, the smell of heated gas, burning innocently. He could have blown the flame out with a kiss, letting the deadly gas fill the chalet.

He looked out of the minibus window through the circular porthole he'd cleared and saw the black peat, a blur to the horizon. 'So you go back that far, do you — twenty years? Is that when Russ arrived?'

'Oh no, I can beat that,' she said, creeping past a police car parked near where a lorry had slewed off the road and into the dyke. The container stuck up at a crazy angle, the cab embedded in the bank.

'I started work at the Dolphin in '69. Chambermaid. I worked for Ruth's father — John Henry. I'm the boss now — twenty staff. I'm running the bus because the driver didn't make it.'

Dryden swung round in his seat. Other than Ruth Connor she was the first person he'd found who could recall the camp before the murder of Paul Gedney.

'What was he like — the old man, John Henry?'

'Nothing like her,' she said, and realizing she'd said too much, she made a show of concentrating on an L-driver ahead on the icy road.

'She's a cool customer,' said Dryden, as lightly as he could. 'It was '75, wasn't it — when Chips was jailed? I've been in to see him — nice guy. What did people think?'

She checked the rear-view again. 'Russ said you were a reporter.'

Dryden looked out of the window. 'That's right. But I'm off duty. You know there were two witnesses who could have got Chips freed – kids at the camp in '74. They were friends of mine. I was here too that summer. I was just a kid.'

'Thanks. Now I feel ancient.'

'Sorry,' said Dryden, smiling into the rear-view. His eyes were tired, and his shock of black hair flattened on one side where he'd slept heavily back at the chalet.

'It's just that I'd like to find out what happened to them. I think someone killed them to stop them coming forward.'

'Russ said.'

'And I think they tried to kill me.'

She looked at him then, the car stationary in a queue tailing back from a flashing police light by the main bridge into Whittlesea. 'Russ said the police didn't think there was anything suspicious – that they'd died naturally. One of them was an alky?'

Dryden thought Russ had done a lot of talking. 'So what did people think – at the time, about Chips?'

She turned off the ignition and they sat in sudden silence in the unmoving queue. 'Chips and Ruth went back a long way, yup? To school. Sweethearts, married at eighteen. And they were happy, you could see that. Then she took over at the camp when John Henry fell ill. Chips was brilliant with kids, a natural. A few years went by, there were no kids. People talk, like they do.'

She bit her lip, sensing the irony. 'She's always been odd with kids. Brittle. Then Chips had the accident. I was in the camp that day, we all came running because they had an alarm by the pool and someone set it off. There was this slick in the water, you know – like from his head.' She turned to Dryden and he could sense the frisson of horror even after thirty years.

'When he got back from the hospital, he was a mess. He was just scared of everything, really jumpy, but he couldn't tell you what was wrong – just like a child.' She blushed suddenly. 'I don't have any, so what do I know – but that's what they say, isn't it?'

Dryden nodded.

'He used to do the poolside duty and the locking up and stuff but anything else, like with people, was too much. He'd end up in the dunes somewhere, and they'd have to send the security guards out to find him.'

'But they stayed together . . . him and Ruth?' said Dryden.

'Sure. But he was ill, and they decided to get some treatment, see if they could do anything. So they took him away. Course, looking back, they said it was the stress – that he'd killed that bloke, beat him to death, and he'd dumped the body out at sea.'

Dryden nodded. 'I've read all about the trial. About Paul Gedney turning up and asking them for help.'

Muriel licked her lips. 'Read about Lizzie Sykes?'

She had a smile on her face now and Dryden sensed the kind of communal thrill that comes from shared malicious gossip. 'Nope.'

She fired up the ignition and they crawled forward again. 'After Gedney went missing the police put out his picture, right? He didn't have a face you could forget. Those eyes. Anyway, this Lizzie Sykes recognized him straight off. She was a bit simple, actually, but I don't think she had the wit to lie. Big girl, but slow. Anyway, she was from Whittlesea too – not like the rest of us, we're all from Lynn – and she'd seen him in the park. This was a bit back, the late sixties, when they were all at school.'

Dryden looked across in the silence and saw that Muriel was smiling, her tongue pushing out her cheek.

'He was sat on a park bench with Ruth Henry – as she was – kissing. Well, the way she told it, more than kissing. Lizzie liked that story. She told it enough.'

Dryden saw the scene differently then, Paul Gedney arriving at the Dolphin by motorbike on a summer's night.

'Did she, Lizzie, tell the police?'

'She told the court. Didn't do her any good though. The other thing about Lizzie was she had light fingers. Petty theft, but then she wasn't the only one. If you knew what they paid chambermaids at a place like the Dolphin, it makes the minimum wage look like a lottery win.'

Dryden had read all the news copy from the trial and there'd been no mention of her testimony, but he knew from experience that newspaper reports were at best a summary, and incidental witnesses were often left out entirely. 'So?'

'They brought it all up in court. Apparently Ruth had caught her once the previous season and docked her wages. Lizzie went round telling everyone she'd get her own back – settle the score. They dragged it all into the court – so the judge said the jury should forget what she said. Ruth denied it flat anyway. But it didn't help Chips, did it? I think a few of us felt he'd clumped Gedney to get even.'

Dryden made a show of checking his mobile for messages, but he took the time to try and think things through. When the phone trilled it made him jump. It was a text message from DI Reade.

RING. NOW.

Dryden checked the incoming call details. The call was timed at 8.48am, Reade was still in Ely, and the rest of his inquiry team was presumably kicking their heels with him. All of which would make a nasty mess of the staff rota.

Dryden decided not to reply and turned to Muriel. 'So,

do you think Ruth was two-timing Chips after they were married?'

'I don't think anyone could have blamed her, although we all did. Chips was popular, yeah? He was drop-dead gorgeous for a start and then after the accident kind of pathetic too, a big kid. Whereas we all thought she was a callous cow. And a rich one, of course – that didn't help.'

'And then along came William Nabbs,' said Dryden.

'Yeah – but he wasn't the first. That's the school . . .' she said, nodding to the side of the road where a set of iron railings ran beside a playground. 'Whittlesea Catholic High School. That's where they all met.'

Dryden was surprised the school was open. Children played, wrapped in scarves and hats. One enterprising teenager was sledging down a frozen grass slope onto the tarmac. As a bell rang he imagined the three of them, a group apart, their heads together, planning.

42

The entrance to Whittlesea District Hospital was an echoing cavern of Victorian marble marred by ill-disguised wiring and a large poster exhorting patients to SAVE YOUR LOCAL HOSPITAL. The Grecian bust still stood, eyes blank, and dust-covered. On one wall the faded colour picture of Elizabeth Lutton hung, the smile still wavering. Dryden dwelt on the white blonde hair, thinking of the bodies entwined in the morning sunlight of the dunes thirty summers earlier. Today the bitter cold had seeped into the hall and somewhere Dryden could hear the trickling of a burst pipe. The WRVS had a stall selling tea and biscuits and he asked for directions to the weekly clinic. Out through A&E, where a single elderly patient sat holding a bloody home-made bandage to his ear, he followed a broken path of sand across the tarmac to a Portakabin. By the ramp up to its doors stood a board.

WHITTLESEA CLINIC.

Clinics morning: 9.15am to 12.15pm. Clinics afternoon: 1.15pm to 3.15pm.

TODAY: Cataract Clinic: Mr Lutton. Medical photography: appointment only. Blood Donors Clinic – all day (Caxton Road Site).

Inside the Portakabin three rows of plastic seats stood empty. In the two far corners paraffin heaters had been lit, scenting the air. The sound of the door closing brought a nurse out from behind a partition.

'Mr Lutton?' asked Dryden. She took Dryden into a consulting room which was also empty.

'Mr Lutton's just at the pharmacy – he'll be five minutes. Take a seat.'

Dryden examined the wall, covered with medical information posters. He winced at the sight of a set of photos illustrating the onset of cataracts. In the final one a blanched retina swam in an eyeball marbled with tiny blood vessels.

Dryden considered what he'd learnt about the human triangle which had been Ruth Henry, Chips Connor and Paul Gedney. Childhood friends in a small Fen town. Ruth leaves school and goes to work in her father's business, and as his final illness deepens, she takes over the day-to-day management of the Dolphin. Chips Connor, handsome, cheerful, and in love, follows her out to the coast. Perhaps they were happy, but somewhere in the background is an unfinished affair with Paul Gedney. Then comes Chips' accident, and his retreat into childhood and manic insecurity. For the young Ruth Henry – a beauty queen and an heiress – it must have been an almost insupportable blow – to be chained for life to a man she would have struggled not to despise.

Dryden covered his eyes and let the cool palms heal the soreness beneath.

A phone rang on Lutton's desk and Dryden jumped. He considered the coming interview without relish. What did he know about Mr George Lutton, consultant ophthalmic surgeon? Paul Gedney's drug-pilfering scam relied on falsified records. Elizabeth Lutton had been the pharmacist at the time Gedney had committed his crimes. The police had gone after Gedney, but she'd been allowed to take early retirement. If Gedney had been found, would his testimony have implicated others? Was it a good enough reason to see him dead? When, and how, had Elizabeth Lutton died?

Impatient, Dryden stood again, and scanned the wall posters. One showed an eye, bulging out in diagram, incisions marked at the side.

Graves Disease, read the caption: *It can be treated.*

You'd never forget the eyes: it's what everyone had said. Dryden began to read the small print but the Portakabin shook suddenly as someone climbed the outside steps.

George Lutton was the wrong side of 15 stone, a bow tie accentuating the stretched white shirt over his stomach. His face was hairless and his cheeks had livid red spots, as if the exercise of crossing the hospital yard had been a significant challenge.

He crashed into his chair and adjusted his glasses.

'Oh yes,' he said, reading a note, and immediately began to pack away pen and documents into an attaché case. 'I'm sorry. I know you rang but I really can't help you now. Elizabeth and I separated in '78. As you know, she died in '89; she'd been ill for several years. By that time she had a new family, and so did I. So you see . . .'

'It was about Paul Gedney.'

Lutton stood, taking an overcoat down from a wooden hat stand. 'Indeed. But I don't want to talk about Paul Gedney, Mr Dryden.'

'I'm sorry, it's just I've never understood why your wife got involved.'

Lutton froze. 'It's almost impossible to slander the dead, Mr Dryden, but be careful. Involved in what?'

Luckily Dryden knew the law of slander better than Lutton. There were no witnesses, so he pressed on. 'Paul Gedney stole drugs over a period of nine months during the winter of 1973–4. I understand that's impossible to do without attracting attention – unless the records are falsified. Your wife was responsible for the records. She retired six weeks after the police inquiry became public. Did she really need the money?'

He walked away from Dryden towards the outer doors. 'Why do you people always assume crime is about money?'

Lutton had a Jag, black and polished like a hearse. He struggled with the door.

'It'll be frozen,' said Dryden. 'De-icer?'

Lutton, angry now, walked to the rear and the boot flipped up automatically.

Dryden was thinking fast: there was something about Lutton's indignation that was intensely personal, a loss of face perhaps, and dignity. He thought again about the unsatisfied smile of Elizabeth Lutton. 'They had an affair, didn't they?' he asked.

Lutton straightened, holding a can of de-icer. Then he leant in close and Dryden caught the whiff of cigars. 'Look. Can I suggest you fuck off. I consider your attempts to gain access to the surgery are improper. I am being harassed. If you do it again I shall make a formal complaint. I wish to get on. I have another clinic at Friday Bridge.'

'She must have been worried when he disappeared,' Dryden persisted. 'Worried he'd get caught, and try to shift the blame. Did he get in touch?'

But Lutton had said enough; he reached up to close the boot but Dryden stopped him. It was packed with kit: sealed cellophane packages of medical equipment, a small carousel for dispensing drugs and an aluminium box, like a picnic cooler, with locks.

'What's that?' said Dryden, touching the cold metallic surface.

Lutton sighed, and crashed the boot down. 'Friday Bridge has a small A&E department for injuries – they're short of blood, I run stuff out on clinic days. It's a blood box. Now goodbye, Mr Dryden.'

43

Humph picked him up outside the hospital gates and drove in silence to the Eel's Foot, parking up on the edge of the long dyke which ran to the horizon: a single white line of ice which seemed to separate the landscape into two equal halves of black, featureless peat. Its surface smoked in the setting sunlight, gently smudging the image of a swan which flew towards them along the arrow-straight track, one webbed foot occasionally touching the ice in its wake.

Dryden fetched beer and juice from the bar. The sun had gone, a vast lid of steel-grey cloud having slid over their heads from the north. A violent gust of wind rocked the Capri on its rusted springs.

The cabbie carefully retrieved a miniature bottle of tequila and added it to the orange juice. 'It's medicinal,' he explained, belching.

'In what sense?' asked Dryden.

'In the sense that it tastes like medicine,' said Humph, adding a second.

Suddenly the ice storm struck, rain thrashing the windscreen and cutting visibility from ten miles to twenty feet in five seconds. As they watched, the water froze on the cab's windows in opaque patterns. Dusk seemed close now, and Humph flicked on the vanity light over the passenger seat.

Humph checked his watch and fiddled with the radio knob. They listened patiently to the national news before it switched to local weather. Dryden's mobile had been off since DI Reade's unwelcome text. He flicked it back on and found a voice message from DI Parlour.

'Mr Dryden. I've just had a brief chat with DI Jock Reade from Ely. I understand you know each other. I'd like to try that statement again, if it's all right with you. Now, please. I'm at the camp, we've set up an incident room in the old dining hall. I'll expect you. Frankly, if I don't see you by dusk one of my officers will come and get you.'

Humph leant forward and turned up the radio volume '. . . and for East Anglia the Met Office has issued a severe weather warning. Freezing rain showers have reached the north coast of Norfolk and will deepen towards nightfall. Ground temperatures are likely to remain at minus 5 or lower, leading to widespread formation of ice on trees, overhead wires, rails, roads and other artificial surfaces. By mid-evening the storm front will have passed from coastal areas, with skies clearing, leading to severe freezing temperatures of minus 10 and below. Police in North Norfolk advise all motorists to stay off the roads unless their journey is vital. Conditions are already described as treacherous.'

'Super,' said Dryden. Humph killed the radio and resisted the language tape: an eloquent, and rare, offer of uninterrupted communication.

'The camp's still crawling,' said the cabbie. 'They want to know what I've been doing parked up on the beach.'

'What did you tell 'em?'

'The truth. That I was keeping an eye on Laura because someone had tried to kill you. I think the copper wants another word.'

'You don't say,' said Dryden. 'I may have overlooked mentioning it in my statement. So I'll look forward to that.'

Dryden closed his eyes, trying to blot out the storm. 'OK,' he said to Humph. 'Stick with me. I see some light at last . . .' He slurped more beer and then balanced the pint on top of the glove compartment, spilling peanuts into the shallow plastic depression.

Humph folded his arms like a Buddha.

'Paul Gedney is – how can I put this nicely – romantically attached to Elizabeth Lutton, Whittlesea District Hospital's senior pharmacist. She's in a marriage she will later escape, she's thirty-five, or thereabouts. He's fifteen years younger – and as far as we know a manipulative and damaged young man. This may not be his fault, but for the sake of the argument, who cares? So what does he see in her? It's only a guess, but I reckon our Paul sees a way of lifting drugs out of the pharmacy without being caught. So Elizabeth is a means to an end; in fact, everyone he knows is probably a means to an end, a fact only marginally more palatable when you remember the object of his little money-raising scheme was to pay for medical treatment for his adopted mother. Then it all goes wrong. The police find some of Gedney's customers reeling around the low spots of Whittlesea and the Fen towns and they're prepared to name their supplier. He gets to hear on the grapevine they're going to bust him, so he does a runner.'

'And ends up at the Dolphin,' said Humph, attempting to winch a four-inch-wide crisp into his mouth without breaking it.

'Indeed. He tries to tap his friends for some money is my guess – which they refuse, and instead offer him refuge for the night. It's just possible Ruth Connor – who is another one of his former conquests – decides that he deserves more help than that, and she slips him the combination to the office safe. Anyway, the plan goes wrong and Chips catches him and wallops him with the stapler. What happens next? My guess is he rides east on the coast road and then doubles back to Lighthouse Cottage, where he dumps the bike – it's still there. Then I reckon, once the police have been and gone, he tracks down Ruth Connor. And that's when they see their real chance.'

Dryden slapped the dashboard and corralled some nuts. Outside, the lights of the Eel's Foot came on, a string of Christmas bulbs swinging violently in the wind.

Humph shrugged, but for once played the game. 'Which was?'

'It's perfect. Two people – two problems. Paul Gedney is on the run and needs to disappear. Ruth Connor is stuck with a husband who – even by his own admission – wasn't happy living in the same world as she was. Emotionally, he's a ten-year-old, with a fragile personality which can break when exposed to the slightest stress. Next stop the funny farm. So Ruth and Paul Gedney figure it out: Chips has got the robbery on the record, the police have got the stapler as exhibit number one if they ever track down the thief. The lovers decide to fit up Chips Connor for Paul Gedney's murder. That way, Chips goes to jail and Paul Gedney gets a new life.'

'How do they fake the murder scene?' said Humph, hooked now, despite himself.

'Blood. Lots of it. Gedney is a trained nurse – or at least part trained. He's done a hundred blood transfusions. She sets him up in the boat – the *Curlew* – over in the marsh, on the riverbank, well out of the way. The police aren't look-ing anyway, they think he's beggared off by motorbike like Chips said. Five pints of blood – that's all it takes. He had nearly six weeks – plenty of time for his own body to have replaced the blood. He stores it in a blood box – a metal container which preserves it at the right temperature. The technicalities are beyond me, but it's not rocket science, all he needs is a generator.'

Humph looked out the driver's side window, unconvinced. 'Why'd he cut himself up with the knife?'

Dryden covered his eyes. 'I don't know.'

Humph, rallying, filled in the gaps. 'So once they've got the blood they choose a spot – the old huts are perfect. Then they spill it all in one go and give it a few days to dry so the police aren't tempted to give it the full forensic treatment?'

Dryden shook his head. 'I've read the trial reports. The examination on site was done by the local man – there's no way they would have spotted the different ages of the blood samples taken at the scene. They'd take three, six, whatever, but only to make sure it was all from one body. That's it. Standard practice.'

'Then they set up the other stuff – clothes, hairs . . . how about the fingerprints?' asked Humph.

'Every item with a print was movable – the clever bit was the iron bed end, but if you look in the old huts you can see they're easy to take apart. They knew where Chips had been working. It was easy enough, and they had so much time. Chips was out of the way by then – at the clinic – so they could choose their moment. And they had time to plant evidence on his fishing boat too – so it looked like he'd dumped the body at sea.'

Dryden took the glasses back and Humph fired up the Capri, but they didn't move. 'Then what?' said the cabbie.

'Good question. He got away – right away. Gedney has to think fast. He's got a face no one can forget. The police have got a picture, and within a week every copper in the east of England has got a copy. OK – he's got some cash, perhaps a lot of cash.' He paused, sensing he was close to something. 'He may have touched Lutton again. She's still got a job, although by now everyone's crawling all over the pharmacy records, so she's heading for the best exit she can negotiate that protects her pension. So he leans on her.'

Humph burped, rocking the Capri. 'Is that where he got the kit, the blood box, the transfusion gear?'

'Brilliant. Exactly. Elizabeth Lutton. It has to be. A quick call, a plea for help not very subtly wrapped up in a threat. The blood box, transfusion gear, even a fresh supply of blood for a full transfusion.'

'Blackmail,' said Humph. He squirted water on the windscreen automatically and the ice cleared, but re-formed quickly between swipes of the wipers. 'Blimey. We'll be lucky to get back in this.'

Dryden felt the blood draining from his face. 'You're a genius,' he said, turning to the cabbie.

'Piss off,' said Humph, sensing an unpardonable excursion into sarcasm.

'No. It was blackmail all right. But Lutton's husband said something to me earlier back at his clinic – "Why do you people always assume crime is about money?" Well, he's right. This time it wasn't. He didn't want money. He wanted something else, and what if Gedney wanted both the Luttons to help?'

Dryden let the glove compartment fall open and twisted the cap off another malt.

By the time they reached the camp gates he was sure; but he needed to be safer than that. 'Drop me over there, beyond the lights by reception – I'll meet you in the dunes at the usual place – give me twenty minutes.'

The ice storm was already causing havoc: a telegraph pole lay across the path to reception, a ball of tangled ice at its head. A bare apple tree stood encased in ice and as Dryden passed a crack rang out like a gunshot as one of the branches sheared away from the main trunk and smashed to the ground like a chandelier. Looking up, Dryden could see the power lines clearly despite the falling night, a luminescent white wire hung with icicles. One half of the canopy over the entrance doors had buckled under the weight of ice above and only a few of the carriage lamps on the chalets still shone.

The rain fell like pellets, tapping at his skull and bouncing high from the hard surfaces of the tarmac and path.

The foyer was empty, the buzz of Muzak replaced by a live local radio broadcast.

'. . . and residents in Whittlesea report a complete loss of power to the Eastfields Estate. A series of accidents has closed the main bridge into the town and police now advise all motorists who are able to leave their cars and find refuge for tonight.'

The lights flickered once and then regained power as Muriel Coverack appeared from the back office.

'How you getting home?' asked Dryden.

'I'm not. I took a busload back a few hours ago but I've got a chalet here for the night. And a free meal. Big deal, eh?'

Dryden nodded and headed for the internet café, where he extracted a large espresso from the vending machine.

Muriel followed him in. 'The police left a message. They said if I saw you to make sure they knew. You've got to go to the dining hall. They're all down there – there's a mobile kitchen and everything.'

The sound of rain clattering against the roof filled the foyer with noise like static.

'Thanks,' said Dryden, not looking up from the computer.

'Shall I tell them, then?'

'Don't bother,' said Dryden. 'I'm on my way.'

The Google search box came up and he punched in the

name of Lutton's private clinic. The website was adorned with a picture of the building, a Queen Anne house in lush grounds with the kind of gravel drive over which only polished cars crunch. There was a Q & A section on Graves Disease, and a cross-link to an NHS site which listed the various symptoms. It was a thyroid condition which could lead to fluctuating sex drive, weight loss, intolerance to heat and sweating. Most symptoms could be kept under control with steroids, but the treatment brought with it side-effects – diabetes, high blood pressure, psychosis, cardiovascular problems and cataracts. Dryden tried another site for Graves Disease and found a more extensive list of symptoms, including proptosis. He clicked on it and found himself looking at a series of before and after mug shots.

'Bingo,' said Dryden. 'Pop eye.'

He read on quickly. Bulging eyes were one of the commonest symptoms of the disease. In most cases patients were treated with steroids or had part of the thyroid gland removed. But if the bulging of the eye continued an orbital decompression – surgery – could be undertaken, an operation which results in the eye sitting back in its socket. The pictures were graphic: in the 'before' version one young woman stared out, the whites completely encircling the iris in both eyes, the lids seemingly unblinking, the edges inflamed and red. In the 'after' version the bulging of the eyes, and the swelling of the face around the eye sockets, was gone. She looked like a different person. If you'd been her brother or sister you'd have walked past her in the street.

Dryden heard voices from the office behind the reception counter, so he hit a printout button and grabbing the sheet ran out into the dusk, down through the camp. The floodlight by the amusement park was still working and showed that the helter-skelter had buckled, the top third sinking down and skewing round. A line of changing booths had collapsed and several telegraph wires lay rigid on the frosted grass. A uniformed PC stood guard down by the water's edge, the scene-of-crime tapes flapping like prayer flags in the wind.

As Dryden looked to the distant lines of white surf just visible at sea the rain stopped. Within seconds the air was completely still and champagne-chilled, the only sound the high-pitched hum of the pylons overhead and the occasional crack of tortured wood. The storm had passed inland, revealing a planetarium of stars. At sea red and green navigation lights came and went.

He thought about the face of Paul Gedney. He thought about thirty years of natural ageing, layered onto a face transformed by an operation to cure the symptoms of Graves Disease. He saw faces, calling them up from the twisting story which had unfurled since the day he had climbed the steps of High Park Flats to the home of Declan McIlroy: and in each he searched for the pale fleeting image of the thief.

Humph joined him at the water's edge, Boudicca racing past them to dance on the sand.

'Nothing moving on the road,' said the cabbie, and they turned to look inland. The usual ribbon of red and white lights shuffling along the coast was still, a few cars stationary. 'It's like an ice rink up there. Copper stopped the cab, wanted to know where you were. I said the chalet.'

A light shone from Laura's room and another PC stood duty on the verandah steps.

'You said blackmail,' said Dryden, digging his hands deep into his coat pockets. 'Blackmail, sure. He needed a new face. I said it was a perfect plan – but it was better than that. They wanted to get rid of Chips, they wanted to make sure the police thought Paul Gedney was dead, and they wanted each other.

'If he went to the police and agreed to a deal Elizabeth Lutton faced jail, but more to the point her husband's career would have been wounded too, perhaps fatally. According to the website the clinic was founded in '73 – he'd hardly got it off the ground. He was on the up. A scandal like that would have meant starting again, at the very least. So he did it for her: he operated on Paul Gedney. They gave him a new face, Humph.'

'So he's alive?'

'Sure,' said Dryden. 'And he lives in Lighthouse Cottage.'

44

The sky was an immaculate blue-black, the cold air super clear so that offshore Dryden could see the coastal lights sinking slowly away to the north with the curvature of the earth. He turned to look inland, along the marching line of pylons, when he saw the first high-voltage flash, an arcing vein of light, high up in the rigging of the nearest tower – the one which Nabbs had inspected the day before. In the half-second it was lit he saw that it was encased in ice.

A moment later he heard the thwap of the cable breaking, and saw it snaking in the air as it jolted and flashed against its neighbours. The pylon beneath shuddered with the release of tension, and Dryden heard ice shards falling in the darkness to the frozen ground below.

The pylon itself stood in a pool of security light splashed within a wire perimeter. Dryden could see a group of engineers working inside to clear ice from the steel housing which protected the ground-level control gear. The ice fell amongst them, and Dryden heard shouts of pain as they dived for cover. William Nabbs was with them, the collar of his yellow thermal jacket zipped up to his chin, his face craned skywards into the superstructure of the tower above, which groaned now as the breaking wires upset the subtle vectors of tension which held the steel frame aloft.

Dryden told Humph to go back to the car, and set off along the coast path towards Lighthouse Cottage. The smell of ozone on the air was thrilling, the air so cold his lips tingled. Dryden turned his fear into energy, running along the frozen sandy path towards the dark silhouette of the house. What did he hope to find? Pictures, perhaps; documents; a careless clue to the former life of William Nabbs. How had he done it? How had he remade a life in the months and years after staging his own murder? Who did he have to fool? Some of the staff at the Dolphin had glimpsed him that night, but only briefly. Lizzie, the maid who'd spotted him with Ruth Connor, was no doubt swiftly sacked. And there was Ruth Connor herself – but then he didn't have to fool her.

A light burned within the cottage and the gate to the walled garden stood open. The palm tree, an exploding ball of crystal spears, had snapped and lay shattered. Dryden looked in the kitchen window. Where the fish had lain on the deal table a bloodstain remained. He pushed open the door and called: 'Anyone?' The echo within told him he was alone, so he walked through the kitchen to the front room and up the narrow wooden stairs to the bedrooms above. One was empty except for a sunbed, the source of William Nabbs' surfer's tan. There was a double bedroom at the front, with two windows – one overlooking the sea, the other the dunes. A set of framed pictures cluttered the landward sill: in one, Ruth Connor and Nabbs sat in a tropical sun, perhaps a decade earlier, perhaps more. Her hand reached under his T-shirt, his fingers through her hair. In another they walked on the beach below, their bodies so close she was almost falling into him, while the huts of the old camp dotted the dune grass beyond.

The electric lights fluttered, blanked out for a second, and returned.

On the bed was the holdall he'd seen Nabbs bring to the Dolphin the night before, empty now. In the bathroom a cabinet of cosmetics. On the tiled edge of the bath itself a plastic case for a set of contact lenses. Dryden prised one out and held it up to the light: a deep marine-blue pigment made it glow like a piece of mosaic.

'The fake surfer,' said Dryden. 'Fake hair, fake eyes.' But something gnawed at his memory, and he tried, and failed, to recall in colour the poster of Paul Gedney.

Back in the bedroom he picked up the picture of the sunshine couple, searching Nabbs' face for the likeness he knew must be there. He heard the footstep at the same moment that he heard his voice. 'What exactly . . . ?'

Dryden was proud of himself. He didn't panic, he just placed the framed photograph carefully back on the sill and picked up the next: a shot of Ruth Connor in a one-piece swimsuit, laughing with delight that someone had caught her on film.

Nabbs, a mobile Velcroed to the outside of his jacket, held a builder's lamp. The streaked hair was matted to his head, and he looked tired, haunted even.

'The pylon's coming down,' said Dryden. 'I came to say.'

Nabbs placed the lamp carefully on the bedside table and something crossed his face which wasn't fear. 'I was unlikely to be in bed . . .'

Through the landward windows Dryden could see the flashing light of an emergency vehicle at the camp gates.

Nabbs re-zipped his jacket. 'Look. The engineers can't shut the power down, the gear's frozen. I need to be out there – I came back for tools and saw the door was open. The police – Parlour – he's looking for you. They're in the old dining hall. He said he'd stay the night. We should go . . .'

'I heard you were planning a trip,' said Dryden, nodding at the holdall. 'But this looks more like a runner. What brought it on? The new witness perhaps – and this time you don't know who to kill.'

He laughed at him then, right in the eyes, and Dryden's heart contracted at the change in tone, the confidence in the voice when he finally spoke. 'I'm not going anywhere, Dryden.'

Dryden, unsettled by doubt, blundered on. 'Birth certificate, driver's licence, National Insurance number. It's only a guess – but you've got none of them. How'd you manage the holiday abroad?'

Nabbs' eyes darted to the holdall. 'So there's a passport – of course, that's where you went after Chips was arrested? Out of the country? A year perhaps, two . . . time enough for the operation, time enough for the hair, an extra stone of muscle.'

'Sorry. What the fuck are you talking about? This doesn't make any sense,' he said, but he was dancing on his feet, desperate to leave.

'It does if you're not William Nabbs.'

A flash, like lightning, lit up the window and the night beyond, although the sound which followed wasn't thunder but the fizz of shorting electricity.

'You're Paul Gedney,' said Dryden, and he saw Nabbs flinch. 'The motorbike you dumped in '74 is still in the garage downstairs.'

Nabbs wiped the back of his hand across his lips. 'The bike's not mine. All the stuff's Ruth's. I just keep the surf-boards in there, for the class.'

Dryden flipped open the top of the holdall. 'Another sunshine holiday then?'

'This is crazy.' Nabbs' voice was brittle, and Dryden guessed his pulse was racing.

Dryden came round the bed to the window and looked out. 'It was something someone said about Gedney, some-one who knew him – knew you – before that night. A kind of arrogance, an ability to rise above the accepted moral code, to take action, get results, to be omnipotent. That's why you did it, because it seemed to solve everything, didn't it? You needed to disappear, you wanted to be with Ruth, you got both. Chips got what he wanted too, didn't he? Or that's what you told yourselves. So nobody got hurt, right? Except the kids. That's where you got it so wrong. You branded them as thieves, ruined their lives, and you could have ruined mine.'

Dryden craned his neck against the window to look east towards Laura's chalet. He could just see the light.

'You thought they'd seen the blood box. If they'd told an adult, found an adult who'd listen, the plan was wrecked. There was no going back. So you had to discredit them, get them away.'

Nabbs looked to the door but Dryden guessed he wouldn't go until he knew as much as Dryden.

'And when they'd gone you met in the dunes.' He looked at him then. 'Was it worth it? Was she worth it?'

Nabbs, finally, was still. 'I don't like being accused of murder.'

'Well done. I hadn't, actually – but yes. You killed Declan McIlroy and Joe Petulengo because they'd seen you that night. If they'd given evidence in court, Chips Connor would have been freed. And if Chips Connor had come home it was all over, wasn't it? Because, despite the surgery and the makeover and the intervening thirty years, he'd have recognized you with a glance: his childhood friend. And you tried to kill me.'

Dryden ploughed on, his confidence returning. 'When you failed, you decided to quit. Run. Find a new life. Again. You couldn't be sure, could you, that I hadn't told someone else. The police perhaps. So you couldn't try again.'

They heard the gate clatter below. 'And when Chips came back he did recognize you – which is why you killed him as well. He'd guessed, not all of it, but enough. Whoever sent him out to search under the chalets had planted the stuff for him to find because they wanted the kids out of the camp. It was Ruth, wasn't it? She paid the security guard to stick with the story – that he'd seen Marcie hiding the stuff under the huts. What was the price? A one-way ticket to the other side of the world? So Chips came back to confront her. But he met you, didn't he?'

They heard the door bang below, but the footsteps which climbed the stairs were oddly delicate. The lights flickered again and they stood in darkness for a second as someone stopped in the doorway, breathing.

The light flooded back. Ruth Connor stood, her hands held out. They were blood red.

'Please come. I think I've killed him,' she said.

45

A wedge of electric light fell across the darkness of the office floor. The man lay on his chest, the body twisted at the waist, the limbs randomly arranged in the awkward sema-phore of the dead. Across his back a line of crimson wounds punctuated the material of the donkey jacket, each edged with a black ring of burnt threads. On the air was the acrid twist of cordite and an undercurrent of urine. In the corner one of the filing cabinets had been pulled clear of the wall and a safe stood open to reveal a pile of black and gold metal safety-deposit boxes. One was open, revealing the purple-orange blush of £50 notes. On the desk a canvas lay half unfurled, two men, naked, stood in a pool of blood.

William Nabbs put down the holdall and flicked a switch. A single neon tube buzzed like a dying insect. Ruth Connor walked to the body and ran a hand into her hair, leaving a streak of livid red on the dry skin of her forehead. 'It was so quiet. I was down in the bar and heard the noise.'

She looked into the corner of the room by a filing cabinet. On the cracked lino lay a gun, the metal a dull silver, the handle clean.

'It's just for pellets, just to scare. Russ kept it behind the bar,' she said, and laughed out of place. Dryden noted the odd tense. He stood over the body, dreading the sightless eyes, but before he could touch him a shoulder jerked, the head lifted, and he rolled over: eyes open, but clouded. It was John Sley. His face held the pallor of butcher's fat, a living waxwork. Dryden noticed that his hand lay over his heart, the fingers feebly trying to massage the chest beneath.

He leant in close. 'John.' The eyes rolled back into the head and the lids closed. 'He needs help – quick. An air gun can't do this. A heart attack's my guess. We need a doctor – or a nurse,' he added, turning pointedly to William Nabbs.

'I'll get a doctor,' said Nabbs, flicking open his mobile.

'Get his wife too – Chalet 18. He may have a condition, there could be pills.'

Nabbs thought for a moment, then fled, leaving the holdall at Ruth Connor's feet.

Sley opened an eye and Dryden glimpsed the iris, struggling to escape the upper lid. Dryden pressed his arm, and felt the cold sweat on his forehead.

'Who did you think it was?' asked Dryden.

Ruth Connor walked to the safe and removed one of the untouched deposit boxes, turned a key in the lock, and revealed that it too was packed with crisp cash.

'For the trip?' asked Dryden.

She tipped the bundles into the first bag, then knelt down and picked up the gun. 'I don't think that is a very clever thing to do,' said Dryden. 'But then you aren't hanging around to answer any questions, either of you.'

Sley groaned and a thin river of saliva bubbled at the corner of his mouth.

Dryden cradled the bony angular skull, listening to the breath rattling in his throat.

'Questions,' he said. 'How long do you think it will take them to put William Nabbs in the computer and find out he doesn't exist?'

She took a cardboard box from the desk drawer and extracted some of the tiny pellets to reload the gun. She laughed once. 'You don't know how wrong you are.'

'I know one thing I'm right about. Three people have

been murdered to make sure the world thinks Paul Gedney died thirty years ago. But there was a worse crime than that, wasn't there? A crime Chips Connor was party to – although he didn't know it at the time. Three other lives – not ended but ruined, right from the start. Those three children who never got a chance, not a real chance thanks to the stigma: thieves. You made them thieves. Just to get them out of the camp, to make sure they couldn't tell anyone who'd listen what they'd seen.'

He put a hand on John Sley's shoulder. 'That's why he's here. Marcie hasn't forgiven you, she never will. Her mum – her adopted mum – thought she was a thief. I don't suppose that troubles you, does it?'

She stood, retrieving another box from the safe. 'You've got the wrong man,' she said, and Dryden noted the implication, that there was a right man. 'William Nabbs was born in Boston, Lincolnshire in 1960. A cute kid – I've seen the pictures. His degree's hanging on the wall. His parents visit at Christmas – his dad's an accountant, his mum a teacher. He's more real than you.'

On the stairs they heard Nabbs returning but Marcie Sley got to the door first. Dryden stood and she came to his voice, and let him lead her hands down to her husband's face.

'I'll check on the ambulance,' said Nabbs, leaving again. 'DI Parlour's on his way too.'

Marcie held her husband's face between her palms. 'John. Here.' She'd brought a bottle of mineral water and she let him sip as she slipped two pills between blue lips. Dryden put an arm around her and felt the gentle vibration as she shook with stress.

'Johnnie,' she said. 'Johnnie, there's a doctor coming.' She turned her head to Dryden. 'What happened?'

Ruth Connor drew back, and as she stood the lino creaked. Marcie stiffened, realizing there was someone else in the room, and then found her with her eyes. She sniffed the air and smiled. 'Don't go,' she said. 'Don't go now. Not yet.'

Dryden's mobile chirruped, he went to kill the call but recognized the Ely number. 'Keep his head up, Marcie,' he said. He left then, knowing that would be what Marcie wanted. Just a minute alone.

Out on the landing there was a fire door. He pushed down the bar, desperate for air, and stepped out onto the top of the metal stairs. The call was from his voicemail box: 'This is a message for Philip Dryden from Father John Martin. I have that information, Philip – I have a service at 7.30 but I'll be free before that. Ring me at the presbytery. Ely 44875.'

Dryden stabbed the numbers into the keypad. He imagined the phone ringing in the chilly hallway of the house, beneath the faded Connemara landscape. There was another flash from the pylon and in it he saw a fire engine extending its ladder skywards.

'Father?' he said.

'Dryden. Yes. Sorry, let me just close the door here.'

Dryden heard the clunk of the old receiver being put down, then a muffled voice. Suddenly he was back. 'I found the records of the child who was fostered with Paul Gedney. An elder half-brother, you recall – different father. He left the foster home in '73 – moved north. Malton, near York. I don't have any records after that I'm afraid.'

'The name?' asked Dryden.

Dryden heard paper crackling. 'Russell Fleet. Russell John Fleet.'

'Dryden?' asked Father Martin, after a few seconds' silence.

'Sorry. You're sure?'

'Yes. Why? The surname was his adopted family's. And there's something else. I remember the child – very different from his half-brother. Timid, really, and not as bright. The real problem was the father – who had access, and abused that trust. Alcohol I'm afraid. Anyway, he made an attempt to take the boy away before he came into care. He crashed the car, there were several internal injuries to the child – he was just three – and one wound which will have stayed with him all his life. The car turned over, shredding the roof, and the metal cut into his arm. In the file there's a picture with the doctor's report which we had for all applicants: the scar is very distinctive, Dryden – like a jagged S.'

46

Ruth Connor was gone, and so was the holdall. A paramedic knelt beside John Sley like a penitent, checking his pulse, while another unfurled a stretcher. In the flickering light of the neon tube Sley still looked deathly white, except for the skin beneath the eyes, which had the purple blush of dead meat. Dryden took Marcie's arm above the elbow, and saw the fingers of her right hand were flecked with blood. 'I hit her,' she said, her voice vibrating with anger. 'I hit her hard.'

Dryden heard DI Parlour's voice below in the bar. He told Marcie to stay with her husband, then slipped out on to the fire escape again, and down to the rear yard. The sky was transformed: a full moon had risen at sea. It was colder again, the landscape ice-white, stiff with frost. He ran down to the old swimming pool and climbed to the first tier of the diving board. The camp lay below, lit by the occasional arc of electricity dancing between the severed high-voltage cables.

Dryden heard an inhuman cry of shearing, tortured metal. The fire engine, parked at the base of the giant pylon, played a floodlight over the superstructure. The tower twisted on its four legs, a single cross-member of steel falling as if in slow motion to the ground below. The lights in the holiday camp flickered once, died, and revived at half power.

He turned back to the sea and saw that the chalets along the crest of the dunes were still marked by their string of pale verandah lights. He thought of Laura within, alone with the glow of the flame from the propane heater, and at that moment Ruth Connor's silhouette broke the horizon, against the grey-silver backdrop of the sea, before dropping out of sight, down towards the old sluice.

He ran, the moon lighting the bone-white sandy path.

The tide was ebbing within the maze of channels in the marsh. Canopies of ice hung over the inlets and pools the seawater had fled. Dryden made his way along one of the fingers of stiff sand until he emerged opposite a wide expanse of open water where the main river emptied into a wide, sluggish pool. He crouched down by the water's edge and saw across the mirror-like surface the wreck of the *Curlew*. The moon caught the gentle curve of the hull, and beside it the sleek black inflated outline of an inshore dinghy, a powerful outboard motor at the rear, silent for now.

Across the water he heard Ruth Connor's voice, as clear and close as if she had whispered in his ear.

'It's all there.' He saw her now, standing on the rotting deck, Russell Fleet beside her, between them the holdall. 'I thought you'd come to get it all,' she said.

Fleet knelt, looking inside the bags. 'Is he dead?'

She shook her head in silence. He held out his hand and she put something in it: the gun perhaps. 'Dryden knows,' she said. 'He knows about the blood.'

Fleet checked the horizon, zipping up a sailing jacket. 'He was always close: and he was there, with the others. Even if he didn't see, he's always known it was the truth. But there's no choice now.'

'You said it was perfect, that nobody would get hurt.' Her voice was louder, a challenge. 'But you killed them.'

'Ruth.' He took a step towards her and she stepped back quickly, the sound of rotting wood creaking under her foot. 'You didn't complain when you got what you wanted – when they took Chips away. You didn't say no that morning in the sand dunes. I was the one who got the butchered face. What did you have to do? Remind me, Ruth. And when the witnesses came forward I did what needed to be done – you didn't have to know.'

She folded her arms, and even by moonlight Dryden could see the chin jut out. 'But when it was all over – when they were dead – you told me then, didn't you, Russ – told me the details, just to share the guilt. Pouring water over the first one after you'd broken his legs, opening the windows and leaving the other to die after you'd laced his drinks with pills. But you didn't have to do any of it. You could have left, melted away.'

He stepped down into the dinghy. 'Yes. I could have gone, Ruth, when the witnesses came forward. Left you two alone. The lovebirds. But then I'd have had to leave the kids as well – my kids, Ruth, my family.

'Because that's where your guilt lies Ruth, or part of it. Telling me that you'd not had children because of Chips. That Chips couldn't. But we found out the truth, didn't we? You couldn't give me a family so I found someone who could.

'And then there was the business,' he said, kicking the holdall. 'Why the fuck should I let two wrecked lives stand in my way? I deserved my share. Just because I don't have the pieces of paper doesn't mean I don't deserve my cut. We'd always been agreed on that, Ruth. I paid in blood. I can't take the family with me, but I can take the money.'

She had a hand to her face and Dryden guessed she was crying, letting his words wound her.

His head was still down, counting in the holdall. 'How did you make Chips agree to the sale?'

'I told him it was what I wanted,' she said, defeated now.

Fleet nodded, standing.

'Did he have to die too?' she asked. 'He came to see me, he wanted to see me. I could have talked. It wasn't about being sent away, it wasn't about what happened to him, it was the kids. He told me when I phoned the prison. He wanted to know why we'd done that to them, Russ.'

'It wasn't a crime, Ruth.'

Dryden let his fingers bunch in fists, knowing that it was.

'A bunch of kids. Jesus,' Fleet said, lighting a cigarette, cupping it so that the flame illuminated the cradle of his fingers. 'He wanted to see you all right. I found him at the back of the flat, under the fire escape, waiting for you to come home. It would have been a long wait, wouldn't it? Telling darling William all about it, were you?'

'He knows now,' she said.

'Oh, *now* – I see. But not *till* now – a mistake, I think. You didn't trust him, did you, Ruth? Didn't trust him with our secrets. It must have been a surprise for him, finding out I wasn't a partner after all. He'll remember that. It's corrosive, distrust; it'll get you both in the end.'

He unlooped a rope and pushed the dinghy clear. 'And we were right. It's been thirty years, but despite what every one of those years has done to my face Chips knew me – knew within seconds. So I said we should talk. We walked here while I explained that we thought it was what he wanted – to go away, to get away from the world. That nobody got hurt that way. We walked here and I took a chance – he was a strong man, Ruth, always was. But I crooked my arm around under his chin and I broke his neck. It echoed, the snap, across the water.'

She stood back then, climbing up onto the bank. 'Go,' she said.

Fleet threw a rope into the dinghy. 'Don't worry about me,' he said. 'I'm gonna become someone else – I've done it before. Perhaps I'll come back one day, for old times' sake.' He picked up the starter line for the engine. 'You'll know the face.'

47

Russell Fleet pulled the starter cord on the outboard engine in a fluid, practised arc, and a harsh mechanical whine filled the night. He left without looking back, guiding the dinghy out into the main channel, skirting the clumps of reeds which crowded the banks, while the sky flickered still with the arcing electric sparks from the overhead wires.

Somewhere, lost now, Dryden could hear Ruth Connor running, the rigid frozen reeds snapping, her breath rasping. He ran too, trying to keep in touch with her sound, and they emerged together, above the old sluice, on the high dune above the chalets.

'He's gone,' she said, knowing Dryden was there. She pulled a hood in close to her face and looked inland where the twin red and green lights of the dinghy crept along the channels of the marsh towards the river. Blood, black in the moonlight, trickled from the corner of her mouth where Marcie Sley had hit her.

'Not yet,' said Dryden. 'Where will he go? The same place he went that summer? How long was he away?'

She shivered. 'You can't prove anything. Not about me.' She took a step away, then another, trying to be alone.

'Where?' asked Dryden again, following.

'Two years. Abroad – travelling. He sent cards. Norway, Sweden – heat was bad for his eyes, after the operation. I said I'd wait and I did.'

Dryden nodded, recalling the expert skater glimpsed through the porthole of *PK 129*. 'That's why he needed the passport,' he said. 'Distinguishing features: a zigzag scar.'

They heard the outboard engine surge as the dinghy reached clearer water.

'I didn't think he'd do that,' she said. 'With the knife. It always scared me; he'd do anything to have a life like other people – he just didn't realize other people aren't like that.'

'I heard it,' said Dryden, stepping closer. 'That night, the cry of pain.'

'I know. I know you're Philip. Russ said he'd seen a picture on your boat. He'd gone out to check you over, knowing you wouldn't drop the case, wondering why, and he said you had that picture – the one with the blood. He said there was a snapshot as well. A child in the sun, by the pool. And Petulengo had a snapshot at home too, the four of you. A match.'

Dryden nodded, thinking that Fleet had taken the newspaper cuttings too, unnerved by the thumbnail picture of his teenage self.

'But I didn't see,' said Dryden. 'I didn't see him – I was there, but I wasn't a witness. I didn't see his face.'

She turned towards him then but never said what she wanted to say.

There was a fresh flash of arcing electricity between the pylons and when the glare had leached out of the sky they saw the dinghy swing out into the main channel of Morton's Leam.

'I offered him money to go,' she said. 'I always said the business was half his – half my share anyway. But we couldn't make it legal – the risk was too great, you need an ID, bank account. Jean's done wonders for him with money over the years, but even she couldn't fix that.'

'Did she know?'

Connor laughed, running a finger over the bruise Marcie Sley had left. 'She's an accountant. Ask no questions, and you hear no lies. Perhaps he told her a story, perhaps he didn't bother. I doubt she's got the imagination to guess. When he's gone she'll tell the kids the truth, just to pay him back for not loving her.'

Dryden shivered. 'So when William arrived you told him Russ was a partner to cover your tracks?'

She nodded. 'It was easier to leave it like that. I paid his salary into a trust Jean had set up. She kept the taxman happy, did the paperwork.'

The whine of the outboard motor shifted key as the inflatable hit an incoming wave and briefly lifted from the water.

'When the witnesses turned up I said I'd buy Russ out of what I'd promised him. But he said that wasn't enough, that we didn't know what the business was really worth until we sold it. So that's what we've done.'

They heard the engine choke and pick up revs as the dinghy breasted the first wave in the channel.

Dryden put a hand through his hair, collecting ice crystals. 'And he didn't drive, did he – again, the paperwork. But he must have driven out to the farm – to kill Joe. That was a risk – he could hardly use his own licence from back in '74.'

'Risks were what he was good at, Dryden.'

'So when he came back, after the operation – I don't understand. What happened?'

'He'd changed. He always said I'd fallen out of love with his face. But it wasn't that. It was the children. The children we didn't have.'

'And then William Nabbs arrived.'

'He didn't know, Dryden. He never knew – till now.'

Dryden climbed up, to the very crest of the dune, and she followed. 'They'll find him this time,' he said.

She shivered again. 'Maybe. But he's been getting ready, since the witnesses came forward. Killing them was the last bet – but he knew it might not be enough. There's a boat, a yacht, somewhere out there, along the coast. By daybreak he'll be gone. He'll become someone else, Dryden; he's good at it.'

They walked towards the curving, twisted structure of the old footbridge over the channel. The ice which hung from the superstructure had twisted the geometry of the wood, and they clung to the rail as they made their way to the centre. Upstream they could see the green and red lights and the white splash of surf at the prow of the dinghy.

A sound of snapping metal drew Dryden's eyes away and he watched as four of the power cables parted simultaneously, the sudden release of tension making the giant pylon shudder and twist at the waist. They heard screaming then, as ice showered down, and the sky filled with the zigzag shorting of the power supply.

Russell Fleet's boat emerged around the last bend in the channel and headed for the bridge. The pylon knelt at its north-eastern corner, metal shearing, and tossed its apex down into the black water. Instantly a sheet of blue lightning covered the surface, a shimmering electric dance, and the visceral thud of the power rocked the bridge. Dryden covered his face with his hands but still the arcing flashed between his fingers and through his eyelids.

When he turned back the world was black except for a single image: in midstream there was a fire licking at the outboard motor on Fleet's boat. He stood, flapping at the flames, which leapt to his arms and head. Then the fuel tank exploded, a dull percussion which popped Dryden's ears. The flames were in Fleet's hair then, so he threw himself into the shimmering water.

Ruth Connor was on her knees when his body passed out to sea beneath them. They looked down through the wooden planking and, by the light now only of the moon, they saw the blackened twisted body, one arm thrown up across the eyes, revealing the ugly black zigzag of the self-inflicted scar.

48

The air, thick with the stench of seared electrics, held a hint of something else which made Dryden retch. He stood with Ruth Connor for a minute, watching the body turn languidly in the tide under the bridge until it was lost from sight. The camp lay half-lit now, the emergency generator rattling in the cold air. By reception the flashing lights of a police car punctuated the darkness. In the silver light Dryden could see fish on the outgoing tide, their dead scales still iridescent.

There was silence but Dryden wondered if he'd been deafened by the explosion. He pressed his fingers to his ears and the pressure popped. Along the bridge he heard footsteps and William Nabbs climbed up from the river-bank. He held Ruth Connor close like a child, looking out to sea.

Dryden rang DI Parlour's mobile. 'Hi. Yup. On the bridge down by the river. Get a boat out, quickly, there's a body going out on the tide. We need the body. There's no time now, I'll be there in ten, but get a bloody boat out.'

Then he ran to the chalet. Laura sat by the window, the COMPASS on her lap where he'd left it.

There was a message again, a brutal repetition: YOU PROMISED

He leant forward to the keyboard and typed: I LIED

Then he picked up the propane heater, killed the flame, and took it outside with his torch. Three flashes into the night were answered immediately from the dunes, the Capri's headlights suddenly blazing, swinging round like a lost lighthouse.

He had time so he walked down to the beach where there was an oil drum used to burn flotsam. He fished out a rope caked in tar and lit it with his lighter, then tossed it in with the propane heater. Looking back at the chalet, he saw the flames reflected in the sightless glass. After a minute the canister popped, a miniature mushroom cloud rising up into the night sky, sparks sizzling on the frosted sand.

The lights of Humph's cab crept down to the foreshore. Dryden went back inside, picked Laura up, and carried her out under the moon. They pushed Boudicca down into the footwell in the passenger seat and slid Laura on to the worn plastic seating. Dryden slipped in beside her and held her.

'The Tower?' said Humph.

'No. The old dining hall. The police are there. It's over. Then we're going home – to the boat. All of us.'

Postscript

The body of Russell Fleet was never found, but a 22-foot ketch, the Saronica, was located anchored off Scolt Head Island, North Norfolk, thirty miles along the coast. It was provisioned for a sea voyage. The burnt wreck of the dinghy was recovered, with the charred remains of an estimated £325,000 in £50 notes.

An inquest into the death of Chips Connor recorded a verdict of unlawful killing. Ruth Connor remained silent and refused to answer any questions relating to the death of her husband, Paul Gedney, Declan McIlroy or Joe Petulengo, or her relationship with Russell Fleet. She was interviewed on six separate occasions but never charged. The case remains open, but DI Parlour sees promotion in other, less intractable investigations. DI Reade endured an uncomfortable interview with the chief constable. He took early retirement, but not on his terms.

William Nabbs claimed to know nothing of Ruth Connor's life before he had met her in 1984. He took a new job as manager of a marina in South Devon. He never saw Ruth Connor again. She bought Lighthouse Cottage from the new owners of the Dolphin and banked the remainder of the sale: £975,000. Under new management the old huts were finally cleared away and a marina built in the old salt-marsh. Most of the staff faced compulsory redundancy, including Muriel Coverack.

Chips Connor was buried at Sea's End parish church, in a plot with a view over open water.

Police interviewed Russell John Fleet at his home in Malton, North Yorkshire. He was unable to produce a passport issued in 1972 when he was eighteen. DI Parlour showed Dryden a picture: even now there was a resemblance to the identically named impostor, and of course there was the distinctive zigzag scar. Fleet had never travelled abroad but denied attempting to pervert the course of justice by selling his passport to his half-brother. He was formally cautioned, but no further action was taken.

An internal inquiry was held within North Norfolk Electricity at the failure – despite repeated attempts – to switch off the National Grid supply when ice threatened to bring down the pylons at Sea's End. A report, subsequently published, found that severe weather conditions had made it impossible for engineers to access exterior switchgear. Automatic electronic safety systems failed owing to a huge surge in consumer demand on the night of the ice storm. Recommendations were made for design improvements to protect systems in the future from freezing rain.

Joe Petulengo's ashes were scattered alongside Declan McIlroy's outside the Gardeners' Arms. Father John Martin conducted the service and Marcie Sley visits daily. In his will, Petulengo left JSK to a trust, with directions for the establishment of a workers' co-operative. John Sley, who recovered quickly from his heart attack although he continues to take daily medication, was elected managing director.

The inquiry into abuse at St Vincent de Barfleur's Roman Catholic Orphanage continues. A preliminary hearing is expected within three years. Whittlesea District Hospital was reprieved following a local campaign run by the town's MP. George Lutton continues to preside over an ophthalmic clinic each Tuesday and Thursday. His private clinic was purchased by a private healthcare company for an undisclosed sum.

The Mid-Anglian Mutual Insurance Company agreed to the conversion of the forward cabin on PK 129 to accommodate Laura Dryden at a cost of £85,000. They also agreed to provide, in perpetuity, a scheme of care including visits by a trained nurse and a remedial physiotherapist. Laura also visits The Tower regularly for hydrotherapy in the pool and to see a consultant neurosurgeon. The *subject of Philip Dryden's broken promise has never been raised.*

Humph's cab is often parked up on the bankside, Boudicca asleep on the tartan rug. Autumn approaches and Humph plans a Christmas trip to the Gulf of Finland and the miniature Estonian capital, Tallinn.

Upon his return he will begin a new language course: Faroese.

Coda

The Criminal Court of Appeal sitting in the Royal Courts of Justice, the Strand, London

Dryden held Marcie Sley's hand as Lord Justice Clark led his two fellow judges back into court. Outside, the Strand's traffic coughed its way towards Ludgate Hill in a heatwave, and the sound of bells marked three o'clock.

The case was of little public interest and Dryden was relieved the court had not, as a result, resorted to a written judgment. There was one journalist on the press bench, two rows of legal counsel, a scattering of the general public and a single persistent bluebottle circling the empty dock.

Dryden and Marcie sat beneath the royal coat of arms opposite the bench, while Laura's wheelchair, brought up by lift, stood in the gangway. Below them, at the front, Ruth Connor smoothed down a stylish black linen jacket.

The judge continued to read the judgment, a process he had begun two hours before lunch. They waited patiently and Dryden took the opportunity to adjust the drinking tube for Laura so that she could sip some water. As she drank she flexed the fingers of her right hand, each one in turn, ending with a half twist of the wrist.

'Finally,' said Lord Justice Clark, his face red with the heat and lunch, 'we come to the evidence of identification itself. Counsel for the applicant have put before us signed statements from two witnesses to the effect that they saw the alleged victim of the crime at issue – Paul Gedney – alive a month after the date upon which the prosecution in the original case alleged he had been beaten to death by the appellant. Another witness, Mrs Sley, has provided corroboration for their statements but is, herself, unable to make an identification in court. We have, however, been impressed by the clarity and consistency of all these statements although we are unable to test them, except in Mrs Sley's case, by cross-examination. We cannot, therefore, allow them as primary evidence before this court, and they do not of themselves constitute evidence which could justify the removal from the record of the original verdict.'

Dryden shifted on the wooden bench and felt the pressure on his hand tighten.

'However, evidence given in this court by . . .' and here he shuffled his papers, 'Mr Philip Dryden has been tested. It is clear that he was present on the night in question with the other witnesses and that he too – according to his sworn testimony – saw the appellant's alleged victim alive on the night of 30 August 1974. He has been able to firmly identify the man he saw that day as Paul Gedney, as featured in the posters and photographs circulated at the time by the police and brought before this court. The appellant's death, and indeed those of the two witnesses first put forward as a basis for an original appeal, are under investigation. Those matters, unresolved, cannot be pertinent to this appeal, but certainly do not add to our confidence in the conduct of the original case.'

The judge closed a file before him and looked first right, then left. All three judges, almost imperceptibly, nodded agreement. 'In these circumstances we find the appellant's conviction was unsafe. We are aware, as must be his widow, that Mr Connor cannot now enjoy this statement of his innocence. But the record will be altered to reflect it, and the conviction set aside. Justice should be done, and it is.'

They rose, the bluebottle fell silent, and the journalist yawned.

Outside, Dryden stood on the steps, the neo-Gothic towers of the Royal Courts of Justice behind him, watching the traffic inch past, climbing the hill from Fleet Street. Marcie Sley leant against him, the glossy black hair swallowing the light. Dryden held the handles of Laura's chair, using his weight to balance it on the step.

Marcie opened her bag and produced a postcard: a picture of Whittlesea Market Place in limp Kodacolour. 'John read it to me,' she said. 'It's from Grace Elliot, my foster mother. She was in the phone book, so I wrote.'

Dryden flipped it over. The handwriting was a tracery of loops and curls.

My Dearest Marcie,

Your letter was the most wonderful surprise. Of course I've never forgotten you, and you're right, you did cause me a lot of pain, but not the pain you think. I shouldn't have let you go, and it's something I've always regretted. I'm alone now, so do come.

Love

Grace.

'Will you go?' asked Dryden.

Marcie nodded, putting the card carefully away. 'If you'll come too. I want her to know the truth.'

Suddenly she was there: Ruth Connor stood below them, skin dry despite the sweltering city heat. She held out her hand for Dryden's and let go almost as soon as they touched. 'Perjury's a crime,' she said.

Marcie stiffened beside him, but Dryden could see Ruth Connor's eyes, and the smile on the thin red lips.

The Capri crunched against the kerb and Humph hooted the horn twice.

'Alone?' asked Dryden, looking beyond her.

Ruth Connor glanced down at the deep shadow crowding in around her feet. Then she said what she'd wanted to say the night Paul Gedney died for the second time: 'I'm sorry,' she whispered, and walked away, the tap of the high heels scattering pigeons into the sky.

THE SKELETON MAN

Jim Kelly

Now available in hardback
Michael Joseph £16.99

For seventeen years, the Cambridgeshire hamlet of
Jude's Ferry has lain abandoned, requisitioned by the
Ministry of Defence for military training in 1990.
The isolated, 1000-year-old community was famous
for one thing – never having recorded a single crime.

But when local reporter Philip Dryden joins the
Territorial Army on exercise in the empty village, its
spotless history is literally blown apart. For the
TA's shells reveal a hidden cellar beneath the old pub.
And inside the cellar hangs a skeleton, a noose
around its neck.

Two days later, a man is pulled from the reeds in the
river near Ely – he has no idea who he is or how he
got there. But he knows the words 'Jude's Ferry' are
important, and he knows he is afraid . . .

As the police launch an investigation into the
skeleton in the cellar, Dryden is convinced the key to
the mystery rests in the last days of the village when
passions, prejudices, guilt and hatred all came to a
head. Everything leads him back to Jude's Ferry. But
who is waiting for him there?

Read on for a taster...

Prologue

It was a child's high stool, commandeered for the execution.

I stood with my back to the wall, part of the crowd, not the mob, but even then I knew that such a line could not be drawn: a line to separate the guilty from the innocent.

Twelve of us then, and the accused on the stool, the rope tight to the neck.

Again the question. 'Why?' Each time marked by a blow to the naked ribs, blood welling up beneath the skin.

I could have answered, ended it then. But instead I pressed my back against the cool wall, wondering why there were no more denials, wondering why life had been given up.

The victim's knees shook, and the legs of the stool grated on the cellar's brick floor. Outside in the night there was a dog's bark, heard through the trapdoor above, and twelve chimes from the church on the hill.

Then the ringleader did it, because he had the right that was in his blood. Stepping forward he swung a foot, kicking the stool away.

The body, a dead weight, fell; but not to earth. The plastic click of the neck breaking marked the extent of the rope, and with it the grinding of the shattered vertebra as the body turned, the legs running

345

on air. The moment of death stretched out, calibrated by the rattle in the throat. Urine trickled from the bare feet, yellow in the torchlight.

I fainted, standing, for a heart beat. When I looked again the arms, bound and ugly in death, were lifeless.

It was justice, they said, licking parted lips.

Justice in Jude's Ferry.

Chapter One

Seventeen years later

St Swithun's Day
Sunday, 15 July 2007
Whittlesea Mere

The Capri shook, and through the fly-splattered windscreen of the minicab Philip Dryden contemplated the Fen horizon. Humph, the driver, slept peacefully, his lips brought together in a small bow, his sixteen stone compressing the seat beneath him. Around them the drained wasteland that had once been Whittlesea Mere, an inland lake the size of a small English county, stretched beyond sight. Overhead a cloud the size of a battleship sailed across an unblemished sky.

The cab was parked in the cool shadow of a hawthorn, the only tree visible to the naked eye. They'd presented themselves at 9.00am precisely that morning at the checkpoint to Whittlesea Mere Military Firing Range, and been directed down a pot-holed drive to the assembly point: the wreck of a wartime tank, ferns hanging from the dark observation slit. They hadn't seen another human being since they'd been waved through the gates, which had not stopped Dryden imagining they were being watched.

The reporter smoothed down his camouflage tunic and felt the familiar anxieties crowding round. This isn't a war zone, he told himself, it's a military exercise. You're here to write about it, not take part. But the sight of a line of soldiers marching towards them, raising a cloud of desert-red peat dust, made his heartbeat pick up. A trickle of sweat set out from the edge of his thick, jet black hair, down towards his eye. He brushed it aside, aware that another one would quickly take its place.

Dryden checked his watch: 10.15am. The time had come. He fingered the webbing inside the blue tin combat hat he held and pulled it down over his black, close-cropped hair. The neat carved features of his medieval face remained impassive. He got out, the Capri's rusted door hinges screaming, and circled the cab to Humph's open side window.

'You can go' he said, the cabbie, waking, struggling to remember where he was and what he was doing.

'Really . . .' said Humph, wiping his nose with a small pillowcase. 'Can't I stick around until they start trying to kill people?'

Dryden tried to smile. 'Just remember. Same place, 5.00pm. And for Christ's sake don't leave me here.' Bodekka, the greyhound, asleep on a tartan rug in the back seat, yawned in the heat, trapping a bluebottle. Humph turned the ignition key, the engine coughed once and started, and he pulled away at speed, leaving an amber-red cloud as he raced towards the safety of the distant checkpoint. Dryden, alone, felt the hairs on his neck bristle.

The soldiers approached the tank and at a word from an officer made temporary camp. They sat, feet in the ditch, and broke out water bottles, while a billycan was set up on a portable gas ring. Little winding chimneys of white smoke rose from cigarettes in the still, hot air. Dryden felt their

348

collective antagonism to the presence of the press, and watched, oddly fascinated, as one dismantled and oiled an automatic rifle. Another stood, walked a few yards down-wind and urinated into a ditch.

Sensing the calculated insult Dryden looked away and heard laughter at his back, then footsteps approaching, so he turned to face a heavy man with three pips on his flak jacket. As the officer made his way through the gorse he picked up his legs and arms as he walked, a self-conscious compensation perhaps for the onset of middle age. Dryden guessed he was in his early forties, but recognized a military uniform had never made anyone look any younger. The major's hair was boot-polish black and shone unnaturally, but his complexion was poor, blotched as if his face had been scrubbed with a nailbrush. Cross-checking his posi-tion on a hand-held GPS with a map in a plastic see-through wallet he looked up at Dryden, unable to hide a frisson of annoyance at the sight of the reporter.

'Dryden?' he asked. 'Philip Dryden – from *The Crow*?' They shook hands, the grip surprisingly weak, but the voice was higher than he'd expected and held some warmth despite the clipped tones. 'Broderick. Major John Broderick.' He seemed embarrassed by the informality of the first name and turned to scan the horizon. 'You've signed the blood sheet?' he asked.

Dryden nodded. At the gate he'd been presented with the official form for signature which effectively removed his right to claim insurance if some idiot with a long-range peashooter turned him into a human jigsaw.

The major smiled, taking five years off his age: 'Just routine. Only with live firing we insist. Regulations. You lot in the press would be the first to get on our case if we broke the rules.'

349

Laughter rolled along the line of men by the ditch, and Dryden wondered what was funny. Excluded, he looked towards the north where the guns must be, hidden beyond the horizon.

'So they'll fire over our heads right?' he asked realizing immediately that there was little alternative. 'Sorry. Stupid question.'

The major nodded.

'When does the shelling start?' Dryden asked.

'Maroon – that's the signal flare – goes up 10.50am. They'll hit it on the pip. Ten minutes later they open fire with an eight-minute bombardment, then we go in to the first line of attack and stop. Then 11.20 another maroon, followed by a further five-minute bombardment at 11.30. Then we move forward to the targets.' Broderick rubbed his hands together. 'Pictures?'

Dryden swung round a digital camera. 'I'm a one-man band.'

'Great.' The major smiled. That was all the military was ever interested in thought Dryden – pictures to send home, pictures for the scrapbook, pictures for the mess wall, pictures in the local paper, pictures for the MoD. Sod the words.

Broderick looked up at the sky: 'St Swithun's Day,' he said: 'Looks like we could have a good month.' The single cloud was a distant smudge to the east, and the noon sun was already compressing their shadows around their boots.

Dryden slapped a mosquito against the back of his hand. 'You Territorial Army too?' he asked, keen to talk about something other than the weather.

'Sure, sure. These are my men,' he said, managing not to make it sound proprietorial.

'So what do you do in Civvy Street?'

The major looked him in the face. 'Business,' he said, ducking the question.

A maroon thudded from the direction of the checkpoint, the signal that they had ten minutes before the bombardment began. The dull percussion in the sky was marked by a purple blotch and matched by a solid jolt through the earth.

The men stood and gathered round, following Broderick up on to the top of the old tank. The billycan was passed around, the tea inside reeked of tannin, had been sweetened with carnation milk, and was the colour of liquid cattle manure. Dryden took a gulp, casually, knowing he was being watched.

Broderick sat on the turret, spreading out a map for the men. 'Right. Listen up. Today's exercise is live firing. This range was requisitioned in 1907. That's a century. So far the number of soldiers who have left Whittlesea Mere in a body bag is four. There is absolutely no law of nature which says one of you can't make it five, so listen.'

Dryden imagined the crumpled body bag, his own hand peeping from the folds of black plastic, blood under the fingernails. 'War games,' he thought, realizing what an obscene juxtaposition of words it was.

The major's briefing was brutally short. The Royal Artillery would bomb the two targets – twice – then the company would move in, conduct house-to-house searches, flush out insurgents, secure the target, and replace the red target flags with blue. All shells would be live, all personal ammunition blank. Blue tin hats denoted Blue Force – those attacking. Red Force, the enemy, was in position. Its soldiers, wooden cut-out targets with concentric rings running out from the heart, wore red hats; a helpful designation Dryden could not help feeling undermined the integrity of the exercise. His own yellow armband proclaimed him a non-combatant.

'And this is our target,' said Broderick, stabbing a finger at the heart of the wasteland of fen shown on the map. 'The lost village of Jude's Ferry.'

JIM KELLY

THE WATER CLOCK

In the bleak snowbound landscape of the Cambridgeshire Fens, a car is winched from a frozen river. Inside, locked in a block of ice, is a man's mutilated body. Later, high on Ely Cathedral, a second body is found, grotesquely riding a stone gargoyle. The decaying corpse has been there more than thirty years.

When forensic evidence links both victims to one awful event in 1966, local reporter Philip Dryden knows he's on to a great story. But as his investigations uncover some disturbing truths, they also point towards one terrifying foggy night in the Fens two years ago. A night that changed Dryden's life for ever …

'An atmospheric, intriguing mystery with a tense denouement' Susanna Yager, *Sunday Telegraph*

'A sparkling star, newly risen in the crime fiction firmament' Colin Dexter

'Beautifully written … The climax is chilling. Sometimes a book takes up residence inside my head and just won't leave. *The Water Clock* did just that' Val McDermid

SHORTLISTED FOR THE 2002 CWA JOHN CREASEY AWARD

JIM KELLY

THE FIRE BABY

Summer, 1976. A plane crashes on a farm in the Cambridgeshire Fens. Out of the flames walks young Maggie Beck, clutching a baby in her arms . . .

Twenty-seven years later, investigative journalist Philip Dryden – visiting his wife, Laura, in hospital – is witness to Maggie's deathbed confession. But some secrets are best kept secret, and what started out for Dryden as a small and curious story about the only survivor of an almost-forgotten plane crash soon escalates into a full-blown murder investigation.

And while Dryden is wondering what other secrets Maggie carried, his semi-conscious wife is trying to tell him something that might just save his life . . .

'Quirky, emotionally intelligent crime fiction that leaves the reader hungry for more' Val McDermid

'A good, atmospheric read. There's a lot to enjoy . . . sense of place is terrific: the fens really brood . . . Dryden is satisfyingly complicated . . . the plot hits all the right notes' *Observer*

JIM KELLY

THE MOON TUNNEL

In the past. A man crawls desperately through a claustrophobic escape tunnel beneath a POW camp in the Cambridgeshire Fens. Above, a shadow passes across the moon, while ahead only death awaits him.

In the present. Philip Dryden is reporting on an archaeological dig at the old POW camp when a body is uncovered. But there is something odd: the man appears to have been shot in the head, and the position indicates that he was trying to get *into* the camp, not escape it.

It's a puzzle which excites Dryden far more than the archaeologists or the police.

That is, until a second, more recent, body is discovered . . .

'The sense of place is terrific: the fens really brood. Dryden, the central character, is satisfyingly complicated . . . a good, atmospheric read'
Observer

He just wanted a decent book to read ...

Not too much to ask, is it? It was in 1935 when Allen Lane, Managing Director of Bodley Head Publishers, stood on a platform at Exeter railway station looking for something good to read on his journey back to London. His choice was limited to popular magazines and poor-quality paperbacks – the same choice faced every day by the vast majority of readers, few of whom could afford hardbacks. Lane's disappointment and subsequent anger at the range of books generally available led him to found a company – and change the world.

'We believed in the existence in this country of a vast reading public for intelligent books at a low price, and staked everything on it'
Sir Allen Lane, 1902–1970, founder of Penguin Books

The quality paperback had arrived – and not just in bookshops. Lane was adamant that his Penguins should appear in chain stores and tobacconists, and should cost no more than a packet of cigarettes.

Reading habits (and cigarette prices) have changed since 1935, but Penguin still believes in publishing the best books for everybody to enjoy. We still believe that good design costs no more than bad design, and we still believe that quality books published passionately and responsibly make the world a better place.

So wherever you see the little bird – whether it's on a piece of prize-winning literary fiction or a celebrity autobiography, political tour de force or historical masterpiece, a serial-killer thriller, reference book, world classic or a piece of pure escapism – you can bet that it represents the very best that the genre has to offer.

Whatever you like to read – trust Penguin.